THE MAJOR ARCANA

THE MAJOR ARCANA

SCATHING REVIEWER BOOK TWO

BananaDragon

*For my parents, Jason de Stefano,
and the lovely community of Royal Road readers*

All rights reserved. No part of this publication may be reproduced, stored in a retrieval system, or transmitted in any form or by any means electronic, mechanical, photocopying, recording, or otherwise without prior written permission from Podium Publishing.

This is a work of fiction. Names, characters, places, and incidents are either products of the author's imagination or used fictitiously. Any resemblance to actual events, locales, or persons, living, dead, or undead, is entirely coincidental.

Copyright © 2026 by Jade Harris

Cover design by Dalia and Sam

ISBN: 978-1-0394-7772-8

Published in 2026 by Podium Publishing
www.podiumentertainment.com

THE MAJOR ARCANA

CHAPTER ONE

"Welcome back."

Feiyu stood up leisurely, twirling the blade effortlessly in his hand. He didn't even bother looking at me, seeming completely uninterested and instead gazing around the room.

I kept my chin tilted up, glaring at him when he finally began approaching. At last, he met my gaze; his eyes squinted, and a cocky grin immediately spread across his face.

"You were fast. I thought it would've taken your party far longer to get through all the dungeon rooms. They're really difficult, even for someone as talented as you, aren't they? I'm really impressed, Peijin. Honestly."

"Ha! You're even more annoying than the last time we met. I didn't realize that was possible."

Feiyu feigned a hurt expression, a pout on his lips as he clutched his chest. "What, did I say something wrong? I was just extending my genuine compliments."

He slowly raised a hand and placed it on my shoulder. His hand was so massive compared to my small frame that my shoulder practically disappeared.

He gave it a tight squeeze. Although the gesture appeared friendly, it felt like a cheap intimidation tactic.

My eye twitched. I put on a fake smile and turned around to face my party. "Go ahead and rest. I'll figure things out from here with Feiyu. I'll update you guys on everything after you wake up."

Yang looked visibly uncomfortable—after all, he was there the first time Feiyu and I met, and he knew how poorly we hit it off.

Yang glanced at me nervously, but I met his gaze confidently. He nodded at me before turning to scoop up Amelia, clearly eager to leave as soon as possible. He quickly ordered the rest of the party. "Let's get off the platform and take some time to recover."

Wei and Yue followed, but not before Yue raised a brow and stared me up and down before leaving.

Now, Feiyu and I stood alone on the platform. He propped his arm on the hilt of his purple sword and leaned against it casually; I clenched a restless Zhige in my hand. The red eye was spinning wildly, looking back and forth between me and Feiyu.

"Where's the rest of your party?" I asked firmly.

"Why not 'how are you?'"

"Excuse me?"

"You're not going to ask how I am first?"

"Why would I?"

"It would be good for us to get along, Peijin. We'll be seeing a lot of each other from now on. I hope I get to see you every single day."

"Not if I can help it."

Feiyu's face lit up boyishly. He rested his chin on the top of his sword, now at eye-level with me. "You know, I'm really curious about you." He teasingly brought up a finger beneath my chin.

At once, my patience ran thin, and my face flushed a humiliating shade of red. "Are you always so r-rash?!"

At the sound of my horrific stammer, we both froze. His already wide smile became even wider, and I was utterly frustrated.

"Do you just get a kick out of teasing me or something?" I exclaimed.

Feiyu stood straight up again, stretching his powerful arms far above his head. "No, but the observers sure do."

A blue screen popped open before him, and he turned it around to face me. It showed his observers chat, as hundreds of messages flooded through.

[Observers Chat]

SJJC: This is my favorite part of watching Feiyu

OwnPen: Keep this up and we'll give you so many more stars!!

Socrates: Aww, she's so cute :)

TarteJuice: HAHA you're the only one that can get a reaction out of such a prickly disciple

CrownFill: That's right she doesn't even show that much emotion for her party members

Ahoy987: Feiyu you can fix her

Landy: FIX HER LOL

UCh888: He can't fix her if he's like the better version of her . . .
APCase29: IM DEAD HE'S RAGEBAITING HER
SonYon: And she falls for it every time lolllll

Feiyu's hand waved before him again. Then, hundreds of smaller blue screens flashed all around him like lights on a Christmas tree.

Observer TarteJuice sponsors 3 stars.

Observer CrownFill sponsors 2 stars.

Observer Ahoy987 sponsors 6 stars.

Observer Socrates sponsors 10 stars.

Observer OwnPen sponsors 3 stars.

. . .

Socrates, you damn traitor. I knew that filthy bastard had no loyalty.

Not only that, but Feiyu was using my reactions to turn a profit for himself? What a sleazy bastard!

Feiyu quickly closed all the chaotic blue screens and tilted his head at me curiously. His signature lazy and mischievous look only intensified. "Get it now, Peijin? Everything's a show, and I'm the star." He winked at me, and I could only imagine how wild his observers chat was getting.

In my peripheral vision, my private chat conversation with a certain observer was blowing up.

[Observers Chat]
Socrates: Jia Li, I promise it's not what it looks like.
Socrates: Wait, Jia Li, don't be mad at me.
Socrates: Isn't it only natural that I support both of you? I read *Surviving My First Run* for Feiyu after all . . .
Socrates: I'm sure Jia Li understands.
Socrates: Right?
Socrates: Please don't ignore me, Jia Li. I'm still your number one fan. Forever and always!!

Observer Socrates sponsors 100 stars.

> [Observers Chat]
> **Socrates:** I know Jia Li likes her stars very much . . .

I crossed my arms before Feiyu. "You're a bit of a stuck-up social media star, aren't you? And you definitely have the ego to match."

Feiyu let out a hearty laugh, and my eyes widened for a moment, surprised by his genuine reaction. He began walking up the stairs leading away from platform one, and I absentmindedly followed him. Because Feiyu was so much taller than me, I had to speed walk just to keep pace with his slow strut.

"Can you blame me?" Feiyu asked. "The stars add up."

"Of course. You're greedy, too."

Feiyu becoming a total sensation among the observers made complete sense. Not only did they already enjoy his character if they read *Surviving My First Run*, but he upped his performance another notch. With the added observer feature, which diverged heavily from *Surviving My First Run*, Feiyu would have both the direct support of his original fans and a steady flow of income.

After all, even in the world before the apocalypse, his only job was to entertain readers. His duty hadn't changed at all.

"Peijin, how old are you?" Feiyu asked suddenly, looking down at me with a ginger smile.

"Guess," I said confidently, tilting my chin up a bit. I was confident I looked younger than my age. If he guessed otherwise, it would look like he was just trying to genuinely offend me. And who liked a rude protagonist? Nobody.

"Barely twenty."

Score!

"I do look very young, don't I? But I'm actually twenty-four. That's why I'm so mature despite my exquisite looks."

"Hmm, is that so? Well, since I'm only twenty-three, I guess I better listen to my senior."

"Obviously! And—"

I winced in pain as we reached the top step. I grabbed onto my side, looking down to see a significant blood stain growing on my hoodie. I pressed onto it firmly, my breath coming out as a hiss.

I was still bleeding from the various wounds that Wei had inflicted upon me. When I pulled my hand back, my palm and fingers were coated in a thick layer of blood.

For a brief moment, I got so swept up in my banter with Feiyu that I had forgotten about the circumstances surrounding us. I could hear my heart beating in my head, and an unsettling thought crossed my mind.

This was dangerous.

Feiyu was dangerous. He was making me weak.

Feiyu's eyes darted down to my wound, but he didn't say anything. I quickly opened the Azure Dragon Store, and instead of making a snide remark, Feiyu turned away like he wanted to give me some semblance of privacy.

I purchased the cheapest healing elixir and downed it quickly, wiping my mouth with my sleeve. I expended more stars to restore my hoodie to its bright blue color.

"Why are you looking away?" I asked finally. "Trying to help me save face? Are you embarrassed for me?"

"And what if I'm trying to help you save face? Is that so bad?" Feiyu answered softly, peeking at where the wound was.

"Yeah, it is. I don't want your pity."

Feiyu ignored my comment, and he instead answered my original question. "My party is waiting by the main security kiosk. There's a total of five people in the party, including me."

I paused for a moment, feeling anxious about the question that had lingered in the back of my mind since I first met Karma. But, I couldn't hold it back any longer. I had to know the truth.

"Feiyu, is there a young girl in your party?"

"Yes. I'm sure she'd get along well with Amelia. They're not too different in age."

A feeling of bitterness swallowed me again, but I did my best to hide my sour expression.

> **Scathing Reviewer activated!**

It wasn't like I could hate my sister for the sins of our mother.

Still, it didn't change how I felt about the whole thing. I was bitter that I wasn't the one with a mother and father. I was bitter that I was never the one destined to be loved. Wasn't I still deserving of some?

It didn't matter. Now, both of us were orphaned. How cruel—it was like some kind of family curse.

At the very least, I wanted to try and love others. My party deserved it.

Lost in my thoughts, Karma's words once again crowded my mind like an angry swarm of wasps.

"Every relationship you forge is your karma because you will always destroy the other person, Liu Peijin."

"No one needs you. They need Feiyu."

Maybe it was best for me to stay away from her. Even if she was my sister, what right did I have to get involved? She could live the rest of her life without knowing I existed, and with Feiyu looking over her, that would be a safe and long life. I couldn't ask for much more than that without being horribly selfish.

I felt the gentle brushing of a hand against my elbow and jumped. I reached for Zhige with wicked speed, my hand tightening on the hilt, before I realized it was only Feiyu who tapped me.

"When you go quiet like that, I don't know what you're thinking," he said softly.

"So, what does it matter? I don't need you to fucking psychoanalyze me now, too."

I grew cold instantly, blocking out Feiyu. I didn't bother to reflect on why there was a flicker of confusion in his normally ridiculing gaze.

We were finally approaching the security kiosk. I saw my party at a separate one a little more than a hundred feet away. Yue was passed out on the ground from exhaustion with Amelia splayed over her abdomen. I could practically hear the two of them snoring from where I was standing.

Wei, still shaken, sat further away, his head resting in his hands as Yang sat just beside him, comforting him and holding a glass with some sort of drink. Wei pushed it away, and Yang winced, staring at Wei desperately. Finally, Yang pulled Wei into a tight hug, and Wei's entire body went stiff—until Wei softened and returned the hug, his body shaking as sobs crashed through him.

Feiyu followed my longing gaze, but I quickly glared at him when I realized what he was doing.

"If your party ever had to struggle for anything, you would know how much seeing that tugs at your heart strings," I said.

"Who said the last arc was easy for us?"

"You were born with a silver spoon in your mouth. You're lucky. Struggle is foreign to you."

"Suffering isn't."

We were just in front of the kiosk when a head popped out from the entrance. It was a young man with messy, straight, brown hair. His eyes were wide and friendly. A giant grin was on his face, and I could practically hear him squealing with delight.

"Hello! Hello!"

He waved his right arm wildly at us before he shot back into the kiosk. An old, grumbled shout could be heard before the young man stumbled out, looking like he had been kicked out from the inside. He quickly rushed over to greet me.

"You're Liu Peijin, right? I'm Huang Cheng!" The boy eagerly took one of my hands and shook it in both of his. Hair from his bangs fell to cover his eyes, but he quickly flicked his head back. "I've been so excited to meet you. I was about to run over to meet you on the platform, but then Feiyu-shushu said he was going to wait for you on the platform instead. Can you believe that? He said I had to sit here and wait for you to come over. I told him I'd leave a much better first impression than he would, but—"

Cheng let out a light yelp as an older man approached behind him, harshly pinching his ear and dragging him away from me. "What did I tell you about running your mouth?"

Cheng instantly pouted and his arms went limp at his sides. "You told me not to do it . . ."

> [Observers Chat]
> **Socrates:** My favorite original duo is here!

> **Divinity Supreme Commander of the Heavenly Hosts voices his fondness for Disciple Cheng.**

> **Divinity Spirit of the Jade Moon looks at Disciple Cheng with adoration.**

The cranky old man was just about the same height as the still growing Cheng, who was no older than seventeen. I knew this because both Cheng and this elderly man were characters from *Surviving My First Run*.

Once his ear was released, Cheng resumed talking but at a slower pace, holding onto his bright red ear. "This is Sun Yuan. I accidentally woke him up from his nap when I came out to greet you, which is why he's a bit cranky, but he's usually very nice," Cheng insisted, casting a nervous glance at Yuan before laughing awkwardly.

Cheng and Yuan formed a powerful attachment as soon as the apocalypse began, mostly due to their traumatic character backstories. Cheng was a seventeen-year-old boy who had been relentlessly abandoned by every foster family he'd had—and he had more than four.

Ironically, it was because Cheng was too sweet, and it manifested into clinginess that overwhelmed all his past families. But with every abandonment Cheng faced, his heart broke more and more, and he overcompensated by loving everyone far too hard and too much.

Yuan, on the other hand, lost his daughter after a long struggle against various mental health issues. Her death led to a divorce from his wife and an eventual spiral into decades of loneliness. Yuan struggled with a crippling addiction to alcohol and was only days from claiming his life before the apocalypse.

It was only natural that these two would find comfort in each other. And, it was only natural that their found-family relationship touched the hearts of many gods, who were fascinated by demonstrations of human struggle and resilience.

I was glad my dungeon room wasn't revealed to all the gods and observers. Thankfully, Socrates didn't know what happened in my dungeon room, or else he would've realized how sickly self-indulgent this duo was.

Once again, my characters were just an extension of my own insecurities and desires.

Yuan grumbled something undetectable under his breath before he scratched the base of his chin. White stubble was poking out, and his skin was speckled from years under the sun, but his eyes were still bright and perceptive.

"So, you are the acclaimed Liu Peijin. Feiyu sure takes an interest in you," Yuan croaked. His voice was incredibly gruff. You could tell that alcohol abuse had burned his throat almost to ruin.

"And you are the legendary Sun Yuan. Feiyu told me all about your incredible accomplishments during our walk up here." I put on a bright and cheery look, trying to mimic Cheng's in the hopes that Yuan would notice our resemblance.

Feiyu tensed beside me from both my lie and sudden change in demeanor.

Yuan let out a pleased chuckle. "Oh, did he really? What did he say? I'm sure there was too much to cover."

"Far too much. I wish we had more time to talk about you. He mentioned how brilliant you were in Cheng's room. You did a lot to save him from that illusion."

"Ha! I'm surprised he gave me any credit for that whatsoever. It's hard when Ruoming is always stealing the stage. That damn kid is always doing things on his own."

I laughed at Cheng's response, but my mind went entirely blank. My bright smile became strained by the effort of trying to remember the details of *Surviving My First Run* because . . .

. . . who the *hell* was Ruoming?

In *Surviving My First Run*, when Cheng was stuck in the horrors of his past in a similar manner to the way I was, Yuan managed to pull him out of the dungeon's illusions. This was the pivotal moment that strengthened their bond. I even cried while writing it, as much as it pains me to confess that.

Feiyu interjected. "Be careful, Yuan. Not only is Peijin the god of fate and fortune, but she is a master of flattery, too. Don't let her sweep you off your feet."

Feiyu's eyes drifted back to the kiosk, and he jerked his chin at a small black point I just noticed, letting out a soft and deep chuckle. "I told you earlier, there's no need for that. Put the gun down. Come out and say hi. Peijin won't bite."

My jaw dropped at Feiyu's casual statement. "You've had a gun pointed at me this entire time?!" I exclaimed. I was dropping my guard far too much around Feiyu. If I had been paying more attention to the information that Hindsight was relaying to me, I absolutely would have picked up on such a stupid stunt.

Feiyu turned to me with a lighthearted smile. "Wouldn't you have done the same? You're so mean and scary, I couldn't help be a bit nervous."

Before I could continue bickering with him, a small figure exited the kiosk. It was a bizarre sight—a little girl holding a massive rifle in two tiny hands.

> **Scathing Reviewer activated!**

CHAPTER TWO

Chills travelled through my entire body, and my heart seized in my chest. My lips parted and eyes widened as I imprinted her face into my brain. I would never forget how she looked at this exact moment.

Honestly, she looked nothing like me. If I hadn't known we were related, I would never have assumed it.

Just as Feiyu said, she couldn't have been much older than Amelia. Her hair was thick, long, and dark brown; her cheeks were filled and face round; and her brows were straight, making her look shy regardless of her expression.

The only thing we shared was our mother's wide, brown eyes. And now that my skills like Hindsight affected my vision, my eyes were normally a glimmering shade of dark blue.

Hindsight deactivated!

My eyes returned to their normal dark brown. I couldn't explain why I wanted so badly to share something with her, even if it ultimately belonged to our mother.

I had no clue how to react. Should I try to win over this girl's favor? But I had no clue what she liked. Would it be weird to ask? Maybe I'd come off too strong? I chewed my lower lip, nervous from all the various options coursing through my head.

She took a few cautious steps toward me, and I did the same. Finally, when I was near enough, I hesitated before slowly lifting a hand to ruffle the top of her head, unsure of what else to do.

It was like making too sudden of a move when feeding a stray cat. Immediately, she cringed and raced back to Feiyu's side, where he quickly lifted her up into his arms and laughed.

> **[Observers Chat]**
> **Nipon23:** meets a random terrified kid and instantly goes in for head pat
> **Aslan:** Okay . . . now why did she do that . . .
> **PhoePot:** Is this Peijin's first time interacting with a human being??

My face turned pink. Was I completely stupid? I was picking between all these different options of what to say in my mind, but when she finally came up to me, I didn't even say a word. I just awkwardly ruffled her hair like some total freak. I really was an idiot.

Feiyu readjusted her, propping her so she was seated on his broad shoulders. "What a scaredy cat you are. Peijin, this is Zhang Qijing. She'll warm up to you quickly, I promise."

So, her name was Zhang Qijing. I could barely hold back my bitter laughter.

Our mother had given us wickedly similar names but with brutally different fates. "Qijing" meant precious, gentle, and elegant jade. My name meant "full of gemstones and fine jade," but it also aligned with failed ambition and tragedy. My mother had decided to damn only one of us.

Qijing clung tightly onto Feiyu's head, and it looked like she wanted to disappear behind him entirely. She cast me an apprehensive—almost hostile— glare. She clung onto Feiyu the same way I had clung onto his character when I was fourteen. Anywhere I turned, there were always echoes of that barbaric man.

Realizing the resemblance between Qijing and I relying on Feiyu, I couldn't stop myself from letting out a cold laugh. "Must run in the family."

I ran a hand through my hair before sighing, shaking my head.

It was beyond me now. There was nothing for me to do but stand back and watch from the sidelines. Feiyu had made that decision for me—he took up any spot by my sister that I might have had a chance of standing in.

But, unlike Feiyu, I was a far more jealous and impulsive person.

I hauled over a nearby bench and dragged it until it was right in front of Feiyu. I stood up on the bench so I was standing face-to-face with my sister, a bright smile on my face. "Qijing is a very pretty name. The 'qi' is for 'jade,' right? My name has a similar meaning. Cool coincidence, right?"

Qijing barely softened her grip on Feiyu's head. "You're Peijin?"

"Yup."

"Feiyu always talks about you."

"I'll assume it's all good things. I have to say, your name is still far prettier than mine. Do you like sweets?"

"Yes, but I'm not allowed to have them. Mom told me they'll give me cavities."

"Well, Qijing, I'm not gonna snitch. Are you gonna snitch?"

The small girl shook her head, her posture finally relaxing. She kicked her feet back and forth now.

"Good. And, Feiyu-shushu definitely won't snitch, either."

I opened up the Azure Dragon Store, quickly buying a massive glass jar of flavored lollipops. It was as large as Qijing's head, and her eyes instantly brightened. I gave it a good shake, popped off the lid, and held it in front of her.

"Which flavor do you like?" I asked. "Orange?"

She quickly reacted with disgust, her face scrunching up. "No way. That's the worst flavor." Finally feeling more at ease, she lowered herself to the ground and out of Feiyu's arms. She peeked into the jar, fishing out a blue raspberry lollipop.

Balancing her rifle against her small body, Qijing peeled off the wrapper, pocketed it, and then popped the candy into her mouth, looking very satisfied.

Noticing the candy jar, Cheng's face lit up, and he quickly appeared beside me, eager to take one the moment Qijing finished. "Whoa! Peijin-ayi, can I please have one? Feiyu, how come you never do this for us?"

He raised an eyebrow. "Do you really need more sweets?"

"That was mean," Cheng answered.

Cheng reached for the jar, but I swiftly jumped off the bench and kicked it back to its original location. I walked over to Qijing's feet and plopped the jar down on the ground right beside her. "You'll have to ask the princess. It's not my candy."

The boy proceeded to plead with Qijing, who returned to her aloof stare and quietness. I snorted, shooting Feiyu an entertained look.

"You better be on the lookout," I told Feiyu. "Qijing just might end up liking me more than she likes you."

"You're always so full of confidence, Peijin."

"I mean it! You should see how Amelia is with me. That girl looks at me like I hung the stars."

"Maybe our kids can have a bit of a play date," Feiyu half-joked.

"Huh? Qijing hasn't met Amelia yet?"

"Qijing was a bit intimidated by your party. None of them have met her yet."

I puffed out my chest cockily. So, Qijing must have really liked me if she had exchanged a few words with me. Of course that would be the case—how could my own sister not like me?

"Well," I said leisurely, "I'm sure Qijing would fit in perfectly with my party. They'd love her."

"It's a shame she's not a part of your party, isn't it?"

I immediately glared at him, pushing past him and walking toward one of the platforms until I found a seat. I was expecting Feiyu to follow me. "You said there were five people in your party, right? I've only seen four of you."

"Our last member works to the beat of his own drum. I'm sure he'll be back in a moment, though." As expected, Feiyu followed closely behind and stood before me as I sat down on the bench, slouching over lazily.

"Hey, why'd you name your party Twenty-Two anyway?" I asked, sitting up a bit and tilting my head. "Is it a reference to something?"

This was something that had been puzzling me ever since I discovered the name of Feiyu's party. That and the fact there was another disciple stronger than me that wasn't Feiyu.

Not only did Twenty-Two deviate from Feiyu's party name in *Surviving My First Run*, but it also coincided with the number of cards in the Major Arcana deck.

Logically, that meant Feiyu must have had some knowledge about the Major Arcana. Since the Major Arcana transcended timelines, it was possible that they reached out to Feiyu because he would have been a pivotal character in all the past timelines.

However, Karma would have theoretically stopped Feiyu from discovering the Major Arcana before I did, since he had less knowledge about the apocalypse than I did—unless he was already a secret member of the Major Arcana.

As far as I was aware, the Feiyu before me wasn't like the Meihua of the Major Arcana. He wasn't some magical, ancient, godly version from another timeline—he was simply the Feiyu I created in *Surviving My First Run*.

Feiyu let out a slight chuckle, his eyes glinting with amusement. "I didn't name the party."

"Huh?"

"I'm not the leader of the party. So, I didn't name the party."

". . . Huh?"

"Huh?" Feiyu mocked my stupid expression. "When did I ever say that I was the leader of the party?"

"Why . . . wouldn't you be? You're Qiu Feiyu. You're a natural-born leader."

"Thank you. But Song Ruoming is the leader of the party. He just wasn't interested in meeting you yet, so he's been sending me to greet you instead."

I sat on the bench utterly stupefied, blinking at Feiyu. My entire body felt frozen in place, and for a moment, I couldn't even form a thought.

So . . . this entire time, Feiyu was never the party leader? He was a casual, boring, good-old member?

I shook my head back and forth. That couldn't be right. It didn't even sound like Feiyu to be following orders that some random disciple was barking at him.

Not only that, but it was a complete upheaval of my understanding of Feiyu and his party. Not once did I doubt his position as the party leader. After all, how could someone possibly surpass him? That was impossible. Feiyu was the main character.

Song Ruoming. I repeated the name over and over in my head, trying to remember if I had ever written a character with that name. If I hadn't, then they must have been someone from the real world.

Maybe they were an avid reader of *Surviving My First Run*, and that was why they had been able to take command of Feiyu and his old party members like this? There was simply no way for a normal person to achieve this big a feat.

Even if Song Ruoming was a reader, I could hardly wrap my mind around the thought that they were so far ahead of the game. Feiyu wasn't someone easily controlled; he valued his power and autonomy more than anything.

I fumbled with the sleeves of my blue hoodie. "I'm guessing Ruoming is the best disciple in your party."

"That's right. Extraordinary really." Feiyu tapped the tip of his sword on the ground again. "Am I a lot less interesting to you now, since I'm not the top catch? Maybe I should have kept my mouth shut."

"I didn't say anything like that." My hand slid up to scratch my tattoo now. It was a bad habit I'd developed ever since it appeared, and it only became worse after my dungeon room. If I could, I wanted to tear the whole thing from my skin, but I knew it was futile.

Out of the corner of my eye, a figure was slowly approaching. It was a relatively tall and lean man wearing gray slacks, black suspenders, and a button-up shirt. But, the most noticeable feature was his platinum hair, blond lashes, and pale irises.

At once, my shoulders fell and eyes widened.

There wasn't a single timeline where I wouldn't have immediately recognized this man.

Scathing Reviewer is flickering!

While Scathing Reviewer normally heightened my emotions and sensitivity, this time, it was trying to dampen them.

As the skill flickered, I only felt an even greater tightening in my chest and dryness in my throat. My stomach dropped. I could hear the rapid pounding of my heart in my head.

> **Scathing Reviewer is flickering!**

After running away from home at fourteen, it wasn't like I could survive on my own. I spent days pathetically wandering around, pleading with strangers for food and water—until I met Zhao Rui on the darkest day of my life. He wasn't much older than me at the time, but he was the only reason I survived.

In fact, he was the very man who inspired Qiu Feiyu. He was the man who inspired all of *Surviving My First Run*.

Once, there was a time in my life when I couldn't imagine a single day without him. The thought never even crossed my mind—I knew that I could live happily with nothing but him. That was until he vanished a few months after saving me. I never saw him again.

> **Warning! Scathing Reviewer is flickering!**

I stood up from the bench and took a shaky step toward him. Then, I took another step forward. I pushed past Feiyu and practically sprinted toward him, biting down on my quivering lower lip.

"Zhao Rui!" I exclaimed, the name coming naturally. When I finally reached him, I slid to a stop. I was terrified that the moment I laid a hand on him, he would suddenly vanish again, and this would be another cruel trick played on me. I ran my hand through my short hair, unable to believe my eyes.

"Zhao Rui," I repeated his name. "Zhao Rui. Rui. Ha! You recognize me, right? It's Liu Peijin. How many years has it been? I really thought I'd never seen you again. I haven't thought about you in ages. I used to think about you every day. Do you know how mad I was?"

Rui stood there, his face completely apathetic. His pale eyes looked at me for a moment before shooting down to my exposed and raw forearm. He grabbed onto my wrist and pulled me toward him, pushing my sleeve further up my arm.

"The Tower," he murmured.

"Rui?"

He released my hand and took a step back. "I don't know who you could be talking about. My name is Song Ruoming, not Zhao Rui."

"Oh."

I stared at the strange man again, my eyes raking over his features.

No—this was certainly Zhao Rui.

I would never have mistaken Rui for anyone else. The mole just to the right side of his nose bridge, the way his lips slightly parted between each word, his naturally long nail beds, the double helix piercing on his left ear, which I pierced for him . . .

I quickly opened the Azure Dragon Store, no longer caring about my star expenditure.

> **You have purchased Lie Detector!**

I looked back up at the man. "You don't recognize me at all?"
Ruoming looked me dead in the eye with zero emotion in his expression. "No."

> **Disciple Peijin activated Lie Detector!**

> **Lie Detector has confirmed Disciple Ruoming's words as truth.**

My face fell and my brow furrowed before a deep frustration burned through me. So, this "Song Ruoming" was the disciple that had been beating me ever since the apocalypse began, was controlling Feiyu like a puppet on strings, knew about the Major Arcana from the start, and was pretending not to know me?

Fucking bastard.

> **Scathing Reviewer has stabilized.**

Ruoming slunk past me, completely uninterested in me and trying to stand beside Feiyu, but I quickly tugged him back, my grip on Zhige tightening.

"Hey asshat, why'd you name your party Twenty-Two? It's named after the number of cards in a Major Arcana deck, right?"

Ruoming paused at the insult and turned to face me. His head was lowered, so he was glaring up at me. "Shouldn't the Tower know more than me?"

I scowled at his snarky reply. "Don't play stupid with me. Not only did you look for my tattoo as soon as you caught a peak of it, but you were calling out to the Major Arcana with your party name."

> **Countless gods express their worries regarding the mysterious Major Arcana.**

"Did I stutter earlier?" Ruoming asked. "I don't know what you're talking about. Feiyu, you didn't tell me that the other party leader was utterly delusional."

"Keep me out of this one," Feiyu said, quickly taking a step back as I approached Ruoming. "Clearly the two of you know much more than I do. I know my place."

"You know I'm not crazy!" I exclaimed at Ruoming. "Deny it all you want. You know exactly what I'm talking about. A normal disciple never could have surpassed Feiyu."

"Then are you implying that you're also an anomaly?"

Ha. At the very least, Ruoming was a reader of *Surviving My First Run*. Feiyu was engineered to be the greatest disciple, no contest. The only people who have met his level are me—the writer—and Ruoming, the must-be reader.

"You're thinking the same thing I am, Ruoming," I answered, keeping my eyes locked on him. "Do you also have a tattoo?"

"Tattoos don't fit my aesthetic."

Both the World and I had our identifying tattoos plastered on our arms. I reached for Ruoming's arm to push up his sleeve, but he reacted with lightning speed, immediately thrusting his sword at my side. I brought up Zhige to counter his attack, and the moment that Zhige made contact with Ruoming's blade, its red eye shot open, spinning wildly.

Ruoming stared at the blade, and for a split second, surprise flickered across his face. Immediately, my gaze narrowed, and I swung Zhige relentlessly while trying to grab hold of Ruoming anytime the distance between us shrank.

Despite engaging with Zhige, Ruoming's movements were wickedly fluid, and he didn't seem to be expending much energy at all. Growing frustrated, I threw Zhige to the side, completely releasing the blade to attack Ruoming on its own.

Ruoming's gaze followed the sword, leaving mine for just a moment. I resorted to my hands—latching onto him and refusing to relax my grip.

I kicked my leg under Ruoming and sent us both to the ground. I recentered myself and clung onto his sleeves, holding on for dear life as he attempted to throw me off. Despite sending Zhige off to hand Ruoming, the blade hesitated, holding itself back.

You have 281,394 cumulative stars.

85,000 stars used.

Strength level 35 → level 43

With my newfound strength, I pushed up, pinning Ruoming's arms to the ground and trying to force his sleeves up. My knee found its way onto his stomach, and I pressed down as hard as I could.

But Ruoming's strength was unbelievable, even with my upgraded skill. He wrapped his arm over my shoulder, and he quickly submitted me in a tight shoulder lock.

I held my breath, not wanting to show weakness before Ruoming. His gaze hardened, and he twisted my shoulder further and further back until I let out a sharp cry.

But, despite the tears brimming in my eyes, I refused to let go of him. Bending until I could feel my shoulder ready to snap, my free hand reached over and tore his entire sleeve off.

CHAPTER THREE

Ruoming instantly let go, and I sat up, grabbing onto his arm and examining it from every angle. I sat beside him, blinking stupidly. Ruoming's skin was perfectly white, smooth, and free of any tattoos.

I double checked. Then triple checked. Absolutely nothing.

If Ruoming wasn't part of the Major Arcana . . . how did he seem to know more about it than I did? He even seemed to know more about it than Feiyu, who was the most likely to have an affiliation with the Major Arcana.

"Happy now?" Ruoming scoffed before sitting up. His large hand wrapped around the back of my head, and he shoved my head into the ground.

My nose crunched against the cement. I let out a pained grunt, but I then planted a foot onto the ground and forced my way up, twisting free from his grip. I quickly grabbed his other arm and pushed the sleeve back to check for any marks.

Nothing.

I stared for a moment longer before releasing him, standing up, and dusting myself off. I shot him a suspicious look, and he scrutinized me with a cold and unfamiliar gaze before standing. Zhige slowly slunk back to my side; it was lucky I was distracted.

Ruoming frustratedly tried to pull down his sleeve, which was now too short, to cover his exposed forearm. My eyes never left him.

I knew Zhao Rui would've never looked at me with such an unrecognizable expression. By this point, everything was pointing to Ruoming being an entirely different person. Still, their resemblance was far too striking to ignore.

If there was just a chance I could see Rui again, I wanted to bet everything on it.

Ruoming shook his head back and forth, his white bangs flying around until they settled effortlessly to frame his face. He adjusted his professional uniform and returned to Feiyu's side.

My gut feeling was telling me this man was undoubtedly Rui, but everything else was wrong.

> [Observers Chat]
> **Socrates:** Jia Li, give it up, he obviously has no clue who you are.
> **Socrates:** And maybe he's just another reader of Surviving My First Run. He just didn't get blocked like the rest of us to end up as poor observers . . .

Now that Ruoming comfortably returned to Feiyu's side, he became even more apathetic and nonchalant. "So, how about *you* share what the Major Arcana is, since you apparently know so much about them?" Ruoming asked, crossing his arms with an unbelievable amount of attitude.

"If I knew, I wouldn't have asked you about them," I answered with equal snark.

"I heard that you are the god of fortune and fate."

"I sure am. You can use Lie Detector if you don't believe me."

"How do your skills work?" Ruoming's tone was perfectly smooth, as though he had the entire conversation contrived in his head already. "Do you see flickers of the future? Hear voices like an oracle? Have a god telling you what's about to happen? Or, maybe you have a special book that gives you all the answers."

> [Observers Chat]
> **Socrates:** Uh oh!

I kept my expression neutral, trying to match his apathetic one. I had no intention of giving any information to Ruoming before I knew more about his character. Unlike Feiyu, where I could guess most of his reactions, Ruoming was a wild card.

"Ruoming, I wonder how you get your knowledge, especially since there seem to be some similarities between us. Do you also happen to be some kind of god? It's really not that unusual. I'm sure you've heard whispers about Wei already." I said.

Ruoming paused, gauging my question before shrugging. "I have no intention of working with you or your party. So why should I answer your questions honestly?"

"You didn't have an issue with fishing for information out of me."

"Clearly you don't either."

It was clear to me now that Ruoming was an avid reader of *Surviving My First Run*. A very, very intelligent one at that; he evidently had no issues playing Feiyu and all the old characters like a fiddle.

Ruoming's understanding of the world and the characters must have been astronomical, and if the Major Arcana was fishing for future Arcana members, he was an obvious contender.

"Well I think we both already got something out of this," I said with a smirk, tilting my chin up. "So, what's your strategy for the next arc? Are you going for the throne?"

Ruoming's face scrunched when I revealed information about the next arc; information that had not been disclosed by the system yet.

"I could avoid it and still win the arc," Ruoming answered.

"You're really confident, aren't you?"

Finally, I'd thrown the bait, and Ruoming had bitten it. He'd confirmed he was a reader. In *Surviving My First Run*, avoiding the third arc's throne was Feiyu's winning strategy, and Ruoming knew that.

> **[Observers Chat]**
> **TekB:** Peijin should not be the spokesperson of the party how is she burning bridges like this </3 she just met Ruoming and the first thing she does is tear off his nice shirt
> **Ahoy987:** What the hell just happened??
> **Ahoy987:** That made no sense are they trying to speak in some kind of secret language
> **CinaA:** wtf
> **Landy:** Wait but this means that Peijin and Ruoming both know the future, right . . .?
> **OwnPen:** OH!!!! Maybe they both read—

Yellow sparks appeared, turning off the Observers Chat. It was as I thought—Karma was still restricting knowledge that the apocalypse originated from my web novel. For the first time, I felt a bit of gratitude toward Karma.

Ruoming looked more than fed up with our conversation, and he didn't bother with responding to me anymore. I didn't mind if he thought I was a fellow reader—as long as he didn't know I was JiaLi1825. For now, he would think he was a step ahead of me in his understanding of the world, but a reader was still fundamentally different from a writer.

Ruoming brushed past me, walking to the kiosk where the rest of his team was. Feiyu lagged behind and watched Ruoming leave before turning back to me.

Feiyu finally let out a loud sigh, clutching his chest like he had watched an intense sports match. "Wow, that was very tense. Mind breaking all that down for me, Peijin? I had a bit of a hard time keeping up with all this future stuff . . ."

"Go ask Ruoming. I'm not your party leader, am I?"

Feiyu let out a defeated and dramatic huff. "Jiejie is so hostile to me."

I paused at the nickname and slowly met his gaze.

"What did you just say?"

"I said you were very hostile to me."

"No, before that."

"I asked you to explain your very confusing conversation with Ruoming."

"You know exactly what I'm referring to," I said, my face flushing bright pink again. "I'm not your 'Jiejie.' Don't ever call me that again, you rude bastard."

"You're a woman, and you're older than me. That makes you my Jie."

"Then don't say 'Jiejie' and make it sound like we're close," I exclaimed in annoyance. "Be more polite!"

"Sorry . . . Jiejie."

Although Jie was usually a respectful term meaning elder sister, calling someone you *weren't* familiar with "Jiejie" was far more teasing and borderline flirty. Feiyu was clearly trying to get a rise out of me.

Demon Great Sage Who Pacifies Heaven tries to hold back his laughter.

Divinity Great Sage Equaling Heaven is cackling and kicking his feet.

Divinity The One Who Fights in Front is embarrassed to be associated with you.

Divinity Supreme Commander of the Heavenly Hosts is starting to think that Disciple Peijin and Disciple Feiyu look good together.

Divinity The One Who Fights in Front casts Divinity Supreme Commander of the Heavenly Hosts a look of horror.

Divinity The One Who Fights in Front says Disciple Feiyu is far too childish.

> **Divinity The One Who Fights in Front says Disciple Ruoming's indifference is a far better trait.**

> **Divinity Supreme Commander of the Heavenly Hosts says Disciple Ruoming's platinum hair looks cheap.**

I looked at the notifications in complete horror, hating the idea of seeing Feiyu or Ruoming anymore than I already have.

"Go bully Ruoming instead of me," I snarled at Feiyu, quickly walking past him. "I'm heading back to my party."

Feiyu's eyes twinkled once more as he chuckled, not bothering to follow me. "You know where to find me, Jiejie!"

If I could have things my way, I would have punched Feiyu in the liver and called it a day, but instead, I walked back to my party, feeling like my social battery was more than drained.

I slowly made my way back to the center of the station. Ruoming's party was stationed at the central kiosk, and I made my way over to the one located a bit further behind where my party had settled. I walked toward them, my heart beating quickly in my chest.

For some reason, I felt nervous. It must have been the combination of knowing Feiyu would be much harder to avoid from now on, as well as the fact that Ruoming was an incredibly powerful but mysterious reader. If I wasn't already stressed from the Major Arcana and Karma, this made everything a whole lot worse.

I smacked myself in the forehead a few times, welcoming the sting. I wanted anything to distract me; I knew it was stupid to let my interactions with Feiyu and Ruoming get to me.

There was no point in stressing over it if I was going to inevitably bump into them for the rest of my life. It wasn't like I could just overpower them, either.

The moment I stepped through the kiosk door, I spotted the entire party sleeping inside, strewn over the floor. Yang was closest to the door and sat up when he heard me. He immediately reached for his staff, but once he realized who I was, he relaxed.

Yang let out a relieved sigh and ran his shaky hand through his hair before turning back to me. "Sorry." His voice was soft, trying not to wake the other party members.

"Nervous?"

"I'm all right."

My expression softened and I sat down next to him, pulling the blue sleeves of my hoodie over my hands. "You can talk about it with me if you want. I can't promise I'll be good at comforting you. You'll probably end up comforting yourself, if I'm honest."

Yang's eyes instantly widened in surprise. I glared at him.

"What?" I grumbled. "Did you think I couldn't say a single nice thing to you or something? What's with that reaction?"

"Yeah, a little bit," Yang said, scratching the back of his neck before letting out a light laugh. "You usually don't say cheesy lines like that. You usually tell us to get back to work or something. What a tyrant."

"That's the last time you'll ever hear that from me."

Yang let out a light laugh, and I watched curiously as his shoulders relaxed, and he finally seemed to truly calm down.

"Did you sort out everything you wanted to tell us?" Yang asked.

"No. I just can't stand Feiyu or that Ruoming kid. I needed to get away from them."

"I don't think we got the chance to meet Ruoming," Yang said, tilting his head curiously. "It was mostly Feiyu talking to us. What does Ruoming look like?"

I waved my hand in the air. "You'll know when you see him. Bright white hair and light eyes. He looks like a ghost, if anything."

"Well . . . I guess anything is possible."

"There's another girl you guys haven't met yet, either. Her name is Qijing. She's very shy, but hopefully she'll warm up to the idea of meeting all of you."

"I think Feiyu mentioned her. He adores her the way you adore Amelia."

I scrunched my nose. "Does he now?"

"I take it back. You love Amelia infinitely more."

"I thought so. How is Wei doing?"

Yang paused for a moment, seeming to pick his words carefully. "I'm sure he'll be back to his old self with enough time. But, he has been on edge and a lot more hesitant to speak up."

"I should have done a better job of protecting him," I muttered, pressing my forehead against my curled-up knees.

I knew I must look pathetic curled up like a child, but with Yang being the only one awake, it didn't feel so shameful.

Moreover, I couldn't blame Wei for feeling betrayed. I was sure that he knew the party always had his best interest in mind, but it was undeniable that I had kept Wei in the dark despite knowing what would happen to him.

Even now, I wasn't going to tell my party the extent of karma or the existence of *Surviving My First Run*—and that was with them having my back regardless of what I did.

Wei, however, could no longer trust that I always had his back. He knew I had been dishonest with him from the moment we met. If I was struggling to trust my party, it would take a lot of work for Wei to trust me again.

It wasn't like I couldn't keep secrets, though. If I told Yue and Wei that they were nothing more than characters I created, their reactions would be terrible.

It would do no good for the observers or gods to know I created this world, either. They would only try harder to ruin me, and my luck was bad enough.

I paused before I wrapped my hands around the back of my head. "This is all so fucked up . . ."

Yang stayed silent, but I could feel his gaze piercing into my back. Before he could say something, Yue stirred beside him, and I instantly sat up normally.

She blindly patted the ground all around her until she felt Amelia's frizzy hair under her fingers, confirming to Yue that Amelia was still there and safe. Then, she rubbed her eyes and slowly opened them, making direct eye contact with me.

"You look like complete shit," Yue murmured before shutting her eyes again, rolling over.

"Huh?! It's because I have to make sure you don't accidentally kill yourself half the time. That would stress out anybody."

"You're so loud, too. Can't you keep it down? I thought you wanted us to get some rest . . ." Yue trailed off, looking like she was about to fall back asleep at any moment.

I reached over and pinched her ear, pulling it toward me as she let out a yelp, slapping my hand away.

"Sorry, I didn't hear you," I said with a fake smile. "Mind saying it again a bit louder?"

"Fine, fine!" Yue whined, sitting up fully now and slapping her cheeks to wake herself up.

Amelia woke up because of the chaos and quietly crawled up beside me. Her hands fisted the fabric of my hoodie before she lay her head on my lap. Dried drool was crusted on her cheeks and chin. I went to wipe it and realized she had already fallen back asleep.

So cute! I wrapped my arm over her small back and gently ran my fingers through her hair. By the time I looked over at Wei, I realized he was already wide awake. But, he didn't say a word to any of us; instead, he just lay on his back, staring blankly at the ceiling above him.

"Wei," I said nervously. "Are you feeling all right?"

A long pause ensued before he replied. "I'm sorry. I'm just trying to sort things out right now. It's all so jumbled still."

Wei's voice was barely audible, but he sat up, his eyes still avoiding mine. His once long and glossy hair was now disheveled and dull, and the bright look in his eyes had vanished.

> **Divinity Supreme Commander of the Heavenly Hosts is mortified by the sight.**

> **Divinity Supreme Commander of the Heavenly Hosts prays for Disciple Wei to feel better.**

> **Divinity Supreme Commander of the Heavenly Hosts sends good wishes.**

Yang looked terribly worried, his eyes never leaving Wei's sorry state for a moment. I wondered what they talked about for that brief moment they were alone together.

"Don't let it eat you up, Wei," I said firmly. "I'll wait for you, but the world won't."

Wei finally met my gaze. "I promised I would be your sword, Peijin. I'm a man of my word. So, tell us what needs to happen next, and I'll execute it."

CHAPTER FOUR

I chewed my lower lip, staring at Wei's sorry state before letting out a sigh. I straightened my back, sitting up all the way now. I had my moment of sulking, but now that my entire party was awake and struggling, I needed to be their symbol of grit.

"There are two main things I want to cover. First, Karma. Second, what happened back in Wei's room, which was tied to the Major Arcana."

I tried to keep my voice as steady as possible. I had kept a lot from my party, and honestly, I was worried about how they might react to the upcoming reveal.

It wasn't like they were stupid—they had obviously picked up on my lies of omission—but they weren't aware of the extent.

"Remember when I was locked with the . . . ghost-version of my dad during my dungeon room? At some point, it changed into an entity known as Karma."

"But, Karma is part of the system," Yue interrupted. "Like karmic restraints, right?"

"That's what I originally thought until my dungeon room. Karma is also an entity. It's capable of shapeshifting. In my room, it looked like me. But in Wei's room, it possessed Daji's deceased form."

Many gods are stunned by Disciple Peijin's reveal!

Divinity The One Who Fights in Front says she did not know Karma interfered in Disciple Peijin's dungeon room.

> **Divinity Great Sage Equaling Heaven asks if Karma shut the dungeon room's broadcast.**

> **Divinity Supreme Commander of the Heavenly Hosts turns to Broadcaster Cheng.**

> **Thousands of gods turn to Broadcaster Cheng for answers.**

Yue gasped, sitting up and slamming her fists on the ground, finally looking wide awake. "So that's why Wei's room was so fucking difficult! If Meihua hadn't stepped in, all of us would've died—"

"Can you let me finish?" I exclaimed, glaring at Yue.

She immediately slumped back down, crossing her arms and grumbling obscenities at me under her breath.

I cleared my throat and continued. "For some reason, Karma also exists as an entity. It's beyond powerful, to the point where I think it could defeat almost all the gods we know. Which makes sense, at least to me, since even gods aren't immune to karmic restraints, unless they possess the appropriate amount of spiritual energy to offset the karmic backlash."

I patted Zhige, who was on the ground just to my side. "Karma recognized Zhige and knew that Zhige was originally named Haimo before coming into my possession. I'll talk about my theory with this later, since it's tied to the Major Arcana."

Yang was staring intently at me, words on the tip of his tongue. I was intentionally ignoring him, anxious about what he might ask me, since it sometimes seemed like he could read my mind. Finally, I left a long enough pause for him to speak up.

"And why would Karma introduce herself to you first?" Yang asked. "You weren't the most righteous person before the apocalypse, but none of us were. If Karma was going to confront one of us for committing evil deeds, I figured it would be Yue."

Yue's jaw dropped, and she immediately shoved Yang. "Are we kidding?! If you're gonna blame someone, blame the person Karma is clinging onto."

Yang shook his head. "It's not Peijin's fault that we have to fight Karma. Karmic restraints target everyone."

"If it targeted everyone *equally*, then why would we need an entire god to save us from Karma's attacks? If it wasn't for Meihua's intervention, none of us would be here, not even Peijin."

"But we're alive, aren't we?" Yang insisted. "How many parties do you think will return with all of their members?"

I coughed loudly again, looking straight at Yue. She rolled her eyes and slammed her back against the wall of the kiosk like a petulant child. I shot her a condescending grin for properly reading the room.

"I don't fully know why Karma targeted me. In all honesty, I think it's unfair, but it's not like I can sue her," I shrugged. "But, there is one thing I can't get out of my mind.

"Karma told me that out of every single being in this universe, I have the worst karma, and I'll never be able to pay it off. In fact, it's so bad that it affects the people around me." I paused, staring at the ground before I looked up at the rest of my party. "And that means it hurts all of you, too. Yue is right."

Wei's face twisted into an unreadable expression, his hands trembling. I avoided his questioning gaze. I knew what he wanted to ask. I knew he wanted to ask if it was my fault things went so far south for him. Although his fate was sealed from the start, my honest answer was still "yes." No matter how I put it, it was my fault Wei had to suffer in the first place.

"That means just by being around me, you're all being hurt. You'll suffer more than you would with any other party." I said softly. "So, if any of you don't want to bear that burden, then now is your chance to leave."

My voice was shaking wildly, and so were my hands. I clasped my hands together and hid them behind Amelia, not wanting to sway the opinions of my party members. The last thing I wanted them to do was stay with me out of a sense of pity or obligation.

Amelia was still pressed against me, but I gently shifted my bodyweight away from her, not looking at a single one of my party members. I wasn't a good enough person to order them to leave, nor was I a good enough person to leave on my own.

I was more afraid of being alone again than I was worried for my party's safety. It was wicked to come to that conclusion, but I still believed they could be safe with me. I wanted to believe that. I desperately wanted to believe that my future wasn't so bleak.

Regardless, it was only right for them to make this decision on their own. I couldn't keep Amelia beside me without telling her that every moment she spends with me will only bring her more agony.

Wei's room was a testament to that fact. Even if I could change his fate in the room, Karma would do anything to hurt me and my party. It was too obvious to ignore.

But for some reason, this felt like my most difficult sacrifice yet. I'd rather slice through my entire body again in Yang's dungeon room or fall into Karma's trap in mine.

The silence in the dark kiosk was heavy. I waited for the moment it would finally break with the sound of rustling fabric and the clicking of shoes as my party members left one by one.

"Why are you acting like that again?" Yue asked, her face scrunched in a disapproving expression.

"Like what?"

"If we cared that much about avoiding a death sentence, we wouldn't have partnered with you in the first place. Look at all the stupid shit you do half the time. I'd say we already have it worse than all the other parties out there," she said, crossing her arms.

I could almost burst out laughing from relief. Despite Yue's biting and critical words, she was still seated in front of me. That was the only thing that mattered.

"Thank you."

Yue groaned. "Shouldn't a sane person feel insulted by what I just said? You're not normal. Maybe you're a masochist or something."

My expression dramatically soured. "First, Yang's a pervert, and now, I'm a masochist. If anything, you're the one who seems to be weirdly obsessed with this sort of thing."

Yang looked exhausted. "Can we leave me out of this, please . . ."

Wei and Amelia hadn't said a word. I wasn't expecting Amelia to, but Wei's silence . . . I'd be lying if I said it didn't terrify me.

Despite our earlier banter, the kiosk went silent once more. It was clear everyone was just as uncomfortable as I was, if not more so.

Finally, Wei spoke up, his voice light.

"Why are you looking at me like that? I told you I'm a man of my word, didn't I? Have some faith in me, then." Wei flashed me a sincere smile, nudging my arm.

I let out a breath I didn't know I was holding. An embarrassed flush crept up my face. I was ready to throw my arms around all of them, but I held myself back.

> **[Observers Chat]**
> **Socrates:** SO CUTEEE!
> **Socrates:** Jia Li made her first true friends. Should I sponsor a cake and set up a celebration? Or would no one else show up to Jia Li's celebration party . . .
> **Socrates:** I'll still be rooting for you! A smaller cake is cheaper anyway.

Socrates was such an asshole sometimes. I quickly swiped the messages away. I could feel my neck and ears heating up now.

"You guys are really embarrassing . . ." I grumbled, rubbing the back of my neck and lowering my head.

"Huh?" Yue said, looking at me stupidly. "So you're embarrassed even when we're nice to you? I should be mean all the time then."

"You already are."

Yue scrunched her nose. "You're not very grateful for all the effort I put into keeping this party running."

I rolled my eyes dramatically. "Whatever you say. Well, still. I'm very . . . appreciative of all of you. I mean it."

"Y-You really mean it?" Yue said, dabbing away her fake tears before I punched her arm firmly.

"In that case," I began, "I'll continue with my theory. If it's totally wrong, though, don't blame me. My guess is as good as yours."

Amelia looked up at me with a teasing look in her eyes, finally speaking up. "That's not true. You're the god of fate and fortune."

"Well, this god isn't omniscient," I said, shrugging my shoulders. "I can only give an outline, and even that might not make any sense."

Yue let out a frustrated groan. "Can you just get to it already?"

I shot her a glare. "The Meihua we saw was a different Meihua from the one that Wei theoretically knew. So, we're playing around with a ton of different timelines, and this might get confusing. Meihua represented the World tarot. I'm the Tower. I still don't exactly know what any of these cards mean, but they're given to people across all the different timelines."

"Do you realize how batshit crazy you sound?" Yue asked.

"We're literally in an apocalypse," I retorted. "Like, with monsters and ghosts and demons. Why is this suddenly far-fetched?"

Yang interjected before Yue and I could spiral. "Then do we exist in those other timelines, and how many timelines do you think there are? Also, what triggers a new timeline, since the World comes from a previous one?"

I figured this must be how quantum physicists felt. I didn't know how to answer any of these questions with certainty, and there was nothing more I hated than this exact dilemma.

Furthermore, I didn't know how to answer Yang's first question. I was inclined to believe that there was only one version of 'real' people who existed outside the world of *Surviving My First Run*. After all, it seemed like the World had been meeting me for the very first time, and I was certainly real.

That being said, if I gave an answer alongside those words, half my party would realize they didn't truly exist. And that I was also the super-secret, in-disguise author of this world.

"I think there might only be multiple versions of some of us," I answered. "Half the reason I'm saying that is because I don't like the idea of thousands of versions of myself existing."

Wei pointed at himself. "What about me, though? If there are multiple versions of Meihua, shouldn't there be multiple versions of me?"

I hesitated, my brow furrowing with the effort of answering. I knew it was easier to be honest with them, and I was doing my best to make those efforts, but this wasn't something I could reveal given the timing of the situation.

"Let's cross that bridge when we get to it," I said. "If there are multiple versions of you, I'm sure all of them more or less have similar character traits, so we don't need to worry. You're a good man, Wei. And if there are multiple versions of Daji, we'll just have to kill every single one."

"At least from my understanding," Yang added, "this is something that should be restricted by Karma, right? For example, a thousand versions of Daji can't just teleport across timelines to slaughter us."

"Gross," I said, sticking my tongue out at the mere mention of Karma.

"Sorry. You know what I mean."

"I agree with you. And other than Karma's personal vendetta against me, the system does seem pretty impartial. So I don't see why a bunch of ancient demons trying to kill us wouldn't be limited by the system."

"It didn't seem very limited a few hours ago," Wei said, his voice bordering on cold.

"I'd rather hope than despair," I answered.

Wei gave me a gentle smile before lowering his head. "I suppose you're right."

"As always."

Yang's eyes drifted down to the tattoo on my arm and Zhige. "Any clue how those two were related?"

"The World acknowledged Zhige earlier. So did Karma. I'm guessing then that Zhige is a ghost weapon that belonged to someone from an earlier timeline. Probably a member of the Major Arcana at that."

Zhige trembled beside me, as if shaking its head nervously, and I gave it a gentle slap on the hilt. "Don't lie."

Zhige shook even more furiously.

Yue huffed, leaning back and crossing her arms. "You must feel really special to have a weapon like that, huh?"

I shot back a bright grin. "I think it's well deserved."

"Was the previous owner also the Tower, then?" Yue asked. "The tattoo only appeared after you came in contact with Zhige."

Zhige flew up in the air and shook back and forth, this time insisting that Yue's theory wasn't true.

"I agree with Zhige on this. There should only be one being for each card. Maybe I'm super magical and immortal now," I joked, laughing dryly. This whole situation was so bizarre to me that I had to find humor where I could.

"Should we test out your hypothesis?" Yue asked, her grin reaching her eyes.

I glared at her and sighed, turning away. "Are you all feeling good enough for the next arc? Any elixirs needed?"

"Could be feeling a lot worse," Yang answered, his hand gently reaching up to rub my shoulder in a friendly manner.

I relaxed into his touch, a great weight being lifted off my chest at such a simple, warm gesture. Amelia looked up at Yang's hand before nuzzling against me once more, her hands gripping my hoodie even tighter now.

"What about you, Amelia?" I whispered.

"Sleepy," she answered.

I laughed. My hand came up to gently ruffle the back of her hair before I rubbed her back to soothe her.

I didn't realize how much my silence was weighing on me, and that I could be so delighted to simply share a few words with my party. But, maybe all I was doing was burdening all of them infinitely more with a truth I could have continued to carry on my own.

I looked up to catch Yang's eyes. They were clear but firm, as if analyzing my every move to see if I was ready to sabotage everything again with my own thoughts. I wanted to burst out laughing the moment I realized what he was doing—I guess I already built myself a bit of a reputation in my party.

"What's with that look?"

"What look?"

I stuck out my tongue. "Liar. You're just like me."

Yang looked briefly taken aback. The jingling sound at the train platform sounded, and we all whipped our heads in its direction. More parties had finally made it back from the second arc.

I got up first and practically rushed to the platform, catching a glimpse of Feiyu already standing at the top of the stairs lazily.

The first person stumbled from the train car.

CHAPTER FIVE

The man looked like he was about to fall, but he quickly caught his footing. He was coated in a dried layer of blood that flaked off with each jagged movement.

But, the moment he spotted me and Feiyu, he instantly straightened his back and cleared his throat. Blue sparks flew around him, and the blood vanished. He expended stars just to look better before us.

I scrunched my nose. I instantly disliked this man. He seemed performative—like every action was dictated by how people would perceive him.

It's not like I didn't do the same thing . . . I just liked to think I was a little more genuine, at least internally. This guy, on the other hand, carried himself like a jackass.

"Hello," he said, not bothering to check in on his various party members leaving the train car, some looking pristine while others appeared wrecked. "Is it only your two parties who have made it out so far?"

I gave the biggest smile I could muster. "Yes. It looks like you did pretty well yourself."

I stepped up to introduce myself properly, extending a hand forward. "I'm Liu Peijin. You've probably met a few of my other party members."

He eyed my hand before finally shaking it. He squeezed my hand as hard as he could, trying to determine my physique stats, and I hid my reaction.

"Nice to meet you. You can call me Owl."

My mouth dropped slightly. "Like, the bird?"

Owl let out a tight laugh. "That's how it's pronounced."

"Is it spelled like that, too?"

"Yes."

"Your mom . . . named you Owl?"

This time, Owl's laugh was even louder, like he was mocking me.

"Of course not. It's a reference to the Bohemian Grove, though I don't blame you if you've never heard of it.."

Ummm . . . what now? I was certain this guy had to be a total loser.

"I definitely have," I asserted cockily, already losing my calm and collected act. I crossed my fingers, hoping that Socrates would come to my rescue with a little information like he always had with the Major Arcana.

> **[Observers Chat]**
> **Socrates:** I can tell my dearest Jia Li wants me to save her.
> **Socrates:** Hmmm . . . should I do it? Jia Li has been a bit mean to me recently . . .

An awkward silence extended between me and Owl.

"Then what is it?" Owl finally asked.

I bristled. Socrates, you bastard.

> **[Observers Chat]**
> **Socrates:** You have to forgive me for the messages I sent in Feiyu's chat.

I gave the slightest nod I could, not trying to draw Owl's suspicion.

> **Socrates:** You're so fun to mess with.
> **Socrates:** Bohemian Grove is an elitist group that meets in California. It's only for the uber elite, and what they get up to is totally unknown. One of their main events happens beneath a giant owl statue, though. It's their main symbol.
> **Socrates:** It's a little bit silly. He's probably trying to paint himself as this big leader in the apocalypse.

I crossed my arms before Owl. "It's the elite social club that meets in California. I just found it unbelievable that you named yourself after their little mascot."

Owl's eye twitched slightly before he let out a slight breath, and his pleasant expression returned. By now, his entire party had left the train car. Some had to be carried out, but in all, it must have been dozens of people trailing behind. Just how many rooms would they have needed to complete?

"I would consider it a satisfactory accomplishment to have led the largest party through the most recent arc," Owl said. "It's not easy looking after so many heads. Remind me again, how many party members do you have?"

At the mention of my party, my expression instantly twisted into a scowl. "What was your hardest dungeon room? Was the last one just about getting over your massive ego?"

Owl feigned a hurt look, and he brought a hand to his chest. "Did something happen in your dungeon rooms? We're all humans here, so if you ever need to talk to somebody, I'm here for you, Peijin."

Owl met me with the performative attitude, and it practically drove me mad. Before I could fully lose my cool, Feiyu stepped forward, gently redirecting Owl with a soft shoulder bump.

"I'll have Cheng take a look at your party members. You know how talented of a healer he is," Feiyu said casually, like he and Owl had known each other for a lifetime.

"Oh, only if Cheng is feeling up to it," Owl reassured Feiyu. "He's still so young. We really need to protect those younger than us. It's only right."

Divinity Supreme Commander of the Heavenly Hosts is wowed by Disciple Owl's righteousness.

Demon Abyssal Kraken of Black Seas says Divinities are not good judges of character.

Divinity Great Sage Equaling Heaven agrees and looks bored.

Behind the duo, Owl's party members looked incredibly relieved by Feiyu's words, whispers spreading among them that practically worshipped Feiyu. God dammit, I would have Yang do all the PR stuff from now on. This was so frustrating.

Cheng popped up behind Feiyu, eagerly chatting up a storm with each patient. I whipped around, scanning for Yang across the crowd.

"Yang! You already met a lot of the other disciples before the start of the second arc, right?"

He rushed over and nodded. "Yup. I'll go talk to them with Cheng," Yang said, bowing his head slightly before rushing past me. Cheng didn't mind one bit, instantly scooting over to make room for Yang and only seeming more overjoyed that he had more people to talk to.

I side-eyed Owl, who seemed annoyed at my intrusion on his plan. If we were going to play a game of appearances, I was going to make sure I'd at least beat this guy.

"I am impressed that you managed to bring back so many people," I said, keeping my eyes glued on him.

Feiyu nodded in agreement, placing a hand on Owl's shoulder. "It really is impressive! I can't even imagine how difficult it must have been to accomplish. You know, even though the party I'm in is so much smaller, I felt truly exhausted by the end. You're really remarkable."

> **Divinity Supreme Commander of the Heavenly Hosts finds Disciple Feiyu incredibly charming!**

> **Divinity Spirit of the Jade Moon nods in agreement with the Supreme Commander of the Heavenly Hosts.**

> **Demon Abyssal Kraken of Black Seas is swooned by Disciple Feiyu.**

> **Demon Abyssal Kraken of Black Seas also wants to earn praise from Disciple Feiyu.**

> **Divinity The One Who Fights in Front says Disciple Feiyu is much wiser than Disciple Peijin.**

> **Divinity Supreme Commander of the Heavenly Hosts emphatically disagrees.**

> **Divinity The One Who Fights in Front rolls her eyes and goes silent.**

> **Divinity The One Who Fights in Front says Disciple Peijin needs to follow through with her promises.**

> **A handful of gods question The One Who Fights in Front about the meaning of her words.**

> **Divinity Supreme Commander of the Heavenly Hosts slams his fist against the table, remembering the promises he made with Disciple Peijin.**

> **Divinity Supreme Commander of the Heavenly Hosts says Disciple Peijin is incredible at keeping her word.**

> **Divinity Great Sage Equaling Heaven asks if they've been watching different broadcasts.**

> **Demon Great Sage Who Pacifies Heaven grunts in agreement.**

I began sweating profusely. It wasn't very easy to forget the promises I had made to both Athena and Archangel Michael. Not only did I have to uncover the Eternal Wish, but I was personally allied with Olympus while the rest of my party was tied to Paradise. And neither of them knew about the contract I made with the other . . .

It wasn't like my hands were completely tied behind my back. After all, there were exit terms to my contracts with Athena and Archangel Michael. In the event of my death, all of the obligations would cease.

Owl let out a sigh of relief at Feiyu's words. "I'm just glad most of us made it back. But now that everyone is on the same page, I'm sure the next arc will be easier."

I perked up at his statement, and I felt a gnawing suspicion in my core. "What do you mean 'on the same page?'" I asked nonchalantly.

Owl's eyes narrowed slightly, as if trying to find the hidden meaning among my words. "Just that there was a bit of a disconnect before. Some of us knew more than others."

"What more did you know compared to the others?"

He smiled, realizing I was testing him. "This setup is pretty similar to those famous apocalypse novels, but not everyone reads those stories. Of course, those who have are equipped with a distinct advantage. Some of these events are much more predictable."

"Is that what makes you the Owl? You must've been quite the bookworm then."

"Ha!" Owl laughed, and we came to the same realization at the same time. "I guess you could say that. Why? Were you also an avid reader?"

My brow furrowed, and my expression hardened. "No. I got bored of it. A lot of stories are recycled."

"Because that's what sticks, right? Who doesn't love a classic tale." Now when Owl spoke, he had a massive grin plastered across his face, like he was utterly delighted by his revelation.

I, on the other hand, looked terribly grim.

Because Owl had also read *Surviving My First Run*.

The meaning behind his words was clear. He had read at least a chunk of *Surviving My First Run*, and so had other members of his party. Perhaps his entire party was made up of readers.

I was surprised I hadn't bumped into more people familiar with my web novel by this point. I wasn't *that* famous, but it wasn't like my work was unknown, either. Now I knew the reason.

Owl probably thought I was also a reader, just like Ruoming did. He could believe that for now. The bigger variable was whether or not Owl or his party members planned on leaking the fact that this whole thing came from my novel.

"All this abstract talk about reading is boring me," Feiyu pouted, now swinging one arm over my shoulder and the other over Owl. "What do we think the next arc is going to be? Hopefully nothing as dreadful as the second arc. Geez, I thought I was going to go crazy in there! All those psychological dungeons are such a drag."

I wanted to roll my eyes. Feiyu was talking like he wasn't constructed solely to thrive in this environment. How annoying.

> **[Observers Chat]**
> **CactusLiver:** Aww, Feiyu is still such a great character. He really plays off the situation without showing how much it affects him.
> **Hedgehog1938:** I know right!! That's my protagonist!
> **BeigeTowel:** Feiyu and Peijin both. Aren't they so similar?
> **Nipon23:** similar how . . . i don't think they could be more different
> **BeigeTowel:** Don't make me type up an entire essay . . .
> **Nipon23:** i take it i'm right then :)
> **BeigeTowel:** They're not the same person or something, but they're similar because they both mask how they really feel about a situation by playing it off lightly. I mean, isn't Feiyu just trying to protect the people around him by downplaying how he feels? I think Peijin does the same to protect her party and herself.
> **Nipon23:** sure i guess but feiyu comes off as charming and peijin comes off as immature
> **Socrates:** Immature?? She's in the middle of an apocalypse. Wouldn't it be difficult for anybody to save the world when they haven't even resolved their character defects yet?
> **Nipon23:** LOLL i know she's livid you just said that

I instantly shut the blue window of the Observers Chat. The last thing I wanted to see right now was these people babbling on and on.

I looked at Feiyu, this time not swatting his arm away. "Whatever it is, we'll all be pitted against each other. The second arc was just scaling us up against one another, so the next one is going to actually test how we fair against one another."

Feiyu's eyes widened. "Wow, you really did read a lot before the apocalypse, didn't you, Jiejie?"

Owl raised a brow at the way he addressed me. I turned away, my cheeks pink from embarrassment. "I'm sure you came to the same conclusion, so there's no need to flatter me."

Feiyu cocked his head toward the Owl, indicating it was his turn to respond. Owl nodded his agreement with me.

"Of course that would be the next level. Anyone would think that, even kids," he began. "More importantly, I think it'll be about the top parties going against one another. After all, there has to be a way for someone to come out on top of all these disciples. There needs to be a true leader, after all."

For some reason, it felt like Owl was taking a jab at me, trying to show off his supreme knowledge in comparison to the god of fate and fortune.

"Mmm, now that both of you mention it, I guess I can see that happening. I never really thought so deeply about it," Feiyu said, pulling back as he stretched his arms in the air, his muscles flexing.

I snorted in disbelief, and Feiyu flashed me a smile.

"Either way," Feiyu continued, "even if some disciple hierarchy is enforced upon us, I hope we can all remain allies. At the end of the day, the only thing people can trust is themselves and the people around them. What use is it if we ruin each other, especially if we're all fighting just to survive?"

I sighed, stepping further back as more and more train cars made it to the station and disciples began unloading by the dozens. If there were thousands of people who survived the first arc, there were now only hundreds who survived the second. But, these people were far more formidable and hardened by what they were forced to overcome.

I turned back to Feiyu. "Spoken like a true warrior, Feiyu. I have to say, I'm impressed. You have my heart pounding in my chest. I'm ready to jump right back in!"

Feiyu's expression lit up, and he let out a bright, loud laugh. It seemed like just about anything could appease him. "The first time we spoke, I thought you were quite funny, Jiejie. I'm glad that my impression of you wasn't wrong."

"H-Huh?" I stammered, turning a humiliating shade of pink again. "What are you even saying? Do you hear the words coming out of your mouth right now? I'm being facetious."

That same arrogant, cocky expression returned to his face, and I let out a frustrated huff, turning around and waving goodbye to Feiyu and Owl. "I'll see you all in the next arc. Best of luck. Let's do our best to keep our parties safe."

CHAPTER SIX

Once Yang saw that my conversation had wrapped up, his head perked up, and he jogged up to me. I approached him leisurely.

"I'm hoping your conversation with Feiyu went better than last time?" Yang asked.

"Every conversation I have with him is a bad one."

"What about Owl? I thought he was a bit eccentric when I first met him. It's noble and a bit crazy to take on such a large party, but it seems like he's done a good job keeping them alive, even if they're in bad shape."

"I hate that guy more than I hate Feiyu. He's so performative."

Yang quirked his brow, and I rolled my eyes at the suggestion behind them. "In a different way than I am. He's just been kissing ass since he came back in third place. What a shame it is to share a podium with that loser . . ." I lifted my head to look at the rows of people from Owl's party, who were now resting against the station's pillars. "How are they doing?"

"They're doing good. Cheng is extremely talented, you know?"

"Yup. Probably the best healer we'll have in these parts. Though," I said, pointing a finger at Yang, "I think you'd have a pretty good knack for it if you decided to pick it up."

"Me?" He exclaimed in surprise, pointing at himself.

"Yup. I think you're special, too, Yang. You could do whatever you set your mind and heart to."

"Did Feiyu cause your brain to short-circuit?"

"No. I'm just kissing your ass. See how annoying it is?"

Yang smiled and looked down at the ground.

"Mind helping me out a bit more in the meantime?" I asked Yang.

"If I refuse, I think you'll really lop my head off this time."

"I want our party to garner more favor with the disciples. Ruoming's party benefits a ton from Feiyu's presence and the fact they set up the entire train-base system when they first got here. It'll be bad if people see us as wannabes that want to uproot everything for power."

"It'll be easier if we work with Ruoming's party to accomplish that. It'll help if we're on good terms with them, and I'm not better than Feiyu when it comes to saying the right things."

"That Ruoming guy . . . how did he get so lucky?" I asked, vividly remembering the first moment I spotted Ruoming.

It was still difficult, if not impossible, for me to think he wasn't Rui. Obviously, a part of me desperately wanted to believe that I'd encounter Rui again, and if I did, he would accept me and tell me why he left me all those years ago.

Ruoming even managed to get my sister into his party. Even if I didn't want to work with Ruoming or Feiyu for a moment longer than I had to, I wanted to be close to Qijing, just to keep an eye on her. If she lost both her mother and father, then it only made sense for her big sister to step up to protect her.

I shook my head. "You're right, Yang. In that case, I think you and Cheng make a good pair, and you two can keep working toward healing the other disciples. But make sure it's clear who you're allied with. This isn't charity work. It's garnering favor."

"I hate to think of it like that, especially if I don't mind helping them."

I remembered our final conversation before the apocalypse—about how Yang didn't mind helping hoarders. About how he simply wanted to propel them forward into a new life that might be a little more kind to them.

For the most part, we were still the same people, even if some pieces of us had been swapped out with new ones.

I smiled softly at Yang, and he looked back at me in surprise. At the very least, I could be reassured that Yang would always be a better person than me, and that thought brought a feeling of great calm to me. There would always be good people in the world, even if they were pushed past the edge.

"You're right."

I opened up my blue profile screen, and quickly navigated to the party chat.

[Party Chat]
Peijin: Let's do our best to leave a good impression on the disciples and work with Feiyu. Yang, keep working with Cheng to help heal the disciples. Yue,

> lightly use Magician's Hand to help soothe patients who might be haunted by what they saw in their dungeon rooms. Have Amelia accompany you. Wei, tail Feiyu for a minute. Or you can rest if you think that's better.

I wanted Wei to be with Feiyu rather than alone with his own thoughts. I figured that no one could better calm Wei than Feiyu, and I knew Wei wouldn't go into too much detail and spill what we knew about the Major Arcana.

I suddenly remembered how Wei received the white robes I originally wanted to give him, and my chest tightened. Was that from Ruoming, then? My lips pressed together in a thin line.

> **[Party Chat]**
> **Peijin:** But I don't want any of you talking to Ruoming, period.
> **Yue:** Keeping him all to yourself? :,(
> **Peijin:** Watch yourself in front of Amelia.
> **Wei:** Thank you, Peijin.
> **Yang:** Understood.
> **Amelia:** Okay!!!

I looked up at Yang and smiled. "All right. Let's secure this win."

"Got it, boss," he answered brightly.

Yang immediately returned to Cheng who greeted him with open arms.

At the same time, a flash of blue appeared behind me, and I instantly recognized it as my personal broadcaster.

"You've got a bit of a collaborative streak going, don't you?" Chang said, hovering behind me with his arms crossed. "I have to say, I'm really surprised."

"Do you have anything important to say to me?"

"Hmph. The next arc starts soon. I'm preparing the arc message to be sent out."

"It's the one about the citadel, right?"

The third arc took place in a citadel, in which the top three parties from the second arc would be competing with each other to conquer the throne. It sounded incredibly simple, but it was a massive location, and the stakes were high. Whoever took control of the throne would rule over all the local disciples; however, they would also be subservient to the gods who supplied them this power.

This time, Chang's face hardly showed any surprise at the knowledge I possessed. He must have gotten used to my antics by now.

"Of course. My dearest Peijin could never be wrong about one of her predictions!"

"Do you have another candy?" I asked, turning to face him and extending a hand.

Chang shot me an exasperated look with a slight pout. "Is that the only way I can get your favor?"

"Yes. I suggest you keep a massive stash of orange lollipops on you now, and I'll keep sending money your way."

"You're so transactional," Chang sighed.

He lifted his two clawed hands and cupped them before his chest. A blue flash appeared before a lollipop fell into his claws. He promptly unwrapped it and shoved it into my mouth without warning.

I was about to scold him before I spotted his one missing scale. I felt a slight pang of guilt until I remembered just how much this little creature was profiting off of my presence in his broadcast, and I instantly felt fine.

Besides, this thing worked for the gods. Maybe I would feel more sympathetic if he wasn't so corrupt. Oh well.

I sucked on the lollipop and savored the flavor for a moment before I grabbed the stick and popped it out my mouth. "Is there anything I should know about the next arc?"

"Hmm, maybe I shouldn't tell you unless you give me something in return."

"Gosh, Chang, don't even pull that on me right now. Or I really will be cranky and mean."

Chang faked a shiver. "Sorry, sorry. Just the thought of that terrified me. But I really can't tell you much because of karmic restraints. All I can say is that popularity matters."

"What?"

"That means you need to be popular."

"I could tell that much. Are you serious?"

"Why would I lie to you?"

"Well, shit."

"I mean, if you think about it," Chang said, bringing up a blue screen before the both of us, "your popularity has grown quite a bit. See this graph? Before, you were at five percent approval, but now you're at twenty percent. It's incredibly impressive if you think about it."

"..."

"I'm not being facetious, Peijin."

"Okay, okay. I get it. I'm sure things will work out."

"You're definitely a great optimist when things are totally hopeless."

I shooed Chang away, and he vanished in a flurry of blue sparks.

Theoretically, if popularity or the votes of gods and observers influenced the next arc, it would have pretty polarizing results. My party had a handful of loyal observers and gods, but at the same time, my party was well-hated by members of both . . .

I let out a heavy sigh and ran my hand through my hair. There was no point in worrying about it yet. I was already trying to improve my party's public standing, and a good performance was always going to curry favor.

As long as my party didn't fumble the entire citadel, we still had a very good chance. And, I had no intention of losing this time around.

I pushed through the crowd of disciples and leaned against a nearby pillar, tapping Zhige on the ground as I stared into its eye.

"Zhige. Do you like me more than your past owner?" I asked, lifting the blade until we were looking eye to eye.

Zhige blinked at me before looking away.

"Zhige..."

Zhige hesitantly looked at me again.

"Zhige, don't you think I've been very nice to you?" I pouted. "Was your old owner that cool?"

Zhige moved its eye up and down, as if nodding. I glared at it.

"Didn't you turn me into the Tower? I think you should take some more responsibility, Zhige. Now, I'm in some super crazy time loop. That really breaks my heart, you know?"

Zhige's eye widened, and the blade quickly shook side to side, vehemently denying my claim.

"Hmm, that's definitely how I see it, though. Maybe I'll find it in my heart to forgive you one day."

Zhige's red eye squinted painfully, like it was getting ready to cry. I let out a laugh and patted the blade gingerly. "I'm just kidding. I trust you. For now."

Before I could continue teasing it, I saw Amelia sprinting toward me from across the platform.

"Peijin!"

I squatted down so I could catch her in my arms and toss her up into the air. "Where's Yue-ayi?"

"Yue-ayi is okay, but I missed you."

"Good girl!" I praised her, a big grin on my face. "Make sure you remind Yue-ayi of that all the time, okay?"

"Okay!"

Amelia buried her face in the crook of my neck again. I smiled.

"Peijin... do you like me more than anyone else?"

Amelia's question caught me entirely off guard, and I looked at her in surprise. "Of course. Amelia is my favorite out of everyone."

"Do you promise?"

Had she overheard my conversation with Zhige? It would be pretty amusing if she was jealous of a simple blade, and a slight smile grew on my face.

"Of course. Why do you ask?"

"Because I'm worried Peijin won't like me as much in the future."

"Huuuh?"

Amelia pulled away from my shoulder, her lips in a pout and her brow furrowed. Her eyes bore deep into mine. "You won't like Qijing more than me, will you?"

I paused, my eyes widening slightly as I looked at her. I quickly brought my expression back to a warm and pleasant one. "Did you see us talk earlier?"

"I heard it."

I cocked my head to the side. "I thought you were asleep. Is your hearing that good now because of your skills?"

Amelia gave a slight nod, but her frown was still present. "You're ignoring me."

"Amelia, you're the dearest to me. Far more than Qijing. If you think I was being extra nice to her, it's only because she's a lot more shy than you. I wanted her to warm up to me."

"But it's not like that," Amelia insisted. "You talk to us in totally different ways. I've never heard you ever struggle with me like you struggled with Qijing. You didn't even talk to Ailun like that, even though he hardly spoke a word!" Her expression twisted into an even bigger pout. "I'm really jealous."

I suddenly burst out laughing, bringing up one hand to cup her cheek while my other still held onto her securely.

"I'm sorry, Amelia. I didn't think you'd feel like that. I only want you two to get along."

"And you promise you won't change your mind?"

"I promise I won't." I brought my hand up and extended a pinky out to her. "I'll even pinky promise you. Do you know what that means?"

Amelia shook her head back and forth.

"It means I can never break this promise. If I break it, I'll have to cut off my own pinky," I said dramatically.

Amelia's eyes lit up in fear. "I would never make you do that!"

"I'm just kidding." I teased, grabbing her pinky with my own and shaking our hands. "But, it means I'll never break this promise, okay? So don't keep Yue-ayi worrying about you. You snuck away from her, didn't you?"

She looked up at me expectantly, and I gently ruffled her curly, blond hair. Amelia didn't say another word, but she reached out and hugged my leg with all her strength before running back off toward Yue, who had since realized Amelia went missing and was desperately scrambling all over the station looking for her.

"Amelia!" Yue shouted once she spotted the young girl, her shoulders tense. "What the hell?! Don't run off like that!"

"I'm sorry, Yue-ayi!" Amelia exclaimed apologetically, her voice trailing off the farther she got from me.

> **Divinity Far Shooting Queen of Beasts watches Disciple Amelia fondly.**

> **[Party Chat]**
> **Peijin:** Yue, how the hell could you take your eyes off Amelia for even a second??
> **Yue:** Oh my god, I swear she snuck away. I was literally watching her like a hawk the entire time
> **Peijin:** Obviously not. I saw her terrified and alone. The poor girl must have been terrified.
> **Amelia:** Yes!!
> **Peijin:** And if you knew she was missing, why wouldn't you shoot a message in the chat, huh? Trying to keep your mistake a secret?
> **Yue:** If I didn't find her I would've sent a message . . .
> **Amelia:** Yue-ayi, don't waste your messages!!
> **Yue:** I actually hate you guys.
> **Yang:** LOL

> **[Observers Chat]**
> **Socrates:** Jia Li, I'm curious. If it ever came down to it, would you save Amelia or Qijing?

"What the fuck kind of question is that?" I gawked at the message, glaring at my screen. "Didn't you hear the conversation I just had? I would try to save them both, but Amelia is my responsibility."

> **[Observers Chat]**
> **Socrates:** I'm just asking . . . Jia Li, you're weirdly kind to that girl. I'm only worried that Qijing could be a weak spot for you.

No one knew that Qijing was my sister. Not even Socrates. It made their doubts all the more frustrating. *Why would I choose a girl they thought I had no connection to over Amelia?*

"My *family* is my *party*," I emphasized. "They're all I have. Apart from them, there is not a single thing left for me."

> **[Observers Chat]**
> **Socrates:** I'm not down there with you, but I hope you know that I always have your back, too, Jia Li.

I let out a huff. "What happened to hating me?"

> [Observers Chat]
> **Socrates:** You've weaseled your way into my heart. Congratulations.

"Your virtual heart?"

Before our banter could continue, a giant blue screen appeared before me, and I instantly read through it.

> **ARC #3—BATTLE OF THE ASCENSION CITADEL**
> **Difficulty: C**
> **Task:** The top three parties will be competing in the Ascension Citadel. Parties will spawn into the main floor of the citadel, and they must fight their way to the throne. Whichever party sits on the Ascension throne first will become the ruling party of China. Both gods and observers will participate in ongoing votes for their favorite party, granting the winners buffs or the losers debuffs.
> **Reward:** Recognized leader of China and
> 100,000 stars per party member.

CHAPTER SEVEN

> **CONGRATULATIONS!**
> Your party, 'Peijin's World Dominion,' placed second at the conclusion of ARC #2—DUNGEONS OF GREAT TURMOIL. You will be competing against 'Major Arcana' and 'Bohemian Grove.'

> Your party will be marked with blue indicators. 'Major Arcana' will be marked with red indicators. 'Bohemian Grove' will be marked with yellow indicators.

> Please meet party leaders Song Ruoming and Owl outside the east exit of Platform 1 to briefly introduce yourself before the commencement of the Ascension Citadel. Arc #3 will begin in half an hour.

> **[Party Chat]**
> **Peijin:** All of you get together. I'll be meeting Song Ruoming and Owl for the next half hour. Take whatever elixirs you need to be healthy and well rested. I can cover the bill if needed.

I scurried toward the meetup location, and I found Ruoming already there. He was standing tall, his hands folded neatly in front of him. He didn't bother looking up at me when I arrived.

"I hope you aren't trying to tear my clothes off again," Ruoming said flatly. The sleeve of his shirt was still missing.

"W-What?!" I exclaimed, lifting a finger to point at him. "That's because I was skeptical of you, so don't make it sound so strange. I'm not some pervert or something, okay?"

Ruoming lifted his head. Those pale, dead eyes seemed to stare right into my soul, and I froze. If there was just the tiniest sliver of warmth in them, I would've accused him of being Rui all over again.

"Don't stand in my way," Ruoming said coldly.

My nails dug into my fists. Who did this guy think he was? To think, I got so worked up seeing him earlier. Even with Feiyu being a patient saint, I couldn't understand in the slightest how Feiyu could bear being in the same room as Ruoming for longer than five minutes.

"Your knowledge won't get you anywhere if you don't have the skill to match it," I shot back.

Ruoming lowered his head and glared up at me. His platinum bangs fell over his eyes, but it couldn't mask their intensity.

Owl finally appeared, a pleasant smile on his face and his eyes squinted shut from his grin. "Ruoming. Peijin. I'm glad we'll be together in this arc. What a truly brilliant trio we have in the making."

I crossed my arms, fed up with Owl. "There's no use in kissing my ass. I already decided I don't like you, so piss off."

Owl's eyes opened a sliver. "That attitude won't get you very far with the gods, Peijin. I hope you can find generosity in your heart."

I bristled at his words. "While you rely on garnering favor, I'll be relying on skill and strategy."

At that moment, Owl decided to ignore me. He turned to Ruoming. "I think it's safe to say that between the three of us, we all care deeply about our parties. So, even if we're competing, how far are we going to be pushing the fight between one another?"

Ruoming looked up, his expression giving away nothing. "I do not care about the lives of your party members. The only thing that matters is that I win."

Owl dispensed a loud, overcompensating laugh. "Of course, of course. I would say the same. But there are women and children in both of our parties."

"So, should I expect you to not stab me in the back when you get the chance?" I asked Owl.

Owl merely responded with a light hum. "You can expect me to treat that young girl of yours kindly."

"Don't you dare—"

"There is no reason for any of us to kill incessantly," Ruoming jutted in. "After all, we aren't the enemy. But I have no plans to go lightly on any of you, and you should hold no expectations of surviving off of my mercy."

Ruoming pushed past us, shoving each of us away with his shoulders. It was hard for me to fathom that a man with such a beautiful, delicate face was filled with an astounding amount of bitterness and resentment, as if he had already been worn down by decades of betrayal and cruelty.

I looked up at Owl with venom, on edge ever since he mentioned Amelia. "This is between Ruoming and me. You are leagues below both of us."

Owl tensed before letting out a sigh. "Don't all three of us have the same advantage, Peijin?"

"I don't know what you're talking about."

"Oh, I think you know exactly what I mean. You, Ruoming, and I all possess the same knowledge about the future arcs. Isn't it such a strange coincidence?" Owl asked, flashing me a large smile. "In fact, I think everybody in my party does."

That meant Owl had come to the same conclusion as I had about Ruoming, and Owl's entire party was certifiably made up of people who had read *Surviving My First Run* in some capacity. My theory was spot on.

Good thing I was such a massive bitch before. Most people dropped *Surviving My First Run* because of my poor attitude, which meant that their knowledge was incredibly limited.

The gods' perception of me was one of my biggest advantages. Marketing myself as the god of fate and fortune was half of my success, and if Owl started threatening that or revealed the truth about *Surviving My First Run*, it would be a massive hit to my reputation.

But, it must have also been a large part of Owl's success.

I took a step closer to him, tilting my head up to face him. "Oh yeah? How about you spell it out for me, then? I'm not quite following."

Owl stared at me for a moment before he let out a single, uncomfortable laugh. "We'll see how this arc plays out."

At that, Owl turned around, leaving me alone at the exit. I waited until he was fully out of my sight before I kicked the wall furiously, watching it crumble apart with a loud boom. These games were really getting on my nerves.

> **Divinity Supreme Commander of the Heavenly Hosts says not to let this get to Disciple Peijin.**

> **Divinity Supreme Commander of the Heavenly Hosts says Disciple Peijin has extremely bad luck, but her grit makes up for it!**

That didn't exactly make me feel better, but I knew Archangel Michael was only trying his best.

I clapped my hands together in front of me. "Thanks, Archangel Michael. I sure hope you're right."

> **Divinity Supreme Commander of the Heavenly Hosts enthusiastically stands up from his desk and begins cheering before Divinity Great Sage Equaling Heaven slams his fist down on the table in annoyance.**

> **Divinity Supreme Commander of the Heavenly Hosts slumps back down in his seat and whispers his cheers.**

> [Party Chat]
> **Yang:** It looks like Owl and Ruoming returned. We're standing outside the JA line if you want to join us.

Not wanting to waste any more of my valuable messages, I didn't bother responding and quickly made my way over. When I finally spotted my party, I gave a big wave, not waiting before I instantly started spewing orders at them.

"Since voting and popularity are pretty big factors in this next arc, I want Yang, Wei, and Amelia to focus on getting the observers and gods on our side. You three are less divisive than me and Yue. On the other hand, all of us need to focus on conquering the citadel."

"Are you going to go for the throne?" Wei asked. "I can guard you along the way from the other parties."

"None of us should sit on the throne," I said firmly, to his surprise.

In *Surviving My First Run*, Feiyu had discovered that whoever sat on the throne would in fact gain incredible power over disciples in their respective country, but that power came at a crippling expense.

The throne was the pet of an outer god. Thus, whoever sat on it would indirectly also come under the control of the outer gods, and their life expectancy would be reduced to a mere five additional years after sitting on the throne.

So instead, Feiyu destroyed the throne. However, the murder of a beloved pet did not go unnoticed, and Feiyu would have to survive the targeted hatred of outer gods for the rest of *Surviving My First Run*.

But, if both Ruoming and Owl were readers of *Surviving My First Run*, it was too easy for them to avoid the consequences of sitting on the throne. Instead, one of their parties would destroy the throne first, and then deal with the wrath later on with similar methods that Feiyu had used.

So, I had to create a brand-new plan. That was nothing for a writer like me. Unlike Yang's dungeon room, I had fully fleshed out the concept of citadels late into *Surviving My First Run*, so I had a distinct knowledge advantage for this arc.

"If we sit on the throne, Karma mandates that we need to give something up in exchange for that overwhelming power, which means there will be some caveat to sitting on the throne. However, if we destroy the throne, we'll piss off the system again."

I twirled Zhige in my hand until it was comfortably pointed right at the ground. I dug the blade into the concrete floor and began to create a diagram.

"This line represents the floor. This structure here is the citadel. It has multiple floors, and the top one will contain the throne. The other parties are going to work their way all the way up, until they either sit on the throne or destroy it," I said, tapping Zhige at the very top of the diagram.

"However," I continued, now drawing a structure beneath the line representing the ground. "The citadel must be getting power from somewhere, right? The theoretical *heart* of the citadel will be located beneath it. It keeps the citadel, the monsters inside, blah, blah, blah, alive. The most important thing is that it controls the throne, too. If we can 'turn off' the citadel by destroying the heart, then we can win the arc without having to destroy the throne and piss everyone off again.

"The way we access the heart is through nodes. Of course, the citadel is doing its best to guard its heart. There are nodes hidden all throughout the citadel, and if we can take control of them, then we're able to control the citadel's size, danger, etc. Most importantly, once we collect all the nodes, it'll form the heart, which we can reveal beneath the citadel."

I let out an exhausted sigh the moment I finished running through it all. "All that making sense?" I asked.

"Wow," Wei said, staring at the diagram before looking up at me with a wide grin. "We've got a really good chance, huh? Do you think anyone else knows about the heart and nodes?"

"Nope. That's from my magical god powers," I said cockily, nodding my head vigorously.

Wei pointed at the top of the diagram, where the throne was. "We should still find the throne room, right? In case there are nodes up there."

"Yes. It'll be a good distraction, too, since the other parties are going to think that we're also trying to sit on the throne. They might have figured out that they shouldn't sit on the throne, but that doesn't change any of our plans."

"How much should we factor in the observers and gods?" Yang asked, his head tilted slightly. "If we're going through this alternative path, then we won't be going head-to-head much with the other parties. In that case, the buffs or debuffs won't have a big impact on us."

"That's the one variable I'm not sure about yet. We'll just have to wait and see how it plays out once we get into the citadel."

Yue nodded, her brow furrowed in concentration as she stared intently at the map, like her small brain was struggling to absorb all the information. "Are our opponents ghosts or demons? I want to know how to make Magician's Hand more effective."

"Could be both. I trust you can go off of vibes once we get there."

"I could also make it look like you exploded or something in there. You know. Just to throw off the other parties."

"That's really twisted, but whatever. Are we all on the same page?"

I checked the arc status and saw there were only a few seconds until it began. I looked around to make sure they all nodded, especially Amelia, who I was worried might not have caught every detail. I flashed them the biggest smile I could.

"Then let's win this."

CHAPTER EIGHT

At once, a flurry of bright blue sparks surrounded us, bouncing off our skin but causing no physical harm.

We were floating in a large cloud of sparks, with no sense of which direction we were headed. I reached out, grabbing Amelia by the collar of her shirt like a kitten and drawing her up against my body.

Wei grabbed onto the sleeve of my hoodie, and Yang pulled Yue tightly against himself, trying to shield her from anything that might suddenly burst through the sparks.

Wei was directly across from me, his face stoic as if this wasn't out of the ordinary for him. That's right—now that he regained his memories, he was the most experienced out of all of us.

He spun his sword in his hand with unbelievable expertise. The long, white fabric of his robes billowed around him almost magically.

Beside him, Yang wielded his staff, his grip firm as he extended it. His eyes were glowing as he sifted through various blue screens, equipping himself with elixirs, skills, and higher levels as though he were about to enter the battle of his lifetime.

The blue sparks moved in a frenzy all around us, going faster and faster until we were spinning rapidly, barely able to keep hold of each other.

I was growing dizzy from how overwhelming the entire sight was and squeezed my eyes shut. Finally, I felt my feet slam down on solid ground, and my eyes shot open.

I placed Amelia on the ground and looked around me, letting out a sigh of relief when I saw my entire party was beside me and safe. All of them had small blue markers above their heads, noting that they were in my party.

Then, I took in my surroundings.

"Wow," I uttered.

"This is so cool!" Amelia exclaimed, jumping up and down in excitement and shooting her fist up in the air.

Around us was a mockup of Venice, with all its narrow streets and roads. Tall orange, blue, and yellow buildings surrounded us. The cobblestone was bumpy beneath our feet. Long green vines with fat red roses wove up and down the buildings.

Above us, the sky was a vivid turquoise. It was also where the citadel's expansive size was made clear. The sky wasn't a never-ending expanse—it was a fabricated ceiling. All the clouds had been painted on it, and it was as though lights were placed behind the synthetic sky to give it the illusion of being outdoors.

We were officially in the Ascension Citadel.

Right off the bat, Bohemian Grove and Major Arcana would break through this fake sky to work their way into the throne room, like Feiyu did in *Surviving My First Run*.

There was nothing to be found on the main floor except a horrific number of beasts and challenges—unless, of course, you knew about the nodes.

Yue let out a low whistle, slowly lengthening her body. "I guess I don't need to book a flight here anymore. Isn't this beautiful?" she asked, taking a few steps until she found a small stone bridge.

Yue ran over to it and peeked over the edge, taking in the murky blue river beneath it, and turned back to us in excitement. "There's no time limit for this arc, right? Maybe it's time for us to take a little break in Venice."

I walked up the windy, narrow roads, dragging my fingertips along the lengths of stony buildings beside me.

With all of us coming from the bustling city of Shanghai, sights like this were utterly remarkable. Even Yang paused to simply admire the architecture. Wei's eyes gleamed with awe, but he was far more restrained in his movements.

"Let's spend a moment here, just to look for any nodes," I began. "Yue, you can use Magician's Hand to detect the illusions that are masking the nodes. Amelia, use Stone's Aura, and you should be able to detect the nodes when they're nearby."

I then pointed to Yang and Wei. "As for you two, I want one of you to follow Amelia, and the other Yue. Make sure they aren't attacked as they look for the nodes. I'm also going to look for the nodes, but I'm going to try to figure out where we are in the citadel, so we know where we go next.

"If any of you bump into Major Arcana or Bohemian Grove, immediately send a message in the party chat, and we'll all come with backup. For now, all of you should stay in this fake Venice location.

"It looks like the voting system hasn't started yet. Once it does, we can get over that hurdle. Does everyone understand?"

> **Disciple Yue has activated Magician's Hand!**

> **Disciple Amelia has activated Stone's Aura!**

Yue and Amelia instantly left, bursting into buildings and hunting for anything out of the ordinary. Wei and Yang followed each of them closely behind.

> **Hindsight activated!**

I wasn't sure how effective Hindsight would be, but it was my best bet at detecting the nodes and staying alert. I ran up one of the narrow alleys before reaching a dead end. A classic Italian building towered over me, ordained with what felt like too many windows and balconies.

For some reason, a dreadful and eerie feeling was flowing through me, but I had no idea what was so off-putting about the current situation.

I leapt up, catching the ledge of the first balcony. Hindsight calculated the distance to the next balcony—too far. I grabbed Zhige and dug the blade into the wall before hooking my heel over the hilt and pulling myself up.

> [Observers Chat]
> **Socrates:** This place is utterly massive. I've been zooming out for ages, and I just caught a glimpse of the end. How many nodes are there?

"I'm not sure how many there are," I answered out loud.

> [Observers Chat]
> **MoldyBlanket:** Who is talking to her privately!! Share with the rest of us!!
> **Aslan:** All of us are curious

> **Demon Great Sage Who Pacifies Heaven scolds**
> **Disciple Peijin for keeping secrets.**

> **Dozens of gods agree with Demon Great Sage**
> **Who Pacifies Heaven's sentiment!**

I huffed, partly from the difficulty of scaling the building and partly out of annoyance. "The question was just about the number of nodes we would need to go through to discover the heart. I'm not sure how many there are."

> **Divinity The One Who Fights in Front is still impressed by Disciple Peijin's knowledge.**

> **Editor's Pen activated!**

> **Ascension Citadel contains 5 nodes.**

> **Error! Impossible within karmic restraints.**

> **Potential Edit: Ascension Citadel contains 10 nodes.**

> **Accept/Deny**

> **Rejected potential edit!**

Ten was far too many. I wanted to minimize the effort my party members would have to go through.

If I remembered correctly, Ascension Citadel had six distinct locations where the heart could be opened: Mediterranean Europe, American city, Arabian Coast, Central American jungle, the throne room, and the limestone caves.

By having only one node in each location, this would minimize the karmic pushback. It wouldn't alter the original design as much as only having five nodes placed randomly, since we would still have to navigate the entire main floor. And, it was much less than having ten total nodes.

> **Ascension Citadel contains one node for each distinct map location.**

> **Edit granted!**

> **[Observers Chat]**
> **GotoKat:** If there are thirty and your party can barely detect them, you are fried
> **Aslan:** True
> **Socrates:** Hopefully there's less than that. For Peijin's sake.
> **Nipon23:** why not 300 :P

I finally made it to the top of the building. I peeked over the edge, using

Hindsight to scan for any potential threats. When none were detected, I threw myself up, pulling Zhige out of the wall and gripping the hilt firmly.

I looked up. I was near the synthetic ceiling now. If I jumped up using all my strength, I should be able to slash through it with Zhige and be closer to the throne room. I surveyed my landscape.

This was the tallest building in the area, but creating that hole now might alert the other parties of where we currently were. I looked around, trying to see where the next map locations were, when I finally realized what had been making me feel so on edge.

In *Surviving My First Run*, the citadel was teeming with creatures. Demons, ghosts, terrifying puzzles—all of it was here, pushing the parties closer together. But from this vantage point I could see that we were totally and utterly alone.

"What the hell . . ." I muttered, shaking my head back and forth.

I walked toward the edge of the building, bracing myself before I leapt down onto the ceiling of the next. I jumped across dozens of feet with each step thanks to my boosted stats until I finally caught a glimpse of the next location.

The tops of various American buildings protruded from above the Mediterranean landscape. That would be our next location, and after that, it would be the Arabian Coast and then the Central American jungle.

> **Observer and god voting will begin in 5 minutes!**

I jumped at the sudden blue screen, my grip on Zhige tightening. Maybe it was through voting that creatures would be spawning. I quickly turned around, leaping off the building. I gripped the side, dragging my fingertips down the bricks to slow my descent until my feet landed firmly on the ground.

> **[Party Chat]**
> **Peijin:** Let's all meet up by the bridge before voting starts. I'm not sure what the voting conditions will be like, so be ready to draw your weapons.

I darted back toward the bridge, and I was the first to arrive. Only moments later, Yue and Yang appeared, Yue panting slightly.

"Any luck?" I asked, staring at Yue.

"Nope. This place is massive. I'm hoping Amelia and Wei had better luck, since Amelia should be able to detect them more easily."

"I'm disappointed."

"Oh, shut up."

I tapped my foot impatiently on the bridge.

"Yang," I said, "I'm using up too many of my messages. I'm going to reach my limit soon. Can you ask where Amelia and Wei are?"

"Got it."

> **[Party Chat]**
> **Yang:** Amelia. Wei. Where are you guys?

I waited expectantly for a message to pop up, but it never did.

"Shit . . ." I grumbled, chewing on my lip.

"Do you think something happened?" Yang asked.

"Maybe they're at the node right now. I don't think Wei would pull anything if he's with Amelia, and Amelia definitely isn't scheming something."

Before I could fully panic, a new message lit up the screen.

> **[Party Chat]**
> **Wei:** Sorry. At node. I'm trying to figure out how to explain where we are.

> **Disciple Wei has adjusted Party Markers.**

At once, the blue party markers that were once floating just a few inches above our heads shot straight up into the sky, flashing brightly.

> **[Party Chat]**
> **Wei:** Can every party see those?

About a mile away, the blue markers belonging to Amelia and Wei shot up into the sky. I turned back to Yang and Yue. "Let's get there before the voting begins. Maybe we can figure out how the node works and get a bit of a head start."

Without warning, Yang suddenly lifted both Yue and I with one arm. We both exclaimed loudly, hitting and kicking him until his other hand extended his staff.

All three of us launched thousands of feet into the air with a scream, and as the staff fell forward, we closed more than half the distance. Yang repeated the movement, and we landed on a roof right beside Amelia and Wei's floating markers.

"I wanted to save us some time," Yang said simply, gently placing us both on the ground.

"Are you fucking crazy?!" Yue exclaimed, pounding his back with her fists furiously. "At least give us a warning!"

"I thought I was gonna die for real this time . . ." I grumbled, stumbling forward.

At the loud crashing sound of our landing, Amelia popped her small head out from a window a few stories below us.

"Here, here!" she exclaimed, waving eagerly. "I found this one all on my own! Wei-shushu didn't even have to help me!"

Yue leapt down, catching the window ledge with her fingertips and swinging herself in. Yang followed after, grabbing onto her outstretched hand and pulling himself in. I grabbed onto his hand and did the same.

The corner of the room was glowing bright blue. In the middle was a glowing cube, spinning slowly and exuding an almost blinding white light.

Wei was standing on the edge of the blue corner. A massive screen was opened up before him. He turned toward me, awe in his eyes.

"Peijin, come take a look."

"Shit, that already looks way too complicated," I said, trudging toward him.

MEDITERRANEAN NODE
Location: Building AK13829 — Floor 2
Description: The Mediterranean node controls the citadel's environment. Use the node's artifact to toggle these settings regardless of the user's current location.
Temperature: 5/10
Weather: 5/10
Gravity: 5/10
Pollution: 1/10
Light: 5/10
Time Loop: 1/10
Owner: Unclaimed

I slowly turned to face Wei. "You know, we could really mess some things up . . ."

Wei looked nervously at the toggles. "If every node is like this, whoever owns one has a terrifying amount of control over the citadel."

"The node's consequences also extend to the owner of that node. So, if I were to set the temperature to 10/10, then everyone, including all of us, would go up in flames. It relies on some kind of mutually assured destruction if you think about it."

Voting shall now commence.

At once, the node exploded and flooded the room with ghosts and demons.

CHAPTER NINE

My party was slammed into the room's walls from the sheer number of creatures that exploded from the node. Amelia let out a startled cry.

"Shit."

I bashed my elbow into the wall behind me, creating a large hole that I quickly fell out of. I hooked onto the protruding stones and drew Zhige, instantly slashing through the bodies of the vicious creatures that spilled out.

They were a hideous sight. Some had multiple eyes across their entire body; others had yellow fangs dangling from their mouths; some had a black, viscous liquid leaking out of every orifice in their bodies.

Demons.

When they met Zhige's assault, they instantly dissipated into black ash, blowing through the air like fog.

I could see purple and black flames erupting inside the building and hear the vicious roar of Amelia's dire wolf as the monsters were quickly reduced.

However, just as quickly as we could kill them, they reappeared.

POLL #1
Which party should face the most difficult monsters?
A. Peijin's World Dominion
B. Major Arcana
C. Bohemian Grove

"What the fuck?!" I exclaimed furiously.

> **Polling ongoing ...**
> A. 35%
> B. 24%
> C. 41%

I used my foot to kick away more of the wall, until the entire thing was practically gone.

The demons began falling straight out of the building and onto the ground beneath, dying on impact. These were some of the weakest and ugliest creatures we'd had to face so far.

But, I didn't want to know what it would be like to fight against monsters not classified as fodder. We still had plenty of nodes left to claim.

"Chang!" I exclaimed. "Are you there?"

I pulled myself back into the building, watching everyone kill hundreds of monsters. I clung onto the ceiling, my hoodie whirring to life as it propelled me upward until I was practically sticking to the surface. I slowly crawled my way over to the node.

The glowing cube was right beneath me now. I strained down, grunting from the effort, until my fingertips finally grazed across the cube. It spun wildly, practically throwing me off.

The sleeve of my hoodie shot forward, wrapping around it and pulling it into the hoodie, placing it right in my grip.

> **Disciple Peijin has claimed ownership of the Mediterranean node!**

At once, the node exuded an incredible white light, and it morphed into a small puzzle piece in my palm. I clung onto it.

> **Polling ongoing ...**
> A. 30%
> B. 22%
> C. 48%

Chang appeared, looking down at the sight and letting out a low whistle. "Look at you go, Peijin! A lovely show as always. It really warms my heart to see."

"You just like seeing your paycheck come in. Speaking of which, does killing all these monsters give us more stars?"

"Definitely. You don't have to ask me about that. It tells you that on its own."

"I was earning too much money, so I turned off the notifications. How much more money do I make if I kill a harder demon in the citadel?"

"Maybe tenfold."

"Tenfold?!"

Polling will conclude shortly!

I pursed my lips, thinking deeply.

"Hey!" I shouted at my party members. "How badly do you guys need more stars!"

Yue glared up at me. "Aren't you one of the richest disciples here?! Leave it!"

"Okay . . ." I turned back to Chang. "Maybe next time."

Polling has concluded! The final votes are as follows.
A. 30%
B. 19%
C. 51%

The tiniest smirk was visible on my face to see that Bohemian Grove was getting the brunt of the poll's consequences. After all, it was probably far more interesting to watch the party that would struggle the most.

But if my party was second-most voted . . . that meant we were still weaker and less popular than Ruoming's party.

"Whatever," I grumbled, annoyed.

With the node now secured, I quickly jumped back out of the building. "Everyone, let's move on to the next location! Follow me!"

I watched as the rest of my party members quickly scrambled out, climbing back onto the roof. The other demons struggled and failed to make their way up and reach us. I looked down cockily.

"The American city is that way," I said, gesturing toward the direction I had scouted earlier. I opened my palm, staring down the node before opening it back up.

MEDITERRANEAN NODE
Location: Building AK13829 — Floor 2
Description: The Mediterranean node controls the citadel's environment. Use the node's artifact to toggle these settings regardless of the user's current location.
Temperature: 5/10
Weather: 5/10
Gravity: 5/10

> **Pollution: 1/10**
> **Light: 5/10**
> **Time Loop: 1/10**
> **Owner: Liu Peijin**

> **Set Temperature: 8/10**

At once, the room elevated to a sweltering heat, and sweat broke out on my upper lip.

Yue's head snapped toward me, and I could tell she was about to yell at me.

> **Set Temperature: 7/10**

"Give it a second," I said. "Let me lower it slowly so the other parties aren't too suspicious. Amelia, how difficult was it to spot the node?"

She shook her head back and forth. "Not too difficult. He could sniff them out if we used Stone's Aura together," Amelia said, patting her dire wolf on the head. It was a humorous sight, given that they were about the same height. He instantly nuzzled her cheek gently, licking her face.

"I do have to activate them, though, in order for the rest of us to see them," Wei added.

"Huh? How'd you do that?" I asked, tilting my head to the side.

Wei pointed at his eye, which suddenly started glowing a deep yellow. "Through the Thirty Aethyrs."

My jaw dropped, and I brought my hands to my head. "What?! Have you already tested that skill?"

> **Set Temperature: 6/10**

I was in complete shock. The Thirty Aethyrs was one of the most complicated skills in all of *Surviving My First Run*. Maybe it was only difficult for a human to wrap their mind around the magical planes, but I was utterly shocked that Wei had managed to enter into the Aethyrs without even seeming fazed.

"I tested it out back in the train station. It only took a moment, and I only managed to enter TEX, which is the thirtieth layer."

Yue interrupted. "What in the actual fuck are you two talking about? Can we please normalize giving context?"

"Shut up for a moment," I said, waving Yue off and turning back to Wei. "So, that allows you to activate the nodes for the rest of us?"

"It's not the only method, but it worked for me and Amelia."

"You're really cool, Wei. I'm happy to be working with you, not against you."

Wei's ears flushed a bright pink, and he turned away, fidgeting uncomfortably. "I'm just doing my part. You don't need to flatter me."

> **Set Temperature: 5/10**

Now that I fully reset the Mediterranean node's setting, I quickly secured it in my Boundless Bag.

Yue clasped her hands together. "Aw, both of you are just soo cute! So, can someone please explain what's happening?"

Yang shrugged. "I have no clue either."

Wei turned to them, still obviously flustered by my compliment. "The Thirty Aethyrs is a magical dimension I can enter with my skills. TEX is the lowest plane, and it's the closest to the material realm. In the center was a massive crystal cube representing Harpocrates, the Greek god of silence and secrecy. There were also four archangels."

"Are you possessed?" Yue asked genuinely.

Wei frowned, looking annoyed. "No. It just gives me mystical insights and lets me communicate with other gods. I can move onto the following planes once I pass a hypothetical test for each level."

"What was the test to enter the TEX level?" Yue said.

"Confront your fears." Wei gave a humorous but also painful smile. "Not very hard anymore, though."

Yue winced. "Sorry. Forget I asked."

I slapped the back of her head. "It's one of the hardest skills to use. It's sort of like a cultivation skill. I wanted Wei to pick it originally because I think it's one of the best when mastered, and Wei is technically a cultivator."

Yang poked Wei's shoulder. "Did you see Archangel Michael?"

Wei shook his head.

> **Divinity Supreme Commander of the Heavenly Hosts says he is too busy slaughtering demons to hold meet and greets in the Aethyrs.**

> **Many divinities from Paradise are criticizing the Divinity Supreme Commander of the Heavenly Hosts' attitude!**

> **Divinity Supreme Commander of the Heavenly Hosts insists he is being honest.**

> **Divinity Supreme Commander of the Heavenly Hosts says it is an incredibly time consuming job to manage the Aethyrs.**

> **Divinity Supreme Commander of the Heavenly Hosts says he is much better at wielding a sword.**

> **Many demons feel incredible animosity for Divinity Supreme Commander of the Heavenly Hosts!**

> **Divinity Supreme Commander of the Heavenly Hosts slumps in his seat and goes silent.**

> **Divinity Great Sage Equaling Heaven bursts out laughing.**

"My sponsor is just a very busy person," Wei said, shrugging.

"Yue, what about you? Can you detect them?" Yang asked.

"Of course I can!" she answered. "I was simply looking in the wrong spot..."

"Sure, sure," I said. "Let's stick together from now on, since we know that Amelia and Wei are a good pairing for this. If we get through this quickly, we won't have to deal with too many polls, and that should benefit us. I'll hold onto the node artifacts for now."

I guided the party through the narrow alley and up the buildings, until I reached the same vantage point I was at earlier. I signaled for them to follow, and we ran across the top. What would've taken hours before the apocalypse now took us only minutes.

Hundreds of creatures swarmed beneath us, piling up to scale the building, but before they could reach us, they would topple down. It was almost hilarious to watch them struggle after such a brutal second arc.

"Zhige, take down as many of them as you can," I said, throwing my blade down into the crowd. Zhige flew all over, slicing them without any resistance. The only difficult part was listening to their horrifying screams and gargles.

I jerked my head at Amelia. "Where's the node?"

She muttered something to the dire wolf, who instantly perked its head up and began sniffing out our surroundings. Its nostrils twitched, and it turned back to Amelia with a blank stare.

Amelia looked at me nervously. "Give him a second. He's just a little shy."

"He can't find it, can he?"

"No, he definitely can!" Amelia insisted, looking incredibly frustrated now.

This time, she whispered in the wolf's ear almost desperately, and he looked back at her blankly before letting out a whine and pawing at the ground.

"It's fine if he can't find it," I reassured her. "We can have Yue give it a shot instead. Or I can try using one of my skills."

Amelia shook her head vigorously. "He's saying the scent is faint, and it's moved around all over the American city. It's not here anymore."

> **[Observers Chat]**
> **Socrates:** Jia Li . . . I don't want to get zapped by Karma for saying this, but you're not the only smart person here anymore.
> **Socrates:** Trust what Amelia is saying. The other parties didn't survive the last arc for no reason.

> **Divinity The One Who Fights in Front is watching Disciple Peijin closely.**

> **Divinity Great Sage Equaling Heaven is growing bored.**

> **Demon Great Sage Who Pacifies Heaven is wondering when the next poll is.**

My voice was firm now. "Amelia. Take us to where the scent originates."

She nodded, and the dire wolf leapt ahead, jumping down onto the road. Various demons attempted to attack it, but the wolf snapped its jaws, and the creatures turned to dust.

Unlike the Mediterranean landscape, the American city was made up of massive glass buildings. In the sunlight, the glass glistened beautiful shades of deep blues and greens. Some buildings were historical, made up of various white stone pillars and detailing.

Further down, a massive beach stretched out. A Ferris wheel broke the horizon. It had been completely overtaken by demons, who were spilling out from one of the gondolas, crashing into the ground, and creating a massive swimming pile of monstrous flesh.

The dire wolf led us down into the sandy beach, and our speed dramatically decreased as we tried to push through the terrain.

Yue let out a frustrated cry. "Ugh! I hate getting sand in my shoes!" she whined dramatically, whipping her spear around and slashing the approaching demon. She spat whenever the demon's black ash blew into her face.

Yang shouted back. "There's a skill you can buy in the Azure Dragon Store to keep your feet clean!"

"What the fuck? How do you even know that?"

"I bought it earlier!"

"What?!" Yue and I exclaimed at the same time.

"B-because I kept getting dirt and mud on my shoes!" Yang exclaimed, trying to justify himself. "And think about it; we don't get proper showers anymore! If anything, you guys should follow my example."

"What the hell did you just say, you stinky bastard?" Yue roared, whacking his back furiously with her spear. "Take that back now, or I'll kill you!"

Yang burst out laughing and began running faster, dodging Yue's subsequent hits by mere millimeters, driving her mad.

> **You have purchased Cleanly Feet!**

I kept my lips sealed as Yang desperately defended himself from Yue's fury.

When we finally reached the Ferris wheel, the dire wolf shakily leapt onto the first gondola, struggling to find his balance as it swayed back and forth. He then jumped onto the next, heading toward the one all the monsters were spilling out of.

"I have a suspicious feeling it's that one . . ." I muttered, pointing at the bright-red one as I turned around and looked at the rest of my party. "Let's get on top of it and tear off the ceiling. Leave the two side doors open so all the demons keep falling out."

We climbed onto it, and I gestured for the rest of my party to stay on the gondola positioned one slot lower.

"Zhige!" I cried out, and the blade flew straight into my hand. I stabbed it into the gondola's metal ceiling and cut out a square, prying it open and peeking inside. Unlike the last node, there was no brightly glowing cube.

Wei's eyes began glowing a deep yellow shade, and yellow sparks began flying out from the gondola until a giant blue screen floated up toward me.

> **AMERICAN NODE**
> Location: Ferris Wheel RN2938 —Gondola #19
> Description: The American node controls the citadel's spatial presence. Use the node's artifact to toggle these settings regardless of the user's current location.
> Alter Layout: Yes/No
> Trap Frequency: 3/10
> Location Size: 8/10
> Location Firewall: 1/10

My eyes drifted to the very last line on the screen.

> **Owner: Song Ruoming**

CHAPTER TEN

"Fuck! Fuck, fuck, fuck! I'm so pissed off!" I exclaimed, rereading that final line over and over. "Are you fucking kidding me?! That stupid unbaked biscuit bastard! He's always walking around looking so smug with his white hair—"

I froze when I felt the eyes of the rest of my party burning into my back. I slowly turned around, laughing timidly.

"Haha, sorry . . . It just seems that Ruoming already took this node . . ."

"What?!" Yue exclaimed, practically mirroring my reaction. "I thought you told us they would be going for the throne."

"Well, I obviously thought that was what they were going to do . . ."

"So, what does this mean?" Wei asked. "If you had that insight about the citadel because of your knowledge as the god of fate and fortune, does that mean that Feiyu, Ruoming, or someone else in that party possesses similar knowledge?"

"No way. That's impossible," I said confidently. Unless, Song Ruoming had read the entirety of *Surviving My First Run* and had it practically memorized by heart.

I was hesitating now. Honestly, I had figured that maybe Ruoming had just really loved *Surviving My First Run* and read a super significant chunk. Maybe even all of it. But, it sometimes felt like Ruoming even knew more than I did, and I could no longer tell if it was just my insecurities talking.

Yue hissed through her teeth. "So, what's the plan now? Only one party is going for the throne. As far as I'm concerned, if Owl manages to sit on it, we *still* lose the arc. Not to mention he becomes our divine ruler or something."

"Yeah, I know that much," I raised my voice. "Just, give me a second, okay?"

I chewed on my lower lip, swinging Zhige back and forth mindlessly.

"Regardless of the situation, there's no time to waste. We have to collect all the nodes before Ruoming does and before Owl destroys the throne. Yang, I want you to figure out where the next map location is. Use your staff to get a view."

I turned to Wei, grasping his large hand in both of mine. "Wei. How are you feeling?"

"Don't worry about me."

"If you don't feel up to it, just let me know. I couldn't survive what you did. Just be honest with me."

"Peijin, if you ever catch me lying, you can lop off my head."

"There's no need for all that."

Yang descended from the staff. "It's not too far from here. It looks like there's an Arabian royal palace maybe a minute west, and we'll arrive soon."

"Then come on, let's go," I ordered, facing the direction that Yang had gestured toward.

However, the node's blue screen flashed before me, the text flickering independently. My eyes widened.

AMERICAN NODE
Alter Layout: Yes
Trap Frequency: 9/10
Location Size: 10/10
Location Firewall: 10/10

At once, the view before us stretched by thousands and thousands of feet, and the placement of each building changed. It switched before us every second.

A giant pit opened up beneath Amelia's feet, and she let out a loud cry. I quickly reached out and caught her, pulling her into my chest to protect her.

But in the next second, a massive building erupted out of the ground, slamming into the both of us. I held back a cry and squeezed Amelia tighter to me. The building disappeared, and we fell to the ground again.

"Shit!" I exclaimed as the ground beneath us now tilted. It was like the desperate frenzy of my own dungeon room, when the room began to spin.

Finally, it all came to a halt, but now that the trap frequency was nearly maxed out, I kept myself still.

"Why the hell would Ruoming max out traps if his party isn't immune? I swear, he's trying to take all of us down with him." I let out a heavy sigh, chewing on my lower lip. "Yang. Can you go up and check where the Arabian royal palace is now, and if you can see it?"

Yang was practically green with motion sickness now. "Y-Yes."

He planted his staff into the ground and balanced on the top, shooting up into the sky until none of us could see him anymore. A few seconds later, he dropped back onto the ground, shrinking the staff in his hands.

"Peijin," he said.

"What?"

"It's all blocked off. There's a massive wall there now."

I pursed my lips before I let out a frustrated curse under my breath. "Let's get there and try to get through it. Either way, it doesn't matter. Ruoming's party will also be trapped wherever they are, and they'll have to lower the firewall eventually."

Yang nodded nervously. "But, what if they've split up? They could be getting to every node first."

I shook my head back and forth. "Then we'll have to do a really good job of protecting our node. They'll have to come to us at some point and take it if they want to create the heart. I'm more worried about what Owl is going to make of all of this," I grumbled.

I took a single step forward when the ground erupted beneath my feet, and I let out a surprised scream. I was instantly covered in a grotesque layer of impossibly sticky slime.

Thankfully, it wasn't a dangerous trap, but it reminded me, nonetheless, that the situation was far more precarious now.

[Observers Chat]
MGirl193: Who gets slimed in an apocalypse. Dead.
OrangePeels: I thought she turned into slime and exploded
Seatdiv: Are you both stupid

"Aw, what the hell," I whined, immediately disgusted by the substance. I slowly blinked my eyes open and opened the Azure Dragon Store, quickly purchasing a skill to get all the gunk off of me.

Yue burst out laughing, slapping her knee and doubling over. "That's what it looks like when traps are maxed out? Oh god, I hope that happens to you another dozen times. It makes you look extra ugly."

"Excuse me? At least I don't look like a wet, long-haired chihuahua."

"A chi—what? What the fuck does that even mean?"

"It just means you're too stupid to understand it."

"No, it just means you're too stupid to insult people properly."

"Hey—"

"We can use my staff to get to the wall quickly," Yang said. "Everyone, grab hold of it."

I grabbed onto the staff. Wei and Amelia did just the same. I shot Yue a glare. She glared back, intentionally stepping on my toe as hard as she could.

"Is that supposed to hurt?" I asked Yue, staring down at her shoe. "I think my physique level is too high compared to your strength level."

Before our childish fight could escalate any further, Yang lengthened the staff as tall as it could go. It slammed against the synthetic sky, no longer able to tear through it. Once we were all the way up there, I took in the view around us.

What was previously a massive map location seemed infinite now. But, the wall stretching to the ceiling was still apparent in the distance.

POLL #2
Which party should receive a boost of spiritual energy?
A. Peijin's World Dominion
B. Major Arcana
C. Bohemian Grove

I scoffed in frustration, quickly turning from the screen. So what, now they were giving us boosts like we were the gods?

"Let's get to the wall. There will be some way to get through it, and they'll have to drop it eventually. It's not like they can stay locked up in their zone either," I ordered Yang.

He nodded and tilted the staff toward the wall, sending us falling toward it. Amelia was clinging onto her dire wolf, who was desperately clawing at the falling staff, and I quickly grabbed onto both of them.

"I got you two," I reassured them as we hurdled toward the ground. Yang repeated the move multiple times until we finally landed on the ground right at the base of the wall. Yang quickly shrunk his staff, bringing it to his side.

I lifted my hand and touched the wall. It was made of a hard material like stone. I brought Zhige up to it and pressed into it to test its strength.

It warped slightly under Zhige's spiritual energy. I pressed Zhige more firmly against it, but the blade began to tremble slightly in my hands.

I cocked my head, grumbling incoherently under my breath. "Wei, can you give it a shot?"

Wei pulled out his sword with complete grace, his sleeves flowing loosely around his arms as he cleanly brought his sword in front of the wall. He gave it a sharp strike, but his sword bounced off of it.

"It's about twenty feet thick, but it's loaded in spiritual energy, too," Wei said. "I doubt any of us could break through it."

"Well, shit," I said, tapping my foot. "I can try to use the seals. But last time, I had the spiritual energy of the demons in my blood to make it effective."

I remembered the poll that was just issued, pulling up the current results."

> **Polling ongoing . . .**
> A. 15%
> B. 64%
> C. 21%

"Chang," I shouted loudly into the sky. "When does the second poll end?"

He appeared before me immediately. "It will take longer than the last. But it looks like you guys are gonna lose it anyway."

I glared at him but didn't say anything else, staring at the dismal poll results instead. Why was there such a disparity? It was evident from the last poll results that my party was the second fan favorite, and that Bohemian Grove was lagging behind. So, why was there such a big lead for Ruoming's party now?

I turned back to my party. "They'll drop the wall shortly. They're planning something in whichever location they're in right now. That's why they're restricting our access to it. So, once the wall drops, we'll likely bump into them and need to be prepared for whatever stunt they pull."

"I'm ready," Amelia said firmly, placing a small hand on her chest. "I can always bring out the serpent." She looked up at me expectantly.

"Wei, you're our trump card," I said bluntly, turning to him immediately. "So, conserve your energy. How good is your control of the Aethyrs?"

"Minimal."

"Then make it adequate. Yue and Yang—you two are going to need to deal with the rest of Ruoming's party. I'm not worried about Bohemian Grove. They're not our competition. Amelia, you can use the dire wolf to support Yue and Yang. Don't get involved in the fight."

"But—" Amelia protested.

"Don't argue about this, Amelia," I said, quickly silencing her.

I knew I was being way too harsh with my party. It was apparent by their silence and the looks on their faces, instead of the typically snarky remarks and questions I'd come to expect. But, if this went wrong, there would be nothing to feel bad about because there would be no party.

I paced nervously outside the wall, running my hands through my hair. I was always a competitive person at heart, even if I was incredibly lazy and could hardly put my passion to use.

But, my anxiety at this moment far surpassed some petty desire to be an enviable person. If I lost this arc, I would lose my credibility with the gods, who had so loyally been following along with my party's story.

I'd be nothing more than Ruoming's bitch. I could already envision the smug look on Feiyu's face, too, when he realized that he put me in my place.

"Ruoming and Feiyu, you are such smug bastards," I cursed them, slicing Zhige across the wall. "Everything's on the line for me."

Only a scratch was left behind by my strike before it was quickly filled in as more rocks appeared to smooth it over.

Suddenly, the ground beneath our feet rumbled. A giant ravine split open beneath the wall, sucking the border back into the ground.

Song Ruoming had opened the barrier.

CHAPTER ELEVEN

I instantly leapt over the ravine, and my party members followed suit without struggle. Amelia had mounted the dire wolf, who powerfully pushed off the ledge onto the other side, clawing into the dirt before pulling itself up.

We had officially entered the Arabian Coast.

Before us stretched a wide expanse of beautiful white and orange sand. Further away, a river was cutting through the sand, and a small city was located beside it.

Now that we were no longer near the American node, I couldn't see the current settings or what the trap frequency was set to.

However, given that Ruoming was now anticipating an altercation between our parties, I anticipated he must have dropped the trap frequency to a negligible level to avoid sabotaging his own party.

I gestured for my party to follow me with a jerk of my head. I dug my feet into the ground to begin running, but my feet quickly sank in the sand.

"It's all getting in my shoes," I complained.

I looked toward Yang, wanting to ask him to use his staff to propel all of us forward again, but as I did, I could see the perspiration on his brow. Unlike Zhige, which had its own spiritual energy reserve, Yang's weapon did not. So, every time he altered its form, it sucked from Yang's very limited spiritual energy.

"Zhige, grow bigger," I ordered, throwing the sword into the air. It instantly expanded, but only enough for three of us to safely get on it. Zhige rotated so it was parallel with the ground and patiently floated a few feet above it.

"Yang and Yue, you two go first. Wei, Amelia, and I will come right after. Don't go anywhere yet, and try not to get into too much trouble, all right?"

Yue brought her hand up to her forehead in a half-hearted salute. "Yes ma'am."

Yang and Yue walked toward the sword, awkwardly shuffling through the deep sand that tried to sink them. Yang lifted Yue onto the sword, who was protesting, before he climbed on himself.

"Zhige, take them to the perimeter of the city. Just make sure we all end up in the same spot, so don't go crazy."

Zhige at once flew forward until it became a speck on the horizon.

"Amelia, can you put the dire wolf away for a moment?"

She nodded. A flurry of blue sparks erupted around the dire wolf. When they dissipated, the wolf was gone.

Amelia looked up at me softly with her big blue eyes. "Peijin, I want to help you more."

"You're already helping me," I answered, still looking at the horizon in anticipation of Zhige's return.

"But I want to help you more," she insisted.

"If there's anything you can do, Amelia, then I'll let you know. Right now, I have everything under control."

I felt something pitch the soft flesh at the back of my elbow, and I let out a startled shout, whipping my head around to see Wei with a disgruntled expression.

"What the hell was that for?!" I exclaimed, rubbing my arm. "That really hurt, you know?"

Wei replied by narrowing his eyes.

"How am I supposed to know what I did wrong if you don't explain?"

"I'll pinch you again."

"For what?!"

Wei let out a sigh. "You see so much and so little sometimes."

"Are you just trying to push my buttons? It's working."

Polling ongoing . . .
A. 10%
B. 69%
C. 21%

Shit. Our poll results were dropping even more now.

[Observers Chat]
Socrates: Jia Li . . .

Wei further narrowed his eyes.

"Why is everyone mad at me right now?" I muttered, turning away as I looked for Zhige on the horizon again.

> **[Observers Chat]**
> **Socrates:** Stop looking for Zhige. Look at Amelia.

Amelia? I looked down and saw the girl practically ready to burst into tears. I instantly jumped in my skin as I picked her up, holding her out in front of me like a puppy.

"Hey, what's wrong?" I asked frantically, turning her all around. Was she injured somewhere, and that's why Socrates and Wei were both acting like I was blind?

She brought her small hands up to her face and, in frustration, swiped at her face. "Peijin is going to replace me," she said simply. Her hands gripped the fabric of my hoodie firmly, until her knuckles were white from the strain.

I paused, looking at her completely dumbfounded. "And why do you think that?"

"Because I'm no use to Peijin."

"That's not true."

"It is true."

"It's because you're very young, Amelia. I'm protecting you, okay?"

Wei whacked the back of my head hard. My head lurched forward, and I let out a grunt.

Amelia's hands released my hoodie. She pushed against me. "Put me down."

A mess of confused emotions jumbled in my chest. I had no idea what I was supposed to do in this situation. Zhige had also not returned yet, even though the blade should already be back.

It was true that I didn't want Amelia to get too involved. It was too dangerous to send her out on her own. That would have been entirely irrational. But it wasn't like I was planning on dumping Amelia if she wasn't useful. If anything, I thought Wei would understand the reasoning behind my actions.

I let out a heavy sigh. "Amelia, listen."

I kneeled in front of her in silence, struggling to find my words. Even though I was a writer, I wasn't the best at comforting people. At this moment, I regretted sending Yang away with Yue.

However, before I got the chance to say anything, Zhige flew before my vision, stabbing the ground right by my side. I instantly stood up.

"Zhige, what took you so long? Is everything fine there?"

The sword flew back up into the air and turned parallel to the ground. It was an understood 'yes' between the two of us.

I picked Amelia up and placed her at the base of the sword. She kept her eyes glued to the ground, her hands balled into fists. This time, I noticed the twisted expression on her face, but I only bit my lower lip.

"Amelia. We'll continue our talk later, okay?"

I stared at her, waiting to see if she would say anything to me. When she didn't, I brought my hand up to her cheek and gently ran my thumb over her face in a comforting gesture.

Wei got on Zhige next, and I pulled myself onto the tip of the sword and held on as Zhige flew forward with surprising speed. The sound of the wind blowing around us was incredibly loud.

I looked behind me at Wei nervously. He reached forward and grabbed my ear, tugging it harshly as I let out a yelp.

"Peijin," he whispered harshly at me. Although we normally tried to avoid serious conflicts in front of Amelia, she thankfully couldn't hear much due to the wind racing around us.

"Yes . . ." I answered like a scolded child.

I probably seemed like nothing more than a kid to Wei now. He had once looked up to me as a symbol of courage, and maybe even morality—but since his memories returned, I probably became far more insignificant in his eyes.

"You're her entire world. You know that, right?" Wei said, forcing me to meet his sharp gaze.

"That's not true."

"You know it is."

"It's not. All of us play a different role to her."

Wei scrunched his nose. "Peijin, you're incredibly smart."

"I'm not trying to act dumb. Do you think she comes to me to grieve? She goes to you or Yang."

"Why do you think she does that?"

"Because I'm not good at talking to people."

"It's because she wants to look good in front of you. She doesn't want you to be disappointed in her. She doesn't want you to think she's not capable. Amelia wants you to rely on her."

"And do you think I should, Wei? Do you think I should rely on her?"

"No, I don't."

"Then I don't know why you're acting like I'm making the wrong decision here. She's so young, Wei. It's our job to protect her and keep her alive. That's the only thing we need to do for her. As long as Amelia gets to live another day—no—as long as Amelia gets to grow old after all of this is over, then we did our job, and we did it well."

Wei lifted a long finger and pressed it firmly into my chest multiple times.

"Peijin, if you asked Amelia to throw herself into the mouth of a vicious demon, she would do it, even if she was kicking and crying the entire time."

"That's not true, and you know it," I insisted, increasingly furious at his comparison.

"It is true. That girl would do anything for you."

"Wei, you're really pissing me off now. This is unfair, and you know it."

"There's nothing unfair about it. Peijin, you asked *me* to be your sword, didn't you? You asked me to put my life on the line for you."

"I asked you to put your life on the line for the *mission*."

> **[Observers Chat]**
> **Cjst123:** What is happening right now
> **CoffeeCatering:** The girls are fighting!!

> **Demon Abyssal Kraken of Black Seas is looking nervously at the scene playing out before him.**

> **Divinity Supreme Commander of the Heavenly Hosts turns away from the broadcast.**

Wei paused, his large eyes searching mine to decode how I really felt. I hardened my expression, annoyed by the fact he was trying to intrude on my emotions.

"Peijin."

We were approaching the perimeter of the city. The buildings were short and made of sun-dried bricks. In the center was a vivid marketplace, full of beautiful merchandise, colorful stones, and delightful food.

"Peijin," Wei repeated when I ignored him. "All those times you sacrificed yourself for us—when you fought karmic backlash alone for Yue; when you almost died to kill the demons in Yang's room; when . . . when you tried to change my fate in my dungeon room—were you not ready to die for us, even though you hardly knew us?"

I stayed silent. I bit down so hard on my lower lip I could taste blood on my tongue.

"I'm your party leader, Wei. It's my duty to protect all of you."

"So, now it's your 'duty.'"

"It's always been my duty."

"Was it about duty in *your* dungeon room?"

I bristled instantly, remembering the way that, in my weakest moments, all I could do was collapse into myself and the world I created in *Surviving My First Run*.

"You're not even talking about Amelia anymore. This is about a problem you have with me."

"Peijin, do you really hate yourself that much?" Wei asked softly, his brow furrowed as he looked at me.

My eye twitched. I held eye contact with him, not saying a word.

"Wei. You don't know a thing about me, so stop pretending that you do."

"Don't I understand you better than anyone else? We're just two lonely people who happen to be gods."

People? Two *people*? Wei wasn't even real.

I wanted to shout at Wei. I wanted to tell him that he had no idea what he was talking about—that I was his powerless god, the one who created him and fabricated all the cruelty he had ever experienced. I was the one who ruined him; I was the one who killed Amelia's parents; I was the one who made Yue furious at the world.

> **[Observers Chat]**
> **Nipon23:** one step forward, three thousand steps back

I let out a slow, steady breath, trying to control my frantically shaking hands. "Wei. Drop it."

> **Polling ongoing . . .**
> **A. 7%**
> **B. 76%**
> **C. 27%**

I couldn't even stand to look at the poll. I turned toward the village. I could see Yang's hand high above his head. He waved back and forth slowly, flagging us down. Zhige slowed, lowering to the ground just beside them. I jumped off.

"Are there no demons or ghosts here either?" I asked Yue and Yang. I was too pissed to bother with niceties.

"Sort of," Yang began. "No demons that Yue and I could sense. But we can both sense the energy of ghosts. No malicious spiritual energy, though."

"What do you mean?"

"It's almost like a ghost village. Maybe some used to live here."

Yang paused and pointed at his own lip. "Are you okay? You're bleeding."

I wiped at my lips, looking down at the back of my hand to see a thin streak of bright red blood. "I'm fine. Just bit it earlier when I was talking."

Yang looked at me hesitantly. He probably knew that the two of us shared the same habit of biting on our lower lips when anxious. Maybe he knew I stole the habit from him, too.

There was the sound of a low, chaotic rumble, and the walls shot up all around us again. It was almost like Ruoming had eyes on us.

"Let's keep going. Tread carefully, and don't go too far alone in case there are traps," I said, cautiously headed up a small street.

CHAPTER TWELVE

I looked around the marketplace curiously, cocking my head. It was full of utterly beautiful items. Not much of it would be of use to my party, since it was low in value and unhelpful in combat.

Yue had the slightest smile on her face. "It almost feels like we're traveling the world. It wouldn't be half-bad if we didn't have to worry about dying at every turn."

"It might not be the most accurate representation, though," I admitted embarrassingly. Even though I based the third arc off of the world's various wonders, I had never left China. In fact, I rarely left Shanghai.

"A place like this would be in shambles now," Yang said softly, the wonder apparent in his voice as he looked around.

As he approached a stand displaying a plethora of beautiful necklaces, a burst of blue sparks appeared under his feet. Instantly, a hoard of demons erupted from the ground, their multiple hands breaking through the ground and clawing for him.

Yang used his staff to shoot himself into the air before swinging it in a small circle, killing all of the demons in an instant. They turned to gray ash, fluttering to the ground by the time he landed.

I let out a low whistle. "Wooow, very impressive. I didn't know a pest controller could get those reflexes in such a short time."

Yang rolled his eyes, but there was a small, proud grin on his face. He picked up one of the necklaces; it contained a beautiful blue stone and was unlike anything I'd ever seen. The stone itself was a deep blue color, but there were royal blue specks and light blue metallic pieces all inside.

We all walked over toward Yang. I made sure not to step on the ash of the demons, instead lowering my head politely over the pile.

> **Divinity Supreme Commander of the Heavenly Hosts praises Disciple Peijin's respect!**

> **Divinity Supreme Commander of the Heavenly Hosts sponsors 5,000 stars.**

Sometimes I felt bad about practically sucking Archangel Michael dry of his stars, but when I remembered how ridiculously wealthy he was, it suddenly seemed fine.

I was now standing at Yang's side.

"Whoa!" I leaned over, staring at the stone. "What kind of stone is that?"

Yang picked it up and held it to the light. "Isn't it stunning?"

Amelia squeezed in beside Yang, her eyes locked on the sign and reading it using her Translator skill. "It says it's imported from Okinawa. It's called a firefly stone."

"Okinawa?!" Yue said with excitement, quickly looking for a purple bracelet. When she found one, she held it up. "Peijin, do you think this would look good on me?"

I nodded. "It's the same color as your skills."

I paused for a moment, staring down at the display before my jaw dropped in excitement. "Yang, can you pass me the blue ones? Those will look good with mine."

Amelia strained to peek at all the ones on the table. "Yue-ayi, which one would suit me?"

Yue brought a hand up to her face, thinking carefully. "Maybe red."

I let out an audible scoff of disapproval. "Are you kidding? It's definitely blue."

Yue scrunched her nose. "I was *going* to say her color is blue, but you already picked that one for yourself."

"There's dark blue and light blue," I retorted, pointing at the table's display. "Light blue suits Amelia perfectly. It's the same color as her eyes."

"I like red more," Amelia answered.

"Ha!" Yue laughed, picking up the smallest red bracelet they had and sliding it over Amelia's wrist.

"Whatever. Wei, what color are you getting?"

"Yellow."

"That's a good one for you," I agreed.

"Shouldn't I get yellow?" Yang asked.

"Oh, maybe," I said, thinking hard about his question. "But I've always associated you with orange."

"Orange? No way. What about me is giving off orange?"

"Your eyes," I answered without thinking. "Everytime your eyes catch the light, they become a deep amber."

Yue nodded her head. "I agree with Peijin for once. It's orange."

Yang stared blankly before turning red, grabbing the orange bracelet silently.

[Observers Chat]
StanDon: So cute!! They all having matching charms TvT
Socrates: Aww. All their picks really fit them well.
CoffeeCatering: I sure hope nothing bad happens after such a nice scene . . .
Napkin: Omg like if someone steps on a trap and blows up
StanDon: Okay so why are we saying such sad morbid things now
Napkin: Just being honest . . . it's been suspiciously quiet

Polling ongoing . . .
A. 14%
B. 65%
C. 21%

Divinity Supreme Commander of the Heavenly Hosts is giggling at the scene playing out before him.

Divinity Supreme Commander of the Heavenly Hosts sponsors Peijin's World Dominion 5,000 stars.

Divinity The One Who Fights in Front scolds Divinity Supreme Commander of the Heavenly Hosts for spending money like water.

Divinity Supreme Commander of the Heavenly Hosts says he can afford to.

Divinity Spirit of the Jade Moon reminds Divinity Supreme Commander of the Heavenly Hosts about his legal fees.

Divinity Supreme Commander of the Heavenly Hosts flushes from embarrassment and says they've already been paid off.

Divinity Great Sage Equaling Heaven is stunned

> that the Divinity Supreme Commander of the
> Heavenly Hosts made a smart financial move.

> Divinity Great Sage Equaling Heaven says that the
> Divinity Supreme Commander of the Heavenly Hosts is
> infamous for making horrible financial decisions.

> Divinity Supreme Commander of the Heavenly Hosts Says Divinity
> Ears That Hear What Comes on the Wind bullied him into
> paying off his legal fees before the interest could accumulate.

> Divinity Great Sage Equaling Heaven is stunned
> to hear the mention of the other divinity.

> Divinity Great Sage Equaling Heaven asked
> when the two became friends.

> Divinity Spirit of the Jade Moon is shocked by the apparent friendship.

> Divinity Ears That Hear What Comes on the Wind says the friendship
> formed after the karmic ordeal with Yue's dungeon room.

> Demon Abyssal Kraken of Black Seas asks if Divinity
> Ears That Hear What Comes on the Wind has been
> okay since sending out their recent distress signal.

> Divinity Ears That Hear What Comes on the Wind
> nods and says it was fired by accident.

> Demon Abyssal Kraken of Black Seas is incredibly relieved.

I turned to the messages, cocking my head as I scrolled through them.

Divinity Ears That Hear What Comes on the Wind? What a long name. I was struggling to remember which god this name could be referring to. They were certainly not a major character in *Surviving My First Run*.

This god clearly had incredible hearing given their title. They were also friendly with the Kraken. The Kraken was generally well liked amongst everyone, given their more humble and shy demeanor, but for a demon and a god to be on such good terms was still an impressive feat. It was likely then that this divinity also had something to do with the seas.

Since Sun Wukong and Chang'e both recognized and were surprised by the relationship between Archangel Michael and this divinity, perhaps it was a Chinese god. Chinese gods of the sea . . .

There was the benevolent Mazu, one of the most well-known Chinese sea goddesses that protected humans. There was the fearsome Gonggong, who wreaked havoc. There were also the four dragon kings, one for each cardinal direction of the China seas.

"Ah!" I exclaimed out loud, turning to the rest of my party. "Ears That Hear What Comes on the Wind is Shunfeng'er."

"Um, who?" Yue asked.

"He's a Chinese sea and door god," Yang answered. "Divine guardian of doors and gates, like the ones you might see when entering a temple. Shunfeng'er typically accompanies Mazu, who is a powerful Chinese ocean deity."

I nodded in agreement. "They're not as powerful as some other gods, though. Maybe Shunfeng'er got caught in a precarious situation and released a distress signal."

> **Divinity Ears That Hear What Comes on the Wind insists that the distress signal was an accident.**

> **Divinity Supreme Commander of the Heavenly Hosts confirms this.**

> **Divinity Supreme Commander of the Heavenly Hosts says he will introduce Peijin's World Dominion to Divinity Ears That Hear What Comes on the Wind.**

I perked up at the message and nodded enthusiastically. I was never going to turn down a good networking and star opportunity. The more stars the better.

> **Polling ongoing . . .**
> A. 27%
> B. 55%
> C. 18%

I cocked my head at the results. It increased significantly just from my little interaction with the party. I guess that's what the observers and gods wanted to see more of.

"All right, all right. We've wasted enough time. Let's find Ruoming," I barked out the order, swirling Zhige in my hand confidently.

I squatted lower, tensing the muscles in my legs before I jumped high into the air, taking in our surroundings.

Further up was a massive white, domed building. Various pillars surrounded it and raised dozens of feet into the air. It was a truly stunning feat of architecture.

Yue squinted as she strained to see the building. "Five hundred stars says that the node is in there."

"And who do you think is going to take you up on that?" I answered. "It's obviously in there."

A flurry of blue sparks flashed beside Amelia, the dire wolf appearing. It lowered its nose to the ground, sniffing furiously before it chittered at Amelia. She gave it a slight nod but said no more.

I brought my hand up to the back of her shoulder, lightly squeezing it. "Is it in that direction?" I asked, knowing that she could confirm it with the wolf.

Amelia shrugged my hand off. She didn't even reply with her words, giving nothing more than a faint, but affirmative, shrug.

I nervously looked up at Yang, my eyes practically pleading with him. He raised a brow at me, as if asking what I had done now.

I shrugged stupidly. Yang deadpanned me before bringing his hand up to cup Amelia's cheek, gently rubbing his thumb across it affectionately. "We'll be relying on you, Amelia. You're the only one out of all of us who can actually locate the nodes, so let us know if we're doing something silly."

Amelia looked down and nodded. It seemed like she planned on staying silent again until she finally spoke up. "Okay."

> **[Observers Chat]**
> **StrawG:** Awwww (TvT) Amelia is my favorite of all the kids. That's the only reason I'm voting for this party
> **Nipon23:** i'm voting for this party because i don't want the next fight to be booooringgg
> **StrawG:** I would be devastated if anything happened to Amelia. We need to do our part to level the playing field!!
> **PinkPineapple:** Am I the only one feeling optimistic for Peijin's party . . . Peijin has more grit
> **Nipon23:** yeah you're the only one
> **Socrates:** I believe in Peijin! Obviously Feiyu is an all-star disciple and Ruoming is just on a tier of his own, but Peijin's resilience is why she keeps winning.
> **Nipon23:** peijin?? resilient??? that girl has a mental breakdown at the slightest inconvenience or human interaction
> **Socrates:** And she still survives! That's resilience and why it's fun to watch.
> **PinkPineapple:** True dat
> **Nipon23:** she's brainwashing all of you smh

> **SnaggleTooth:** Peijin can brainwash me. She's bad
> **StrawG:** What???

I quickly clicked the glowing white X at the top of the screen to close the chat.

"Zhige, pinky promise you won't snap?"

The red eye squinted at me like it was grinning.

"Grow longer but stay thin."

The blade shifted instantly, representing a staff more than anything. I held it out in front of me, dragging it across the ground to sense for traps. The moment it came in contact with the ground, a giant hole opened beneath me.

I let out a surprised yelp as I looked down, noticing a raging river that was ready to sweep into the underworld of the Arabian Coast.

Yue quickly stabbed through my hoodie with the tip of her spear until I was hanging on the end of it like a kitten grabbed by its scruff.

At once, my hoodie began to thrash violently, furious at Yue. Yue quickly flung me back up, and I shot her a thankful look.

"Zhige. A bit longer please."

Zhige obliged.

"Yang, use your staff in the same way."

We headed toward the building just like that—the two of us dragging our weapons on the ground to check for any traps and rescuing one another from the ones we did stumble across. We slowly headed to the dome.

Miraculously, it still seemed like there were no mobs. The number of traps decreased, as well, until we were hardly running into any. Perhaps someone already controlled that node, and that was why they were spawning at such a minimal rate. That was my only working hypothesis.

The closer we got to the dome, the more I could feel a rumbling beneath my feet.

"Do you guys feel that?" I asked.

"Nope."

We continued to advance. The rumbling only grew stronger. I perked up.

"Did you guys feel it this time? It just happened again. I swear that the ground is shaking beneath us."

"So, that's actually called an earthquake," Yue said facetiously. "And, I still don't feel a thing."

"Shut up. Wei, did you feel it?"

He paused and went as still as a statue; he must have been focusing all of his energy into sensing any anomalies. A few yellow sparks flew off of him as he used his overextended spiritual energy to increase his sensitivity.

The ground rumbled again.

The white band wrapped around Wei's forearm began unwinding like a snake getting ready to strike.

"It sounds like footsteps," Wei finally said.

"Footsteps?"

"Yes."

"That's the worst thing you could have said. *Those* are footsteps? It's like an entire earthquake."

Yue looked increasingly confused. "I still can't feel what you guys are talking about."

"Honestly, I can't either," Yang answered.

Amelia reluctantly nodded.

"Are you all being serious?" I asked.

"If anything, things feel eerily silent," Yang said. "Hasn't this entire arc so far been painfully easy? Maybe it's because we leveled up so much in the last dungeon room, but this room doesn't feel like much of a challenge so far."

"I agree," I said, "but I can only imagine it ramping up."

Nothing Yang was saying was untrue. I fundamentally agreed with him. In *Surviving My First Run*, this was a frantic and violent room. However, it was feeling more like an incredibly stressful vacation rather than an apocalyptic challenge.

The ground rumbled. This time stronger—I felt it throughout my entire body.

> **Divinity Supreme Commander of the Heavenly Hosts has granted all members of Peijin's World Dominion a minuscule amount of spiritual energy.**

At once, the rumbling became apparent. Amelia, Yang, and Yue all jumped, surprised by what now felt like the constant trembling of the ground.

So, it was only detectable if someone held a certain threshold of spiritual energy, which was why Wei and I felt it first.

"The ghosts?" I speculated out loud. "Are they trying to hide from—"

The sound of deep, banging drums rang out all around us.

CHAPTER THIRTEEN

The banging of the drums was rhythmic and far off. It got louder and louder, surrounding us until I could feel the bass tremble in my chest.

A deep, almost groaning sound echoed like a chant. The sounds of smaller drums followed suit, banging wildly.

"What the actual fuck," Yue said, utterly dumbfounded.

All of us looked around frantically, trying to locate where the sound was coming from until what felt like millions of blue sparks flashed all around us.

Ghosts instantly appeared, but instead of being aggressive, they were looking around aimlessly, like they were just as confused as we were.

"What is this?"

"Where are we?"

"Are we finally back?"

"My stand! Did someone rob me? Which one of you twisted bastards stole my jewelry!"

"Is this one of those new challenges?"

"Haven't you heard the news?" A young male ghost called out eagerly, bringing his fists up to his chest like he couldn't contain his excitement. "Apparently, there's a new king!"

"A new king? King of what?"

"Who cares, but there's a new king!"

The ghosts were all humanoid, though some were more deformed than others. A good chunk of them had missing limbs; some were odd colors; and others were incredibly stunning, looking like they were still alive.

But, none of them exuded a dangerous energy.

"Um, Peijin," Yue said, leaning in to whisper in my ear, "should we kill all of them? Or . . ."

"Hold on," I said, hyperaware of my surroundings.

> **Hindsight activated!**

The world turned translucent all around me as I frantically surveyed my surroundings for any threats. However, not even Hindsight was picking up on anything urgent around me.

The ghosts buzzed with excitement all around us. Some had taken up the stands in the marketplace and were selling their goods, but with each transaction, they whispered more and more imaginative rumors of the king.

"A new king? For us?"

"Should I light a candle?"

"Or make an offering?"

"Or say a prayer?"

"I heard he rivals the Four Great Male Beauties of China!"

"Oh, please. I'll believe it when I see it."

"Well, I heard that even Aphrodite fell in love with him."

"Aphrodite has so many lovers. Who cares about what she has to say?"

"Apparently she broke karmic restraints just to favor him in the last arc."

"Broke karmic restraints?!"

"Will he be making an appearance soon?"

"I heard a rumor that there's going to be a parade."

"I heard the same."

"Selling prayer candles here! Buy some now, and curry favor with the new king!"

> **Hundreds of ghosts are speaking of the new king.**

> **Many gods are growing excited at the news of a new king.**

> **Divinity Great Sage Equaling Heaven is asking if there is actually a new king.**

> **Demon Great Sage who Pacifies Heaven says he hasn't heard of any new kings.**

> **Divinity Great Sage Equaling Heaven is scratching the inside of his ear with his pinky.**

> **Divinity Great Sage Equaling Heaven is asking if the king is trying to become a god.**

> **Divinity Supreme Commander of the Heavenly Hosts gasps in excitement.**

> **Divinity The One Who Fights in Front gazes on with great skepticism.**

I stared blankly, having never been more confused in my entire life. What in the world was happening?

Dozens of ghosts bumped into me and shoved me on the street, swarming the candle shops and buying dozens at a time. It was rare for there to be such a big event in a ghost's mundane existence, and their excitement was infectious.

"Should . . . I buy candles?" I asked mindlessly, staring blankly at the scene.

I turned around to face my party and saw Yue already holding dozens of candles.

"You wouldn't even buy those for me in Wei's dungeon until I blackmailed you!" I protested.

"You told me I was supposed to worship the gods, right?! I want to curry favor with this king, too! If he likes us, can't we get to the node easily?"

> **Thousands of gods are now watching the stream with bated breath.**

> **[Observers Chat]**
> **Socrates:** Jia Li . . . did we ever see an ascension ritual this early in *Surviving My First Run*?
> **Socrates:** Not that I'm complaining, of course! This could be a great opportunity for you to make another divine ally!

The blaring sound of trumpets rang out all around us, and finally, Hindsight picked up on a completely chaotic sight rounding the top of the hill in front of the dome.

"Up there!" I exclaimed, pointing.

Dozens, if not hundreds, of ghosts dressed in beautiful, glistening uniforms were lined up in two rows outside the dome. They all moved perfectly in sync, swaying with the grand music.

In the middle was a stunning float parade. Toward the front, giant, golden statues were being carried and thrown up and down by a group of ghosts. Behind them was an impressive display of massive floating creatures.

One of them displayed beautiful female masks with golden wings protruding from the head. Another showed skeletons in massive fields of flowers. It seemed to stretch on and on, with no end in sight.

Did we seriously stumble into an ascension ceremony? Typically, ascension ceremonies were used to gain a sufficient amount of spiritual energy to become a divinity, or someone had already acquired enough spiritual energy and wanted to make a show of it.

In front of all of this was a massive line of animals and ghosts. Beautiful women stood in the front, dancing as their thin but colorful robes flew around them effortlessly, drawing in the eyes of thousands of ghosts. The men were dressed up as swordsmen, pulling off impressive tricks on the sidelines.

Tigers prowled behind them; a line of elephants adorned with intricate fabrics, jewelry, and beads stomped through; and camels swung their heads back and forth with the music.

Amelia let out an excited gasp as she pointed to the creatures. "I'm going to get those!" she exclaimed with newfound determination, blue sparks already lightly fluttering around her.

"Wait a minute," I said, staring at the jaw-dropping sight. I squinted. I couldn't believe my eyes. "Is that . . . Is that Cheng?!"

Leading the charge of this very chaotic sight was Cheng, shouting and riling up all the ghosts around him with more rumors of the king.

Cheng brought a small trumpet up to his mouth. "Make way for the king! Clear the bazaar!"

He began clapping his hands to the music and chanting, and it didn't take much for all the ghosts to replicate him.

He practically skipped down the road, talking to every single ghost near him. His energy was absolutely electric, his once playful demeanor now wickedly charming as he grabbed the hands of women and wrapped his arms around the shoulders of men. "A brand-new star is here, so come be the first to meet his eye!"

At once, all the ghosts around us sprinted toward the parade, stomping over one another greedily. My entire party followed suit, thankfully faster than all of the stampeding ghosts.

Cheng spotted me surprisingly fast, and he waved at me eagerly, looking far too overjoyed to be seeing his competing party.

"You're gonna love this guy," he shouted, a bright grin plastered on his face. Although I knew Cheng was genuinely delighted to be putting on a show like this, given his character, it felt like adding insult to injury.

Polling ongoing . . .
A. 20%
B. 62%

| C. 18% |

| **Demon Bearer of the Thousand Hungers is roaring with excitement at the broadcast!** |

| **Divinity Clock-Handed Judge is asking if the king is a ghost.** |

| **Demon Hollow Herald is wishing for a wicked king.** |

| **Divinity Star-Eyed Watcher is looking at her screen for the first time.** |

| **The Divinities of Paradise are all watching the broadcast.** |

| **The Divinities of Olympus are all watching the broadcast.** |

| **An unprecedented number of gods are watching the broadcast!** |

I could practically imagine the expression that must be on Chang's face right now, floating in all the stars he could ever want. Ruoming and I had turned him into a millionaire overnight.

I jerked my head to my party. "Follow my earlier instructions, and don't worry about me!"

They quickly dissipated into the crowd, with Wei lurking behind, not too far from me. But, with the amount of ghosts present, it wasn't hard to lose track of where everyone was.

I moved my way to the front, shoving ghosts over with my shoulder. Although they'd normally protest and cry out in rage, they were far too fascinated by the spectacle before them. For a population typically extremely impoverished, this must have been the most brilliant display they'd seen in centuries.

Cheng smiled and extended a prayer candle to me. "Care to celebrate our king?"

I snatched the candle from his hand and pulled out a lighter from my Boundless Bag. "Give these blessings to Divinity Blessed Martial Guard of Salvation." I smiled as I handed the candle back to Cheng. "Sorry, but I'm already loyal to a god. Besides, does your king even have an epithet?"

Cheng's smile faltered when I sent the candle's spiritual energy to Wei, but he quickly recovered and offered his hand once more. A flash of blue sparks appeared on his palm and another candle took its place.

"No worries. There are thousands of these to go around."

I gave him a tense smile. "Aw, Cheng, you're far too sweet. Anyways, where is he?"

"Where is who?"

"The king." I pulled Zhige around from my side, the blade ringing at the swift movement.

"Ah! He'll be out in just a moment."

"Cheng—"

Bang!

I moved before I could process what had occurred. The bullet sliced through my cheek before striking a ghost, who turned into ash instantly without a sound. Hindsight flickered wildly with an overwhelming amount of information.

> [Observers Chat]
> **Socrates:** OMG
> **Sapling123:** WAS SHE HIT???
> **MagicTape:** Peijin!! You need more spiritual energy!!

> **Polling ongoing . . .**
> **A. 33%**
> **B. 50%**
> **C. 17%**

> **Hundreds of gods scream in shock!**

> **Divinity Supreme Commander of the Heavenly Hosts is dumbfounded.**

> **Divinity The One Who Fights in Front grants Disciple Peijin a minuscule amount of spiritual energy.**

Although it would have normally caused a panic, in such a chaotic parade, the gunshot didn't faze any of the ghosts, who were still in a frenzy over the new "king."

I brought up two fingers and gently swiped them over the stinging wound. It should have healed by now, but instead, I could feel it burning, and the wound only grew deeper and deeper. I stared at the blood on my fingers before slowly turning my eyes back up to Cheng.

"Sending out your child soldier to kill me, now?" My voice was ice cold. Based on the way the bullet traveled toward me, Qijing must have been camping at the building just behind me. That was, of course, assuming she didn't have a skill that could redirect her bullets.

Bang!

With the boost from Athena, I dodged instantly, my perception terrifyingly fast.

The thought of my own little sister trying to kill me publicly sent a wicked bitterness coursing through me. I spun around, Hindsight frantically analyzing all of the buildings until it finally pinpointed the tiniest gun barrel peeking through the dried bricks.

My grip tightened on the hilt of my blade. Knowing that Wei was still surveying me from the crowd, I lifted Zhige and pointed straight at the barrel.

Boom, I mouthed before smiling. I watched the barrel instantly retract behind the security of the wall.

> **[Party Chat]**
> **Peijin:** Don't kill her. I want her alive.

I brought Zhige before me, assuming an appropriate fighting stance. "Planning on firing another headshot?"

Cheng gulped audibly before laughing anxiously. "I'm a really great healer."

"Right."

I lurched toward Cheng, my blade aimed right at his eye. He let out a nervous squeal and quickly ducked. Blue sparks erupted around him. One of his skills activated.

I swung at Cheng with killing intent, and yet he seemed to dodge it all just the same—no matter how fast I moved.

> **Agility level 30 → 40**

Hundreds of thousands of stars instantly drained from my account. Blue sparks erupted around me.

Still, I couldn't land a single hit on Cheng.

I let out a frustrated groan.

"Your skill," I began. "You have Prey's Insight, don't you? You sense my killing intent and can tell where I'm planning on striking."

Sweat formed on Cheng's brow. Even if he could predict my moves, it wouldn't stop an overuse of the skill from completely exhausting him. I stopped my movements, pulling back and staring at him.

"You're not a challenge for me. Quit running."

> **[Party Chat]**
> **Peijin:** Yue, take care of Cheng. He can sense killing intent, so he'll know where you're planning on striking him. But if you use Magician's Hand and trap him in an illusion flooded with killing intent, you'll blur his senses.
> **Yang:** Peijin, you're going to run out of messages. Keep it in check and don't

> die. We'll take care of things. Just trust what we're doing from behind the scenes.

My fight with Cheng drew him away from his job of leading the parade, and the ghosts noticed.

"What is that woman doing?"

"Is she trying to stop the parade?"

"Why stop the parade? We haven't even seen the king yet!"

"Get this bitch off the road!"

"She's disturbing the show!"

I scoffed at the conversations, entirely ignoring Cheng now as I turned back to the parade. The ghost singers and dancers were now chanting the praises that Cheng had been singing.

"Here he comes—ring the bells and bang the drums!" they chanted, clapping loudly in time with the beat. They continued moving forward, each step precisely calculated.

The ghost women adjusted their veils and outfits, polishing their appearance. The men attempted to push their way to the front, dying to know what the king would look like after such high praises were being sung.

Behind me, I could hear Cheng let out a startled yelp. He whipped around in confusion, his brow furrowed as he struggled to locate whatever was bothering him. I knew Yue had him now, and I continued pushing the opposite way of the parade, looking for the king.

Finally, I saw it. The comically sized, gold and red carriage. Hundreds of finely dressed ghosts were carrying it by the long poles that extended out of it, taking slow steps, as if merely touching the carriage was the greatest privilege of their lives.

I walked directly in front of its path.

CHAPTER FOURTEEN

The speed of the drumming and the music increased rapidly until it finally reached a dramatic climax.

"There it is!"

"He's coming!"

"The king is here!"

At once, a giant elephant covered in gold jewelry burst through the doors of the carriage, bellowing and trumpeting. On its back was Qiu Feiyu, that bastard, his expression bright and gorgeous.

Feiyu stood on the back of the elephant, balancing easily as the elephant stomped and stampeded viciously, throwing its head back and forth. It was a wild, overdone, and wasteful display. I had never seen something more embarrassing. How his party even managed to pull this off was far beyond me.

> [Observers Chat]
> **SJJC:** Oh my god
> **Aslan:** This is incredible
> **Peenut:** How do they keep pulling off incredible stunts every time??
> **MGirl193:** Guys are we changing our votes . . .
> **Socrates:** No!

Feiyu grabbed his stunning purple sword, throwing it into the air and catching it as his black clothing fluttered around him. His perfectly layered hair flowed in the wind, giving him an effortless but wild charm. Feiyu looked at the crowd and gave his first, bright smile, and the ghosts went utterly mad, screaming wildly and trying to reach him over the parade barrier.

"He's beautiful!"

"He's a disciple? From the apocalypse challenges? That man?"

"His physique!"

"Selling prayer candles! Help this man become a god!"

"How many do you have?"

"Give me all you got."

"Here, here, save some for me!"

"Don't hog it, you cow! You won't catch the eye of the king!"

"Cow?! Who are you calling a cow, you fucking bitch!"

My entire body was almost shaking with anger. I looked up at Feiyu as he approached. I was entirely unmoving. Feiyu finally saw me, perking up before winking and blowing me a kiss.

I flushed bright pink in anger.

The various ghosts around me instantly stopped fighting one another and stared at me instead.

"W-who is that skank? Get out of the road, whore!"

I whipped around to the ghost who shouted that. "Skank? Whore?!"

Feiyu slid down the trunk of the elephant, who was now in sync with the rest of the parade, and gracefully landed. He slowly walked up to me.

Scathing Reviewer activated!

For some reason, even though seeing Feiyu filled me with an unspeakable rage, I could never act on it when he approached. He infuriated me, but he also made me weak. I could only blame it on my attachment to *Surviving My First Run*.

Even though it was entirely irrational, he was the only constant in my life for the last decade, and seeing him gave me a sense of security and made me want to wipe him off the Earth at the same time.

"Tch," I scoffed. I was turning meek, and it was this ugly bastard's fault.

When he finally stood before me, I had never felt smaller. He towered over me, far superior, both internally and externally. I knew I could never reach his tier. Feiyu had something he was born with that I simply lacked.

"Jiejie," he muttered, leaning down until we were seeing eye to eye. "I'm so happy. I didn't know you wanted a front row seat for my ascension."

Divinity Supreme Commander of the Heavenly Hosts gasps and covers his mouth in shock.

> **Divinity Supreme Commander of the Heavenly Hosts gets a nosebleed.**

> **Divinity Supreme Commander of the Heavenly Hosts says Disciple Peijin and Disciple Feiyu look extremely good together.**

> **Countless gods are scolding Divinity Supreme Commander of the Heavenly Hosts!**

> **The Divinities of Paradise are warning Divinity Supreme Commander of the Heavenly Hosts not to have sinful thoughts.**

> **Divinity Supreme Commander of the Heavenly Hosts is doubling down.**

> **Divinity Supreme Commander of the Heavenly Hosts is scheduling a fan club meeting.**

> [Observers Chat]
> **Socrates:** Jia Li . . . please don't fall for Feiyu's teasing again . . .
> **Socrates:** Jia Li, don't do something stupid. Pretty please. Jia Li?

My eye twitched. I held myself together.

"Trying to ascend, huh?" I answered coldly.

"It does seem like that. Are you here to stop me, Jiejie?"

"I'm going to kill you, Qiu Feiyu."

"Is Jiejie jealous? I'm sorry. I didn't mean to steal the spotlight from you. But Jiejie is already a god, so Jiejie doesn't need a parade. Jiejie already has millions of devoted worshippers."

Suddenly, thousands of burning lights pointed straight at me. It was blinding. I moved my arms up to shield my eyes.

I was spotlighted, and all of the ghosts who hadn't been watching me before were now staring straight at me.

Cheng, panting, stumbled back into the picture, standing only a few feet away from me and raising his hands into the air. "A wicked disciple has decided to challenge the king! Watch the king rightfully defend the ghosts and what he stands for. The king will need all the spiritual energy in the world from his people, so send all your prayers to him at this moment!"

Cheng flung out hundreds of thousands of prayer candles into the crowd. I scanned around for my party, panic welling in my chest. Was it that easy for a mere healer to strike down Yue?

I finally caught sight of Yue. The skin of her arm had turned a grotesque purple shade, and she was clawing at her throat, evidently struggling to breathe. Yang stood just beside her, desperately administering concoction after concoction of elixirs. Yue's expression was desperate, her face turning bluer by the second.

I looked back at Cheng, my jaw dropping. Cheng was . . . a poison user now?

> **Divinity Spirit of the Jade Moon insists she is helping Disciple Yang heal Disciple Yue.**

> **Demon Great Sage Who Pacifies Heaven is shouting at his screen.**

> **Demon Great Sage Who Pacifies Heaven is spamming messages to both Disciple Yue and Disciple Yang.**

> [Party Chat]
> **Yang:** I won't let her die. Take care of Feiyu.
> **Amelia:** FEIYU HAS THE AMERICAN NODE!

My eyes jumped back and forth between Feiyu and Cheng. I couldn't fight both of them at the same time. Feiyu was already going to be the hardest fight I've had against another disciple, and if Cheng was truly an adept healer and poison user, one strike could incapacitate me.

> **Polling ongoing . . .**
> A. 20%
> B. 70%
> C. 10%

At this rate, depending on how much spiritual energy this poll awarded, Feiyu really might become a god.

That must've been the master plan. This entire setup, the parade, the spotlight—all of it was a specifically curated show meant to make Ruoming's party look like the most brilliant and prestigious disciple group the universe had seen.

They were truly playing their role in the broadcast. They were entertainers. This was a game, and they had rigged it in their favor.

This theme was evident all throughout *Surviving My First Run*. The more one entertained and the greater story they told, the more success came their way. Feiyu's secret to success was always telling the best story.

But, not once has the system so blatantly rewarded a fabricated performance like this.

The poll questions were tailored to awarding the greatest show, and Feiyu's party must have known that.

It was like a live popularity poll used to pit streamers against one another. Nothing about this was organic. In fact, it lost all of the charm that *Surviving My First Run* had, and it infuriated me.

"Qiu Feiyu, did you know about the poll?"

"Know what?"

"Ha. I should've checked *you* for a tattoo. You really get me going, Feiyu."

> **[Party Chat]**
> **Peijin:** Do anything and everything. I want the greatest story these gods will ever witness. Amelia, summon the serpent.

A massive cloud of blue sparks erupted from the top of a nearby building. The sea serpent appeared, roaring viciously and instantly crashing down. It pinpointed Cheng and let out a vicious roar, spit flying everywhere.

At once, the surrounding ghosts dissipated, terrified for their lives, and Amelia ensured she wouldn't accidentally harm them. If she did, it would only make us lose ghost support.

Feiyu's head jerked toward the serpent. In that moment of distraction, I lunged at him, swinging my sword for his ribs. He blocked my strike effortlessly, pivoting his blade for my head. I scrambled back, readjusting my grip on Zhige and muttering to the blade.

This time, when I moved to strike Feiyu, I intentionally struck too short. Feiyu attempted to block a swing that would never land, and in that moment, Zhige lengthened, nicking Feiyu's arm before Feiyu promptly retreated.

Some of the ghosts, who were still watching after avoiding the serpent, gasped in shock.

"She's struck the king!"

"The king got hit?!"

"Did she strike his face?"

"Your blade can change sizes, too," Feiyu said with amazement, blood dribbling down his arm. "I'm so jealous."

I didn't even want to think about how Feiyu was now wielding my initial dream sword.

"Stop wasting your breath and fight me," I spat.

He let out a low whistle. "So feisty. Like a cute little kitten."

We exchanged blow after blow, neither of us seeming to get closer to the other. I spat curses at him, and he stopped responding, too focused now on the battle raging between us.

I pulled back for a moment, analyzing the situation. In terms of raw strength, Feiyu could beat me. Both of us could certainly level up our stats more, but that would just result in an arms race.

I frowned slightly. Feiyu adjusted his grip on his sword, jerking his head at me as if beckoning me to continue my assault. Why wasn't I stronger? Why couldn't I be just a bit taller so I could at least fight him head on?

In terms of skills, I wasn't sure if his skillset had changed from *Surviving My First Run*, but he was much more adept for offense than I was. Apart from the information that Hindsight could provide me, I didn't have many skills useful for combat.

I couldn't rile him up, either. It was obvious that I would fall victim to his verbal taunts before he ever fell for mine. The situation was looking more and more bleak by the moment. Should I have Wei deal with him instead, and I could handle Qijing?

That would be a much more ideal situation for me, but it would be terrible in terms of my perception. It would make me look weak and like I was hiding behind Wei's strength. I wanted to prove that I could at the very least match Feiyu.

"You're the first god I'm fighting," Feiyu said with a little smirk. "You can actually keep up with me."

"Yeah, wanna send me a prayer candle, so I can be even better?"

Feiyu gave a breathy laugh, his eyes sparkling. "How many do you need to catch up?"

I glared at him, and he shrugged halfheartedly in reply.

I suddenly perked up. That was it. It wasn't that I was far weaker than him in strength or level—especially not with Zhige—but I didn't have enough spiritual energy to compete with him. Considering the amount of ghosts that must be lending him spiritual energy right now and the ongoing poll, I was far behind.

Just like I told my party to put on a show, I needed to do the same, even if I couldn't rely on my strength or skills to do so. And, I still needed that goddamn node.

"Feiyu, should we play a game?"

Feiyu perked up, curious and always excited by the prospect of a game. "What is it?"

"The ghosts can bet on who they think will win our fight with a candle. I'll even throw in an additional one hundred thousand stars into the pot. That's the same as the reward for winning the arc. Can you match that?"

Feiyu grinned. "I can double it."

I awkwardly looked at my balance, a drop of sweat falling down my forehead.

264,498 stars.

I crossed my arms, trying to keep my best poker face. "You're just trying to fund the entire ghost economy, huh?"

"Jiejie, I think you'll win. I'm just trying to give you more stars."

"Fine. I'll double it too. four hundred thousand stars in the pot total."

I opened up the system screens, quickly creating a contract and turning it toward Feiyu to sign. I didn't want him to have any tricks up his sleeve.

LIU PEIJIN AND QIU FEIYU CONTRACT
Liu Peijin and Qiu Feiyu will each contribute
200,000 stars into the betting pool.
The winner of the fight will receive 400,000 stars.
The winner of the fight will receive respective
spiritual energy from all wagered bets.
The winner will be declared when a disciple
is able to land a killing blow.
No outside influence of other party members is permissible.

"Am I missing anything?" I asked, turning the screen toward him.

My hand rested on my hip, and my eyes travelled all over Feiyu as he read the contract. Where could he be hiding the American node? The nodes were so small that it could be anywhere.

Feiyu let out a deep hum. "How interesting. 'Able to land a killing blow on the other.' So, we aren't trying to kill each other? Jiejie, I thought you said you were going to kill me."

"I'll make that a slow and agonizing death."

"Jiejie is so mean."

"Are you planning on killing me right here?"

Feiyu didn't reply, only smiling at me.

"The contract is perfect, as I expect from Jiejie."

All signatories have signed! The contract is now
in effect until a winner is declared.

CHAPTER FIFTEEN

Feiyu let out a loud whistle, throwing a hand up in the air. "To everybody and anybody watching, place your bets on the god of fate and fortune or me, Qiu Feiyu, by purchasing prayer candles for one of us. Feel free to create your own mini gambling rings. Just imagine how much you can win with this many players."

At his words, the ghosts stilled for a moment, looking at one another in surprise. Feiyu was right—if they started betting on one of us, with this many people involved, millions of stars could be won.

Ghosts were fallen humans. Fallen humans loved gambling.

The crowd was still until there was a trail of smoke from somewhere in the crowd. A candle had been lit. The first ghost had made a wager.

I hoped Chance Sought Gold Serendipity didn't hate me for stealing his future income.

At once, the crowd went wild, thousands of candles being purchased in rapid succession. I would need to act fast, before all of it went to Qiu Feiyu.

I could already see him breathing out a sigh of relief, without a doubt feeling the effects of all the spiritual energy being directed at him.

"It's such a warm feeling, Jiejie. It's like receiving the biggest, warmest hug. I hope you can relate, yes?" Feiyu smiled at me.

> **Divinity Supreme Commander of the Heavenly Hosts is buying as many candles as he can!**

> **Divinity Great Sage Equaling Heaven
> reluctantly opens the system store.**

> **Divinity The One Who Fights in Front is
> waiting for a more impressive display.**

> **Divinity The One Who Fights in Front threatens that
> Disciple Peijin cannot lose without severe consequences.**

> **Divinity Ears That Hear What Comes on the Wind
> publicly voices support for Disciple Peijin.**

> **Divinity Ears That Hear What Comes on the Wind has granted
> Disciple Peijin a minuscule amount of spiritual energy.**

> **Demon Great Sage who Pacifies Heaven is too busy
> shouting at the screen for the fight to seriously start.**

"Only the sting of karma excites me." I slid my back foot on the ground and gripped Zhige, slowing my breathing and lasering my focus until all I could feel was the beating of my heart in my ears.

I felt the warmth of spiritual energy flowing through me, relaxing my muscles and providing relief from the constant soreness I'd felt since the apocalypse had begun.

> **Card Dealer activated!**

All of Feiyu's fifty-six Minor Arcana cards opened up before me, and almost all of them were lit up. They were colored beautifully, floating before him and encircling the two of us until it felt like we were surrounded by all his stories, and not a single other person in the world existed.

Of course, Feiyu had no clue this was happening. But, for a moment, his face contorted, and he shook his head in confusion.

I'd hardly interacted with Feiyu, but since I was his creator—as long as there wasn't a significant shift in events that had happened to him since the apocalypse began—I still had an incredibly high understanding of his character.

Evidently, I didn't know some of his memories weren't known, since they were formed with his party. I didn't have access to those cards. But luckily, the apocalypse wasn't far enough along for too much to change.

I was going to erase Qiu Feiyu.

I swirled my hand around me, selecting all of the lit-up cards. I was surprised to see our first interaction on the Page of Cups card, a card representing unexpected inspiration, new emotional connections, and a childish wonder.

> **You have selected 48 cards!**

> **How would you like to alter these cards?**

> **Delete.**

A furious flurry of yellow sparks appeared all around me. Karma was pissed.

At once, I felt all the energy drain from my body. Card Dealer was one of the most powerful skills I knew of, and it required an utterly ridiculous amount of spiritual energy.

Furthermore, my usage of the skill on Feiyu was an overstep. The only reason I had access to so many of his cards was because I created him, not because I had taken the effort to understand him. It was a wicked advantage, and I was being heavily punished for it.

The Tower tattoo on my arm burned terribly, lighting up so much that it was visible even beneath the sleeve of my hoodie. I clamped my teeth together, barely able to hold myself upright.

Feiyu stared at me in shock before he stumbled back, a hand coming up to grip his head.

I turned back to the blue screen, altering the command.

> **Cancel skill.**

> **Card Dealer cancelled!**

None of Feiyu's cards had vanished yet. My spiritual energy, although a significant portion depleted just from triggering the skill, quickly returned to me. I could feel my tattoo sucking up the majority of it, and I tightened my grip on Zhige as I swung at Feiyu.

Yellow sparks erupted all around me the moment I struck him, but they vanished not long after that, once the skill was successfully cancelled.

But, to outsiders, it would look like, for just a moment, that I learned how to wield Karma. If blue sparks represented genuine skills and the system, then yellow signified punishment and horror. But there I was, striking a disoriented Feiyu after a sudden eruption of yellow sparks around me.

Feiyu barely reacted in time. Zhige cut through his side, the length of the blade extending to dig deeper into his flesh, but Feiyu leapt back and quickly deflected Zhige. Apart from his shock, now that the skill was cancelled, Feiyu returned to his usual alertness and focus.

"Ha... what kind of skill is that?" Feiyu stated. "You should teach me that one sometime, Jiejie. Not a single blue spark. What a monster you are."

I panted heavily, my arm feeling like it was on fire. I did my best to tune him out, hardly having the energy to focus on anything but the feeling of Zhige in my hands and my skills swirling around me.

"She really struck him!"

"Is it a psychological skill?"

"Why didn't the king react sooner?"

"That girl really is a god. Of course the king doesn't stand a chance against somebody like that. It's an unfair fight!"

"She's a god?!"

"She sure doesn't look like one."

"The king mentioned it, too."

"Well, my money is on the line now, you bastard! Do I switch my vote?"

"She still couldn't land a true strike on him. I'm giving the king more spiritual energy."

"What an idiot you all are! A disciple could never beat a god!"

> **Card Dealer activated!**

> **You have selected 48 cards!**

> **How would you like to alter these cards?**

> **Delete.**

Feiyu let out another pained groan. This time it took me longer to recover from the activation of Card Dealer, and my entire body trembled violently.

I let out a loud cough, blood sputtering from my mouth. I instantly wiped it away, not wanting to show Feiyu how much each attack was draining me.

> **Divinity Supreme Commander of the Heavenly Hosts is shouting at you to get up!**

> **Dozens of gods are clamoring, unable to believe what they were witnessing.**

> **Divinity The One Who Fights in Front is remembering when you first revealed your identity as god of fate and fortune.**

For the first time, Feiyu's eyes went dark and serious. His lips were pressed in a thin line. Before I could cancel the skill and recover, he jerked his sword at me, thrusting it straight for my neck.

> **Cancel skill.**

> **Card Dealer cancelled!**

I quickly ducked as yellow sparks burst all around me. But Feiyu's reaction time also increased as he grew used to my attack. He pivoted his sword, slashing it deep into my back as I wrapped around him. Zhige flew out of my hand, slicing into Feiyu's leg before flying back into my grip.

I let out a loud groan, but I struggled back onto my feet behind Feiyu. Feiyu stumbled before regaining his balance. He stared at the blood gushing from his leg before he slowly turned around to face me. He cocked his head, analyzing me the way a predator watches its already dying prey.

I could feel the hot blood dripping down the skin of my back, and I smirked. "What's wrong? Your first time taking a hit over there?"

"I can tell you're a professional. Look at how well you're handling that wound, Jiejie."

> **Card Dealer activated!**

> **You have selected 48 cards!**

> **How would you like to alter these cards?**

> **Delete.**

I inhaled deeply before practically soaring at him, yellow sparks bursting all around me. I extended my arm out all the way, aiming for his collarbone.

Feiyu's recovery to my trick was getting faster and faster each time, and I was only getting weaker. Zhige sliced into his collarbone before Feiyu pulled away again, scoffing.

> **Cancel skill.**

> **Card Dealer cancelled!**

> **Card Dealer activated!**

> **You have selected 48 cards!**

> **How would you like to alter these cards?**

> **Delete.**

I didn't even give myself a moment to breathe. My arm erupted into yellow sparks, and they traveled up my blade, crowding over Zhige, whose red eye now moved in a total frenzy. Blue sparks flew out from Zhige, who was now tapping into its own spiritual energy, leading to a completely destructive hit.

> **Hindsight activated!**

I finally spotted the American node, trapped securely in the inner pocket of his coat.

I aimed for his hip, trying to drag my blade up vertically to cut through his entire front side.

The disoriented Feiyu lowered his stance, and he breathed out a wisp of ominous, dark gray smoke. His eyes glowed a deep purple, almost red, and locked right on me.

Panic took over me when I registered his actions over the flurry of blue and yellow sparks. He was getting ready to use his signature offensive skill.

Before I could complete my original move, I threw Zhige forward, now focusing solely on surviving Feiyu's next attack.

> **Cancel skill.**

> **Card Dealer cancelled!**

Zhige stabbed straight into Feiyu's hip, exactly where I was hoping. The yellow sparks travelled up Feiyu's body, tearing into his skin, but it didn't faze him in the slightest.

It was like nothing could break his current state of focus. His now clear gaze remained locked on me as a red thread appeared between the two of us.

He was going to land the next hit. His skill Thread of Malice guaranteed it.

He lunged forward with horrific speed, his blade aimed right for my heart. Instead of making a completely futile attempt to dodge him, I moved toward him, slightly turning my torso so the blade would just miss my heart.

I felt his sword slice straight into my body and a horrific, searing pain in my lung. I let out a shallow wheeze, frantically trying to keep my breathing calm.

Feiyu had punctured one of my lungs.

I let out a violent cough, bright red blood flying from my mouth. My saliva began to froth in my mouth, and I could hardly breathe.

> Countless gods are gasping in shock.

> Countless gods are staring at their screens in disbelief.

> Divinity Supreme Commander of the Heavenly Hosts lets out a mortified cry.

> Divinity Ears That Hear What Comes on the Wind is holding Divinity Supreme Commander of the Heavenly Hosts back from interfering in the arc.

> Divinity The One Who Fights in Front stares at her screen with a solemn expression.

> Divinity Spirit of the Jade Moon covers her mouth in horror.

> Polling ongoing . . .
> A. 43%
> B. 44%
> C. 13%

I gritted my teeth, pressing myself deeper into the blade of his sword as I reached for Zhige, who was still stuck deep in his hip. I grabbed Zhige, dragging the blade straight up Feiyu's side in hopes that the pain would make Feiyu retreat.

Without hesitation, Feiyu pulled his blade out of my body to block Zhige. Zhige clattered to the ground. In that split moment, I reached into Feiyu's pocket and took the American node. He hardly noticed—thinking I was simply flailing around stupidly.

But, the damage was done. I took a few, weak steps forward until I hit the ground, grabbing my chest. I was choking on my own blood. I was going to suffocate to death.

> **LIU PEIJIN AND QIU FEIYU'S CONTRACT CONDITIONS HAVE BEEN FULFILLED!**
> **Winner: Qiu Feiyu**
> Reward: 400,000 stars and respective spiritual energy.

> **Polling ongoing . . .**
> A. 11%
> B. 81%
> C. 8%

Feiyu looked down at me, stepping closer and getting down on one knee. His face was only inches from mine, so the only thing I could make out through my fading vision was his bright smile. He must have felt an unbelievable surge of spiritual energy.

> **Divinity Supreme Commander of the Heavenly Hosts is attempting to descend into the arc!**

> **Divinity Ears That Hear What Comes on the Wind is attempting to descend into the arc!**

> **Warning! Severe karmic violations!**

> **Warning! Severe karmic violations!**

> **Dozens of gods attempt to subdue Divinity Supreme Commander of the Heavenly Hosts!**

> **Divinity Great Sage Equaling Heaven warns that Divinity Supreme Commander of the Heavenly Hosts is about to summon a calamity!**

"Jiejie, I really like you a lot. So, just grovel a bit, and I'll save you, yeah?"

Just one more move from Feiyu, and I would be done for. Everything I worked toward was already lost. Feiyu had defeated me.

My lip trembled. Blood was welling in my throat and lungs, and the pain was excruciating. There was no way I could die like this—not after everything I already survived. And to die at the hands of Feiyu . . . that was the worst shame I could bring myself.

Blood gurgled out of my mouth. With my last few seconds of consciousness, I reached into my Boundless Bag, my fingers squirming with the effort of finding a certain small object.

I felt the little puzzle piece grace my fingertips.

> **MEDITERRANEAN NODE**
> Location: Building AK13829 — Floor 2
> Description: The Mediterranean node controls the citadel's

> environment. Use the node's artifact to toggle these settings regardless of the user's current location.
> Temperature: 5/10
> Weather: 5/10
> Gravity: 5/10
> Pollution: 1/10
> Light: 5/10
> Time Loop: 1/10
> Owner: Liu Peijin

This was my last hope.

> **Set Time Loop: 2/10**

Feiyu looked down at me, stepping closer until he got down on one knee. "Jiejie, I really like you a lot. So, just grovel a bit, and I'll save you, yeah?"

By increasing the setting to two, time unwound by a mere second. So, in total, I had nine seconds to fix this because I couldn't surpass the maximum time loop setting.

In that case, I had one chance.

I reached into my Boundless Bag and found the Mediterranean node.

> **Set Time Loop: 10/10**

My body slowly repaired itself, our movements going in reverse until I was standing before Feiyu once more.

One.

The red thread appeared. Feiyu's hit was guaranteed.

Two.

I reread the contract. "*The winner will be declared when a disciple is able to land a killing blow.*"

Three.

Feiyu got into his stance.

Four.

I flipped Zhige around, pointing the tip of the blade straight against the side of my neck.

Five.

There were six main vessels in my neck. If I sliced far back enough, I would theoretically miss all of them and survive.

Six.

Feiyu lunged forward.

Seven.
Zhige attempted to dull itself and shrink, realizing my plan.
Eight.
I plunged Zhige straight through my throat.
Nine.
The red thread snapped.

CHAPTER SIXTEEN

"No!" Feiyu shouted, lowering his sword and reaching out to grab me. I twisted Zhige, and the blade tore through the nape of my neck. Then, I redirected it, threatening to slice through the front.

Divinity Spirit of the Jade Moon lets out a horrified cry!

Divinity Supreme Commander of the Heavenly Hosts is tearing up!

Countless gods are waiting with bated breath.

LIU PEIJIN AND QIU FEIYU'S CONTRACT CONDITIONS HAVE BEEN FULFILLED! **Winner: Liu Peijin** Reward: 400,000 stars and respective spiritual energy.

Feiyu grabbed onto me and forced my hand off the hilt, his expression serious. He sheathed his sword, and his hands frantically squeezed me, like he couldn't believe what I had just done.

I let out a pitiful groan, wincing at Feiyu's touch. The pain was agonizing, though not as bad as having Feiyu pierce through my lung. A significant amount of blood was dripping from the sloppy wound.

I didn't know why Feiyu was reacting this way when he had no issue with nearly killing me only seconds before. Was it only okay when my life was in his hands? What a sadistic bastard.

But surely I wasn't stupid enough to actually lop my head off, right? The blood flow was alarming. I was pretty sure I stayed far enough back.

Right?!

> **[Observers Chat]**
> **Socrates:** OMG
> **MGirl193:** IS SHE OKAY??
> **Seatdiv:** Peijin get back up
> **Aslan:** Peijin you can't die like this
> **Socrates:** Peijin, come on. You're not this weak.

"Cheng!" Feiyu shouted, attempting to locate him in the crowd. He pulled Zhige out of my neck and threw it to my side, ensuring I wouldn't make another effort to slice my head off entirely. His trembling hands cupped the back of my neck, applying firm pressure. He frantically scrolled through the Azure Dragon Store.

I gave a feeble whine, rolling into Feiyu. He held me tightly like he was worried I'd turn into ash and vanish. I snaked my hand up, inconspicuously taking the American node out of his pocket and sliding it into the sleeve of my hoodie. My hoodie took care of the rest, slowly transporting it up my arm.

Since I won the game, the warmth of spiritual energy was now flowing through me, filling me with an incredible amount of peace and strength. The blood flow began to slow. The pain subsided almost entirely. I looked up at Feiyu to find he was still preoccupied with the Azure Dragon Store.

I feigned a gurgle in my throat, and Feiyu let out a small but panicked sound. "Cheng!"

I redirected the spiritual energy to the wound on my neck, tightening the tiny muscles around the area to slow the blood flow until it was manageable. I had received a truly miraculous amount of spiritual energy, yet so much was immediately redirected to healing my body from the strain that Card Dealer demanded.

I slowly reached for Zhige, my fingers inching closer to the blade until I could finally feel its cold metal in my hand. The muscles in my legs tensed, prepared to launch me.

I leapt up into the air with absolutely unprecedented speed, lifting Zhige far above my head in preparation to strike.

"Qiu Feiyu, I swore I'd kill you!"

I plummeted toward the ground like a rocket, my eyes wide and locked onto Feiyu's wide and open back.

A white figure appeared, moving so fast it was just a blur. It smashed into me, sending me hurdling to the ground.

I yelped, the wound on my neck instantly opening up again. I saw the battered bodies of my party members nearby, and at once, the ribbon on Wei's arm unwound to wrap itself around my neck. It tightened, making it almost impossible to breathe, but it helped stop the bleeding.

I rolled across the rocky and sandy terrain until I finally slammed into some of the observing ghosts. When I finally tried to stand, all I could see was the flash of white hair before I felt a horrible, searing pain in my arm.

There was Song Ruoming, his face completely indifferent and calm. He grabbed his pale sword, which was so thin it resembled a saber, and dug it straight into my tattoo, like he wanted to tear it off.

"You are one of them," I smirked. "I was right. Where is it? Where is your tattoo?"

I tore my arm away, letting his sword rip through it before I gave my arm a good shake, redirecting my spiritual energy to help heal it. My wounded tattoo healed abnormally fast, like it was especially adept at channeling spiritual energy. If only I had it on my neck.

Ruoming looked at me blankly. For a moment, I thought he was entirely unaffected by the fact his entire plan had been unraveled, but then I saw his slight eye twitch, and I smiled.

"How old are you?" I asked before Ruoming struck me again. Unlike Feiyu, whose movements I could keep up with despite struggling, Ruoming was on an entirely different level. He far surpassed me in technique, strength, and speed—if I hadn't been fighting him, I would've been in awe. Luckily, I was now the one with all the spiritual energy.

All of my senses were unbelievably heightened, even without me leveling anything up. The processing speed for all my skills was remarkable. Ruoming's movements looked like they were in slow motion.

"Only beings who can die keep track," Ruoming answered. His thin sword stabbed into my side and dragged up, creating a deep gash through my entire front side. I winced, pulling back and stumbling.

I redirected my spiritual energy, slowing the bleeding but not fully closing the wound to avoid depleting my resources too quickly. Zhige, who was typically so in tune with my fighting style, hesitated with Ruoming.

"Ha! Well, aren't you just as cocky as Feiyu is?"

Blood was seeping from the wound on my front and on my neck, coating Wei's ribbon and my hoodie in a deep maroon color. Although these injuries would usually render me out of commission, spiritual energy truly made all the difference. I was really feeling like a god now.

Polling ongoing . . .
A. 45%

> **B. 45%**
> **C. 10%**

Feiyu flew before me, his purple sword aiming to shatter my collarbone. I easily parried his slash, but Ruoming followed up behind his attack, his saber making a series of cuts that grazed me over and over again as I matched his pace.

I could hear the roar of Amelia's serpent behind me. Without even thinking, I leapt up, and the serpent appeared beneath me perfectly, scooping me up. I held onto its whiskers, my feet dangling while I looked down.

The world around us began to blur, and the ghosts let out terrified cries. The ground warped beneath them, turning into steep dunes. Various spikes burst from the ground, targeting Feiyu and Ruoming.

"Yue!" I looked around frantically until I spotted her standing near the middle of the serpent's winding body. Yang was beside her, holding her still. Blue sparks erupted all around her from the effort of creating the illusion.

Her skin was still a sickly purple hue, but the swelling had gone down significantly, and she was no longer struggling to breathe. Thankfully, Yang and Chang'e managed to diffuse Cheng's poison.

Hearing my cry, Yue looked around for me. She finally spotted me and gave a weak smile before flipping me off.

I could taste the metallic tang of blood in my mouth. I pressed my hand against the wound on my chest and winced. I looked down at my hand to see it coated in blood.

Before I could attempt to heal the wounds again, Ruoming appeared before me.

"Huh?"

He dug his blade into the serpent, which let out a brutal cry and instantly shook its head. Ruoming reached for me while I dangled from the serpent's whisker.

I held on tighter, looking down to see if I could survive the fall. Before I had to make the decision between falling or fighting, white robes blurred before me.

I let out a cry of relief at the sight of Wei.

He gracefully jumped from the snout of the serpent, intercepting Ruoming's strikes. Unlike me, Wei did have thousands of years of technique and skill under his belt. He was the best match for Ruoming.

Their blades clashed loudly against one another, and Ruoming scoffed, annoyed.

I squinted, getting a closer look at Wei. There was a small figure dressed in all black in one of his arms.

When I realized who it was, I instantly perked up. "Qijing?" I muttered under my breath in surprise.

The little girl was dangling there, struggling to pry Wei's arm off her, but Wei held her in a vice grip. She was still clinging onto her rifle.

> **[Party Chat]**
> **Peijin:** We ned to get the Araban node and lefe 4 Central American jungle. Amelia, get it???

I cringed at the message full of typos. I was far too panicked to send anything proper.

> **[Party Chat]**
> **Amelia:** Yes!! Cover me for 5 minutes!!
> **Peijin:** Wei, go with her, I can cover things here. Bring the kid with you.

Wei froze and turned back to look at me, doubt written all over his face. I nodded my head. After all, Wei was the only one in my party who was actually capable of activating the node.

The serpent vanished from beneath us, and my entire party hurdled toward the ground. I extended my arms, grabbing the bricks of a building and dragging my hand down to slow my fall.

Ruoming pursued me, leaping off the buildings with his gaze razor focused on me. I gulped audibly. This guy was really scary.

I made sure both the nodes were secure in my Boundless Bag, and I held it close to me.

"Ruoming! Can't we talk this out?" I laughed nervously, trying to put some distance between us to browse the Azure Dragon Store for something that could heal my injuries. I was really doing my best to keep my reserve of spiritual energy high.

I wove in and out of the buildings, but he slammed through walls, sliding in front of me and forcing me to engage with him. Sweat clung to his platinum hair, and it finally looked like I was giving him a challenge.

Zhige, however, also seemed intent on challenging me.

My sword dutifully worked with me when I blocked Ruoming's attacks—growing in size, shifting, or adjusting its position to mitigate most of his blows—but, when it finally came time for me to strike Ruoming, it hesitated, pulling back slightly so I would just miss.

I became increasingly frustrated as more and more small cuts appeared all over me. At this rate, I'd have to use even more of my spiritual energy. *What a waste.*

Feiyu appeared behind me. Unlike Ruoming's blows, which were highly technical and exact, Feiyu relied on his brute strength and grit to push through.

Combined they were formidable.

I moved even faster, refusing to hesitate for even a moment. Even if I wasn't as strong as them and lacked their technical skills, I had more spiritual energy than both of them combined, and that made *me* formidable.

On the next hit, my blade and Ruoming's flew from our hands from the impact. We both stared blankly for a moment until I grabbed Ruoming's hair, smashing his head into the ground.

Feiyu advanced, and I dodged his blade by mere millimeters. I raised my hand, and Zhige flew back into my grip. Rocks began jutting out of the walls of the building as Yue and Yang located us, and her illusion returned.

Yang leapt forward, wielding his spear—he thrust himself between Feiyu and me, and Feiyu instantly stabbed through him. Yang winced, smashing his staff down on Feiyu's shoulder, but Feiyu tanked the hit.

Panic welled in my chest at Yang's injuries until I saw what looked like another dozen versions of Yang fanning out through the room. It was rare to see him use his Alternates skill, but it was already like he had mastered it with how well every single one of his copies moved.

Many swarmed Ruoming, blocking his range of sight. I took the opportunity to slink in behind them, now convinced that Ruoming had his own tattoo from the Major Arcana.

I glared down at Zhige. "You're being bad. Did you know Ruoming previously?"

Zhige's eye avoided my stare.

"Look left for yes. Look right for no. And don't bother lying to me."

Zhige's eye slowly shifted toward the left.

"Then you know where his tattoo is."

Zhige shook back and forth, disagreeing with me.

"Have I not been nice to you? I even gave you a pretty name. Look up for arms. Look down for legs. Look to the left for the chest. Look to the right for the back."

Zhige stared straight at me.

I crossed my arms. "Do you want to go back and live with him then, huh? Am I that much worse?"

Zhige shook back and forth again.

"Then where is it?"

Zhige reluctantly looked to the right.

"His back?!" I exclaimed, looking up at Ruoming and Feiyu killing all of Yang's alternates. "How am I gonna see that . . ."

I was starting to feel like a total pervert now. Everytime I had the misfortune of bumping into Ruoming, I was scouring his body for this stupid tattoo.

> **Divinity Supreme Commander of the Heavenly Hosts demands you remain loyal to Disciple Feiyu.**

Loyal . . . ?

I opened the Azure Dragon Store, quickly sifting through until I found a potent enough healing elixir. If the normal ones cost five thousand stars, this one was almost thirty-five thousand. I would have to thank my dearest Qiu Feiyu for funding this healing elixir.

It appeared in my hand with a flurry of blue sparks. I stared down at the glass bottle, inspecting the pink liquid inside with a small sense of awe. Thanks to the contract with Feiyu, something like this seemed so trivial now.

With the amount of spiritual energy I now held, it wouldn't be too long until I could start calling myself the god of fate and fortune with some degree of conviction, rather than it being a complete and total lie.

Furthermore, for the first time, I held a victory against Song Ruoming and Qiu Feiyu. Although the arc was still ongoing, and it hadn't reached its conclusion yet, the Arabian Coast was the first time we had gone head-to-head; and to my surprise, it had somehow worked out.

I knew I was going to face a strict scolding from Yang and Wei for being entirely irrational, but I was also glad they believed in my plan. Even the first time around, when I'd hardly survived my punctured lung, they hadn't interfered, just like I'd asked.

I shivered at the thought. My win was still a horribly fragile one. I was reminded that in the end, Feiyu and Ruoming were still stronger disciples than me, even if I walked away with a victory in the Arabian Coast.

I snuck up on Ruoming as fast as I could, knowing I only had seconds to act before he would pick up on my presence amongst all of Yang's alternates.

He whipped around.

I was still underestimating him. He noticed me far earlier than I'd expected.

I quickly darted behind him, trying to slash the fabric covering his back. Sensing what I was trying to do, Ruoming spun around, instantly parrying my hit but not before I could nick the fabric.

A sliver of his tattoo peeked through. A lonely man covered in dark, bloody robes trekking forward in a background I couldn't make out.

The Hermit.

I pulled back, feeling entirely satisfied now.

The earth seemed to rumble before a terrifying selection of massive beasts erupted from the ground.

CHAPTER SEVENTEEN

The beasts were horribly large, and they were much stronger than the ones we encountered at the previous nodes. Their eyes skimmed past all the ghosts and instantly locked on us. Some charged instantly; others let out vicious roars with their spit flying everywhere and their expressions manic.

Wei and Amelia must have located the Arabian node. Given the sudden burst of mobs we were facing, the Arabian node was evidently the one that controlled the citadel's mob settings, including their strength, appearance, frequency, and aggression.

"Yang! Yue!" I shouted, grabbing onto both of them. "Let's go! They have the node!"

All of Yang's various forms turned to me, and I awkwardly looked at all of them, not able to decipher which one was Yang, before I turned to Yue.

"That one," she said, pointing to one of the carbon copies.

A row of beasts lunged at me, and I instinctively raised Zhige to slice through it. But, the monster was surprisingly powerful—I held onto Zhige with both hands and strained before slicing the creature apart and turning it to ash.

How high did those two set the mob strength?!

I began sprinting through the narrow streets, the two of them following suit as I heard Ruoming and Feiyu chase after us. I grabbed my Boundless Bag and pulled it to my front, quickly sifting through it. There was so much junk in it now that it was hard to find anything.

I grabbed the Mediterranean node, and my hoodie deposited the American node into my hand. I quickly connected the puzzle pieces at their respective sides. Then, I opened the American node with a quick tap.

> **AMERICAN NODE**
> Location: Ferris Wheel RN2938 — Gondola #19
> Description: The American node controls the citadel's spatial presence. Use the node's artifact to toggle these settings, regardless of the user's current location.
> Alter Layout: No
> Trap Frequency: 1/10
> Location Size: 10/10
> Location Firewall: 1/10
> Owner: Liu Peijin
> Set Location Size: 1/10

At once, the entire map shrunk, until the Central American forest was clearly visible. Wei and Amelia were waiting for us across the border, waving frantically. Beasts were rapidly approaching behind them.

Wei repeatedly looked over his shoulder to make sure they didn't get too close, but his growing panic was apparent. Qijing still hung from Wei's arms, having given up a long time ago and now lying there limply.

Feiyu and Ruoming were just behind us. Cheng and Yuan reappeared, Yuan protecting Cheng from the overwhelming number of beasts. In the shrunken Arabian Coast, hundreds of ghosts and beasts were pressed right up against each other.

The beasts were salivating, driven by the desire to consume premium disciples who were just in front of them. Their ravaged growls and screams echoed all over.

Our feet thumped against the ground, and behind us, we could hear the quickening pace of Ruoming and Feiyu over the stampede of beasts. None of us had ever run faster, until our feet finally crossed over the border.

> **Set Location Firewall: 10/10**
> **Set Location Size: 3/10**

The ground at the border divide split apart, and the wall erupted from it. I grabbed onto Yue and Yang, pulling them both under me to protect them from the flying debris and earthquake. Once it settled, I let go of both of them, shakily kneeling on the ground and panting.

Wei was hunched over, two obvious figures protected under the sleeves of his robe. He pulled them back, revealing the two small children.

Amelia was shakily holding onto the Arabian node, trembling like a leaf when she adjusted its settings. The mobs all disappeared in an instant, and I let out a sigh of relief. Amelia turned her attention to Qijing, her expression unreadable.

Thankfully, my entire party was present, and even Qijing didn't have a single scratch on her. I fell backward on the damp soil and burst out laughing, my hands covering my face. My feet kicked up and down in the soil, sending the jungle's moss flying all over in large clumps.

"Oh my god," I sighed, letting my hands fall to my side. I looked up at the forest canopy, feeling horribly serene for the first time. "We did it."

It had been so long since I'd been able to revel in such a victory. Well, not that I could *really* call it a victory, but for a moment, I didn't feel like I was playing catch up with Feiyu.

Beside me, Yue let out a small sound, and it almost sounded like a burp. I turned to her in annoyance, but then she gagged and brought her hand to her mouth.

Yue hurled all over the ground beside me.

I let out a startled shout and scrambled onto my hands and knees, looking at the viscous yellow pile in complete disgust.

"Are you *trying* to vomit all over me?"

Yue wiped the drool hanging from her lips, her eyes teary and her hair sticking to the sweat on her forehead. She plopped down beside me, legs straight out. "That stupid kid!" she cried loudly, pounding her fists against the ground. "Peijin, you didn't tell me he was a goddamn poison user!"

"How was I supposed to know?" I instantly defended myself, my nostrils flaring at her accusation.

"Don't you know everything? I seriously thought he was going to kill me this time, Peijin."

"Does it look like I knew he was a poison user?"

"I was absolutely kicking his ass, right?" Yue continued, ignoring me entirely. "And then he pretended to retreat, but then he must have thrown something at me. It felt like a tiny sting, so obviously I ignored it, but a few seconds later, poof. I couldn't see anything, my throat started closing up, and I really thought it was over."

She got up and crawled toward me, placing her hands on both my shoulders. I shivered, disgusted and trying to swat her off, but her grip held firm. She started shaking me back and forth.

"And do you know the worst part, Peijin?"

Her eyes were wide and crazy. A chill travelled up my spine. "What?"

"I thought I was dying, and I thought about you. My last thought was almost, 'Peijin is going to be so mad at me.' Can you believe that? You've brainwashed me. I've gone crazy. Totally crazy." Yue now shouted at me, shaking me as hard as she could. My head bounced back and forth, and I became terribly dizzy.

"You are batshit crazy," I shouted back, kicking her off. "And, you're still purple—go get fixed!"

Yang appeared behind her and pried her lingering fingers off me, dragging her through the dirt before looking at me. "Cheng is really dangerous. If it wasn't for Chang'e, I really think Yue would have died. And given her current state, she must still be affected."

Yue pouted dramatically before a puff of blue sparks appeared before her. She pulled out a virtual mirror she must have previously purchased and examined her appearance. "I look horrible," she whined. "My eyebags are even bigger than Peijin's now."

Immediately, the Azure Dragon Store popped up, and she wriggled out of Yang's grip. Her hand began swiping through the store, purchasing as many beautification skills as she could find. Her complexion instantly brightened, her hair sorted itself, and her eyes became lively once more.

I scrunched my nose. "You're too young to be worried about that stuff."

"I just don't want to be an ugly old hag like you."

I practically teleported in front of her. My grin was far too wide. "Did I hear that right? Should you be talking to your elders like that, Yue?"

She shivered. "Never mind . . . scary old hag."

I brought a fist up and hit the top of her head lightly. She brought her hand up and rubbed the spot.

I turned to look up at Yang and gave him a soft smile. Exhaustion was etched deeply all over his face and eyes. "Are you all right?"

"No."

I snorted, rolling my eyes. "Well, you did a damn good job."

"I thought I was going to die from a heart attack," he confessed, looking down at Yue. We really need a good healer. I appreciate Cheng's work infinitely more now. I figured we could get by without one, but having a good healer makes all the difference."

I cocked my head. "What makes you think you can't be one?"

Yang's eyes narrowed. "Are you just trying to make me carry more weight?"

"I'm just very selective with new members. I don't think there's a single thing we can't do."

"Speaking of new members," Wei interjected.

Everyone's heads snapped toward him. He was holding onto Qijing like she was a kitten—his hands were under her arms, holding her a few feet in the air before him. Qijing was kicking furiously, her chin tucked in tight to keep a hold of her rifle.

"What do I do with the girl?"

Amelia looked up from the ground, eyeing Qijing suspiciously. Picking up on Amelia's stare, I gave a little smile, picking up Amelia and launching her into the air.

"First, I need to celebrate this girl. How brilliant you are!" I exclaimed, nuzzling my nose against Amelia's soft cheek. Her face flushed pink with pride until she remembered that she was supposed to be mad at me, and she pressed her hand firmly against my cheek to push me away. I let out a light laugh, putting her back down on the ground and rubbing her head.

"Can you hand me the Arabian node?" I asked, smiling at her.

She apprehensively placed it in my hand, and I pulled the other two nodes from my bag to connect them all. Now, we had more than half the nodes. This was looking more like a cake walk with every single node we collected.

But, the one in the throne room and next to the heart were the most important for us to bring this arc home.

I placed the nodes back in my bag and secured it. I headed over to Wei, bumping his shoulder playfully before I looked at Qijing. To me, Qijing felt more imaginary than any of my characters.

I still couldn't wrap my mind around her existence.

"You're a good shot," I said, meeting her large black eyes. I grabbed her gun and pulled it out of her grip, and Qijing let out an infuriated shout. "But it's rude to fire at your friends. I'm really hurt, honestly."

"Take me back to Feiyu!" she cried out furiously, her face twisting. Her hands reached out, like she wanted to grab onto me and pummel me. It looked like she was ready to burst into tears at any moment.

Earlier, Qijing had been so shy and timid. When I first approached her, it felt like I was reaching the back of my hand out to a stray animal. But now, caught in my party's trap, she was completely wild.

Her jaw trembled, and she furrowed her brow. "You tricked me."

"How did I trick you? There's not a scratch on you. Wei-shushu here did such a good job protecting you."

"I trusted you."

"Enough to fire a kill shot at me?"

Qijing went silent, glaring at me. "I could've made the shot."

"I believe you. I'm not going to test it."

I chewed my lower lip and looked over my shoulder toward Yang for help. After all, I did just kidnap the poor girl, and I wasn't really sure what kind of reaction I was expecting out of her.

Yang rolled his eyes and walked up, taking the gun from my hand. He examined it thoroughly, even looking through the gunsight.

"This is a very big gun for a kid," he said, looking down at Qijing with what almost looked like pity. "You're very impressive, Qijing. Who taught you how to shoot?"

Qijing refused to answer.

Yang's eyes remained glued on the gun. "They must be incredibly skilled. So, it certainly couldn't have been Feiyu . . ."

"Yes it was!" Qijing immediately interjected.

Yang smiled. "Wow, really? I was totally mistaken. Feiyu must be incredible, then. How does he even know how to shoot something like this?"

"My Gege is good at everything."

I stiffened. "Gege." For Qijing to call Feiyu such an adoring term for older brothers . . . it set my blood on fire.

"Feiyu is your Gege?" I asked her.

"Yes, and he's the best one ever."

"Did Feiyu tell you I was his Jiejie?" I asked with a cheeky grin, trying to mask the anger behind my expression.

Qijing's face twisted in horror. My grin widened.

"Don't you hear Feiyu refer to me as his Jiejie all the time? That means you should listen to me, too."

"Then why did Feiyu try to kill you?"

I looked away. "Feiyu told me you were very shy, but you're very talkative."

"Because I'm very angry."

"I'm always angry. That makes two of us."

I booped her nose, instantly agitating her. She clawed at me furiously, but I only let out a light laugh, ruffling the top of her head before lifting her into my arms and placing her on the ground. I took the gun back from Yang and handed it back to her.

She instantly aimed it straight at me and fired. With the tip of my finger, I pushed the barrel out of the way, and the bullet went flying into the jungle before smashing through a tree.

A wide smile spread across my face. I kneeled down to look straight into her eyes. With Qijing's hand still on the trigger, I grabbed the tip of the gun and pointed it straight against my temple.

"Peijin!" Wei shouted, instantly moving toward me. I lifted a hand to stop him in his tracks.

I continued smiling at Qijing. "Next time, aim here."

Qijing's finger trembled on the trigger, her eye twitching furiously before she pulled the gun away.

I stood up, dusting the mud from my knees. "That won't kill me so easily anymore. You can thank your Gege for that. He did me a big favor." I ruffled the top of her head and pulled her until she was standing just before me. I looked up at Wei.

"Both of us have the most spiritual energy here, Wei. We should focus on getting more like what Ruoming attempted to pull off."

"It's easier for me because I'm a cultivator," Wei said. "You'll need to rely on worshippers until you get enough spiritual energy to prove yourself."

"I have a lot already," I grumbled.

Wei raised a brow, and I sighed, rubbing the back of my neck.

I felt the soft fabric of Wei's ribbon beneath my fingertips and was instantly reminded of my earlier wound. Thanks to the elixir, it was now healed over. Wei's ribbon unraveled and comfortably wrapped around Wei's arm again. At once, its brilliant white color was restored.

"Ah!" Yang exclaimed suddenly. "Don't do something that rash again!"

"Do what?"

"Slash your own neck. Are you kidding? I could hardly diffuse poison. There was no way I could have fixed that."

"Don't worry. I was pretty sure I wasn't going to die."

"'Pretty sure.' Like that makes me feel much better."

Without warning, Wei stepped forward and grabbed my arm, pulling my sleeve all the way up past my elbow. He inspected my tattoo curiously.

CHAPTER EIGHTEEN

"What are you thinking?" I asked.

"Your spiritual energy was going insane the entire time you were fighting Feiyu."

"I think my tattoo manages most of it, or it lets me tap into it more easily. I thought my arm was going to fall off earlier, though."

Wei continued to look at the tattoo, his hand gently examining it.

"You were losing tons of spiritual energy and then suddenly recovering it. That would kill almost anyone."

I puffed out my chest and shouldered him. "I must be pretty incredible, then, right?"

I was relieved that after surviving the fight, tensions amongst all of us seemed to have lightened up a bit. It would've been agonizing to come out of that just to enter another fight, only less manageable.

"I was trying to figure out how you were doing it."

"Card Dealer."

"You know Feiyu well enough to use that skill?"

I flushed with embarrassment. "He's not a very complex character."

Wei cocked his head. "Really? I can't for the life of me figure out why he does anything he does."

Well, of course not. In *Surviving My First Run*, Wei dutifully followed Feiyu's every command, regardless of how much he understood. Since Feiyu was usually right, it was a safe bet for his party members to blindly trust him.

Wei challenged me much more because I was usually wrong, and going along with my plans usually meant some great consequence. It wasn't like I could help my terrible luck or something, though.

"Feiyu wears his heart on his sleeve," I finally answered.

"What did slicing your own neck have to do with anything?" Yang interrupted, walking over and crossing his arms.

"It was a bet I made with Feiyu. Whichever disciple was able to land a killing blow would win four hundred thousand stars and all spiritual energy from the bets."

Yue sat up. "Four hundred thousand stars? You're loaded!"

I whacked her head again, and she went silent.

"Couldn't you have just tried to kill him instead of slicing your own throat?" Yang asked, narrowing his eyes.

"Of course."

Qijing's face twisted in horror, and she raised her gun at me, but I instinctively flicked the barrel away again.

"Why didn't you?"

I went suspiciously silent.

Yang glared at me. "Why didn't you?"

"No reason in particular."

Yang turned to Yue.

> **Disciple Yue has activated Lie Detector!**

> **Lie Detector has confirmed Disciple Peijin's words as false.**

I flinched.

Yang stared into my soul. "Peijin . . ."

"It's not that serious."

> **Disciple Yue has activated Lie Detector!**

> **Lie Detector has confirmed Disciple Peijin's words as false.**

"Okay, it was serious, but nothing to be concerned about. I handled it perfectly."

"Don't make me use the skill again. I'm so exhausted," Yue groaned.

"I don't want you guys to worry about this sort of thing."

"It was absolutely terrible," Yang decided.

"Yup," Yue agreed.

Wei nodded, and Amelia sighed. Qijing looked as though she wanted to cause my next catastrophic injury.

"Fine. Feiyu killed me. It was the result of a series of bad calculations."

My entire party looked at me like I was an alien.

"What?"

"You *died*?"

"No, I'm being dramatic. I didn't die. I was one hit away from potentially dying."

"Where were we?" Yue asked, stunned.

I shrugged. "You guys trusted me to handle it, and I did."

"You're not gravely injured right now, right? Other than your neck wound, obviously, but that was self-inflicted." Yang's expression was one of total mortification, like his anxiety was about to eat him alive.

"Yes. I used the time loop setting on the Mediterranean node to give myself a second attempt. That's when I stabbed myself to fulfill the contract conditions without giving the win to Feiyu."

"Contract conditions? What? You're unbelievable," Yang sighed, rubbing his temple. "What if it didn't work? You could have died!"

"Didn't you see how overjoyed I was that I survived just now? It's not like I'm trying to die."

"It's not like you're trying to live, either," Yang argued.

I waved my hand in the air, brushing him off. "Whatever. Let's get this next node. Now that the firewall is up, we'll be fine until we have to leave this area."

I pushed past all of them and looked around the jungle. There were no more mobs, so this would be an easy location to get through.

"Amelia, guide us to the node."

Amelia's dire wolf appeared and hopped through the forest, occasionally pausing to aim its nose high into the air and recenter itself. It led us to a large Mesoamerican pyramid.

I was following almost absentmindedly as we began to scale the stairs, looking down at the tattoo on my arm. I used my nail to pick at it, wondering why Ruoming was trying so hard to destroy it. I still could hardly grasp the full meaning of it.

> [Observers Chat]
> **Socrates:** Is Jia Li still bothered by the Major Arcana?

"I'm bothered by both Major Arcanas," I grumbled.

"What did you say?" Yue asked.

"I'm talking to some observers. Don't worry about it."

> [Observers Chat]
> **Socrates:** In order from your biggest worry to least, it's Karma → Major Arcana → Ruoming and Feiyu → Eternal Dream.

"Eternal Dream last?"

> **[Observers Chat]**
> **Socrates:** I mean in terms of importance . . . they've been pretty MIA, don't you think?

I shrugged, rubbing the back of my neck. The wound had closed by now, and all I could feel was the bumpy texture of healing skin.

> **[Observers Chat]**
> **Socrates:** Karma definitely hates you. The Major Arcana hasn't been super involved, though, right? I mean, other than the World.

"Yeah, but there must be twenty-two of them. Maybe less, since I became the Tower recently, but there has to be at least a dozen."

> **Many gods express annoyance at Disciple Peijin's secrecy.**

> **Many gods express that Disciple Peijin should explain the meaning of her words for the rest of the broadcast.**

I glared down at the message. "I'm a god. Since when do I have to disclose my every thought? I'm not beneath you."

> **Divinity Supreme Commander of the Heavenly Hosts nods his head.**

> **Divinity Great Sage Equaling Heaven bursts out laughing at your confidence.**

> **Divinity The One Who Fights in Front tells you to remember your place.**

> **[Observers Chat]**
> **Socrates:** Yeah, but what are you going to do against them . . . they're millennia old, and you're just twenty-four. You're like an insignificant baby to them.

I pouted at Socrates's message before closing the tab and letting out a heavy sigh, running my hand through my short hair.
"Wei."
My party was now scaling the pyramid, climbing each massive gray stone. Wei turned around and looked down at me expectantly.

"Now that you have all your memories back, do you look down on the rest of us?"

"What do you mean 'look down?'"

"Do we seem young and insignificant? After all, you hardly know us."

"Is that what you're worried about now?"

My frown deepened. "I think it's a valid question. I'm trying to understand the real Major Arcana better. What does time feel like to someone who has lived for thousands of years?"

Wei turned back to the steps before him. He dug his fingers into one of the large gray stones and hauled himself up, hooking his foot on the edge and pulling himself up. "Don't you already know what it's like? You're the god of fate and fortune."

"Well, I'm not *that* old. Why are you being so difficult?"

"I don't see any of you as insignificant. Sometimes, I think you guys are much more mature than me. How many times have all of you saved me? I may be the oldest god here, but I became a god when I was just a boy."

"So, you still feel like a little boy?"

"No."

"Okay, then you're confusing me."

Wei huffed and turned around. "I like being here, and I like all of you. The only thing I care about is that all of you survive. Nothing else matters to me. I don't think of any of you as smaller than me."

I stopped climbing the stairs and simply stared at Wei before I laughed. He turned around, face flushed from embarrassment.

"What's so funny about what I said?"

I slapped my hand over my mouth to stop myself from laughing. Once I got myself under control, a finger came up to wipe the joyous tears from my eyes. "You're so sweet, Wei."

Yue let out an audible snort, and Wei only became more flustered, turning around to glare at Yue.

I cleared my throat audibly. "There's a reason I've never given you such a fond compliment, Yue."

"Hey!" Yue exclaimed. "I almost died for you that last round! That damn Cheng . . ."

Qijing was lagging a few steps behind us, clinging to her gun. Each step was at least five feet tall, making them wickedly difficult for myself to scale, and infinitely harder for such a small girl as Qijing.

Amelia, who was riding on the back of her dire wolf, wasn't struggling near as much. The giant creature easily ran up and down the steps, carrying Amelia with ease. She was leading the way, if anything.

Qijing looked up, and seeing that I was waiting a few steps ahead, instantly stopped advancing. Her fatigued expression instantly turned into one of rejection.

"Don't wait for me," she grumbled softly. "I can get up by myself."

"I'm not waiting for you. I'm exhausted, so I'm taking a little break here. You're doing better than me."

Qijing silently continued forward, until she finally reached the same step as me. She grabbed onto my sleeve and pulled me forward, dragging me up with her.

She was certainly an interesting character.

I was practically beaming from ear to ear now. It had been a while since I felt so happy with how things were going. I wanted to hold these few minutes close to my heart because I knew it would all end soon, with my luck.

"Qijing, how did you end up in the same party as Feiyu?"

"The apocalypse hit when I was in my class. I ran away, and Gege found me. He's my hero," she said pridefully.

"So, Feiyu saved you?"

"Gege saved my life," she affirmed.

Scathing Reviewer activated!

Instantly, my eyes softened when I looked at the back of her head, as she carefully led me up the steps. The idea that Feiyu, my dearest creation, would also leave such an impact on my little sister's life gave me a fuzzy feeling in my chest.

"Is that so? Feiyu is very good at saving people, isn't he?"

"Yes. That's why I have to go back to Gege. Even if you're his Jiejie, I like him much more than you."

I smiled brightly, squatting down to meet her eyes. I pulled my sleeve out of her grip and brought my hand up to gently glide it down her cheek before I gave her chin a gentle squeeze. Her skin was so soft, and her features so delicate.

She had the exact same nose I did. And, now that I was taking a closer look, she also had the tiniest little mole beside her eye, just like me.

I didn't even know this girl existed her entire life, but now that I'd found her, I knew I couldn't let her go. She was so fragile, and the thought of something in this cruel world even laying a finger on her filled me with an unprecedented dread.

"Qijing, I promise I'll look after you and reunite you with Feiyu, okay?" I gently rubbed the top of her head before my fingers combed through her long hair.

"You're a liar."

"I'll always tell you the truth."

"That's also a lie."

"Then let's make it a pinky promise," I said with a large grin, holding out my pinky.

Qijing stared at me hesitantly before she took my pinky around her own and shook it.

"There," I said. "Now I can't break the promise."

Qijing's brow furrowed, but she said no more. She made sure to grab the sleeve of my hoodie again before turning away and dragging me up the steps. My chest bloomed, and I couldn't stop myself from beaming at the little girl before me.

"Every relationship you forge is your karma because you will always destroy the other person, Liu Peijin."

Karma's words echoed through my mind, and I flinched instinctively. I hated the amount of control that Karma could exude over me. Even the tiniest, greatest interactions of my life were constantly overshadowed by the notion that I was ruining everything.

I heard the sound of growling and looked up, noticing that both Amelia and her dire wolf were staring down intently at me.

Although Qijing was leading me through the proper path, she had done an exceptionally poor job at it, and we were now dozens of steps behind.

I pulled my hand away before I grabbed Qijing and flung her onto my back. Using a small burst of spiritual energy, I caught up to the rest of the party.

"Sorry," I instantly apologized.

Amelia's blue eyes stared through me before she turned away, continuing to guide the dire wolf.

When we finally reached the top of the pyramid, Amelia pointed down into it. "The node should be in here."

Wei stepped up and kneeled before it. He shut his eyes and lowered his head. Moments later, his white robes fluttered around him wildly, and light blue sparks burst from his skin.

The activated node flew up into his hand, and he threw it at me.

CENTRAL AMERICAN NODE
Location: Pyramid WJ85638 — Top
Description: The Central American node controls the citadel's psychological influence. Use the node's artifact to toggle these settings regardless of the user's current location.
Fear Effect Intensity: 5/10
Hallucination Probability: 3/10

Sanity Drain Rate: 2/10
Memory Suppression: Enabled/Disabled
Ally Trust Sync: 4/10
Owner: Liu Peijin

CHAPTER NINETEEN

"What a scary node," I said, reading the screen. "Good thing they didn't get this one. Geez, the entire thing is only psychological settings."

I poked around the node settings for a moment, the rest of my party peeking over my shoulder to assess it.

"Sanity drain?" Yang murmured, glaring. "Should we lower that?"

I scratched the top of my head. "Um, are you feeling a bit insane?"

"No, but doesn't it sound quite bad?"

"If we have stronger mental resolution than the other parties, I think we should crank it up."

"Keep it down," Yue grumbled, leaning on my shoulder and resting her chin on top of my head. "That's the stupidest thing you've said, Peijin. We're all crazier than Ruoming and Feiyu."

"Fine. What about the fear effect? We can crank that one up. I think it'll get to Bohemian Grove quite a bit."

Set Fear Effect: 8/10

My existing anxieties instantly tripled, but it wasn't a serious hindrance to my thinking. It definitely would have had a larger effect if my party hadn't won the fight on the Arabian Coast or if I didn't have as much spiritual energy. I looked around my party to check on their reactions.

Amelia was shaking her head back and forth. "Turn it down," she whined.

Surprised, I immediately turned back to the screen.

> **Set Fear Effect: 3/10**

"Are you okay?"
Amelia gave a shaky nod. "Can you lower it more?"
"Let's keep it here."
"Okay."

Hopefully the other parties didn't have such a severe reaction. If someone in Ruoming's party did, they would have certainly realized that we'd gotten a hold of the psychological node, and that was always a reason for panic.

However, in the same way that Ruoming's usage of the past node was rather conservative, I also had to use the Central American node conservatively. If I didn't, the harm it would cause my party outweighed any benefits, which could be seen in Amelia.

I opened my bag and paid attention to the Central American node compared with the other three. Now, the cube was only missing two more faces. It was almost complete.

> **ATTENTION: Bohemian Grove has entered the throne room!**

I stared at the notification. "Uh-oh."
Well, clearly I had startled somebody in Bohemian Grove.
There was no way Owl was stupid enough to sit on the throne, right . . . ?
Unless he thought the fight against Ruoming and me was pointless . . .
"Let's go. No time to spare. We'll make sure we grab the node in the throne room, and then we can make a run for the heart."

> **Divinity Ears That Hear What Comes on the Wind says Song Ruoming will go for the heart node.**

> **Divinity Ears That Hear What Comes on the Wind says Disciple Peijin will need to pick which node matters more.**

I nodded, showing that I received his message. Shunfeng'er was such a minor character that I was surprised to see any involvement at all. This help was extremely appreciated though, and if Shunfeng'er could help connect my party to Mazu, that would be the ultimate opportunity.

> **Divinity Supreme Commander of the Heavenly Hosts says to go for the throne.**

> **Divinity Supreme Commander of the Heavenly Hosts says Disciple Peijin has already defeated Disciple Ruoming's party.**

"I appreciate the sentiment, but it was all of us against Ruoming and Feiyu."

> **Demon Abyssal Kraken of Black Seas sponsors 1,000 stars for your humility.**

> **Divinity Ears That Hear What Comes on the Wind sponsors 1,000 stars for your humility.**

I shut my eyes and exhaled. I wasn't trying to be humble, but I wasn't going to complain about more stars.

"We're going to the throne room," I began. "First, we'll need to break through the artificial sky. Then, we'll need to ascend to the top floor as fast as possible. Our objective is to make sure Bohemian Grove does not sit on the throne, but we also have to make sure they don't destroy the throne, either. It'll be easiest if we get control of the node located there, so we're one step closer to shutting down the whole thing."

Yue raised her hand. "What's stopping Ruoming from doing that?"

"The fact that we have all the nodes. If you don't have control of all of the nodes, you can't access the heart."

I shuffled through the Boundless Bag again, slightly annoyed at the prospect of rummaging for the nodes all over again.

When I finally found them, I held up the joined form for Yue to see. "Once we get all the nodes, it'll form the heart."

Yue pouted. "If only I was a god, then I could do such cool things. How would I ever figure out these things on my own? It's so unfair."

"I'm going to make you a demon soon. Hopefully in the next arc."

"Huh?!"

"Yang, use your staff to break through the ceiling and get us into the next citadel level, since that's where the throne room will be. I'll take Yue and Qijing on Zhige. You take the rest."

"Hey, wait—" Yue interjected, grabbing my shoulder. "You're going to make me a demon? You really mean it, Peijin?"

I let go of Zhige, and the blade flew in front of me, instantly quadrupling in size until Yue, Qijing, and I could fit on it. It floated parallel to the steps, making it easy for us to board. I placed Qijing on top before I sat with my legs around her, ensuring she wouldn't fall.

"Are you scared of heights?"

Qijing didn't respond, but she didn't get off Zhige either.

I tapped on the American node once more, opening it up.

AMERICAN NODE
Location: Ferris Wheel RN2938 — Gondola #19
Description: The American node controls the citadel's spatial presence. Use the node's artifact to toggle these settings regardless of the user's current location.
Alter Layout: No
Trap Frequency: 1/10
Location Size: 3/10
Location Firewall: 10/10
Owner: Liu Peijin

Set Location Size: 1/10
Set Location Firewall 1/10

At once, Yang extended his pole; Wei and Amelia grabbed on as it shot into the sky. The golden staff tore straight through the artificial clouds and background like it was tissue paper.

Zhige soared up, though at a speed significantly slower than Yang's staff, since it was wary of throwing us off at the steep incline.

I sat furthest down the sword, with Yue in front. I held onto Qijing tightly in front of me. Although she tried not to make it obvious, it was clear that Qijing was deathly afraid of heights. Her eyes were squeezed shut tightly, and she pressed against me to ground herself.

Yue spun around at the tip of the blade to face me. She slammed her hands down eagerly, and Zhige bounced unsteadily. "What did you mean earlier? You meant that in a good way, right? I'm getting a promotion?"

I narrowed my eyes, not wanting her to feel too special. "Turning into a demon is never a good thing."

"Sure, but you made it sound like some goal of yours. Do you have these big, crazy, and ambitious plans for me? Can I please hear about them?"

"Don't put it that way," I grumbled, my face turning a light pink color.

"So you do!"

Demon Great Sage Who Pacifies Heaven shouts in delight.

Demon Abyssal Kraken of Black Seas sits up straighter.

Divinity Supreme Commander of the Heavenly Hosts hesitates slightly.

> **Divinity Ears That Hear What Comes on the Wind reassures Divinity Supreme Commander of the Heavenly Hosts.**

"Ah, wait, PR announcement," I declared to the sky. "For full transparency, I have every intention of turning Yue into a powerful demon. Although I might be a divinity, I don't think labels will divide my party."

Yue's eyes glimmered in excitement. "You really mean it?"

"Of course I do, unless you don't want to."

"I do!" Yue leaned forward even more, until Qijing was awkwardly squished between the two of us. "I can't wait! Can you imagine? I'll have thousands of temples built for me, all over the human and demon realm. And I'll be wickedly powerful. I'll even be able to shut you up when you're rude."

I sighed loudly.

"Is that why you were okay with the Bull Demon King sponsoring me?"

"Yes. I think it's good for divine relations, too."

> **Demon Great Sage Who Pacifies Heaven is offended by your comment.**

"Why . . . ?"

"Because Yang has Sun Wukong as his sponsor, and the two of you get along exceptionally well. It's hard for the rivalry between Sun Wukong and the Bull Demon King to reveal itself when both their disciples work well together in the same party."

> **Demon Great Sage Who Pacifies Heaven screams at his screen in rage.**

> **Divinity Great Sage Equaling Heaven stops picking his ears.**

> **Divinity Great Sage Equaling Heaven screeches loudly.**

> **Demon Great Sage Who Pacifies Heaven sends Divinity Great Sage Equaling Heaven a threatening message.**

> **Divinity Great Sage Equaling Heaven reaches for his Ruyi Jingu Bang.**

> **Divinity Great Sage Equaling Heaven reminds Demon Great Sage Who Pacifies Heaven who won their last battle.**

> **Demon Great Sage Who Pacifies Heaven screams until spit covers his screen.**

> **Divinity Supreme Commander of the Heavenly
> Hosts struggles to mask his apprehension.**

> **Divinity Ears That Hear What Comes on the Wind
> tells Disciple Peijin to trust her judgment.**

We still had a bit more time before we would catch up to Yang. By now, his staff had retracted, and I figured they were already exploring the citadel.

I let out a loud and dramatic sigh. "Aren't you so glad I saved you, Yue? I could've killed you right there on the bridge. I thought about it."

"Should I really be thanking you for not killing me?"

I shrugged, a faint curve at the corners of my lip. "You've grown on me. That's what I'm trying to tell you."

Yue turned to me, a totally disgusted look on her face like she was about to be sick.

"What?! Should I call you a cunt instead?"

"You look even more ugly when you're trying to be nice."

"Maybe divinities and demons can't get along after all . . ."

Yue's eyes finally wandered down to smushed Qijing. "You," she said, spinning her spear and pointing the tip at the girl's heart. "You should try to get along with Amelia more."

Qijing opened her eyes just a sliver before shutting them again, ignoring Yue.

Yue huffed. "Peijin, why did you take such a liking to her? She's so rude, even for a kid. The rest of Feiyu's party came out to greet us except this girl. It's bad if you and Feiyu spoil her too much."

"I feel bad for all the kids stuck in the apocalypse."

"Yeah, but you get all tender and sappy with her."

"Well, she almost blew my head off a few hours ago. I think I should be nicer to her to save my own life."

Qijing shifted forward, putting space between the two of us, and I snorted.

"Awww," Yue cooed. "She's like a mini me."

"Don't ever say that again."

Zhige finally reached the top of the fake ceiling, approaching the small hole Yang's staff had made. Zhige instantly tilted vertically, and I hooked my legs onto the guards to stabilize myself and Qijing. Yue held on, already used to the drill, given the extensive number of times she's had to hang onto Yang's staff.

Zhige pushed through the entrance Yang's staff created. We finally entered the throne room.

It was a vivid red color. In the center was a large, luxurious golden throne. It had ornate golden carvings of dragons and various swirls all around it.

Beside it were carvings of various deities, protecting whomever sat on the throne. These gods served a similar role as Shunfeng'er.

Behind the throne was a large canvas upon a wooden wall. The top had two golden dragons that met in the middle—a symbol of incomprehensible wealth, power, and fortune. The stairs that led up to the throne were painted red, and the overall room was massive.

AMERICAN NODE
Location: Ferris Wheel RN2938 — Gondola #19
Description: The American node controls the citadel's spatial presence. Use the node's artifact to toggle these settings regardless of the user's current location.
Alter Layout: No
Trap Frequency: 1/10
Location Size: 1/10
Location Firewall: 1/10
Owner: Liu Peijin

Set Location Size: 3/10

Set Location Firewall 10/10

At once, the hole we entered quickly shut behind us. I lifted Qijing and gently placed her back on the ground. She nervously reloaded her gun, instantly fearful of her new surroundings.

She was much more timid than Amelia, and that made me want to protect her even more. Although the two were around the same age, Qijing was more like a fish out of water.

Before I could say anything, I felt an uncomfortable tingling sensation travel up my spine. I perked up instantly, looking all around the room.

Hindsight activated!

CHAPTER TWENTY

My eyes moved up and down each wall, but I couldn't pinpoint the source of the unsettling feeling creeping up my back. It was like someone was watching me, and I could feel their gaze burning into my back.

Was it Ruoming? No way—Ruoming's presence almost felt serene. Even if all of Ruoming's energy was focused on me, I never felt an ominous prickle. Sometimes, it was like Ruoming didn't even exist. Other times, it hit me like a dead calm that I wanted to sink into.

Feiyu's presence was overwhelming like a fire. It blocked all my senses until the only thing I could think about was Feiyu's terrifying and dominant existence. At the same time, there was an addictive pull to it. Once you entered Feiyu's circle, you couldn't escape.

Wait, what?

I blinked in surprise, looking down at my hands for a brief moment. Since when did I start picking up on people's presence like this? Was I more in touch with their spiritual energy?

I looked at Yue. She was like a fine poison. It was as though she was the most delicious fruit in the world, but by taking a bite, you would be accompanied by an agonizing pain.

Qijing was the rain pattering on a windowsill. She was sometimes chaotic and violent, but it also delivered a soothing calm. You could lose yourself in the sound.

As for myself . . . It was completely empty. I couldn't detect a thing. I looked down at my tattoo, wondering if it was storing pieces of me.

Finally, Hindsight picked up something in my vision. There was the tiniest hole in the throne, and a yellow eye was peeking through. It stared right through me.

I turned to Yue slowly, jerking my head toward the throne. The room was silent. Far too silent. Where was the rest of my party?

I pulled out Zhige and walked across the room, dragging the tip of the blade across the ground and letting the scraping sound ring out. I waited to see if whoever was hiding behind the throne would act, but it remained fixed on me.

"Yue, is this an illusion?"

Disciple Yue has activated Magician's Hand!

"No."

"Ask in the party chat where they are. I'm running out of messages."

[Party Chat]
Yue: Squad where we at
Yang: Throne room
Yue: ?? Are you hiding in the throne or what??
Yang: No. All of us are here waiting for you. The hole sealed up after the firewall closed, but we figured you guys entered through a different entrance using Zhige.
Yue: We came from the hole your staff made. We're in a gold and red throne room with various dragons. There's somebody in the throne, and Peijin looks like she's about to shit her pants

---

"Qijing, hold onto me," I ordered. "Yue, I'm gonna mess around a bit."

AMERICAN NODE
Location: Ferris Wheel RN2938 — Gondola #19
Description: The American node controls the citadel's spatial presence. Use the node's artifact to toggle these settings regardless of the user's current location.
Alter Layout: No
Trap Frequency: 1/10
Location Size: 1/10
Location Firewall: 10/10
Owner: Liu Peijin

Alter Layout: Yes

The room we were in immediately began spinning and flipping around. The various decorations that surrounded the throne even changed, warping into tigers instead of dragons. For a split second, I could see a human figure in a meditative pose before they vanished behind the throne again.

"Yeah. Fuck this." I turned to Yue. "All right. Somebody must have some godforsaken skill if they're able to genuinely manufacture this entire structure. It has to be an illusion to some capacity, right?"

"It could be," Yue admitted, "but it's not like we can tear through it. It's solid."

"It's cold," Qijing suddenly complained.

"Is it?" I asked, surprised.

MEDITERRANEAN NODE
Location: Building AK13829 — Floor 2
Description: The Mediterranean node controls the citadel's environment. Use the node's artifact to toggle these settings regardless of the user's current location.
Temperature: 5/10
Weather: 5/10
Gravity: 5/10
Pollution: 1/10
Light: 5/10
Time Loop: X
Owner: Peijin

Set Temperature: 6/10

"Is that better?"

"No."

"Oh." I looked at Yue. "Do you feel cold?"

"No."

"Qijing, are you talking about having chills?"

The girl nodded.

So, she could feel it, too. "Yue, do you feel like somebody is watching you? I have this horrible foreboding feeling."

"Maybe you're going through menopause. I don't feel it."

"Fuck off."

I slunk forward until I approached the back of the throne. I lifted Zhige until it was properly aligned with the top center of the throne and brought the blade down, slicing the throne in half.

The throne split apart to reveal a hollow interior, but it was perfectly suited for a person to fit in. The foreboding feeling vanished.

"Huh. So—"

The sound of a deep drum rang out, and the floor vanished beneath us. Yue let out a startled scream before she stabbed her spear into a nearby wall, catching herself. Qijing and I continued to fall further down.

"Peijin!"

I threw Zhige beneath me, and it instantly expanded, catching me. Qijing let out a pitiful sound, about to smash into the metal. I quickly moved Zhige to the side and grabbed onto Qijing with my hand, pulling her onto the sword.

"Yue, jump down here! We can't lose each other!"

Yue leapt down, landing on the sword. We were floating in the middle of two throne rooms now.

"Does somebody already have the throne node?" I wondered. "But, this is something only I should be able to do with the American node."

Bang.

The sound of the drum rang out once more. The rooms spun all around us, forcing Zhige to make jerky, last-minute moves. Qijing let out a loud shout, but both Yue and I kept our hands on her.

The feeling of being watched returned, and chills travelled up my back.

Bang.

More rooms opened.

Bang.

The ground beneath us disappeared and opened up into what looked like an infinite fall.

Bang.

Ruoming appeared before me, and I let out a startled cry before crashing straight into him.

The impact threw me off the sword.

"Peijin!" Yue shouted, her grip still on Qijing.

Ruoming's eyes widened in shock as we were pressed together until we hit the ground.

Bang.

Yue and Qijing vanished behind a newly formed wall.

At once, I felt a sharp, searing pain in my side.

Ruoming had stabbed his saber straight through me.

"H-Hold on!" I shouted, scrambling back to my feet with the blade still sticking out of me. "Don't stab me yet. I'm not ready!" I grabbed onto Ruoming's hand, preventing him from pulling the saber out of my body and worsening the bleeding.

Bang.

Ruoming and I were floating in the air before we were flipped around, smashing into thrones, gold decor, rugs, and pillars. I couldn't tell which way I was facing, but I held onto his sword like my life depended on it.

I frantically looked around, trying to catch a glimpse of who else might be in the same room. Then, I felt a large, steady hand grab me by my hoodie and dangle me in the air like a kitten.

I let out a breath I didn't know I was holding. I was hanging off one of the side halls with a large drop beneath me. "Thank you—"

Feiyu's joyous expression popped into my vision, and he wiggled his fingers in greeting. "Jiejie, I missed you so much."

> **[Observers Chat]**
> **Landy:** LOL
> **Ahoy987:** There is our charmer
> **SJJC:** Feiyu to the rescue

> **Divinity Supreme Commander of the Heavenly Hosts is watching Disciple Peijin and Disciple Feiyu with bated breath.**

> **[Observers Chat]**
> **Socrates:** Jia Li, don't let Feiyu set you off course again.

Bang.

I was flying through the air again, but Feiyu easily grabbed a ledge and held onto me. He curled both my and Ruoming's weight easily, enabling us to grab a hold of the same ledge.

Ruoming's sword was still poking through the entirety of my torso.

"Zhige!" I shouted, raising my hand and expecting Zhige to fly into it like always.

My hand remained outstretched and empty.

I cleared my throat. "Zhige!"

Zhige never came.

I swallowed loudly, looking at Ruoming. Although we were both hanging from the wall with our free hands, and our other hands preoccupied, I was still in the losing position with a sword sticking through me.

"Ruoming . . ." I laughed nervously. "You're a really great swordsman. I don't think I've complimented you properly yet."

Ruoming cocked his head, his eyes narrowing. I laughed even louder out of sheer fear. I heard Feiyu's sword ring out behind me as he unsheathed it.

> **[Observers Chat]**
> **Aslan:** Oh no

> **Nipon23:** GG
> **CannedWorms:** Our Jiejie is cooked
> **Socrates:** Peijin, just tank the wound and get out of there!
> **MoldyBlanket:** DISCIPLE PEIJIN PLEASE DON'T DIE AGAIN
> **CactusLiver:** Holy Moly. Bohemian Grove is insane.

I felt Feiyu's calloused fingers trace the back of my neck where I had sliced through it to escape him. I let out a startled gasp and immediately jerked away, but I couldn't go far. Feiyu let out a light chuckle.

"The wound healed up nicely, but it could be better. Do you want me to ask Cheng to take a look at it for you?"

I raised my voice at him, looking over my shoulder with a glare. "I have an entire sword sticking through me right now! I have bigger problems."

"Oh, sorry. I didn't notice."

I got ready to shout at Feiyu, but Ruoming took my moment of distraction to pull his sword out. I instantly felt blood drip down from the wound, and I clamped my hand over it. Normally, I would've taunted this evil duo, but without Zhige, I was hopelessly weak.

I could still use the dao that I acquired from the previous arc, but that would require me opening my Boundless Bag. Given that I was holding all the nodes in there, that was absolutely *not* an option right now.

"The Hermit. How'd you earn that one?" I asked Ruoming, trying to distract him.

He simply ignored me and moved to strike me again.

Feiyu wrapped his arm around my shoulders and swung me to the side over the abyss. Ruoming's blade missed me by mere millimeters. My feet were dangling over another drop, but Feiyu's grip was tight.

"Ruoming, don't kill Jiejie yet," Feiyu pouted, poking my cheek with his free index finger. "She's really like a baby divinity now, right? With all that spiritual energy she took from me, I want to test the true limits of a divinity."

Was this guy planning to torture me? A shiver travelled up my spine.

"Tch." Ruoming sheathed his sword, readjusting his hold on the wall. "You just like having a shiny new plaything."

Feiyu grinned from ear to ear. "That's true. Can we keep her?"

I kicked my legs and tugged at his arms furiously, infuriated by how dehumanizing he was. "Let me go, you bastard! I'm not some toy—"

Feiyu slapped his hand over my mouth to shut me up. I screamed against the palm of his hand, but he didn't move it.

"She's a baby divinity," Feiyu repeated with wonder. "And look. She's like a kitten."

I was screaming a flurry of horrific curses into his hand, but unfortunately, he couldn't hear any of them.

Bang.

The room shifted again, and Feiyu held me tightly beneath my arms. I finally kicked free and landed on the ground with a loud grunt. I scrambled onto my feet and quickly opened the Boundless Bag, whipping out the dao as fast as I could before shutting the bag once more.

Ruoming and Feiyu followed me down, landing on the ground gracefully one after the other. I turned around, breathing heavily and tightly gripping the dao.

Despite having more spiritual energy, I was undoubtedly cornered by these two and lacking my main weapon. The wound at my side was quickly healing thanks to my heightened status.

"I won't let you torture me for your own sadistic pleasure!" I shouted at Feiyu and Ruoming.

Ruoming slouched and turned away, rubbing his temples like he was suffering from a severe migraine. "She's your problem, Feiyu. Her voice gets on my nerves."

Ruoming stepped back to begin inspecting the room, eyes roaming over every detail; Feiyu took a few steps forward, his hands held in a placating gesture like he was approaching some rabid animal.

"Calm down, Peijin."

Calm down??

My eye twitched. *Last time I fought this man, he cut me apart and told me to beg for my life. What the hell did he mean "calm down?!"*

"You tried to kill me!"

"When did I do that? The citadel has sanity decay as one of its debuffs. Are you sure that isn't getting to you?"

I wanted to bash my head into a wall. I couldn't describe how utterly infuriated this man could make me.

"I've spoken to you enough. I want to talk to Ruoming."

Feiyu pouted. "Am I not interesting enough? Just because you and Ruoming have matching tattoos doesn't mean you two are suddenly super special."

"Yes, it does."

"If I get one, will you talk to me?"

"Yes."

"I'll work very hard then to impress you, Jiejie."

Divinity Supreme Commander of the Heavenly Hosts is giggling at his screen.

> Divinity The One Who Fights in Front rolls her eyes.

Feiyu had a big, mocking grin on his face. It was like he was playing with his food. I lagged a few steps behind Ruoming, following him as he inspected his surroundings.

> **POLL #3**
> **Who should Peijin be placed with?**
> A. Her party
> B. Disciple Ruoming
> C. Disciple Feiyu

"What?!" Feiyu and I cried out at the same time but for entirely different reasons. I whipped around to face him, glaring and pointing my dao at his face.

"What are you shouting for?"

"I'm only in a third of the options," Feiyu answered, feigning worry.

"And, so what about it? I hope you fuck off!"

> Divinity Supreme Commander of the Heavenly Hosts is campaigning for C.

> Divinity Ears That Hear What Comes on the Wind affirms Divinity Supreme Commander of the Heavenly Host's message.

> Polling ongoing . . .
> A. 3%
> B. 60%
> C. 37%

> Divinity Supreme Commander of the Heavenly Hosts is threatening dissenters.

Feiyu looked at the ongoing results, biting the inside of his cheek. "Only thirty-seven percent?"

"That's already too fucking high, bastard!"

At the sound of our bickering, Ruoming suddenly turned around and glared at us both. We went silent instantly, looking at him nervously like scolded children. I trailed behind Ruoming silently for a moment before I spoke up hesitantly, wanting to know more about him.

Although the two could have easily subdued me by now and stolen the nodes, they hadn't. And, perhaps my sense of security was misplaced, but I wanted to believe that I wasn't about to be brutally slaughtered like a lamb.

Furthermore, I wanted to signal that I wanted to speak to Ruoming. I also wanted to return to my party, but it was rare to get an opportunity like this.

"How did you get your tattoo?" I asked.

"I don't remember."

"Are you a regressor? I hate your kind, by the way. You ruin every story, strutting in here already knowing the solution to everything."

"This run is different from before."

"Oh, sure it is. You must be at such a disadvantage."

Ruoming bristled, but his expression calmed right after. He was a total expert at masking his emotions, and it only made me more eager to dissect him. I wanted to know every little detail about Ruoming.

Whether or not he was Zhao Rui didn't matter anymore. Ruoming had entirely captivated me on his own. So, I continued to speak, even though most of my words seemed to die in the air before reaching Ruoming.

"I got my tattoo when I came in contact with Zhige."

"I'm surprised to hear that," Ruoming said absentmindedly, searching the room for something.

"Why?"

"Because Zhige was never *your* sword," Ruoming answered bitterly, his voice suddenly cruel. "I'm sure you've pieced that together by now."

"Zhige likes me a ton, so does it matter? Besides, spiritual weapons are bound to their owners. If Zhige is still bound to me, then it's not a mistake. What, did Zhige used to be your blade or something?"

Ruoming froze, turning to me with those completely dead, haunting eyes. "It's not Zhige. It's Haimo. If you keep talking, I'll slice your tongue off."

CHAPTER TWENTY-ONE

I'd like to see you try touching a divinity," I taunted before quickly shutting up and changing the subject. "Do you like books?"

"I love books!" Feiyu called out from behind me, making every futile attempt possible at earning my attention. I easily tuned him out.

Polling ongoing . . .
A. 10%
B. 72%
C. 18%

Feiyu's jaw dropped in shock. It must have been his first time losing a popularity contest.

"Are you reading during the apocalypse?" Ruoming asked me. "You really have that much free time? You should spend more of it trying to level up."

What a total dickhead.

"The Owl is an avid reader. I think that's why he's so prepared, don't you? Maybe he read a lot of apocalyptic novels in the past, and that's why he can predict some things."

Ruoming remained silent for an uncomfortable amount of time. He must have known what I was digging at. Sure, he might have been a regressor, but I was almost sure he also read *Surviving My First Run*.

The way he was navigating this apocalypse was as if he'd taken the blueprints of *Surviving My First Run* and tweaked them over and over again until he found the ideal outcome. Still, it wasn't perfect. That meant he either hadn't been a regressor for as many runs as I'd thought, or the variables had changed significantly.

Ruoming turned to me, a slight frown apparent on his face now. I smiled in response. He turned away and continued his inspection.

"I'm right, aren't I? Did you come to the same hypothesis as me?"

"I have no interest in speaking with you."

"I don't have any interest in speaking with Feiyu, but you keep sending him after me."

"I don't send him after you. He decides that on his own."

"That's true," Feiyu interjected.

I continued. "So, Ruoming. Something is different in this run compared to all the previous ones, right? What is it?"

"I don't know what you're talking about."

"There's no point in hiding it from me anymore. Unless, of course, you're trying to keep it a secret from your party. The Major Arcana, your past runs, the new variables . . . It must all be so difficult for you to process. But, I'm sure you'll manage. After all, how old are you? Five hundred years old? A thousand years old?"

At my incessant rambling, I finally got a reaction out of Ruoming. He practically teleported right in front of me, a snarl on his face. The tip of his blade pressed into my neck.

I was shaking, but not from fear. I was giddy with joy. I finally incited a reaction out of Song Ruoming. I looked up at him, my eyes squinting from the excitement.

"I think we have a lot in common. Can't we talk about it? Why are you so cold and self-isolating?"

"You'll only drag me down."

"Maybe you were a god in one of your past runs, but you're not one now. I am. We should get along with each other instead of fighting all the time, shouldn't we?"

"You're no god. You're too weak."

"I'm the god of fate and fortune."

"Is that what you told everybody at the start? I've done the same strategy before. It doesn't work."

Divinity The One Who Fights in Front looks down at Disciple Peijin slowly.

Disciple The One Who Fights in Front asks if you tricked her.

I instantly shook my head back and forth at the notification, terrified by the potential implications. "It's not a trick. I know more than anybody else here. Even you, Ruoming."

I grimaced at the bold lie. Ruoming's face twisted with silent anger, but he withdrew his blade, and I let out a shaky sigh of relief.

Then, the ominous sensation returned. My grip on the dao instantly returned.

> **Hindsight activated!**

Similarly, both Ruoming and Feiyu tensed up, now looking for the source. I spotted the throne, now hanging from the ceiling, and I leapt up, slashing it in half. This time the inside wasn't hollow. I fell back onto the ground and caught myself.

I shared the information I had gathered earlier with Ruoming and Feiyu. "It's not a standard illusion. It could be a highly advanced one, but it's most likely a legitimate skill."

"It could also be a defense mechanism of the citadel," Ruoming murmured, the distant look in his eyes telling me that he was searching for any past memory of this.

Feiyu strolled around lazily. "It's the Owl's skill."

"How do you know that?" I asked.

"He's named 'Owl.'"

I shot him an exasperated look.

"He's also used it against me before. It's one of his observatory skills. It must have strong synergy with the citadel, since he's using it to watch us."

I was reminded of Wei's dungeon room. During the conflict with Daji, she would often survey us using trees. By leaving behind strands of her white hair, she was able to turn it into an observation point.

"I fought something similar last arc," I added. "It was against the demon Daji. I can only assume her skill is analogous. If it is, then by destroying the object he's possessing it'll sever the tie."

"That doesn't solve how we get out of this," Ruoming said, gesturing all around him. He frustratingly pressed his hand against his temple, rubbing it. "Cheng must be terrified. Not to mention Qijing, since you rudely kidnapped her."

"Rightfully so!" I protested. "You made her blow my head off!"

"She didn't succeed," Ruoming answered curtly, like we were talking about our to-do lists.

I tried to punch his arm, but he grabbed my wrist and twisted my arm back until my elbow locked, shoving me into the ground. I let out a distressed groan, but then Ruoming sat right on top of my back, keeping me pinned to the ground.

"Feiyu, you said you encountered this skill already?"

Feiyu nodded. "I followed Owl's spiritual energy until I found the room he was hiding in."

"Why didn't you kill him?" I grunted out the words from beneath Ruoming, straining for each breath. Ruoming looked fairly lean, but it felt like he weighed far more than Feiyu, who was far larger and infinitely more muscular.

"Can I kill Owl?" Feiyu asked Ruoming, cocking his head to the side.

"Yes," Ruoming answered without hesitation, getting up. Ruoming made sure to step on me as many times as possible while doing so.

I thought more deeply about Feiyu's question. Again, I was no hero. I didn't care about righteousness or fairness, unless it was in Karma's case. But, the more I got to know someone, the harder it was for me to easily dispose of their life.

"Why are you killing him?" I turned to Ruoming.

Ruoming didn't even bother looking at me. "He's a variable."

"Am I a variable?"

"Yes."

"Ha! Are you going to send Feiyu after me next?"

"I'll kill you myself once the consequences aren't so steep."

Usually, whenever I swore I would kill Feiyu, the only emotion that dominated that decision was sheer rage. It was incredibly evident in my voice every time.

But Ruoming, however, seemed entirely calculating in his response. There was no anger or spite in his tone—just sheer logic. I was something that diminished the success of this run.

This run . . . The World's words suddenly echoed through my mind.

"I'm not supposed to tell you this. In the run just before this, we made it. But right at the end, this unknown rogue skill sent us back."

I reached out, grabbing onto Ruoming and looking up at him. "Wait. This run. You're trying to make it your final one, aren't you?"

Ruoming stared at me cruelly, his eyes wide and wild with anger. "Who did you hear that from?"

"The World."

"Of course," Ruoming let out a dry laugh, dragging his hand down his face. "What else did she spill this time? I knew it was a mistake letting her join us."

I firmly slapped Ruoming across the face, glaring at him. "Don't talk about Meihua that way."

Ruoming's head jerked back, and his eyes remained glued to the ground for a long moment, his cheek turning a humiliating shade of pink and purple as a bruise already began to form.

He brought a tentative hand up to gently touch his cheek, like he couldn't believe I had just slapped him.

"You've known her for only a few minutes," Ruoming said coldly. "I've known her for decades. Don't talk to me about the World."

"What was the rogue skill called?"

"What?" Ruoming asked.

"What was the rogue skill called? The one that sent all of you back once you finally reached the end."

Ruoming's dead eyes became distant now, too. It was as if each question I asked him sent his mind hurdling back through all those runs that he'd failed, and each one was a wound on his mind.

He looked down, his eyes reflecting what I could only interpret as a morbid and twisted emotion.

"Scathing Reviewer."

CHAPTER TWENTY-TWO

Many gods look toward one another with the same question in mind.

Divinity Supreme Commander of the Heavenly Hosts scratches the back of his neck nervously.

Divinity Ears That Hear What Comes on the Wind asks what the issue is.

Divinity Abyssal Kraken of Black Seas says Scathing Reviewer is the name of Disciple Peijin's skill.

Divinity Ears That Hear What Comes on the Wind looks stunned.

Divinity Supreme Commander of the Heavenly Hosts is worried Disciple Ruoming might kill Disciple Peijin.

Divinity Ears That Hear What Comes on the Wind scolds Divinity Supreme Commander of the Heavenly Hosts for doubting Disciple Peijin.

[Observers Chat]
MoldyBlanket: So . . . Peijin has the skill that single-handedly set back everyone who won the last run?

Aslan: RIP
MoldyBlanket: Peijin is not making it another day
Seatdiv: It's not like Ruoming knows about Peijin's skills. Do we even know what Scathing Reviewer does?
Landy: It makes her nicer right?
MoldyBlanket: Only sometimes. Sometimes I think it makes her even more cruel
Landy: I wonder how much autonomy she has over her personality then . . .
Socrates: Scathing Reviewer isn't a skill that clashes with Peijin, though. Even if it acts on its own, it hasn't deliberately harmed Peijin in any capacity.
MoldyBlanket: For now. If Peijin tries to win the apocalypse, who knows what will happen

All the notifications flooded in, and I let out a heavy sigh, knowing this was one of the worst things Ruoming could have revealed. Archangel Michael and the observers were right.

If Ruoming found out that I now wielded Scathing Reviewer, he would definitely kill me. If he was irrational, he might even indirectly blame me for getting sent back.

"Oh," I laughed, awkwardly rubbing the back of my neck. "Do you think it'll appear again if you make it to the end of this run?"

"I'll make sure it doesn't," Ruoming answered bluntly.

I peeked up at Feiyu. "Does Ruoming tell you everything about his other runs? Or do you just go with it."

"Depends on the day."

"Well, aren't you easy to handle? So obedient."

"I pride myself on being a team player."

Scathing Reviewer activated!

And there it was—Scathing Reviewer making another appearance.

I watched Ruoming curiously, my eyes picking up on every slight movement. I even used Hindsight, so I could notice every slight twitch in his muscles and the calculation behind the moves he was making.

Sometimes, people had slight "stutters" in their movement; people decided a different move was better, abandoned it entirely, or simply couldn't keep still. Even Feiyu, whose movements were always so precise, had stutters.

It was part of Feiyu's charm, if anything. He was so human, and at the same time, he was the most perfect specimen.

But with Ruoming, every movement was precise. There was no doubt or hesitation. He never changed his move—and it made him so fascinating to watch with Hindsight.

I let out a heavy sigh. I really wished Feiyu wasn't here so I could have a proper conversation with Ruoming. I wanted to pick through every single detail in his brain and piece it all back together again. I wanted to be the only person who knew everything about Ruoming . . .

I must have been going crazy. I needed to turn down the sanity drain rate the moment I could access the nodes again because it was certainly getting to my head now. What the hell was up with me?

If Ruoming didn't look so much like Zhao Rui, I wouldn't be thinking about him at all. It was unfortunate that after running away from home, Zhao Rui had become my entire world for a few months.

It was the first time I let myself care for something—someone—without restraint, and it ended up with me being abandoned and left alone all over again. It was like the world wanted to teach me the same lesson over and over again. There was no one for me to rely on but myself.

But with both Feiyu and Ruoming beside me now, I felt sick to my stomach. These were two shadows of the most important people in my life, and neither of them knew that. It was like my one-sided love hit me in full force again, and I wished I had a place to call home with a warm bed to sink into.

I felt Feiyu's finger brush against my cheek, and I instantly jerked up, slapping his hand away and looking up at him furiously.

"What the fuck are you plotting now?"

"You're crying."

Feiyu brought his finger up before my face, showing the large tear perched at the end. He flicked his hand, and the tear splattered to the ground.

"It's because I'm sleepy. I really want just one good day of rest."

"Aw, Jiejie, is this arc too difficult?"

I shoved him away. "You weasel your way into everything."

"I try my very best."

"You should give up."

I looked up nervously and caught Ruoming's eyes trained directly on me. I only felt even more embarrassed about my sudden emotional breakdown. Scathing Reviewer was a horribly unwelcome skill.

"What are you looking at?" I asked sharply.

Ruoming didn't respond, but his eyes began to subtly glow.

Disciple Ruoming activated Lie Detector!

Lie Detector has confirmed Disciple Peijin's words as false.

His voice was incredibly monotone. "You are crying."

"You asshole!" I shouted, standing up and reaching out to latch onto him and pull him down to my height. He easily sidestepped me.

Bang.

The room shifted again, and I let out a startled sound as the ground shifted beneath me once more. Ruoming whipped around and grabbed onto my collar, quickly catching me and gripping the wall to keep the two of us secured. Feiyu, of course, managed perfectly all on his own.

Once the room settled, I turned to Ruoming. "Since you've already done this a million times, how do we get out of this?"

"I haven't dealt with this before."

"Huh?" I said dumbfounded. "You've done this so many times, and you don't even know how to get past the third arc?"

Ruoming's eyes narrowed. "Do you know any better?"

"No . . ."

Ruoming let go of me, and I gasped as I hurtled toward the ground fifteen feet below. I smacked into the ground and grunted upon impact.

"You're the god of fate and fortune, but I've never met you before."

"And you've never encountered this skill before. So, what's your point?"

"You're not a god."

"Yes I am."

"Only because you stole Feiyu's spiritual energy."

"Stole? I beat him fair and square."

"You weren't a god before that."

"I was. You don't know everything."

Disciple Ruoming activated Lie Detector!

Lie Detector has confirmed Disciple Peijin's words as truth.

My face was horribly smug now, and Ruoming's eye twitched slightly. I still didn't know why Lie Detector worked in my favor for my boldest lie yet, but I was absolutely not going to complain.

Polling ongoing . . .
A. 4%
B. 84%
C. 12%

Polling will conclude shortly.

Feiyu perked up, finally sensing something. He whipped around and found the glowing yellow eye in seconds, quickly stabbing through it. His eyes were glowing purple as he activated a skill that heightened his analysis.

"There's a pattern," he finally concluded.

Bang.

The rooms shifted again. Mid-fall, Feiyu's eyes locked in on a small gap in the wall, and his sword pierced straight through it in an instant.

Bang.

The room shifted. Feiyu understood it.

I, however, was getting horribly queasy.

"Shit . . ."

We were flying through a now never-ending series of changes. Feiyu only became more and more attuned to his environment, practically gliding through the air as he struck eye after eye.

He flipped in the air, until he finally spotted me frantically flapping my arms around. "There's a thread connecting through all these rooms directly to Owl!"

"Well, are we almost there?!"

"No! Don't worry about me, I'll handle it."

Polling has concluded! The final votes are as follows.
A. 3%
B. 90%
C. 7%

I stared at Feiyu with wide eyes after the final results were released. At once, a wall erupted between Feiyu and Ruoming and me like a divider. Trusting entirely in Feiyu's abilities, I looked over my shoulder to face Ruoming.

Ruoming grabbed the back of my hoodie like he was holding onto a kitten by its nape, keeping me close enough to him that I was no longer flailing around. "You're incompetent," he hissed into my ear.

I looked over my shoulder at him, grateful for the opportunity to speak in an unfiltered fashion with him. "Is that how you should be speaking to your fellow member of the Major Arcana? We're allies."

"Not everyone with a tarot is automatically a good member of the Major Arcana."

"How many slots are left?"

"A lot."

"Can I get multiple?"

"You don't even know what it signifies."

I smiled. "You're talking so much now. You only responded to me occasionally before."

Ruoming went silent instantly, a slight frown on his face.

"It must have been exhausting," I continued, "going through this so many times."

Ruoming's silence stretched out.

I looked down. As the rooms kept flipping, Ruoming did a good job keeping us secure, and it was an indicator that Feiyu was managing well on his own now. So, I continued to speak.

"I'm already anxious whenever I think about what my party members might be going through," I confessed. "I can't imagine how it might feel to be in your position."

Ruoming hesitantly replied, "It doesn't bother me."

I snorted. "Well, that's obviously not true. You might tell yourself that, but look at how you interact with your party members. It couldn't be further from the truth."

Ruoming scoffed. "Are you going to spend this entire time psychoanalyzing me?"

"I just want to get to know you. And we've never met in a previous run, so this can't be too boring for you."

"How many people do you think have said the same thing to me by now? It's in the thousands. There are trillions of beings out there. Don't act like you know me."

I smiled solemnly, knowing that for someone as tortured and old as Ruoming, there wasn't much he hadn't experienced or people he hadn't met. "I guess I'm still too young. When I was younger, I thought I would meet many people that I'd connect with. But now, I realize it only happens a few times."

I looked up at Ruoming before quickly breaking eye contact. I was far too embarrassed by my sudden series of confessions.

"I've only found those connections here," I said. "At the very least, you must have met one person here that you can say the same about."

It wasn't like what I was saying was entirely true. I was just trying to tug at Ruoming's heart strings, of course. I would never be this sentimental.

"You're right," Ruoming finally said. "You are too young."

I pursed my lips. "What do you think then?"

"What?"

"I mean, where do you think I'm wrong in what I'm saying? I'm curious to see what an old, old, old man like you has to say."

Ruoming let out a heavy sigh, like he wouldn't be able to stand me for a moment longer. But, his grip on my hoodie remained firm, keeping me anchored to him.

"Being alone is better than sitting next to someone and feeling lonely," Ruoming answered.

"You're kidding. Do you feel lonely right now? I'm right here, talking to you."

"We can talk as much as you like. But we'll never understand each other. Nothing can change that fact. At any moment, one of us could die, and I'll be the only one knowing you ever existed."

"But I won't die," I asserted.

I didn't know why Ruoming's mindset was frustrating me so much. Most of the time, I had the exact same thought process as him. But now that I was face-to-face with such a brilliant mind, it felt like he was speaking complete nonsense.

"Tch. Do you think anyone else wanted to die in the previous runs? You're nothing more than a record player."

I grabbed tightly onto Ruoming's sleeve. "I mean it! You said it yourself. Things are different this run, right? This time is different. This will be your last run, Ruoming, so stop acting like everyone is going to die and leave you again."

"Ha!"

Ruoming burst out laughing, bringing a hand up to shield his eyes and mouth from my view. I frowned slightly, looking at him. He laughed manically, and for a moment I was worried he was never going to stop.

> **[Observers Chat]**
> **Socrates:** Jia Li sure is speaking an abnormal amount . . .
> **Socrates:** This is almost scary to witness. I've never heard you be remotely honest with yourself.
> **Socrates:** And to a man like Ruoming at that. Scary! This is the real apocalypse.

"Even if I die," I said softly, "this place is still my only salvation. I never lived life as a good person, and I've never had anything to lose until now. And I think a part of me will always love this story because of that, even if it takes everything from me one day."

" . . . This story is the only thing we have in common," Ruoming said bluntly.

> **Divinity Supreme Commander of the Heavenly Hosts is tearing up at Disciple Peijin's sudden compassion.**

> **Divinity Ears That Hear What Comes on the Wind is amazed at Disciple Peijin's vulnerability.**

> **Demon Great Sage Who Pacifies Heaven is intrigued by Disciple Ruoming's stoicism.**

"I've been dying to know one thing," I continued. "Is everyone the same in every iteration?"

"No."

If Ruoming wasn't going to be philosophical and ponder the purpose of life with me, then I was going to revert to being as insufferable as possible. I wondered if this was the same psychological warfare tactic that Feiyu defaulted to when speaking with me.

"Even you? Have you done things you regret?"

Ruoming's lips pressed into a thin line, but I only looked up at him curiously. My hair was whipping all over my face, and we had flown through so many rooms that I didn't even bother with orienting myself anymore.

"My party and I will survive this round."

"That wasn't my question."

"You're getting on my nerves."

"Did I steal half of your would-be party? I have Wei and Yue, after all."

Ruoming slapped his hand over my mouth, and I attempted to speak through it, but nothing more than an unclear grumble came out. I flung my arms furiously, finally prying his hand off.

"Are you going to kill Owl?" I blurted out. "He's obstructing you, isn't he?"

"You're of bigger concern than Owl."

"Are you going to kill me . . . ?"

"I'm pondering it."

"Why pondering? You're not a very good decision-maker. It didn't take long for me to decide to kill Feiyu."

Ruoming didn't respond to my taunts.

"Have you done that before?"

"What?"

"Have you killed them? Is that your biggest regret and how you got the Hermit tarot?"

Ruoming's grip on me tightened, but I didn't loosen my questioning. If anything, I only became more persistent.

"You must have been terribly lonely this entire time, Ruoming. You're closer to a god than a man, and not even the gods would be able to understand you. Including me, apparently."

"You don't know a thing, Peijin."

"I know this much. Am I wrong?"

"Yes."

Disciple Peijin activated Lie Detector!

Lie Detector has confirmed Disciple Ruoming's words as false.

Ruoming slapped my arm firmly. "This is my nightmare, but it must be your dream come true. Is that what you're trying to get at?"

"Yeah. I'm trying to remind you of your misery, actually."

"Well, it doesn't affect me anymore."

"Have you fallen out of love with the story?"

Ruoming's eyes widened, and he intentionally avoided my gaze. I stared at him expectantly, about to repeat my question.

I had long fallen out of love with *Surviving My First Run*. It had been a number of years since the promises of the story could keep me going. At the same time, that story was my only lifeline. In all twenty-four years of my life, there was nothing else waiting for me.

I could only imagine how much worse it would be for Ruoming. After all, how old was he? A few hundred years old? Thousands? Even millions?

Every moment he found solace, it was all stripped away with each run, and he was only left with the shadows of people in bodies that couldn't recognize him.

"My party and I will survive this round."

"A story doesn't die until its final reader gives up on it. So, don't give up, or your story will end here, Song Ruoming."

Ruoming scoffed. "And who's reading my story? The gods who torment me?"

"I will," I said earnestly. "Knowing that there are good stories and people who will read them motivates me."

"Peijin."

"Yes?"

"You are a woman of complete and utter nonsense."

CHAPTER TWENTY-THREE

Ruoming released me and lifted his leg, instantly driving it into my lungs and kicking me across the room. I coughed violently before a giant beast crashed into the room, causing a wall to splinter apart mid-rotation.

It flung itself right in front of Ruoming—exactly where I had been just moments before. It reached a powerful, clawed hand up into the air and brought it down against Ruoming.

Although Ruoming lifted his sword to defend himself, the creature was wickedly powerful, still managing to grip Ruoming within its claws.

The demon instantly tightened its grip, crushing Ruoming's lean body in its grasp. Ruoming let out a pitiful groan before breaking free, the demon's hand splitting apart into dozens of small chunks at the expert maneuvering of Ruoming's sword.

I grabbed my dao, looking around for something to grasp onto. I landed on a freefalling chair and gripped onto its back, bracing myself to attack the beast.

But, before I could, Feiyu must have cut the final string.

The entire room around us vanished entirely.

Many gods are protesting!

Divinity Spirit of the Jade Moon wishes Disciple Peijin and Disciple Ruoming had more time.

| Divinity Spirit of the Jade Moon is feeling very melancholic. |

| The World is watching Disciple Ruoming with an unreadable expression. |

| The World turns off the broadcast without a word. |

| Divinity Spirit of the Jade Moon is worried by the World's reaction. |

| Divinity Spirit of the Jade Moon wants to check on the World. |

| Demon Great Sage Who Pacifies Heaven reminds divinity Spirit of the Jade Moon to live with her choices. |

We were dropped into a massive golden throne room once more, ordained with illustrious red fabrics, jade stones, and striking statues. Most notable was the massive golden throne in the center. It was carved to complete and utter perfection, each side reflecting the light and catching all the stones around it beautifully.

Feiyu landed near me, and I could see the thick beads of sweat dripping down his forehead. His breathing was labored, and his perfectly styled hair was out of place. For once, it looked like Feiyu was struggling. I let out a sigh of relief.

My attention was quickly drawn back to the throne. It was surrounded by dozens of members of Bohemian Grove, who turned to us simultaneously. Some of their faces showed mortification at the appearance of Feiyu, and others idiotically seemed delighted by the opportunity to finally challenge him and see if he deserved to be the protagonist of *Surviving My First Run*.

| **Hindsight Activated!** |

I scanned the crowd, but I couldn't spot Owl. He must have been hiding somewhere in an attempt to figure out what the nodes were and how to access them. Given that he didn't already possess one, he hadn't read far enough into *Surviving My First Run*.

At once, Feiyu was swarmed by at least a dozen different disciples, blue sparks flying out all around them as they instantly activated their skills in an attempt to subdue him.

He brought his sword up to his head before the disciples could land and crush him. The clanging of weapons could be heard as every single disciple made an attempt to land just a single blow.

However, with a slight rumble of the ground beneath their feet as their only warning, Feiyu's body crackled with power before he swung his first hit, instantly slashing through nearly all of the disciples.

Ruoming's face was stone cold once more, completely laser-focused on detecting Owl. If Owl was looking for one of the nodes, he still must have been within the vicinity, since the node must have been located near the real throne.

I let out a small sigh. If only Amelia were here. I was wondering how the rest of my party and Zhige were doing. It would've been much easier if I'd been trapped with them instead of these two, but once Owl was dealt with, we wouldn't need to gruesomely work through the throne room for a moment longer.

My eyes roamed around the throne room, analyzing the situation. Although a handful of disciples attempted to jab at me, thanks to my new degree of spiritual energy, just releasing some of it could send them flying back into the wall.

Traces of Owl's spiritual energy were present all over the throne room, like he had split himself up into various little parts and distributed them to throw us off. I couldn't pinpoint exactly where he was.

Was he using a skill like Stone's Aura, which could make it infinitely harder to detect his true location? I turned to Ruoming.

If Ruoming was anything but stupid, he would go for the node first while I looked for Owl. Owl was a temporary hiccup in the road, but getting the node was the ultimate goal. If anything, I was shocked he didn't rob me when I was with him and Feiyu.

I kept glancing around the room. I couldn't detect or activate the node on my own, which meant I *had* to find Owl first so my party could reach me. That would only make this infinitely easier for Ruoming, who wouldn't even need to lift a finger.

But, if I had all the other nodes, it wouldn't matter who got to the throne node first. We were both going for the heart, and that required owning all of the nodes. It would be a head-on clash between the two of us if Ruoming accessed the node first and the entirety of our parties arrived.

I scoffed. I had won once, and I could win again.

If Hindsight was weaker against Owl's skills, I would have to rely on my raw power. I shut my eyes and took in a steady breath, letting my spiritual energy spread evenly throughout my entire body and tuning out the chaos surrounding me until I felt lost in the sensation of my own body.

I opened my eyes slowly, looking around for any anomaly. In the throne room, the walls were made of various large slabs. Some were wood. Others were stone.

But, in the very back, tucked behind the throne, one of the slabs was slightly tilted, not quite aligning with the rest. Although this could have been the result of poor construction, it also could have been the result of replacing the slab.

I tucked the dao by my side and leapt forward, my fingertips gripping the edge of the slab. I slowly moved my fingers down the entire edge, gripping and tugging to see where there was the most slack.

I used more and more strength with each pull, but the slab hardly shifted. It was as though someone was holding it in place. I shifted until my eye was right over the slight gap where the slab connected to the rest of the wall.

I leaned in closer and closer until my nose was squished against the wall. A large, glowing yellow eye was staring right into mine.

A sword stabbed straight through the slab and into my torso. The slab crumbled into smaller chunks of stone instantly.

I grabbed onto the blade, not even feeling it slice through my hand. It would take far more to hurt me now.

My grip tightened. I tore the sword from my torso but kept a firm hold on the blade and pulled it toward me. The person who was holding it was thrust forward, slamming into the mountain of crumbled rocks and tripping.

"You're easy now," I said, my voice cold and expression grim. "Did you really think you were cut out for this world?"

Owl trembled before me like a leaf, fighting to regain his composure. Finally, he succeeded, and he managed to calm his frightened expression and give me a warm, pleasant smile, like we had been friends for the longest of times.

"I'm glad to see you're doing well. This arc has been quite a challenge, hasn't it? I've heard there was quite the battle for the Arabian node."

I didn't even want to attack this bastard. He wasn't an enemy worthy enough of being slain with a blade at my hand. Even if Ruoming was also a fellow reader, at the very least Ruoming did *Surviving My First Run* justice. Owl was nothing more than a narcissistic poser.

I lifted my leg and kicked him across the ground, and he let out a loud shout as he tumbled forward.

He grit his teeth and held onto his side, letting out a low laugh. "You've really surprised me. You're on the level of Ruoming and Feiyu, aren't you?"

"Of course I am. Why wouldn't I be?"

"It's all starting to come together," Owl said, looking up at me with a large, smug grin. "Your conversation with Ruoming makes a lot more sense now."

"What the hell are you talking about now?"

"You're going to regret not killing me. You should have murdered me like you murdered Wang Ting, yeah?" Owl let out a manic laugh, finally standing up and bringing a hand to his face to cover his laughter, his eyes wild. His eyes continued to glow an ominous yellow hue. "I'm already a dead man! Fuck!"

I flinched at the brief mention of Wang Ting. That was one of my earliest displays of cruelty after the apocalypse had begun, and that decision had followed me throughout the rest of the arcs.

Still, I wouldn't say that I regretted it. I don't think I could have ever learned to love someone who was such an idealized image of my mother, especially after finding out about my father's suicide and Qijing.

He must have some kind of observation skill similar to the array that Daji had. But, Owl didn't seem particularly clever, and I wasn't sure what could have awarded him with any sort of major revelation.

"I already am regretting it," I said. "You're fucking nuts."

I lifted my leg once more, getting ready to stomp his head into the ground. He looked up at me one final time, his trembling hand coming up in a futile attempt to protect his head.

"Come on. Do it already, Peijin. Or should I call you Jia Li?"

[Observers Chat]
AYaNg: Jia Li???
WarningLights: What is he talking about?!
Routined: It has to be JiaLi1825 right
PineBlvd: Oh my god
Peenut: Wait, isn't that the author of Surviving My First Run?
Aslan: Is he saying that Peijin is the author??
MGirl193: Is that how she's been able to know everything?
OwnPen: WHAT

You have received a new review!
ROUTINED: ★ ☆ ☆ ☆ ☆
Like I could EVER support Jia Li are we kidding??? Wtf

You have received a new review!
PEENUT: ★ ☆ ☆ ☆ ☆
Lmao, she triggered the apocalypse and has been taking advantage of everyone. I wouldn't expect any better.

"Ha!" Owl cried, grabbing onto his abdomen to control his wide laughter. "It really is true. Wang Ting... dammit!"

Owl looked up at me, repeatedly pounding his chest with his hand. "Murder me. Murder me like you murdered Wang Ting. Come on, Jia Li, don't hesitate now!"

I stared down at him in utter shock. Now that Owl had pieced together the information, karmic restraints couldn't stop the rapid influx of messages and the deterioration of everything I had worked toward.

I could feel the control over my spiritual energy quickly waning, now entirely reliant on support from the beings originally in *Surviving My First Run*.

[Observers Chat]
CrownFill: She really is despicable. Through and through. Deceiving all of us like this??
Ahoy987: There's no way she's actually Jia Li though, right??
OrangePeels: It all makes sense. No wonder she knew everything.
Socrates: Peijin can be a reader, just like Ruoming and Owl are. Who says that Owl is right?
TarteJuice: Of course you'd say that. You're ALWAYS on Peijin's side. Are you her fan or something? If she really is Jia Li, don't forget that the reason you're on this end of the apocalypse is because she blocked you
Socrates: And so what if she is Jia Li? Are we not all watching her?
MoldyBlanket: I would have NEVER helped her if I knew who she truly was
Socrates: You KNOW who she truly is now. You've never known her as Jia Li, but you've watched Peijin this entire time.
MoldyBlanket: TarteJuice is right. All you have been doing is dick ride Peijin!!
Socrates: I've been blocked, too. It's not like I have some alternative incentive than the rest of you.
TarteJuice: Fuck off. We've been rooting for that bitch this entire time?? This has to be a joke

---

You have received a new review!
TARTEJUICE: ★☆☆☆☆
As wicked as always. Dooming everyone around her and for what?

An observer has edited their review!
MOLDYBLANKET: ★☆☆☆☆
Edited Review: I would have NEVER EVER supported Peijin had I known she was JiaLi1825. How could she do this to all of us? It's such a pity only we know. Just wait until everyone else finds out! That'll be her Karma!

Original Review: Before Peijin gets overrated, I want to say I was here since Day 1. Never doubted her!! Don't forget me!!

> **I was completely frozen. My lower lip trembled slightly, and my breathing became more rapid. Panic welled all through me, but showing it would only draw even more suspicion.**

Owl's smile widened even more. "Why are you hesitating now, Jia Li one eight two five? Come on, kill me. Kill me already. Kill me!"

"Is this your last ditch effort to save yourself? Next time, find the right person, you motherfucker."

I brought my foot down, instantly crushing his skull. His limbs twitched, his hands instantly reaching out. His dying body was still fighting with every ounce of power to survive.

Fuck.

My heart was beating in my ears, and my entire head was ringing. This bastard. The moment I met him, I should have killed him. He was entirely self-centered and losing—and that made him wildly unpredictable.

Fuck, fuck, fuck.

> **Hundreds of gods look at one another in confusion.**

> **Divinity Supreme Commander of the Heavenly Hosts asks what Jia Li 1 8 2 5 means.**

> **Demon Great Sage Who Pacifies Heaven is looking into the title.**

> **Divinity The One Who Fights in Front cannot remove her eyes from Disciple Peijin.**

> **Divinity The One Who Fights in Front has a tense expression.**

I couldn't react. I couldn't hesitate in killing Owl, and I couldn't show an ounce of recollection at the words that Owl had just spoken. If I had, that would have been acceptance of the accusation.

But in an apocalypse centered around turning everything into tools of entertainment, this would undoubtedly spread through all the observers like it was a fact.

When I finally looked down, Owl was nothing more than a massive pile of gore beneath my feet. I had absentmindedly blended him into a pulp.

A small ghost fire floated up from his corpse. It was a tiny, flickering flame, hardly visible. It floated further up and up into the sky, but I grabbed my dao and forced it to dissipate, ensuring that Owl would never, ever return.

I felt cold fingers wrap around the back of my neck and tighten, instantly making me lightheaded. A terrible presence slowly approached from behind until I saw the few strands of white hair in my peripheral vision.

"Peijin."

Ruoming's voice was utterly terrifying.

"Yes?"

"You're going to tell me that Owl is terribly mistaken."

"Yes."

"Because that's the truth."

"Yes. It is."

"Good. And I'm not going to use Lie Detector because I believe you."

"Of course. You have no reason to doubt me. Don't we understand each other?"

CHAPTER TWENTY-FOUR

I turned my head to catch a glimpse of his expression.

I had never seen a more haunted look on anyone's face before. His already hollow eyes were wide and trembling slightly; the lines of exhaustion in his translucent skin were terribly clear.

"That's right."

Ruoming's hand fell from my neck, and I intentionally held my breath for a couple of extra moments until he stepped back. I didn't want him to hear the sigh of relief I was about to let out.

> [Observers Chat]
> **CrownFill:** She really is despicable. Through and through. Deceiving all of us like this??
> **MocFra:** What the fuck just happened
> **Ahoy987:** Is it seriously true
> **MocFra:** If Ruoming is a reader too then he's going to be totally pissed
> **FloraFau19:** How many years has he had to suffer???
> **Foek485:** This must be nothing to him. Imagine the amount of stories he could tell
> **Ahoy987:** Imagine how manipulated he must be feeling after what Peijin asked him earlier. Suddenly her concern for him became curiosity about how her work ruined his life . . .

This time, not even Socrates came to my defense.

> **Demon Great Sage Who Pacifies Heaven is pounding his fists against the table in a fit of rage.**

> **Demon Great Sage Who Pacifies Heaven exclaims that Karma is interfering with the results.**

> **Divinity Great Sage Equaling Heaven says Demon Great Sage Who Pacifies Heaven is too incompetent to find the results.**

> **More gods attempt to discover the meaning behind the title.**

Now that Owl was dead, the illusion immediately began to dissipate. As the walls swirled around us like liquid, the faint sound of screaming grew louder and louder, and both my and Ruoming's party members landed on the ground with a loud thud.

Although I wanted to throw myself straight into the arms of my party members, I held back, still horribly shaken up. I was still only moments away from losing everything I'd worked toward. All I needed was one stroke of bad luck—and I was notorious for that.

Zhige saw me and flew into me, throwing its weight against me. I quickly wrapped my hands around the blade, but instead of greeting it warmly, I only stumbled back, terrified. Zhige picked up on my apprehension, and its wild red eye slowed and squinted in concern.

Sensing my sudden meekness, Ruoming returned and gripped my arm tightly, his face still furious. "You're going to let one bad thing set you off? Are you that shallow?"

"I—"

"You don't have another shot. You'll never be able to start over."

"You think I don't know that? Fuck off."

"You asked me what my biggest regret was. Are you going to make this yours?"

"Let go of my fucking arm," I spat, shoving him back.

I looked in front of me and saw Feiyu, looking utterly exhausted. He survived the attack of the disciples, but he was now covered in blood, and even his perfectly groomed clothes had been torn in the scuffle.

Time and time again, it was much easier for the three of us to give up than to keep pushing forward. But something drove us to continue.

I scowled and turned away, focusing on putting my dao back into my Boundless Bag.

"Peijin!" Yue shouted, looking terribly relieved to see me.

There were cuts littered all over her skin, and just behind her, Yang didn't seem to be doing much better. His torn suit was full of patchwork pieces of fabric keeping it together. I really needed to buy him a new one when I got the chance.

Spotting Yue, Cheng perked up instantly and pointed at her. "It's you again!"

Yue whipped around, looking mortified to see him. "You fucking kid! I'm going to kill you this time for real!"

Yang would be the first of us to grow a full head of gray hair, and this was going to be one of the catalysts. Yue shot toward Cheng, but her fear was apparent in her erratic movements, not wanting to be subjected to his vicious poisons again.

Wei and Ruoming instantly engaged in a vicious one-on-one fight, their techniques matching one another's with brutal precision. It was another battle of knowledge versus strength, with Wei being far stronger but Ruoming knowing every single one of Wei's weaknesses.

Qijing and Amelia stood side-by-side, but now that Qijing's main party had returned, Qijing immediately pulled out her gun and pointed it straight at Amelia. Amelia let out a terrified squeal before quickly maneuvering out of the way, her silver cuff glistening as she summoned a massive elephant from the parade.

The elephant billowed, using its long trunk to whack the rifle out of Qijing's hands. It lifted up its large feet, preparing to crush Qijing's small body.

Qijing looked up, her eyes widening slightly before she ducked, bringing her arms above her head.

Feiyu sped toward her, but I quickly slammed my shoulder into his back, tackling him to the ground before I grabbed a hold of Qijing. I ran over Feiyu and pulled Qijing to my chest, rolling out of the way.

I looked down at her and brushed strands of her long black hair off her sweaty forehead, my hand trembling slightly.

"Peijin!" Amelia shouted from behind me. I whipped around, and Amelia's large eyes were glaring down at me. "You're getting in my way!"

Feiyu stood back up, and he grabbed onto my leg, pulling me to the ground. I instantly let go of Qijing, not wanting to drag her down with me. My chin slammed into the ground, and I winced. Qijing scrambled back to her feet, running for her gun with an outstretched hand.

Amelia lifted her arm into the air, the silver cuff flashing as the dire wolf sprung out a cloud of blue sparks, its jaw wide open and ready to latch onto Qijing.

I kicked Feiyu's face with the base of my foot and threw myself in front of Qijing, the dire wolf latching onto my arm before quickly letting go at the realization of who it attacked. The elephant stampeded toward me, but I again used my body to protect Qijing, throwing the animals into a flurry of confusion.

"Neither of you should be killing each other!" I shouted at Amelia.

I grabbed onto Qijing's gun and snapped it over my knee. She let out a mortified cry behind me as Feiyu held her back. I stomped forward, grabbing Amelia's shoulder firmly and squatting down. "Find the node. That's the only thing you should be doing."

"Let go of me! I'm not going to!" Amelia cried back, tears brimming in her eyes as she pulled away sharply.

"Amelia," I practically pleaded. "Please, just focus on the nodes! I don't want you fighting!"

"You don't want me doing anything," Amelia replied furiously. "Just replace me already!"

Wei and Ruoming's conflict erupted violently, and Wei's body smashed into the ground, hurdling toward Amelia. I instinctively moved to grab her, but she responded just as quickly, avoiding me and putting herself in Wei's path. She'd rather be struck than depend on my help.

Thankfully, Wei managed to reorient himself before anything could happen to Amelia, but it didn't stop the frantic beating of my heart in my head.

> **Disciple Yue has activated Magician's Hand!**

The entire room around us began to warp, and the members of Bohemian Grove spun around in shock and surprise.

Yue mimicked the Owl's skill, causing the room to flip and the walls to vanish into seemingly never-ending pits. Some of the members let out startled shouts, not fully aware of the capacity of the Magician's Hand skill. Others, who had read further into my story, pieced it together instantly and charged toward Yue.

In response, Yuan, who finally activated one of his skills, brought up a large, glowing shield before him. He slammed it into the ground, and all of Ruoming's party members instantly had a glowing blue box formed around them, equipping each of them with various buffs.

Cheng finally relaxed his shoulders slightly, letting out a heavy sigh of relief. Yue's fists were glowing with Demonic Fire, yet when she finally got close enough to throw a hit, her fist deflected off the invisible barrier around Cheng.

The space around him warped slightly, his protective shield taking damage but not yet being destroyed.

"Huh?" Yue mumbled stupidly.

Cheng closed the small distance between them and pricked Yue's hand with a thin needle.

"Goddammit, Yue!" Yang cried.

Yue stumbled back, staring at her hand. Then, her arm erupted with massive purple welts and hives and turning a fiery red color. She immediately cast Yang a sad, pleading look.

> **Divinity Spirit of the Jade Moon sweats heavily.**

Ruoming caught up to Wei and jabbed at him furiously. Finally, Wei's ribbon uncoiled from his arm and snaked up into the air before shooting down as sharp as a dagger. Now, Ruoming needed to fight on two fronts.

Feiyu, however, had already managed to kill or scare off most of Bohemian Grove, and now his eyes were set on me. I frantically stuck by Amelia's side, despite her repeated attempts at throwing me off her tail.

"Amelia, stop it," I whispered softly, reaching out to grab her small hands. "Just for right now, please look for the node. Everybody here is counting on you."

"You say that every time," Amelia said in a low tone, tears welling up in her eyes. "You just want me to listen to you."

Feiyu's sword came swinging down, and I grabbed Amelia, tugging her into my chest as I quickly dodged Feiyu's attacks. I threw Zhige down, and the sword began to hold its own against Feiyu.

My hand came up to cup Amelia's cheek, gently brushing her tears away. "How can I make it up to you?"

"You can't. I'll be mad at you forever."

"You can hate me forever. That's okay. But I'll always be here for you, so please don't think otherwise."

Amelia slapped my hand off. "I want my *real* family back."

I winced at her words, feeling a terrible degree of guilt for how her life was unraveling. "Amelia . . . I understand if you're mad at me, but please, for everybody else in the party, help them survive this. You're the only one who can do it."

Amelia stared at me for a long moment, the tears in her eyes still present but not spilling. She was doing her absolute best to not cry.

"I wish . . . I never met you," Amelia hissed with conviction.

> **Scathing Reviewer is flickering!**

With a raise of her hand, the dire wolf immediately appeared at her side before it lifted its nose into the air, searching for the node. In one movement, Amelia swung herself onto the back of the dire wolf, riding it toward wherever the node was located.

> [Observers Chat]
> **CrownFill:** This is what you deserve. Never forget it.
> **FloraFau19:** Did you really think you could pretend that you lived a good, noble life? No wonder your luck has been bad this whole time
> **Foek485:** This is why Karma hates her guts. Good

I trembled slightly, squeezing my eyes shut at the influx of messages. I ignored the countless negative reviews coming in, unable to deal with them.

> [Observers Chat]
> **Nipon23:** cat is out of the bag!!
> **Nipon23:** you really are a fool if you thought you could reinvent yourself here loll

Before I had enough time to pull myself together, I could feel the sharp pain of a sword slicing straight through my back before pushing through the front of my chest.

I looked down and the glistening purple blade before it retracted. Zhige flew straight back into my hand, and I whipped around, face-to-face with Feiyu once more. Using my spiritual energy, I quickly stopped my wound from bleeding.

"Have you learned nothing?" I asked.

"I don't want to kill you."

I thought back to the one timeline where Feiyu did, in fact, kill me. My expression twisted into one of disbelief.

"I'm serious," Feiyu replied sincerely.

"The heat of the moment gets to you."

I swung at Feiyu, my eyes locked on a perfect opening. But, due to Yuan's skill, Zhige was deflected instantly. I let out a scoff, digging my sword into the barrier in an attempt to pierce it.

Feiyu instantly pushed me back, and I watched him carefully adjust his stance and take in a deep breath, getting ready to use Thread of Malice. I swallowed nervously and upped the speed of my attacks to break his focus repeatedly, though I knew my attempts wouldn't last long.

Amelia pinpointed the location of the node, the dire wolf circling it.

> [Party Chat]
> **Amelia:** Over here Wei!

Wei did his best to keep his expression stoic to avoid drawing suspicion from Ruoming. I turned away from Feiyu, running toward Ruoming. With a burst of spiritual energy, I broke through Ruoming's defense and slashed up the length of his side. He let out a sharp hiss.

His protective barrier had already been weakened by Wei, and with a single hit loaded in spiritual energy, it shattered under Zhige.

Wei broke away, leaping over to Amelia and instantly activating the node before taking it into his hands. However, the moment he grabbed hold of it, the entire room began to tremble violently.

CHAPTER TWENTY-FIVE

The large throne in the center of the room rumbled back and forth before its legs extended, and it leapt up.

"Huh?" I stared at it dumbfoundedly before it turned to me and attempted to run me over. I let out a surprised squeal and quickly jumped out of its path of destruction.

It continued to run in the same direction, plowing through layer upon layer and growing larger with every passing moment. It destroyed Yue's illusion instantaneously, and she let out a frustrated groan while clutching onto her loosely hanging and diseased arm.

Various colorful elixirs were dripping from her mouth as Yang fought furiously to protect her from Cheng and Yuan. But, anytime Yang was about to successfully land a hit, Yuan would instantly jump to Cheng's defense, ensuring no harm came to him.

I turned to Ruoming, but he had vanished. Instead, all that remained was a gaping hole beneath where he once stood.

"The heart!" I shouted for the rest of my party to hear. "Get to the heart node! We're almost there!"

My party turned to me, and without a moment's hesitation, Wei brought up his sword and stabbed it straight into the floor of the throne room. But, it didn't break through.

Shit. The nodes.

I looked over my shoulder, and Feiyu was quickly gaining distance. I redirected my spiritual energy into my feet and darted forward, opening my bag and quickly finding the nodes.

> **AMERICAN NODE**
> Location: Ferris Wheel RN2938 — Gondola #19
> Description: The American node controls the citadel's spatial presence. Use the node's artifact to toggle these settings regardless of the user's current location.
> Alter Layout: No
> Trap Frequency: 1/10
> Location Size: 1/10
> Location Firewall: 10/10
> Owner: Liu Peijin

> **Location Firewall: 1/10**

I quickly shut the nodes in Boundless Bag once more, and only milliseconds after did, I felt Feiyu's body crash into mine. I went flying across the ground, and I drew my limbs in to roll and minimize my injuries.

"Wei! Again!" I shouted before Feiyu grabbed onto me and lifted me into the air, slamming me back down into the ground.

With another strike, a massive hole appeared beneath Wei, and he leapt through. Amelia followed only moments later, and Yang pulled Yue down.

Once I was sure they had all made it, I turned around to grab onto Feiyu's coat. I pulled him down on top of me. I extended my leg into his hip before he could land and flipped him over my body. He hit the ground with a grunt.

I looked him dead in the eyes, flipped him off, and leapt into the hole Wei had created without a second to spare.

After jumping through the layer holding the throne, I plummeted through the open skies, watching the Arabian landscape open out beneath me. My entire party was free falling through the citadel once more.

I watched as many of them were intercepted by members of Ruoming's party and the occasional Bohemian Grove member, but I knew they could handle it as long as Ruoming and Feiyu weren't involved.

I lengthened Zhige and threw him beneath me, riding him like a hoverboard. Once we were about to hit the ground, I balanced on Zhige's hilt and pointed the tip straight down, hoping a mixture of spiritual energy and momentum would help break through the next layer into the limestone caves. Either that, or I was about to die on impact.

I pulled my arms tight against my chest and pressed my feet together. Zhige lengthened more and more until the tip was a sharp point a few feet long. On impact, it sliced through the ground, and the thick layers of dirt whizzed past me.

Finally, the space opened up into what resembled a vast limestone cave.

Stalactites of various lengths were hanging from the ceiling, massive formations that had taken thousands of years to form. There were even some sharp stalagmites jutting from the unsteady ground.

It was pitch black, apart from the occasional torches placed throughout. But, thanks to my skills, my vision adjusted quickly.

I leapt off of Zhige, and at once, Ruoming was by my side, his wide and pale eyes staring straight at me. Although seeing him was usually accompanied by a horrible amount of physical pain, he didn't attack me yet.

We were the only two who made it to the lowest floor of the cellar so quickly. The rest were still making their way down or presumably attempting to stop one another from making it.

"Are you the one who moved all the nodes from their usual locations?" he asked calmly.

"No . . ."

"One per location is much easier than it was before. It took me a lot of runs to memorize where all of them were placed."

"I'm just trying to level out the playing field. It's a bit difficult when you're the competition I'm facing."

"What skill lets you change the story?"

I flinched at his final word, but thankfully, it was too ambiguous in this context to be limited by karmic restriction, so I figured I was still safe among the gods for now.

"Why would I tell you?"

"Maybe you were very dissatisfied with the original series of events."

"Of course. I'm just trying to improve it."

"That makes you a bit of a scathing reviewer, doesn't it?" Ruoming asked with a slight smile on his face.

I could hardly describe it as a smile. It was horribly icy and distant, just like every other aspect of him.

He must have come to the conclusion that the Scathing Reviewer skill had been adopted by somebody in this current run. Given that he now suspected I was Jia Li, and reasonably so, it would make me the most likely suspect.

He was growing more skeptical by the second, and that meant my chance of dying was also increasing accordingly.

"I wouldn't say that," I answered. "I don't dislike anything. I like finding the positive everywhere."

[Observers Chat]
UCh888: Most bullshit phrase ever said by Peijin . . .
Seatdiv: LMFAO

"Tell me, god of fate and fortune," Ruoming said, gripping his weapon even more tightly, "will I regret not killing you?"

"Yes. You will, in the same way I already regret not killing Feiyu."

"I think so, too."

"Then kill me," I stated simply. "If you really tried to, you could."

"What holds you back from killing Feiyu? Attachment?" Ruoming asked, an almost mocking tone in his voice.

My eyes narrowed. Anything would sound silly, given that Ruoming had spent forever at Feiyu's side. My attachment was terribly insignificant in comparison, even as his creator.

"Is that what keeps you from killing me?" I taunted right back. His smug expression quickly soured.

"I haven't survived the apocalypse for nearly as long as you," I continued, "but, there's only so much we can hold onto in a world like this. Whatever that is, if we can cling onto even the idea of it for the rest of our lives, we can live forever."

"Ha! So, your attachment to Feiyu is keeping you alive. You're nuts."

"No, my hope is."

"Hope wanes."

"Conviction doesn't."

"If you die, what do you think is going to happen to everyone you've brought together?"

This question reflected the earlier conversation I'd had with Ruoming. Ironically, back then I was trying to convince him there was still more to this world. Oddly enough, he managed to flip the narrative on me.

I often thought about my own death, even before the apocalypse. I thought about my own death so much that I stopped fearing the idea of dying.

I wouldn't say I was *trying* to die. But there were many times that nothing kept me living. In that respect, my party was right.

I walked on a tightrope hanging far above the ground where death would await me. I would tease the edge and teeter until I was certain that even the smallest wind would send me hurtling toward the ground. But it never happened.

I certainly was not an optimist. I was bitter, resentful, and plenty angry. While I was writing *Surviving My First Run*, I wanted everybody to love Feiyu because I wanted to believe that if I could write someone lovable, then I could mimic them until I was also deserving of love.

There were many long, arduous nights I spent curled up in a thin sheet, restlessly throwing myself all over the mattress. I would struggle to open my eyes, afraid of the nothingness that awaited me. When I finally did open them, I was enveloped by total darkness.

I'd bring one of my hands up just before my face. Then, I'd bring the other, and I would clasp them together until I was holding my own hand in the dark. I would imagine that it was somebody else's hand—my mother's, Dad's, Qiu Feiyu's, even Zhao Rui's—and I pretended that they would never let go.

And, in the dark, when I could make out nothing around me, I'd have them tell me everything I always wanted to hear, until I had to bury my face into my pillow to stop myself from wailing. I wanted to suffocate in the soft feathers of my pillow and let it smother me. But, when it became unbearable, I always pulled back and caught my breath.

I was, first and foremost, a coward. So, no, I never feared my death. But, I feared everything else. And I never thought about a world after me.

I hesitantly lifted my head, biting my lower lip before I finally spoke up.

"You'll take care of them for me, won't you?"

I finally met Ruoming's eyes, and I could feel the exhaustion etched into my expression. Ruoming looked down at me, wide-eyed, not saying a word. It wasn't like I expected him to answer anyway. What was I thinking?

I flashed a wide, bright smile at Ruoming, lifting a hand and repeatedly patting him on the shoulder. "What's got you so philosophical? Don't worry. I'll surely kill you and Feiyu, and I have no plans on dying."

Ruoming looked down at me solemnly. I'm not sure what I could have possibly said that he hasn't heard before that would get him so worked up. He frowned slightly.

"Who was Zhao Rui to you?"

The question caught me off guard, and I looked up at him in surprise, my head cocked to the side slightly.

"Huh?"

"When we first met, you mistook me for Zhao Rui. Who was he?"

"Huuuh?" I repeated stupidly. "When did my background suddenly matter? He was just someone I knew growing up."

"Was he important to you?"

"Maybe."

"Maybe not," Ruoming shrugged. "Especially since you don't remember what he looks like."

"Shut up. You two could have been identical twins."

"Then it was one-sided. He left you. Am I wrong?"

I let out an infuriated huff, crossing my arms. "How the hell did you survive this long with such a wicked personality? You just piss me off the more you talk! One moment I'm pitying you, and the next moment I want to torture you. No wonder you and Feiyu get along so well. Two sides of the same coin."

Ruoming let out the softest chuckle. I jolted at the sound and faced him.

It was hardly audible, and when I first heard it, I thought I must have been mistaken.

I didn't think I said anything that funny. Thinking back on it, there was no humor in what I said. I stared at Ruoming, a hint of both fear and disgust on my face. Laughing hardly suited him.

"Don't do that again," I said.

"What?"

"Laugh. It's terrifying when you do it."

"Did Zhao Rui laugh?"

"No. But he's nothing like you. He was never cruel."

Ruoming tilted his head slightly, like he was trying to think of his next words. "I hope you can find him again," Ruoming finally answered bluntly.

I couldn't get a read on this guy at all. At one moment, he was threatening me like I was the only hiccup in his road to victory. Next, we shared what felt like an intimate conversation two friends would hold with one another. I could hardly believe what I was hearing.

"If I do die, I hope it's at the hands of you and Feiyu," I said simply. "I'll come back as a ghost and torment everybody otherwise. My ego couldn't handle losing to anybody lesser than you two."

The roof above us began to rumble, massive limestone formations, dirt, and stone crumbling down as our party members rapidly approached. Simultaneously, I brought Zhige out before me, pointing it straight at Ruoming.

"Ruoming, I will win this arc. And after that, I want us to be allies."

"That sounds like a miserable proposition."

I smiled.

Wei's ribbon burst through the roof, bringing an avalanche of debris down alongside it.

CHAPTER TWENTY-SIX

The ribbon shot straight at Ruoming, expanding until it was a large sheet attempting to entrap him.

Wei followed not long after, his white robes whipping all around him. He was practically glowing, standing out like a lantern in a dark cave. His entire body was crackling with spiritual energy, yellow sparks flying off of him as he tested the limits of karma over and over again.

> **Divinity Ears That Hear What Comes on the Wind is lending Disciple Wei spiritual energy!**

> **Divinity Supreme Commander of the Heavenly Hosts is lending Disciple Wei spiritual energy!**

> **Divinity Supreme Commander of the Heavenly Hosts is lending Disciple Peijin spiritual energy!**

> **Divinity Ears That Hear What Comes on the Wind is lending Disciple Peijin spiritual energy!**

My entire body filled with a serene sensation, and I quickly charged Zhige with more spiritual energy, topping off the blade's reservoir. Its red eye squinted joyously. Now that my observer reviews were ruined, I was truly dependent on the help of the gods.

I felt a puff of hot air on the back of my neck. "Jiejie, why do you keep running away from me?"

I let out a mortified gasp, instantly grabbing the back of my neck and rubbing it. Goosebumps travelled all the way down my back, and I couldn't help but shiver at the terrible sensation.

"What the fuck are you doing?!"

"Reminding you that I'm still here."

Feiyu's large blade crackled until a bolt of lightning stretched out from the tip, breaking into a long line. It let out an ominous purple glow around the bright white bolts.

He swung the blade at me, and the lightning burst out until it connected with my skin. At once, it travelled all over my body, sparks flying off me. I entire body shook violently, and I groaned from the pain. The lightning left long burn marks all over my body before they vanished with a bit of spiritual energy.

"If only I got that spiritual energy," Feiyu pouted, his sword crackling again. "Just imagine what I could do."

Hindsight activated!

A massive force was quickly approaching from above. I flattened Zhige until it looked more like a large metal sheet and brought it over the top of my head like a shield.

The throne burst through the ceiling, crashing down and causing the entire cellar to rumble. Massive chunks of debris fell along with it, and I struggled to hold Zhige above me without caving into the massive amounts of pressure being forced down.

Without any cover, a chunk of debris clipped Feiyu's shoulder, and he gave a small groan. He stumbled slightly, one of his arms now limp. His other hand was still gripping his sword, and he looked up, instantly destroying the rest of the falling debris before it could strike him.

The throne was alive—the pet of an outer god. At the realization that its beloved home was about to be destroyed by the assembly of the heart, it came out in full force to defend it.

The throne ran on its long golden legs, mindlessly crashing into every single wall, not caring about who or what it was about to plow through. It was of such massive size that each step made it feel like the entire cave was about to fall apart.

Ruoming and Wei broke apart as the throne charged between them. It whipped around, seeming to latch onto Ruoming and sprint toward him.

The throne made it to Ruoming faster than he could dodge, and it prepared to smash him into the wall of the cellar until he was nothing more than a smashed corpse.

Feiyu broke away from me, his one arm still weakened, and a lightning bolt stretched out from the tip of his sword. He aimed it straight for the throne.

Like a wild animal, the throne completely panicked at the sight of the impending hit. It leapt into the air, smashing up against the stalactites and throwing itself against the walls. It shook terribly at the resulting wounds.

Feiyu's hit missed the erratic throne, and the lightning shot straight into the roof, sending sparks travelling all the way down the cave. It lit up like a firework show, and everyone ducked out of the way of the disastrous sparks and falling limestone.

Through the hole above us, which the throne had created, a loud roar sounded. The massive snaking body of the sea serpent appeared, screaming and launching itself toward the throne.

Amelia was riding on the back of the serpent, her hands gripping the whiskers atop its head. She let go and jumped down to the base of the serpent. With a flash, the dire wolf appeared beneath her legs before she landed.

The serpent dove toward the throne, mouth hanging wide open. Amelia clung onto the strong neck of the dire wolf as it darted down the serpent's long body, until it finally hit the cave floor.

Noticing her arrival, Wei ran to accompany her while his ribbon defended his back from the attacks of Ruoming and Feiyu.

Yue, Yang, Yuan, and Cheng appeared only seconds later, but the four of them were deeply entangled in a fight. Although Yue and Yang had incredibly strong defensive skills, Yuan and Cheng were optimal at defense and healing.

Combined with their occasional offensive skills and poison use, none of them seemed to surpass the other. Thankfully, the effects of the poison on Yue were predominantly mitigated with Chang'e and Yang's medical assistance.

I followed closely behind Ruoming and Feiyu, ensuring they couldn't catch up to Wei and Amelia. The throne was temporarily preoccupied with the serpent, but it was making quick work of Amelia's beast, bashing its head in with its long golden legs.

Despite the massive size and aggression of the serpent, the throne had successfully crushed half of its skull in, and its movements made it infinitely more difficult for the serpent to keep track of it.

Finally, Amelia's dire wolf located the node. She whipped the beast around, checking for Ruoming and Feiyu. However, they were still engaged in a deep battle with Wei. Wei looked at Amelia, sword drawn as both Feiyu and Ruoming attacked him at once.

Wei's body was already marred with blood. Various small cuts appeared all over his skin as he was worn down by the onslaught. However, just as quickly as they appeared, he channeled his spiritual energy into healing them.

> **Divinity Supreme Commander of the Heavenly Hosts is lending Disciple Wei spiritual energy!**

> **Divinity Ears That Hear What Comes on the Wind is lending Disciple Wei spiritual energy!**

Wei was able to challenge karmic restraints with the influx of spiritual energy, dampening karmic backlash against him. Regardless, both Ruoming and Feiyu were utterly formidable disciples to face alone.

Amelia was repeatedly flinching, her complexion weak and pale, especially as the sea serpent took more and more repeated blows from the throne. Amelia's spiritual energy must have been practically depleted by demanding that the sea serpent continue fighting despite the injuries it was sustaining.

> **The World is lending Disciple Amelia spiritual energy!**

My eyes widened at the notification, my head whipping up to stare at Amelia. Like the one time that Artemis had partially descended in the ghostlike image of a girl to help Amelia tame the serpent, the faintest gold shadow of the World was behind Amelia now, her hands gently grabbing Amelia's shoulders and guiding her hands.

Blood dribbled down Amelia's nose, her breathing haggard. But, at the delicate touch, her posture straightened and determination set in her eyes.

"Meihua!" Ruoming shouted furiously, his grip tightening on his saber as all of his attacks became even more precise and frantic.

The transparent and glistening image of Meihua jerked up, looking at Ruoming. The World shot him a sheepish grin, and Meihua stuck out her tongue before vanishing.

Ruoming's expression twitched, and the tattoo on his back began to glow, visible through the thin layer of his button-up shirt. His movements became more charged.

> **Divinity Far Shooting Queen of Beasts watches The World sourly.**

> **Divinity Far Shooting Queen of Beasts is lending Disciple Amelia spiritual energy!**

> **Divinity The One Who Fights in Front glares at Divinity**

| Far Shooting Queen of Beasts for her interference. |

| **Divinity The One Who Fights in Front reminds Divinity Far Shooting Queen of Beasts of the consequences of her actions the previous time.** |

| **Divinity Far Shooting Queen of Beasts states that the threshold for intervention is far higher now.** |

It was good to see these two still bickering, especially since there would be another opportunity to pick a sponsor after this arc.

| **[Observers Chat]**
Socrates: Poor Amelia . . . this arc has been so tough on her.
Socrates: Jia Li should really try to amend her relationships after this arc is over. Why are you suddenly having such a hard time?
Socrates: Also . . . I don't want to stress Jia Li, but almost all of the observers believe that you're Jia Li now. If the gods and your characters find out, it might be a big hit before the next arc. |

| **The World is watching you.** |

I jumped between Wei, Ruoming, and Feiyu, and at once I could feel Ruoming and Feiyu's blades slash through my skin. I winced, but Wei picked up on my intentions. He pulled away, turning toward Amelia.

Amelia quickly guided him to the heart node, and he activated it, taking it into his hands. He now held the throne and heart nodes. I had the rest.

Wei looked up at me, opening his mouth to shout something before the throne burst through. Its long gold legs instantly smashed into Wei, shoving him to the ground. He looked up at Amelia in a panic, and his ribbon quickly scooped up her and the dire wolf, pulling them into the air and out of the throne's reach.

"Wei-shushu!" Amelia shrieked, her small hand outstretched for him.

The throne continued its sprint forward, crushing Wei under its long legs. The sound of the stampeding throne masked the brutal crunch of Wei's body.

"Wei! Wei!" I looked frantically at the mangled state of his body, and in that moment of distraction, Ruoming and Feiyu both slashed deep wounds into my back.

CHAPTER TWENTY-SEVEN

"Augh!"

My blue hoodie tugged me further away, sparing me from what could have easily been two deadly strikes.

Blood burst from my back, and I sputtered, blood pouring from my mouth. I wiped it in shock before healing my injuries.

Divinity Supreme Commander of the Heavenly Hosts lets out a mortified cry!

Divinity Supreme Commander of the Heavenly Hosts frantically looks at the other gods.

Divinity Supreme Commander of the Heavenly Hosts refuses to let Divinity Blessed Martial Guard of Salvation die.

Divinity Supreme Commander of the Heavenly Hosts begins his descent into the mortal realm.

Warning! Severe karmic violation!

Warning! Severe karmic violation!

An outer god stirs.

> **Divinity Ears That Hear What Comes on the Wind supports Divinity Supreme Commander of the Heavenly Hosts.**

> **Many gods are outraged at the sudden interference!**

> **Demon King of the Nine Hells is infuriated by Divinity Supreme Commander of the Heavenly Hosts' appearance!**

> **Demon Great Sage Who Pacifies Heaven is unsure what to do.**

> **Divinity God of Thunder begins his descent into the mortal realm.**

I hiccupped nervously at the flurry of notifications. God of Thunder was none other than Thor—Yuan's sponsor. Although it was late enough in the arcs that descents wouldn't be as seriously punished as they had been during Artemis's first interference while saving Amelia, the situation became infinitely more precarious.

Worst of all was that the outer god who most likely owned this throne was beginning to take notice of the chaos.

Shit . . . at this rate there might be an entire holy war down here, especially if the outer god decided to get involved. There was no coming back from that. And my status as the lowest of low-tiered gods was not helping me at all.

> **POLL #4**
> **Which party's descended gods should receive a critical injury?**
> **A. Peijin's World Dominion**
> **B. Major Arcana**
> ***Bohemian Grove has been restricted due to zero interference by the gods.**

My eyes widened at the poll. I instantly panicked, knowing the observers would vote against me. But, more importantly, this was about which god had built better rapport. This would further deter gods from acting further.

> **Many gods are shocked by the poll!**

> **Divinity Ears That Hear What Comes on the Wind asks when polls could harm gods!**

> **Demon King of the Nine Hells asks when gods started saving disciples.**

> **Various gods express great frustration at Divinity Supreme Commander of the Heavenly Host's constant interference!**

> **Divinity Great Sage Equaling Heaven shouts that Divinity God of Thunder is a thuggish, prideful, arrogant brute.**

> **Demon Great Sage Equaling Heaven casts a glance at Divinity Great Sage Equaling Heaven's self-reflective comments.**

> **Various gods agree with Divinity Great Sage Equaling Heaven's comment!**

> **Divinity The One Who Fights in Front looks nervously at the poll.**

Feiyu and Ruoming attacked me once more, but I dodged, scrambling toward Wei.

"Wei! Come on, heal!" I finally reached him, and I lifted his ruined body. Some of his limbs had fully detached from his torso, while other parts of his body had been entirely skinned.

It reminded me all over again of his dungeon room and the torment he'd faced at the hands of his worshippers. I could only hope that his spiritual core hadn't been destroyed, or Wei really was about to die.

"Yang!" I cried out desperately, frantically looking around for him and holding Wei close against my chest. In my moment of weakness, Ruoming's attacks became more relentless, and I could hardly hold him back by swinging my sword back and forth desperately while clinging onto Wei.

I finally caught sight of Yang. Yang looked like a complete and utter mess, sweat dripping down his brow and tears brimming in his eyes from the horror of the situation. But, he couldn't escape his current predicament.

The growing shadow of Thor was appearing behind Yuan, and Yuan was becoming a terrifying offensive threat that neither Yang nor Yue could even get close enough to attack.

The throne was circling back around, attracted to the amount of energy that Feiyu, Ruoming, and I possessed. Viewing us as the main threat, it charged straight for us.

I wanted to lift Wei into my arms and pull him to safety, but with the fragile state of his body, I was terrified that if I lifted him too far up, he would fall through my arms in a mess of shredded organs and skin.

A red string appeared, connected right in the center of my chest. I looked up to see Feiyu's perfect stance, his eyes locked on me.

"Shit."

An enormous cloud of blue and gold sparks flashed before me. A massive angel dressed in a thick metallic layer of silver armor was forming.

Long blond hair flew all around his perfectly chiseled face; a pair of massive and beautifully feathered wings stretched out behind him, at least a dozen feet long; a massive golden halo gave off a blinding glow, following the smooth movements of his head.

Archangel Michael.

> **Divinity Ears That Hear What Comes on the Wind lets out a thunderous applause!**

> **Hundreds of demons are screaming collusion and interference!**

> **An outer god has awoken from its slumber.**

The angel lifted a massive sword made of what looked like flames. But upon closer inspection, it was made of the tormented souls of devils burning in hell. Archangel Michael held hell in the palm of his hand.

> **Warning! Severe karmic violation!**

The golden throne smashed into Archangel Michael, shoving Archangel Michael back by dozens of feet. However, Archangel Michael didn't seem affected in the slightest, tanking the hit before lifting his sword and driving it into the side of the throne, sending it flying back.

A loud eruption sounded out from behind me. I whipped my head around to see lightning burst out from Yuan's body as Thor appeared behind him.

Archangel Michael looked over his shoulder, and it was my first time catching a glimpse of his face.

If I had to describe Feiyu as handsome, then Archangel Michael was otherworldly.

Literally.

I brought my hands up to protect my eyes from his blinding looks.

Wei stirred in my arms, and my eyes shot open. I looked down at him, my hand brushing off the blood-stained strands of hair from his face. His body was slowly pulling itself together, and I let out a relieved cry, burying my face into his robes.

"Wei," I whispered softly, reassured by the thought that he could hear me. I lifted my head and opened the Azure Dragon Store, quickly sending dozens of prayer candles his way.

"If you want to see his story continue, then give us more spiritual energy, goddammit!" I shouted into the sky, knowing that hundreds, if not thousands, of gods must have been looking down on us now.

If Feiyu and Ruoming could orchestrate the entire Arabian parade, then at the very least, I hoped some of these gods and a few observers still held a fraction of empathy for my party members.

> **[Observers Chat]**
> **Nipon23:** who is going to be donating to jia li of all people? aww, does kindness suddenly matter when you're on your hands and knees begging?
> **Aslan:** Me.

> **You have received a new review!**
> **ASLAN: ★★★★★**
> **I don't blame you. Make right by this life, and I can only hope that things will turn out well for you and your party.**

> **Polling ongoing . . .**
> **A. 42%**
> **B. 58%**

Spiritual energy surged through me once more, and I looked down at Wei, who was healing faster now that he was receiving a greater dosage of spiritual energy from the audience.

Wei's arms slowly reattached to his shoulder, and he began to wiggle his fingers. He moved at an agonizing pace until his fingers gripped the long fabric by his waist.

"Node," Wei croaked.

Archangel Michael drove Ruoming and Feiyu back, but only for a moment before Thor lifted his hammer and aimed it straight for Archangel Michael's side. The two gods were now in a formidable battle, and Ruoming and Feiyu were trying not to become collateral damage.

To my surprise, Ruoming and Feiyu didn't make any attempts to approach me when the opportunity presented itself. Although they were previously trying to wear me down as much as possible with what I assumed would culminate in an attempt to take the nodes, they now held back.

But, it wasn't that noticeable. To anyone else, it would still look like they were trying to break through the surrounding chaos.

Did they want me to assemble the heart?

I reached into Wei's white robes and pulled out the throne and heart nodes. I sifted through my Boundless Bag until I found the rest of the nodes, and I instantly assembled all of them together until they formed a cube.

At once, my entire body seized up.

I was frozen in place.

In my hands was the heart of the citadel, and it was a massive, red, and beating organ. I could feel the heat radiating into my own palm, and I wanted to recoil in response, but I had no control over my movements.

All I could do was stare at the heart, immobile. I tried to signal to Wei that something was wrong with my eyes, but his recovery was strenuous and ongoing.

Behind me, I could hear Archangel Michael's conflict with Thor. Archangel Michael was never worried about interfering with the arcs, having always tested Karma since the apocalypse began. For Thor, however, this was a massive violation.

"Have you forgotten your place?" Archangel Michael said simply.

I could hear a deep rumbling coming from where Thor was, and fear filled me. What the hell were these gods doing using the citadel as their playground?

The injured throne slowly stumbled back onto its legs. Terrified of the overwhelming spiritual presence of Archangel Michael and Thor, it hesitated. It took a few steps back like a startled stray dog, looking around for an escape or easier prey.

Wei was recovering steadily now, and for the most part, he was pieced back together. He must have been receiving serious aid in the form of spiritual energy.

On the contrary, Archangel Michael shrunk down until he was only a foot taller than Wei. Thor did the same, and the two appeared behind their respective disciples.

Thousands of gods and observers are roaring with excitement at the fight!

Polling ongoing . . .
A. 47%
B. 53%

Their material forms had faded into a golden sheen to conserve spiritual energy usage. One could hardly distinguish the outlines of their bodies, but upon closer inspection, both Archangel Michael and Thor were gearing up and preparing to fight a proxy war for their disciples.

Yuan's personality matched perfectly with Thor—both were gruff and fought with everything on the line, and now that Yuan had someone to protect, he would stop at nothing.

Wei and Archangel Michael didn't have nearly the same synergy. Archangel

Michael could be immature and mischievous, whereas Wei was introspective. But, the two of them were united in the idea that justice always prevails.

Wei's ribbon returned, slithering back up his arm. Amelia and her dire wolf had been securely bound at the corner of the cellar, unable to move until Wei was better.

Archangel Michael made the first move. Lifting his sword, Wei mimicked the movement, and Thor forced Yuan to defend himself. It was a battle between sword and shield. Wei had unparalleled technological knowledge, but Yuan was unreachable.

Through the chaos, Feiyu snuck through, approaching me curiously.

"Jiejie, what's got you all frozen up like a statue?"

He stalked around me, and when I evidently failed to respond, a wide smile appeared.

"Jiejie is so quiet. Cat got your tongue?" The tip of Feiyu's blade gently pressed into the center of my torso, like he was reminding me that with one swift movement, he could kill me. So much for us being friends. Ruoming wasn't far behind, and he watched the entire situation with his complete attention and arms crossed.

"Get the fuck away from her!"

Yue suddenly slammed down straight on top of Feiyu, her legs extended as she dropped down from the sky. Feiyu immediately slammed into the ground, letting out a pained grunt. Yue's hands burst with purple flames, and she punched Feiyu's face, sending him flying back.

. . . Since when did Yue get that strong?!

> **Divinity Great Sage Equaling Heaven is screaming at Demon Great Sage Who Pacifies Heaven for being rash!**

> **Demon Great Sage Who Pacifies Heaven plugs his ears.**

Upon closer inspection, a shadow of the Bull Demon King could be seen behind Yue, guiding her movements and giving her the necessary spiritual energy to match Feiyu's unbelievable skill level.

I could practically scream from rage at the unbelievable amount of interference occurring before me, but I was still frozen. Ruoming burst forward to strike Yue, but she dodged and grabbed onto me, taking the heart from my hands.

Instantly, my limbs relaxed, and I finally regained control over my body. I let out a sigh of relief, but when I turned to face Yue, I realized she was now frozen in place.

CHAPTER TWENTY-EIGHT

"You never figured out what this heart's defense system was, did you?" Ruoming said simply. "You must have figured it wasn't important at the time."

Demon Great Sage Who Pacifies Heaven is pounding his screen in a fit.

Demon Great Sage Who Pacifies Heaven is cursing Disciple Yue.

Ruoming stalked closer, looking up at me. He poked Yue, and she remained entirely still, unable to retaliate. "It took me a long time to figure this arc out. First, I had to realize that I needed to use the nodes. Then, I had to find dozens of them and learn to activate them. How many runs do you think that took me? When I finally did all of that, I ended up in this pathetic state. Worst of all, I once did it solo without a party to free me. I was frozen for what must have been years."

"What are you getting at?"

"I'm saying that I'm still better than you."

I couldn't tell if he was joking.

But, now that the heart was here, all I had to do was destroy it. Although if I would freeze the moment I touched it . . . perhaps I needed my entire party to help me.

That was impossible with the current state of affairs. Everyone was stretched terribly thin by the circumstances.

"Have you ever destroyed the heart?" I asked Ruoming suddenly, doubting his claims.

"Of course. Why would I lie?"

"Because it's not a very interesting story if you're frozen for half of it. I don't believe you."

Suddenly, it all began to come together. There was a reason that Ruoming and Feiyu allowed me to assemble the heart. If there was a true advantage in being the one to do it, they surely would have done it on their own. They were more than capable of taking the nodes from me at multiple points, and it would explain why they were holding back.

In that case, this specific heart must have had a powerful defense mechanism. Perhaps more than just freezing anyone who touched it.

Warning! Severe karmic violation!

Divinity Great Sage Equaling Heaven is wondering if he should interfere.

Divinity Spirit of the Jade Moon warns all gods of the consequences for karmic violations.

Demon King of the Nine Hells swears vengeance against the involved divinities.

Demon Great Sage Who Pacifies Heaven insults Demon King of the Nine Hells.

Demon Great Sage Who Pacifies Heaven is infuriated with Disciple Yue.

The gears in my head were turning. If I couldn't destroy the heart, and Ruoming was waiting for me to make that mistake, I needed to come up with another way.

Suddenly, despite holding onto the heart, Yue could finally move again. She looked at me with both surprise and anger, her face twisted. "What the fuck is this?!"

Yue looked like she was ready to berate me, but the heart stopped her. It grew larger and larger in size until long tendrils burst from the beating, wet organ. They instantly latched onto Yue's arms, digging into her flesh.

Yue let out a surprised yelp, instantly trying to throw it away, but its tendrils began to snake their way beneath her skin.

I sliced through the heart with Zhige, but the moment the blade came in contact with the heart, I froze once more. However, the heart withdrew the tendrils from Yue's body, and blood instantly gushed from her wounds.

Yue grabbed onto her spear and flung it against the heart, throwing it onto the ground far from me. Yue quickly picked her spear back up, and I could hear the rumbling of the throne as it made more frantic laps around the cellar like a desperate wild animal. I looked back and forth between the throne and the heart.

I was about to do something incredibly rash.

"Wei! Attack the throne! Destroy it!"

"What?" Wei shouted back, unable to hear me.

"Destroy the throne!"

"What?!"

"The throne! Destroy it!"

Wei turned to me in utter confusion, and Yuan landed a firm blow against Wei's back. Wei went flying into a wall, slamming into it and crumpling into the ground. He let out a surprised gasp, but he got to his feet only a few moments later, his hands trembling as they gripped his sword.

With the shadow of Archangel Michael present, it looked as though a pair of long white wings were stretching out from Wei's back. Paired with his flowing white robes and glowing eyes, he truly looked like a horrifying god.

He looked back at me, and I pointed to the throne. "Destroy it!"

"You'll anger the outer gods!"

"Get them here!"

If multiple severe karmic violations were to culminate, then there was no denying that a calamity could occur. Getting an outer god involved, especially with the number of gods and demons that now had a hand in this arc, would undeniably throw the karmic limit over the edge.

The god most likely to intervene, especially with the threat of an outer god, was evidently Archangel Michael. If I could get him to unknowingly expend even more spiritual energy, it would trigger an overreaction at the hands of the other demons and gods present.

With that, the karmic violation would only worsen, and one of four main calamities would spawn. That was a surefire way to destroy the entire citadel.

Yue turned to me in surprise. "Are you sure—"

"Guard the heart until the throne is headed for it. We need them to clash."

Ruoming turned to me wide-eyed before his expression quickly hardened. All of a sudden, he came at me full force, no longer holding back.

The weight of his attacks hit me and pushed me back, but I lengthened Zhige and began meeting his strikes head on. I let out a burst of spiritual energy, and Ruoming was pushed back slightly. Still, even with my obvious power advantage, I couldn't surpass his practiced techniques.

I looked over my shoulder to see Feiyu headed toward Wei, who was still fending off Yuan. Feiyu assumed his signature stance, and before he could lock a thread on Wei, I jumped over and tackled Feiyu to the ground.

Feiyu was caught off guard by the sudden attack, but my landing was poor, and I ended up beneath him. He instantly drove his blade into my shoulder, and I winced, attempting to throw him off.

Feiyu's eyes glistened a deep purple, and his blade crackled. Instantly, I felt a horrible jolt of electricity travel through me, and I let out a distressed cry, unable to get him off.

Wei appeared, immediately throwing Feiyu off. I lay on the ground for a few seconds, recovering from the vicious attack. A pattern of burn scars covered my entire body. It looked like the branches of a tree extending out all over me, even overlapping with my tattoo.

> **Warning! Severe karmic violation!**

> **[Observers Chat]**
> **SJJC:** GET HER FEIYU!!!
> **TarteJuice:** Feiyu, you can't lose. You're so much stronger. All the observers are cheering for you!!
> **Ahoy987:** GET BACK WITH RUOMING
> **Landy:** Omg . . .

It was now Ruoming and Feiyu versus Wei and me. For a moment, Yang, Amelia, and Yue managed to distract Cheng and Yuan.

I looked at Wei, who had a cloud of blue and yellow sparks around him. He was no doubt facing the consequences of the karmic backlash, but Archangel Michael must have been taking most of the hit. I shivered as I remembered the agony from Yue's dungeon room.

"Wei, get to the throne. I'll handle it here. Archangel Michael, stick with Wei. Don't leave his side. I hope I can trust that you want your disciple to live."

My words triggered Archangel Michael, and I could see his translucent shadow only grow in size behind Wei. I wouldn't be surprised if Archangel Michael suddenly appeared in his full form again. If anything, I welcomed it with my current plan.

"Peijin!" Ruoming roared.

I jumped at the sound, having never heard him raise his voice or show more than the most minimal sliver of emotion. For a moment, I felt timid before him.

"Are you trying to get us all killed?!" Ruoming screamed.

"You won't die."

"You will!"

What was up with this guy?

"I won't," I insisted. "My kid is mad at me. I pinky promised I would make it up to her, so I have no plans on dying!"

Ruoming stared at me stupidly before letting out a bitter laugh, running his hand through his platinum hair. "Things like that still matter to you?"

Feiyu moved at the same time, headed for Wei, but I intercepted him.

Wei ran for the throne, his ribbon striking it first. The throne instantly whipped around, locking on Wei and charging at him. Wei's apprehension was obvious—having nearly died once already to it—but with the power of Archangel Michael, he managed to get out of its way.

Wei raised his sword far above his head and brought it crashing down on the throne. A giant crack split through it, but it was still holding itself together.

> **An outer god has been disturbed.**

> **An outer god has taken notice of the arc.**

> **An outer god is rapidly approaching.**

The throne threw itself around back and forth, reeling like a child throwing a tantrum. It was clearly in agony, and it was drawing the attention of its owner.

> **Disciple Yue has activated Magician's Hand!**

Suddenly, it seemed as though the heart was in front of the throne. The moment the throne stepped over the illusion of the heart, Wei teleported dozens of feet back.

Wei's brow furrowed in confusion before he realized Yue's plan and played into it. Like a dog being taught a trick, the throne fell for Yue's tricks. It searched around for the heart until it found it, and once stepping on it, Wei would be teleported further back once more, saving the throne from Wei's onslaught.

Yue's illusion slowly dissipated into reality, and the throne chased after the real heart, finally reaching it and trying to crush it. Yet, it froze upon contact. However, the strength an outer god—even if it was solely its pet—possessed was unparalleled. It strained against the heart's control, and the crack Wei had created only grew larger and larger.

The entire world seemed to rumble below our feet. Feiyu's actions slowed, and he looked to Ruoming with a look of defeat on his normally cocky face.

"Ruoming," Feiyu said firmly. "We're going to summon a calamity if this continues."

Ruoming's thin brows drew together, and the stress on his normally stoic face was apparent. "We can't destroy the throne."

"I can do it."

"No," Ruoming insisted. His eyes were distant, like he was remembering something from a previous run.

The throne finally broke free from the heart, one of its legs tearing off of it. At this point, the throne was going to end up killing itself. Wei circled around it, threatening to strike and driving the throne back to the heart like a dog herding sheep.

> **Divinity Spirit of the Jade Moon is urging Divinity Supreme Commander of the Heavenly Hosts to retreat!**

> **Divinity God of Thunder is threatening to slay Divinity Supreme Commander of the Heavenly Hosts!**

Yang, Amelia, and Yue were unable to hold back the vicious duo any longer. Yuan and Cheng appeared behind Wei. Yuan lifted a large shield and brought it down on Wei's back.

Wei whipped around, wings still stretched out behind him. With a burst of his sponsor's spiritual energy, he sliced straight through Yuan's protective barrier, jousting his sword through Yuan's side.

Instead of healing Yuan like expected, Cheng slid between Wei and Yuan. He dragged a small, sharp object across Wei's legs.

At once, Wei's legs expanded grossly, massive bubbles appearing and causing him to collapse. It looked terribly similar to the disease in Wei's dungeon room. Wei instantly panicked, his eyes growing distant, his hands trembling while he helplessly watched his body get taken over by the toxin.

CHAPTER TWENTY-NINE

Archangel Michael's shadow became less and less translucent as he spent more spiritual energy to return to his real physical form, yellow sparks bursting behind him.

The god's glowing blue eyes latched onto Thor, and Archangel Michael cocked his head to the side. His long blond eyelashes couldn't mask his horrifying stare.

"You're getting on my nerves. Do you want me to kill your disciple?"

His voice was low and menacing. Archangel Michael whipped his sword around to throw Cheng back. Without even touching him, Cheng flew dozens of feet, slamming into the wall and letting out a sharp cry. He slumped onto the ground, his eyes fluttering shut. Yuan instantly tried looking over at Cheng, his gruff voice shouting out for him.

Warning! Severe karmic violation!

Thor, however, stopped Yuan from turning, continuing to control his body and bringing him up to face Archangel Michael. After a few seconds, Cheng's eyes opened, and he stumbled back to his feet, blood seeping through his shirt. He must have broken a handful of bones, but he quickly healed his own injuries.

"You think you run this place?" The deep, bellowing voice of Thor called out. "You're nothing! How dare you lay a hand on a disciple?"

Archangel Michael clicked his tongue, not seeming to have a single care in the world. After all, Archangel Michael thought he could avoid most consequences by virtue of his just intentions.

A low roar sounded from far beyond the citadel. The sound of thunder, having nothing to do with Thor or Feiyu, rang out.

The entire cave split apart, limestone crumbling down. I instantly ducked below Zhige, and the rest of us took cover.

But, it didn't stop there. More and more layers of the citadel split apart until all the upper layers of the citadel were exposed. A horrifying avalanche of debris tumbled straight for us.

With a flap of his wings, Archangel Michael quickly rushed around my party, scooping us into his arms. He brought his wings out all around him and used them to cover my party. One of his hands gently cupped my back and pulled me close.

Amelia was buried in the soft fur of her dire wolf, and she was utterly exhausted. Her entire body shook with the amount of effort it took to have summoned both the dire wolf and the serpent for such an extended period of time. She quickly retracted the dire wolf and collapsed against Archangel Michael.

Yang didn't look much better. He always looked effortlessly put together; but now, he wore the exhaustion in every part of his body. Yue, however, looked fine thanks to the help of her sponsor and Yang's healing. Wei took a moment to catch his breath, now that Archangel Michael was no longer directly supporting him.

Last was Archangel Michael. I finally met his eyes, and I was blown away by all that they held. They were just like the World's; they were so deep with so many variations of blue that it looked like they held the entire ocean.

His eyes twinkled brighter than stars in the night sky, and he flashed the most beautiful smile I'd ever seen.

"Peijin!" he said, thrilled. Cascading debris was smashing onto his body, but he didn't even flinch, his eyes fully trained on me. "This is such a blessing. I can't believe I finally get to meet you. I'm so excited that my heart is ready to burst from my chest."

I could see the karmic backlash eating into his flesh, but with each chunk it tore from his body, it was replaced instantaneously thanks to his unbelievable reserve of spiritual energy.

"You're going to end up in court again. Probably in jail, too," I said, trying to remain suave despite my own excitement at meeting him.

"Shunfeng'er said that's the point."

"Huh?"

"You're trying to summon a calamity, right? I can do a lot more if it'll help."

"Are you nuts? That's the last thing you should want."

"Are you kidding? Watching you is the most fun I've had in millennia. Things get so boring when I win all the time," he sighed dramatically.

The downpour of rocks finally stopped, and Archangel Michael folded his wings behind his back. I couldn't stop staring, utterly amazed by his full form.

However, it had become unsustainable by this point, and there were larger and larger chunks of flesh missing from his body with each passing second, even if they lasted for only a few moments. He returned to the smaller, semi-translucent form and scoped out Ruoming's party.

Thor didn't need to bring out his full form to shield his party members, since Yuan was already a very capable defender and the pair had good synergy. Thus, Yuan was able to protect the entire party with minimal interference.

Suddenly, a horrific moan sounded out—so deep I could feel it rumble through my entire body. With the citadel now ruined, the sky was finally visible.

I looked up to see a massive tentacle tearing a hole through the sky. It was black but with an iridescent sheen, making it appear white, green, or blue at different angles. It managed to grip onto the sky like it was something material and shatter it, sending black cracks through it.

I gulped loudly. A terrible chill travelled down my spine at the overwhelming display of power before us.

"H-Hey, Peijin?" I heard Yue squeak, gently moving closer until her hand was gripping my arm. "This is all a part of your plan, right?"

"I sure hope so."

"You better do more than hope, or I'll fucking kill you!"

"You might not be able to with how that thing looks . . ."

Yang interjected, looking up at me while clutching his stomach, evidently out of breath and cramping. "Peijin, I swear to god . . ."

Amelia was trembling like a leaf as she looked up at it. She squeezed her eyes shut and brought her hands over her ears to mask the horrible sound of the outer god's groans.

> Divinity Far Shooting Queen of Beasts contemplates interfering.

> Divinity The One Who Fights in Front warns Divinity Far Shooting Queen of Beasts to stand down.

> Divinity Far Shooting Queen of Beasts bristles.

> Divinity Far Shooting Queen of Beasts argues that Divinity The One Who Fights in Front has been trying to take Amelia as her disciple the entire time.

Archangel Michael, sensing the impending chaos, walked up behind Amelia and gently placed his hands on her shoulders. Although he was far smaller than earlier, his presence had its own powerful effect. Standing beside him felt like being wrapped in a warm weighted blanket. It was unbelievable how comforting just the sight of him was.

Wei looked up at his sponsor, his eyes glimmering slightly with admiration. Wei, too, was a divinity. Once upon a time, he might have even rivaled Archangel Michael. But Wei had long fallen from those heights and was not a protector. Being able to rely on the security of another must have been terribly reassuring.

The throne burst out from the rubble, leaping up and down at the sight of its beloved parent. One of the massive tentacles reached down slowly, searching for the throne.

"Wei, Yue—same plan. Let's wrap this up quickly," I said before turning to Archangel Michael. "Will you hold back Ruoming's party?"

"Wow, you really do ask for the impossible. I thought to myself many times that your party members must be crazy to carry out your ideas. But now that I'm here, how can I possibly say no?"

"I'm glad to hear that you find me convincing."

"You're even more witty in person! You're so charming. I knew you were a perfect match for Feiyu."

Despite the stressful circumstances, my jaw dropped, and I stared at Archangel Michael in utter silence. My mortification was obvious, but he only gave me another one of his brilliant smiles before vanishing. He wasn't even in his full form, but I had complete faith in his abilities.

"Yang and Amelia . . ." My eyes slowly travelled to Amelia, but I looked away before our eyes could meet. "I'll need the two of you to rescue us when we need it."

A rumble echoed out once more as the sky split apart more and more, and lightning appeared from the black smoke forming around the outer god.

Wei charged toward the throne, his ribbon flowing out beside him for support. He brought his sword high up above him and slashed at the tentacle of the outer god. Spiritual energy erupted from his blade, slashing the outer god, which instantly recoiled.

Wei's hit split the tentacle apart, but it easily meshed back together, ultimately unaffected by his attack. Still, his mere presence terrified the throne, which instinctively searched for the heart.

Using the same trick, Yue created an illusion of the heart. She turned around, signaling for Amelia to assist.

"Amelia, find where the heart is! Is it lost beneath the rubble?"

Amelia used her silver cuff to spawn the dire wolf. She hopped on and let it guide her toward the heart while Yue moved in her general direction.

Yang whipped around, using his staff as a barrier for Ruoming's party. The moment they tried to pass Archangel Michael, he'd smash them straight back with an invisible border.

"Peijin! Liu Peijin!" Ruoming shouted, his expression wild. "What the fuck are you doing?!"

It wasn't my fault I was more creative than Ruoming. No wonder it took him so many arcs to eventually "win" the apocalypse. He was merely a reader, confined to the world inside the pages.

Disciple Yang has activated Alternates!

Dozens of copies of him sprung out from his real body, which quickly got lost in the chaos. They all worked on keeping Ruoming's party restrained. Archangel Michael did not make any attempts at harming the disciples. Rather, he worked alongside Yang to keep them trapped like animals in a playpen.

Yue and Amelia led the throne to the heart, and it quickly attempted to destroy it once more. Once again, the heart defended itself, sending the throne spiraling as it took more and more damage.

An outer god is infuriated by the behavior of numerous gods and disciples!

From the body of the outer god, disgusting black liquid was dripping down, plopping onto the ground. When it landed, the ground would smoke before the black liquid sank through it, burning straight into the center of the Earth.

The outer god reached for its pet, and the throne was struggling to find it through its clouded judgment and fear. At once, I spun Zhige and leapt up, dragging it down the outer god's entire tentacle.

With Zhige's potent spiritual energy, it took longer for the outer god to heal, since Zhige's strikes burned the outer god's flesh. The outer god let out what could only be described as a shriek—but it sounded much more like a haunting cry. There was nothing comparable to the sound that it let out.

One of the tentacles aimed for me, but instead of coming straight for me, it branched out into dozens of different sharp branches. One skewered straight through me, and I winced.

After piercing me, it continued to branch off inside my body. I struggled to stay calm, despite the sensation of dozens, if not hundreds, of knives piercing deeper and deeper into my body.

> **[Observers Chat]**
> **Socrates:** Jia Li, did you think you could fight an outer god??? Get out of there!

> **Polling ongoing . . .**
> **A. 49%**
> **B. 51%**

I squinted at the poll results. With so many gods getting involved on behalf of my party, more were voting on behalf of my party since there were more connections.

My party was legions ahead of Ruoming's party. At the very least, there must have been hundreds, if not thousands, of gods and observers invested in my story. I was confident that more would continue interfering. Well, I guess I just lost all the observers . . .

Blood burst from my mouth. I tried to pull myself off the main branch, but it was like the tentacle was barbed. Each tug viciously tore through my flesh; even with my heightened healing, the internal injuries would be utterly devastating.

> **Divinity Spirit of the Jade Moon is deeply conflicted!**

> **Divinity the Blessed Martial God of Salvation reminds Divinity Spirit of the Jade Moon of her history of inaction.**

> **Divinity Spirit of the Jade Moon flushes red at the mention.**

A golden staff burst up from beside me. Yang, or one of his alternates, appeared, spinning the staff in his hand. He slashed through the main branch protruding from me.

CHAPTER THIRTY

I began falling toward the ground, and I quickly reoriented myself, landing on Zhige and having him lift me.

Yang spawned more and more alternates of himself, but with each one, the agony strewn across his face was apparent. His alternates' breathing was ragged, and blood was streaming from their noses from the exertion.

Although detached from the main body of the outer god, the branches inside of me continued to move and grow. At this point, I could feel them travelling into my chest, and I could hardly mask my panic anymore.

> **Divinity Spirit of the Jade Moon is descending into the arc!**

I collapsed onto my loyal blade, clutching my chest. Blood was coming out of my eyes, nose, and mouth now—falling onto Zhige in flat droplets. Zhige's red eye swirled back and forth in a complete panic.

> **Warning! Severe karmic violation!**

A woman in swirling white robes with blue detailing fluttered before me. Her skin was ghostly pale, but her cheeks and nose were a beautiful and rosy pink. Beside her was a large floating white rabbit, whose red eyes stared into me.

"Consider this amends for my past errors," Chang'e said, her voice so delicate and soft I could hardly hear her.

I wanted to reply to her, but I couldn't muster the strength to speak. My eyes began to flutter shut. Her hands worked meticulously to pick the branches out from deep beneath my skin and quickly heal the wounds.

The branches came out in long, blood-covered strands; it was like Chang'e was pulling parasites out of my skin. The sight disgusted me, and I quickly turned away and stopped myself from vomiting in my mouth.

Each brush of her skin against mine sent a cooling and soothing sensation through my entire body. It was the most divine and relaxing feeling I'd ever experienced. I let out a sigh of relief, shutting my eyes again.

Chang'e's white rabbit came to my side and bit my finger firmly. I let out a startled yelp and jolted up, looking surprised. Chang'e's lips were pursed in a thin line, like she was annoyed that I was truly taking advantage of her presence at this moment.

But just beside me, Yang wasn't faring much better.

His head had gone limp, and he could no longer keep his eyes open. One of his alternates vanished into thin air. Then another. And another.

With less potential targets, it only became harder to keep Ruoming's party in check and the outer god distracted. Not only that, but Yang was critically injured now, too.

I knew Chang'e would have wanted to get out of this situation as fast as possible, especially with the poll putting her at risk. After all, she was the sensible one and the one insisting the other gods didn't get involved.

But here she was, whether it was out of sense of duty or pity, treating my wounds.

Now, she had to treat Yang as well. She couldn't walk away from his suffering now that it was so apparent. Yang was whimpering from pain, his body twitching wildly while he fought to keep himself awake.

After only a few moments, I felt significantly better, but nearly all of Yang's alternates had vanished until none remained.

His staff shrunk, and he began hurdling toward the ground.

> **Divinity Great Sage Equaling Heaven is descending into the arc.**

> **Warning! A calamity is forming!**

> **Warning! A calamity is forming!**

Sun Wukong appeared as a small boy with wild blond hair and a long blond tail. But, the moment he caught Yang before he could smash into the ground, Karma had finally had enough.

All the descended gods were viciously attacked by a powerful wave of karmic restraints. Yellow sparks appeared all over their bodies, instantly tearing into their skin.

> **[Observers Chat]**
> **Aslan:** Quick!! Give the gods more prayer candles!!

Sun Wukong let out a mix of a shriek and a howl before quickly disappearing, instantly giving up now that Yang wasn't a guaranteed fatality.

> **Divinity Great Sage Equaling Heaven has been expelled from the arc.**

> **Divinity Great Sage Equaling Heaven is shrieking and howling at his screen!**

> **Divinity Great Sage Equaling Heaven is pounding his keyboard.**

> **Divinity Great Sage Equaling Heaven says he has never been treated in such a manner.**

> **Demon Great Sage Who Pacifies Heaven points and laughs at Divinity Great Sage Equaling Heaven's weakness.**

In truth, Sun Wukong was probably the strongest god following my party. That also meant he was punished the most for interfering.

Chang'e worked frantically, looking with great fright at the yellow sparks that quickly appeared all around her. She let out a gasp and brought her hands up as if trying to shield herself, but they quickly tore into her body.

Not even her small rabbit was spared. It let out a terrified squeal as thousands of sparks tore it apart. But, just as quickly as it was injured, it regenerated. It glared at me before flying over to Chang'e, checking on its master.

Chang'e was trembling slightly, tears in her eyes. Her wounds healed almost instantly, but for someone trying to avoid conflict, this was the worst possible outcome. Her rabbit affectionately licked her, and her mood improved somewhat.

"My debt to you is paid off," Chang'e said smoothly, her face contorted. "But I still can't let Yang die. Your debt is to me now."

"Yang needs you."

Chang'e flew down, her robes fluttering. She found where Yang was lying unconscious on the ground. If it weren't for Sun Wukong, he would have been long dead. She quickly got to work.

The outer god, however, continued its onslaught, more and more of it slowly descending as its long tentacles reached toward the ground. It thrashed violently, reaching for any moving creature in its vicinity.

The throne ran toward it, leaping up at the tentacles every time they got low enough. However, Yue and Amelia would quickly redirect it back to the heart.

Wei ran up to Chang'e, protecting her from the outer god while she created the tiniest barrier around her to keep herself safe from the attacks.

I lifted Zhige when I finally made it to the ground. Our spiritual energies intertwined, but Karma quickly latched onto me next, biting into my skin. I winced from the pain, but I only fed Zhige with more and more of my spiritual energy.

> **Warning! A calamity is forming!**

Ruoming turned to me from behind the strong defense of Archangel Michael, his eyes wide. "Peijin. Goddammit, stop it! You're going to kill all of us!"

> **Divinity Far Shooting Queen of Beasts contemplates interfering.**

> **Divinity The One Who Fights in Front is threatening Divinity Far Shooting Queen of Beasts.**

> **Divinity Far Shooting Queen of Beasts is descending into the arc!**

The body of a young girl with long ginger hair descended, resembling the one that had previously interfered to save Amelia. She raised a glowing gold bow into the air, and it glimmered beautifully.

"You don't need to protect me!" Amelia cried, noticing the actions of the god. Amelia brought a hand up to protect her face from the ever-increasing winds. One of the tentacles approached her, but through the dire wolf, she easily dodged its movements, opting to run up the tentacles.

But, with one powerful flick, the outer god sent Amelia flying with a shriek, and she flew through the air while clinging onto the dire wolf, trusting it to land safely.

Artemis didn't focus on saving Amelia. Rather, she loaded an arrow and pulled it taut against the string. She closed an eye and aimed it straight at the outer god.

The shimmering golden arrow shot straight at the outer god. Behind it, a beautiful trail of glistening blue and white sparks erupted like stars in the night sky. The arrow struck a tentacle of the outer god, and golden lightning travelled up its entire body.

Its tentacle shriveled back, shrinking in size before vanishing into a massive pile of black goop. Artemis looked over her shoulder to check on Amelia, who safely landed with the dire wolf, before preparing her next arrow.

> **Divinity The One Who Fights in Front is infuriated by Divinity Far Shooting Queen of Beast's interference!**

> **Divinity The One Who Fights in Front warns that Divinity Far Shooting Queen of Beasts is making enemies with powers far stronger than her.**

> **Polling ongoing . . .**
> **A. 49%**
> **B. 51%**

Artemis's face twisted into a scowl as she pulled the arrow taut against its string. Unlike the previous arrow, this one was entirely different. Golden birds, bears, and deer appeared behind her as she drew the arrow.

When she finally released it, the heads and bodies of forest creatures appeared all around the arrow. It exploded as it struck the outer god, the various creatures travelling up its body.

> **WARNING!**

> **WARNING! A CALAMITY IS FORMING!**

If the outer god's entrance wasn't horrifying enough, the calamity was far worse. The repeated karmic violations had reached such a degree that a calamity was now forming.

Dark storm clouds began to swirl in the sky like a forming typhoon. The cloud reached down, swirling around violently. The wind picked up faster and faster until I could feel myself being swept up into it.

I instinctively drove Zhige into the ground, trying to keep myself rooted. But, the wind was picking up far too fast, and it tore both me and Zhige from the ground.

I let out a startled gasp as I was thrown into the air, being sucked into the violent typhoon. Water began to rain down, whipping against my skin with such force that it was slicing right through me despite my high amount of spiritual energy.

I looked around frantically for my party, but I could hardly orient myself with how violently I was being flung around.

"Zhige!" I exclaimed, staring at the blade as it grew larger, attempting to hook onto anything. My hoodie was dragging me forward as well, but both of their powers were futile in the face of the calamity. Even the long arms of the outer god were being pulled into the powerful typhoon.

For a moment, it felt like Zhige and the hoodie might pull me out from the worst of the storm, but the winds picked up even more, and I went spiraling into it, unable to even open my eyes without fear of them getting sliced apart by flying pieces of water and debris.

I let out an accepting sigh. There was only so much I could do. Having taken the gamble of summoning an outer god and calamity with nowhere else to go, I had acted rashly. If this was my punishment, so be it.

Suddenly, I felt a hand grip my hoodie, pulling me back in. For a moment, I opened my eyes in shock and saw Feiyu.

His large hand was gripping onto the front of my hoodie, struggling to pull me in. His other was wrapped around his sword, which was embedded deep into a massive piece of debris. His eyes were squinted, struggling to stay open and on me.

I turned around, wondering how he'd bypassed Archangel Michael. I immediately got my answer.

By now, everyone was simply focused on avoiding being sucked into the storm. Even Archangel Michael was straining, flapping his massive wings to keep himself rooted to the ground.

"Let go! I'll be fine!" I shouted, Feiyu's grip on me slipping with every second.

"Grab onto me!"

"I can't!"

I reached out my hand, trying to move it forward to latch onto Feiyu before the wind would tear it back. I winced painfully, feeling my muscles tear with the effort. I forced my eyes open, looking around frantically. A tiny but sharp piece of limestone instantly sliced across my left eye, rendering me half blind as blood poured down my face.

"Jiejie!" Feiyu cried out. He was using his entire body's strength to try and pull me back into him.

"Where are the kids?"

"Fuck, Peijin! Grab onto me!"

Feiyu strained, his jaw clenched tightly from pain. Finally, he was forced to let go of me. I felt my breath catch in my throat before I relaxed, accepting whatever was to come.

Then, I felt his calloused hand grip mine, pulling me in firmly before his arm wrapped around my shoulders. I looked up at him, my brow furrowed.

Blood was streaming from various cuts all over his body. His eyes, especially, had been torn into from the water droplets and limestone shards. Feiyu attempted to blink away the blood, but he couldn't mask the pain.

My jaw fell slightly. "I told you to just let me go. Look at yourself!"

"If you're going to die, die somewhere far away from me," Feiyu said, his voice tense. His grip on me tightened.

I wanted to call him out for being the same bastard that was willing to kill me if it meant winning the arc, but he wouldn't know what I was referring to anyway.

> **Divinity Supreme Commander of the Heavenly Hosts is lending Disciple Peijin spiritual energy!**

With the gifted spiritual energy, I created a thin, protective barrier around me and Feiyu. "Where's Yuan?"

"You sucked all the spiritual energy out of him."

I huffed, struggling against Feiyu's arm, but he held me tightly against him. For now, the thin barrier was protecting both of us from the storm.

The storm split apart, and right in the center was a bright orange beast.

The faceless being had eyes that could not see, ears that could not hear, a torso with no organs, and intestines that could not digest. It was pure, unadulterated chaos.

Its only undebatable trait was its resemblance to a dog—petite, coated in orange fur, and on all fours.

Hundun. One of the Four Perils.

Apart from its nonsensical appearance, its mind was also a muddled universe. It antagonized the upstanding and befriended the corrupt, with no ability to distinguish from right or wrong. It was a creature completely beyond redemption.

Artemis turned her small head to stare straight through me. Shivers instantly travelled up my entire body.

Must I strike that, too?

Her deep voice echoed through my entire mind, and I jumped, terrified by the sound.

"What's wrong?" Feiyu instantly asked.

"Nothing."

Although Artemis only spoke a few words without any malicious intent, I could sense how much power she held just from the way she spoke. It was truly horrifying.

I quirked a brow. So, she was also fully aware that I was trying to destroy the entire scenario.

You know what I want.

At the end of the day, Artemis had her eyes set on Amelia this entire time. At the end of this arc, Amelia would have another opportunity to choose whether or not she finally wanted a sponsor.

I met Artemis's eyes with much effort, doing my best to not tremble before her and show my inferiority. I gave her a curt nod, and she turned away, pulling the bowstring taut once more.

CHAPTER THIRTY-ONE

Hundun was one of the four main calamities that could be summoned in the case of major karmic violations. There was also Qiongqi, Taowu, and Taotie. The four of them were monstrous beings that represented different forms of chaos and evil, greed, aggression, and cruelty.

They had been banished to the four corners of the universe, but they would be temporarily freed to wreak havoc as a result of the karmic balance being severely disrupted.

Hundun was the symbol of primordial chaos and disorder, although it was certainly the cutest of the Four Perils. Qiongqi embodied aggression, cruelty, and evil intent, enjoying slaughtering the most righteous people.

Taowu was known for recklessness and stubbornness, holding a complete disdain for all authority. Taotie symbolized gluttony and excessive greed, consuming every single thing in its path.

Now, Hundun was flapping its four white wings frantically in the air, as though it was struggling to keep its meaty orange body afloat. It hadn't made a significant move yet—it was far too stunned at being summoned for the first time in what must have been a millennium.

The outer god temporarily flinched back at Hundun's presence before it became even more aggravated. Outer gods and calamities were the most powerful beings in all of *Surviving My First Run*, and they despised one another. Even the most powerful gods like Archangel Michael couldn't stand a chance against their wrath.

Artemis drew in a tight breath, one of her large, green eyes twitching from what I could only assume was sheer rage at being manipulated once more by me. Her long, golden eyelashes fluttered as her hand pressed against her cheek and she fired the glistening arrow.

It struck Hundun straight in the chest, and its six legs immediately jolted.

> **Divinity The One Who Fights in Front is descending into the arc.**

"You've bitten off more than you can chew, Peijin."

Feiyu's soft voice was clear over the chaos, and I could feel him loosen his tight grip on me.

"You and Ruoming were the ones who stopped me from executing my original plan," I replied.

"Ruoming is going to kill me . . ."

"Ha!"

Before I could come up with a snappy response, Athena's form appeared in full armor. She was wearing a large silver helmet, and she must have stood fifteen feet tall. Her sword and shield were drawn, and large, fluttering brown robes whipped around in the chaos behind her.

"Artemis!" Athena roared.

> **Polling ongoing . . .**
> **A. 50%**
> **B. 50%**

> **Polling will conclude shortly.**

Finally getting its bearings, Hundun grew massively in size until it rivaled that of the outer god's tentacles. At once, it slammed into the ground, causing a massive earthquake beneath our feet.

Feiyu wrapped his body around me, leaping off the ground as a massive ravine split open beneath us. Lava burst out along with hot rock fragments and toxic gases. I could feel its heat singe my skin, and I ducked into Feiyu's black coat to shield myself.

Hundun reoriented its body until—where I could only assume his head would be—it was facing Artemis. Artemis flinched but drew her bow and loaded an arrow. She pulled in more and more of her spiritual energy to grow in size, while Athena charged toward her.

With lightning speed, Hundun darted forward, attempting to slam into Artemis's body with its own. Artemis attempted to dodge, but Hundun was far too large and powerful. It reached Artemis, and Athena leapt in between, drawing her sword to block the attack.

Lava continued to erupt from the ravine, but Feiyu lifted me, dragging me away. I peeked over his arm, surveying my surroundings. Among this destruction, I needed any of these gods to destroy both the throne and the heart to leave the entire scenario in ruins.

I scanned the chaos for my party, which was made easier thanks to the bright colored indicators above their heads. Yue and Amelia were still doing her best to guide the throne to the heart, though the outer god was now a major distraction, as the throne was torn between its fear and desire to run to its owner.

The outer god brought down a tentacle, trying to slam it straight down on Yue. She quickly created an illusion and slipped out, but only by a few millimeters. The illusion quickly flickered, wavering as her exhaustion grew.

The storm was pulling her in as well. Although she was further from its center than Feiyu and me, she undoubtedly felt the effects, doing her best to stay rooted with her spear.

Amelia, however, was lagging behind. The dire wolf was dragging its claws into the crumbling ground, but it couldn't help but be tugged slowly, closer and closer to the storm. However, upon spotting Artemis, Amelia's gaze hardened.

She jumped from the back of the dire wolf and lifted her silver cuff into the air, the dire wolf quickly vanishing into the cuff. Then, one of the creatures on the cuff began to glow, and the serpent appeared, no longer injured. Amelia must have exuded an incredible amount of spiritual energy to heal it.

It threw Amelia into the air, and she grabbed onto its whiskers. Artemis's eyes quickly lit up with surprise before they filled with warmth. It must have been fulfilling to see how much her earlier sacrifice had paid off, helping Amelia grow into herself.

Artemis used more of her spiritual energy on her attacks and Amelia, but Hundun was far too powerful. Now growing accustomed to what it felt like to move freely once more, Hundun became more and more violent, smashing its large body against any surface near it, including the enraged outer god.

I looked around for the rest of my party members, wanting to ensure their safety, as well.

Yang now stood straight up, Chang'e just behind him. Chang'e was shivering like a leaf, utterly horrified at the scene playing out before her, but she hadn't returned to the heavenly realm yet. As far as I was concerned, that was more than Sun Wukong could say.

Her white and blue robes flew out behind her, and with all the fire and lava spreading around us, they caught their light and reflected beautiful hues of gold and oranges. The lava had the same effect on Yang's eyes, and his jaw was firmly set now that he was reassured by her presence.

The outer god flung out its large arm straight at Chang'e and Yang. Yang lengthened his staff, striking it just enough to slow its speed.

Chang'e let out a frightened cry and moved to cover her face, sending massive waves erupting from behind her as they crashed straight into the outer god's tentacle.

Chang'e sniffled, looking at the retracting tentacle with great fear, her hands trembling. Her white rabbit was nestled into the crook of her neck and shoulder, trying to hide from the chaos. "This is terrifying!"

Yang ignored her, raising his staff to strike again at the overreaching tentacles.

"Where's your party?" I shouted at Feiyu, my voice getting drowned out by all the chaos.

"I don't know! Your hair keeps getting in my face—" Feiyu began spitting, strands of my hair getting caught in his mouth. I jerked away in disgust, slapping his arm.

"Let me go, then! I didn't ask for you to hold me."

"But you're so small. You'll just fly away!"

"What the hell did you say to me? I'm above average height, you rude bastard!"

I kicked and pushed against him while he began running further from the storm, doing his best to pull us out of the terrible winds. I scanned around for his party.

Ruoming, Qijing, Cheng, and Yuan were all huddled together, with Ruoming fighting directly against the outer god.

Ruoming managed to bring his blade down on the outer god multiple times, leaving deep cuts in the tentacled flesh. It was clearly not his first time battling one, and I couldn't help but freeze for a moment in amazement.

"Whoa."

But, it wasn't long before the outer god sent Ruoming flying with one connecting hit.

Ruoming brought his arms to his chest to protect himself as he went flying, spinning in the air to try and latch onto something and avoid the bursts of fire and lava. At once, Yuan, aided by Thor, fabricated a protective layer around him to prevent any catastrophic injuries.

I pounded furiously on Feiyu. "Let me go! I need to get to my party!"

As always, he completely ignored me. He clamped his hand over my mouth again to shut me up. This time, instead of just trying to pry off his hand, I bit down firmly on the flesh of his palm.

He let out a surprised yelp before dropping me instantly. I rolled across the ground, quickly steadying myself. My grip tightened on Zhige as I ran back toward the storm, where all the gods were, along with my party.

I couldn't be concerned with whatever Ruoming's party was doing on the outskirts. It was far more important to find my party members and Archangel Michael, since he was supposed to be watching over Ruoming.

As I got closer, the winds picked up their deadly speeds once more. The small shield of spiritual energy around me flickered, growing worse with each strike. Finally, I caught a glimpse of the glowing halo.

I wanted to cry out in relief at the sight of Archangel Michael, still on the battlefield. Behind him were Wei, Chang'e, and Yang. He had fully extended his wings, creating a barrier around the group.

Yang was already looking much better, and I gulped, knowing that Chang'e might decide to quickly jump ship once she knew he wasn't going to die.

Wei was standing back to back with Archangel Michael. He fought back furiously against the relentless onslaught of the outer god, but all of us knew how futile the fight was.

None of us could win against the outer god. It was only using a percentage of its strength. And the calamity was far, far stronger.

Hundun was now jumping up and down on the citadel grounds. It leapt dozens of feet into the air before crashing back down, creating vicious quakes with each landing. The floor beneath it split deeper and deeper, yet Hundun continued relentlessly.

I suddenly felt a hand on my shoulder, and expecting it to be Feiyu or Ruoming, I whipped around furiously. But, it was the bruised and battered Yue looking up at me. One of her eyes had swollen shut, and clinging onto her leg was an equally beaten Amelia.

CHAPTER THIRTY-TWO

"Peijin. What the fuck?!"

I grabbed onto Yue's hand, and at once, a spiritual energy barrier appeared around both her and Amelia.

"Amelia, where's your wolf and serpent?"

She looked up at me, completely drained. Her typically lively blue eyes were almost a dark gray, reflecting no light. "I can't summon them. They're too injured."

Suddenly, Amelia teared up and furiously wiped at her face with a tattered sleeve. "The outer god struck my wolf."

I bit my lower lip, looking at Yue. She avoided my gaze before finally speaking.

"Peijin. I don't think we're going to make it through this one."

"Just hold on a bit longer. It's almost over. The citadel can't handle much more of this before the entire thing is destroyed."

"It's going to take us down with it."

"That's why I'm telling you to hold on."

"You're fucking crazy. Sick in the head," Yue snapped before she sighed and rested her forehead on my shoulder. "Can I have some of that?"

"What?"

"Your spiritual energy. It feels so good," she murmured, practically dozing off on me.

I shoved her back. "Ask Chang'e. Leave Amelia with me."

Amelia wanted to refuse, but she was too exhausted to start another fight. And now that the situation had become this dire, she relented.

"Are you leaving me alone?" Yue asked.

"I'm going to resolve this. I'm the one who started it," I said simply, lifting Amelia.

I piggybacked Amelia and adjusted her arms around my neck. I moved my Boundless Bag so it operated like a seat for her, and she hooked her legs around my torso.

"Don't tell me you're going to do something rash again," Yue grumbled.

"I won't," I promised.

Disciple Yue activated Lie Detector!

Lie Detector has confirmed Disciple Peijin's words as false.

"Peijin . . ."

The ground rumbled violently beneath us. I could feel the air around us getting hotter and hotter. It was finally getting to the point where even the air was toxic from all the fumes, and I could feel my lungs burning.

"I have Amelia with me," I reassured Yue, "so, just trust me. And buy something to protect your lungs if you're going to stay near the ground."

"Peijin," Yue repeated nervously, grabbing my sleeve.

"Go to Chang'e. She's about to leave the moment Yang is better."

"Yang? What happened to Yang?!" Yue asked nervously, worry written all over her face. My eyes widened in surprise at seeing such an expression from her. It didn't suit her one bit.

I let out a loud groan. "How about you go over there and see? Stop chit chatting with me right before we all die."

Yue looked like she had a million more things to say to me, but all she did was grip my shoulder for a moment before running off.

I adjusted my Boundless Bag slightly, opening it to pull out the pigeon's lung. It felt like so long ago that I fought the serpent.

"Amelia, put this in your mouth."

She bit down on it and began to breathe through it. I didn't bother buying one for myself. With the amount I would be speaking, it would only hinder me.

Divinity God of Fate and Fortune is lending Disciple Amelia spiritual energy!

Her eyes widened at the notification, and I stuck my tongue out at her cheekily. "I'll look out for you. Heal the serpent and the wolf. Let me know if you need more."

I threw Zhige forward and, reading my mind, it quickly grew. I stepped onto it, leading it toward where Artemis and Athena were currently fighting Hundun.

Athena originally descended to punish Artemis, but now both of them were fighting for their lives against Hundun. It must have been the first time that these gods have had to fight against a calamity.

"Athena! Artemis!" I shouted, flying toward them before leaping off Zhige, running. The winds were terribly strong again, and at any moment, I could be swept off my feet.

> **Divinity Ears That Hear What Comes on the Wind is lending Disciple Peijin spiritual energy!**

I dug my feet into the ground, one hand holding Zhige and the other clutching Amelia.

"Liu Peijin!" Athena roared furiously, glaring at me. The moment she turned to face me, Hundun shot a blast of dark spiritual energy straight at her.

It was almost like Athena teleported. One moment, she was in the path of Hundun's strike, and the next, she was right in front of me, her sword pointed at my throat. She was countless feet taller than me, and I swallowed loudly.

"Do you want to drag everyone down with you?!"

"Not exactly . . ."

I watched as Artemis loaded another arrow. What looked like miniature moons of all different phases spilled from the arrow. She shot it straight at Hundun and struck the beast. It shook violently before flying straight at her.

"Kill me and lose your contract," I told Athena, bringing my hand up to brazenly push her sword from my neck. "I want you and Artemis to restrain the throne. I'll handle Hundun."

She looked at me for a moment before letting out a booming, mocking laugh. She placed a large hand on her stomach and howled with laughter.

"Are you going to kill Hundun? Such hubris. You may have been able to get away with manipulating the gods to do your dirty work, but this is no joke. You've caused true mayhem."

Amelia's grip on my shoulders tightened, and my hand that was wrapped around her legs gently patted her.

"Restrain the throne. You'll fail otherwise," I said slowly.

> **Polling has concluded! The final votes are as follows.**
> **A. 51%**
> **B. 49%**

My eyes shot wide open at the results. My party . . .

Before Athena could fire a quippy response, she suddenly froze. Blue and yellow sparks burst straight through her chest.

Her eyes went wide. Right in the middle of her body, extending from her chest down to her hips, was a massive hole. Blood immediately poured from the wound, and she stumbled back, bringing a hand up to touch the edges of the wound, as if not believing what just happened.

"No!" I shouted, quickly looking around.

It wasn't just Athena. Archangel Michael, Chang'e, Artemis . . . All of them had suffered the same mortal wound.

With a loud crashing sound, Archangel Michael collapsed onto the ground, blood pouring from his chest. Still, he kept his wings extended to protect my party members. Just beside him, Chang'e was wailing loudly, her robes soaked bright red with blood and her rabbit failing to comfort her.

Wei turned around in shock, instantly running to the two of them. Yang and Yue were left to defend the rest of the group.

Thousands of gods are in complete shock, witnessing the scene.

Demon Great Sage Who Pacifies Heaven is relieved he returned before the poll ended.

Divinity Great Sage Equaling Heaven is looking at the scene in complete and utter shock.

Demon Abyssal Kraken of Black Seas is trembling.

Divinity Ears That Hear What Comes on the Wind is staring blankly at his screen.

The World brings her hands to her mouth.

Divinity Ears That Hear What Comes on the Wind is descending into the arc!

[Observers Chat]
MoldyBlanket: And that's exactly what Jia Li deserves ^^
CannedWorms: Athena right as always. Displays of hubris
BMelv: Lmao she's trying to get everyone killed at this rate

I ran forward to try and catch Athena, but all I could do was soften her fall.

Artemis was just behind her, collapsed onto the ground. Various forest animals swarmed all around her, protecting her body from further injuries.

"Surely your core isn't where your heart is, right?" I laughed in a panic, looking down at Athena's injuries in complete and utter shock.

With how many gods became involved in the arc, I figured there was no way I would have lost the poll. Especially against Thor? Only Thor??

Athena mouthed a threat at me, but thankfully I couldn't read her lips. I frantically scrolled through the Azure Dragon Store, but I knew anything that could heal a god of her strength was probably far out of my budget.

You have purchased Elite Healing Elixir.

50,000 stars used.

I poured the elixir into her mouth, and her wound healed. But, it was at an agonizingly slow pace. The inflicted wound must have also had spiritual energy infused to prevent healing.

"W-Wait," I said frantically, "don't return yet."

Athena snarled.

"You haven't restrained the throne yet."

"I'm . . . going to kill you."

I rolled my eyes. "Don't tell me you can't even restrain a throne. It's going to be embarrassing when I accomplish it on my own. Besides, do you want to be the first god to return? The rest are still down here."

I was using the exact same tactic as when I'd first met Athena. Baiting her into a game always guaranteed her involvement, because her ego wouldn't allow anyone to think less of her.

Besides, my words were true. Chang'e was bawling her eyes out, but her hands still diligently moved to repair Archangel Michael's wounds. I squinted and noticed a bright red figure standing just beside Archangel Michael.

It must have been Shunfeng'er. Before becoming one of the gods serving Mazu, he was a demon she destroyed. Thus, he still had the appearance of one. His skin was a fiery red, and he had short white hair.

Honestly, he was quite ugly.

He knelt down beside Archangel Michael and Chang'e, saying something inaudible to the both of them. Chang'e looked at him in surprise before nodding her head repeatedly, and Archangel Michael reached up to grab Shunfeng'er's hand.

I watched in complete and utter shock as blue sparks swarmed around Shunfeng'er until they covered his entire figure. Then, what emerged was an entirely new being.

Sort of.

Instead of the red demon, a divinity appeared. With the long wings of Archangel Michael, the flowing white and blue robes of Chang'e, and luscious blond hair, ordained with beautiful traditional jewels. It was a merged version of Archangel Michael and Chang'e.

" . . . Since when could that guy do that?"

I turned back down to Athena and pointed. "Do you want to be known for being lesser and weaker than that C-tier god? Get up, Athena."

Despite my harsh words, I was trembling like a leaf. She really was going to kill me one day.

Athena's wound healed slightly faster, and she struggled for her sword. But, Shunfeng'er landed just beside the two of us with a loud thud. He was now holding Archangel Michael's sword. I looked at him in genuine shock.

"It's temporary. It'll be gone soon. Peijin, end this now."

"Uh-huh . . ." I said, stunned by the creature beside me. It leaned over Athena, and using Chang'e's skills, Shunfeng'er managed to stop Athena's bleeding, though he was still unable to heal the wound. He moved to Artemis next, parting the animals and reaching her battered body.

For a moment, I was frozen with amazement. That seemed like a terribly overpowered skill. I certainly didn't assign it, and I was stunned that Karma wasn't throwing a fit.

Beside me, Athena stood up shakily, her breathing coming under control. Without a word to me, she turned toward the throne, hobbling toward it. I could see the massive throne through the hole in her body.

"Peijin," Amelia's squeaky voice called out. She removed the pigeon's lung from her mouth to speak to me clearly. "Feiyu-shushu and Ruoming-shushu are coming."

I practically jumped out of my skin. If those two wanted to kill me right now, there was no way I could survive. But instead, Feiyu appeared before me, a stupid grin on his face.

"Wow, pissing off the great Athena. Who knew you had the balls to do that?"

Ruoming was next, not even looking at me. "This is all wrong."

Once Athena and Artemis were back on their feet, though still only a percentage as powerful as they had been, they searched for the throne. Thankfully, now that they had been significantly weakened, karmic restraints weren't acting as harshly on them.

I shot them a look, and once Artemis gave me a slight nod, I turned back to Shunfeng'er, Feiyu, and Ruoming.

[Party Chat]
Peijin: Stay alive. I'll take care of the rest.

Amelia was clinging onto me, and Feiyu cocked his head. "Carrying your kid into a cosmic war is a bold move."

"I'm the best person to take care of her right now." I looked at Shunfeng'er. "How long do you have?"

"Fifteen minutes."

"Well, shit."

Ruoming was eyeing me silently.

Feiyu tapped his foot impatiently. "So, what's your genius plan this time?"

"Artemis and Athena will restrain the throne with the heart. We provoke the calamity until it destroys the entire citadel, including the heart and the throne. It'll be banished afterward, since the karmic violation will end, and we can return to the station before the outer god kills us. We need to use the calamity because the outer god will never kill its own pet."

"And you did this just to beat me," Ruoming said coldly.

"This wasn't plan A."

Hundun, realizing the lack of attention he was receiving, awkwardly turned its body to face us. It was both hilarious and mortifying how clumsy and deadly Hundun was.

He flapped his small wings and flew right at us.

CHAPTER THIRTY-THREE

I quickly ducked beneath it. I thought of raising Zhige to slice open its underbelly, but at the speed Hundun was moving, he could have snapped Zhige right in half.

Ruoming grabbed onto one of the tentacles of the outer god, swinging himself onto it. He drew his saber and cleanly jabbed up its body.

The outer god reacted violently, immediately shooting out branches to dig into Ruoming's flesh.

Ruoming leapt from the body of the outer god, the branches still reaching for him. But, instead of trying to fight them off, he ran at Hundun.

Hundun spun around to attack Ruoming. At that moment, the outer god's branches struck Hundun, causing the creature to jump in shock.

Its tiny little legs splayed out before it hobbled around to face the outer god. Its small wings propelled it into the air before it charged at the outer god.

The moment it made contact with the outer god, a massive explosion rang out. The entire arm of the outer god was severed in an instant, black goop falling onto the ground to coat it in thick, sticky layers. It covered some pools of lava, leading to massive billows of smoke.

Multiple of the outer god's tentacles flew forward to grip the calamity, wrapping around it and constricting like a python. It lifted Hundun into the air and aimed it straight at us.

Ruoming quickly scrambled to his feet. Feiyu grabbed onto Ruoming and threw him across the ruins before sprinting as fast as he could. Ruoming landed and skidded across the ground, sweating profusely.

> **Divinity God of Fate and Fortune is lending Disciple Amelia spiritual energy!**

"Serpent!" I shouted.

At once, Amelia lifted her cuff, and the massive serpent appeared before us. I leapt onto its head and redirected it from the path of the outer god.

However, before the outer god launched Hundun's massive body for us, it used its tentacles to rip Hundun into a dozen pieces. Then, it threw all of them at once like the pellets of a shotgun blast.

The landing points were unpredictable. One struck the side of the serpent, slicing a third of its body off. Another landed just beside Shunfeng'er. The impact caused a massive crater to open up beneath Shunfeng'er, and he desperately flew into the air.

Another struck just beside the throne. The throne was utterly terrified by the chaos happening all around it. It struggled to attack the heart and dodge the chaotic attacks. Thankfully, Athena and Artemis were still herding the two pieces closer and closer. They mimicked Wei and Yue's earlier actions, continuing to deceive the throne.

> **Divinity God of Fate and Fortune is lending Disciple Amelia spiritual energy!**

Amelia healed the serpent, and I led it up into the sky. It snaked wildly, jaws open and snapping at any tentacles that got too close.

Amelia clung onto me even tighter. "Is it dead?"

"I have no clue."

I squinted down at the various pieces of Hundun lying all over the ground. Even the outer god seemed to hesitate for a moment, probing one of Hundun's severed legs.

But, instead of fading to ash, all of Hundun's body parts twitched. They began regenerating rapidly.

Out of one of Hundun's legs, a torso formed. And then another leg. And another, until a brand-new version of it was created.

Until there were at least a dozen copies of Hundun scattered all over the area.

> **Demon Abyssal Kraken of Black Seas is stunned by Hundun's power.**

> **Demon Abyssal Kraken of Black Seas states this is the first display of calamity power he has witnessed.**

> **Demon Great Sage Who Pacifies Heaven is sweating bullets.**

> **Divinity Great Sage Equaling Heaven has
> food spilling from his mouth.**

Amelia's jaw dropped as she watched all of the copies form. "Shit," she whispered, and the word sounded incredibly unnatural from her mouth.

"Don't say that. But yes, shit."

Shunfeng'er flew up next to me, both Feiyu and Ruoming hanging off of his torso. They both leapt off next to me, grabbing onto the serpent's head to avoid falling to the ground.

Shunfeng'er whipped Archangel Michael's sword, and I could hear the sound of millions of damned souls from the blade. "Artemis and Athena are ready."

I looked down, and I could see that both Artemis and Athena had trapped the throne right beneath us. It was crowded by hundreds of forest animals weighing it down, and Athena and Artemis were on either side, using all of their remaining strength to pin it down. Right beneath it was the glowing red heart.

One of the Hundun copies flew up into the air and flapped its wings faster and faster until the wicked winds returned. Debris was lifted into the air, and I could feel the serpent getting sucked into its pull, but I redirected it, pushing it beyond its limits as I brought us to the center of the storm.

Another one of the Hundun copies grew larger before it began leaping up and down on the ground again, causing massive quakes once more. However, now when fire and lava burst through the Earth, Chang'e raised her hands up into the sky.

Massive waves came crashing down, turning it into obsidian. A gaping hole remained in her robes, but it appeared that her wound had healed. Beside her, Archangel Michael was still overlooking my party, but he was about half the size as earlier. Evidently, the poll resulted in a massive hit to his spiritual energy.

With the threat of Hundun, I knew the duo couldn't last much longer. None of us could.

My tattoo began glowing under my sleeve once more. And upon closer inspection of Ruoming, I could see the faintest light peeking through the clothes on his back. Moreover, I could feel my spiritual energy pooling in my arm and its constant fluctuation.

Shunfeng'er spun Archangel Michael's blade in the air. Although I could only assume that this was Shunfeng'er's first time wielding it, he handled it with the same expertise that even Archangel Michael did.

He lifted the blade, and its flames immediately extended dozens of feet into the sky. The screams of the damned echoed as Shunfeng'er swung it down and straight through the middle of the citadel. At once, the outer god was struck with a devastating blow and a handful of the Hundun replicas were sent flying back.

My eyes widened at the display of power.

As if that wasn't enough, waves began to swirl around Shunfeng'er—one of Chang'e's powers. He swirled them all around himself until he had various water tentacles surrounding him and defending him from any of the attacks.

Beside me, Ruoming twitched, his eyes locked on Shunfeng'er.

I could feel a draining of spiritual energy from my arm before it surged once more. I still had practically no clue what the tattoo could do, but I knew it was related to my spiritual energy reserves, and I was beginning to get the vaguest of ideas.

At least three copies of Hundun turned their focus to Shunfeng'er, as well as the outer god. They struck out for him at once, but he swung Archangel Michael's sword in a wide circle around him, and they were thrust back with a wave of spiritual energy.

I removed Amelia from my back, gently placing her on the head of the serpent. I looked up at Feiyu.

Feiyu met my eyes, and his brow furrowed. "Hey—"

"I'll be right back."

"Hey!"

I threw Zhige down and leapt onto it, driving it forward and higher until it reached Shunfeng'er.

Hindsight Activated!

Each of the different copies of Hundun held a different one of the original's abilities. One controlled the wind, another controlled energy bursts, and so on. I locked my eyes onto the one capable of shooting immense amounts of dark spiritual energy.

I had Zhige fly right over it. The moment it got close enough, I dropped down onto the surface of the calamity. At once, its entire body trembled as a dark layer surrounded it.

Editor's Pen activated!
Before Hundun launches his energy attack, a bell will chime.
Edit granted!

Ding!

I pulled an abundant amount of spiritual energy from the reserve in the tattoo—far more than I was granted even from winning against Feiyu—and smashed my legs into the top of Hundun.

Hundun went hurtling toward the ground at a wicked speed. At the moment of impact, Hundun erupted into a powerful explosion of dark spiritual energy. Zhige caught me before I could follow Hundun all the way down.

Hundun was driven thousands of feet beneath the surface, leaving a massive crater in its wake. But then, a line appeared, cracking down the entirety of the citadel. Then, the entire earth split once more.

Artemis and Athena held steadfast, bracing against the vicious earthquake. The entire ground was rippling out like it was made of water.

My party was lifted into the air by Archangel Michael and Chang'e. Ruoming's was being protected by Yuan, Thor still looking over them, though he had shrunk a considerable amount.

I turned to Shunfeng'er. "We hit the throne and heart with that."

Shunfeng'er looked at me like I was crazy.

"Bring me back to Ruoming!" I shouted at Shunfeng'er.

Shunfeng'er quickly snapped out of it, grabbing onto me and launching me at them. I flew through the air before latching onto the serpent's whiskers, looking up at them.

Amelia was sweating again from overexerting herself while controlling the serpent. Ruoming and Feiyu were battling the long tentacles of the outer god, which had wrapped itself around the serpent.

"I'm going to strike the throne and heart with Hundun," I shouted over the chaos. "I need you to get the outer god to focus on all the versions of Hundun. If we can trigger all of their skills at once, it'll completely destroy the citadel. And I need you to convince Yuan to shield all of us."

Feiyu let out a low whistle. Ruoming stared at me like I was stupid.

"You want Yuan to shield all of your party members?" Feiyu asked.

"Yes. Amelia can bring them onto the serpent to guarantee them the best chance of survival. No one on the ground will live through this."

"Tch," Ruoming scoffed. "And you think we will survive by flying?"

"Our odds are better."

Ruoming snapped. "You're reckless. This time, you've dragged all of us into it."

"It's a good thing you don't have to worry about dying," I answered tensely.

I turned to Amelia, kneeling down and cupping her face in my hands. "Amelia, I need you to push through for just a bit longer. Fetch the rest of my party and Ruoming's, and make sure to protect them with the serpent. Feiyu-shushu, Ruoming-shushu, and I are going to end this, but it's going to be very dangerous, and I'll need you to go far away as fast as you can."

"You promise you'll be okay?"

"I promise."

Amelia extended her pinky out for me. I latched onto it and shook it firmly before I stood up, patting her on the back.

I signaled for Shunfeng'er to return, and he quickly lifted Feiyu, Ruoming, and me into one arm.

"Peijin," Shunfeng'er began, "I only have a few minutes left."

"This will all be over by then."

The Hundun replica I had kicked was finally resurfacing from the crater. With how long it took, it must have been thrown far deeper than I had initially imagined, likely blown further down by the impact of its own blast.

I wiggled from Shunfeng'er's grasp, jumping onto Zhige. "All three of you need to trigger the outer god to attack Hundun. I don't care how you do it, just get it done."

"Got it, Jiejie," Feiyu said, saluting me. He turned to Shunfeng'er. "Drop me off in front of the one controlling the winds. He's been getting on my nerves."

Certain that they had their front covered, I flew with Zhige down toward the Hundun duplicate that I had previously kicked. Despite the fact that it had been driven through the Earth, it didn't seem to have sustained any injuries. If anything, it only seemed to feed off the chaos, becoming larger and stronger than before.

I audibly gulped. This was fine. Even if it was stronger, that just meant its impact on the throne would be heightened.

"Yoohoo!" I shouted at it, letting out a tiny burst of spiritual energy. It instantly turned to face me, sensing my presence.

I got chills, the hairs on my arm standing up. This could very well be my final show. I let out a steady breath, trying to calm myself to the best of my abilities.

Instead of flying straight at me, Hundun fired up an attack, its hair sticking straight up as the energy coursed through its body.

Ding!

A massive ball of dark energy hurtled toward me.

CHAPTER THIRTY-FOUR

I instantly swung Zhige to the side, practically flipping through the air to avoid the trajectory of Hundun's attack. However, rather than the dark energy flying straight past me, it did a quick U-turn toward me.

I hiccupped out of panic and grabbed onto the edge of Zhige before throwing my body off. The dark ball whizzed right past where I was standing moments before. But, it turned again and shot back at me. I pulled myself back onto Zhige and continued to dodge the attack.

Ding!
Ding!
Ding!

Three more headed straight for me. At this rate, I knew I couldn't dodge them all. I was a dead man walking.

As fast as I could, I flew Zhige down to the throne, but I realized that wouldn't work either. Athena and Artemis would certainly get caught in the blast, and realizing that, they would escape and let the throne go before I even got there.

I knew I couldn't depend on just destroying the heart either, like I'd originally planned. For example, if the heart was able to deflect Hundun's energy ball right back at me as one of its defensive mechanisms, I would never survive. I would be too close to it to escape.

The only thing I could do was fool the throne and the heart, and then tear down the entire citadel.

Just another day's work.

Think, think, think!

My heart was pounding so fast in my chest I thought I would die of a heart attack at any moment.

I looked over my shoulder to see the four dark energy balls quickly gaining speed. I looked down at Zhige, sweating bullets. Its red eye was tearing up, like it knew it wasn't going to survive whatever suicidal plan I had in mind this time.

Fuck! Think! You're the author!

There had to . . . There had to be something I could do.

I looked down at my tattoo. It served as a safe haven of spiritual energy, pulling from reserves I didn't even know it held. Theoretically, even though the observers now despised me, I was still a god. A real god of fate and fortune, though a terrible one.

I wiped the tears forming in my eyes. For the first time, I felt like I was connecting with others. Dying right after feeling that comfort would be too pitiful, even for a damned bitch like me.

> **Card Dealer activated!**

This time, I turned the skill on myself. All fifty-six cards opened up before me. To my surprise, there were still a few cards blocked off from me, so I only had access to forty-three. That was even less than what I had for Feiyu . . . Thankfully, most were still glowing beautifully. I wondered if that was another puzzle piece for me to solve, or if it was due to my lack of self-awareness.

Both possibilities would have been tragic.

By using this skill, I would likely lose one of my cards to backlash. I wanted to know what it would be ahead of time, but I guess I would never find out. I could only hope it wasn't something too important.

I quickly sifted through the rest of the cards, looking for the most insignificant one—a memory that I wanted to lose, if anything.

The Ten of Wands caught my eye. It was a representation of a time I would have been overburdened, fighting an uphill battle, despite losing all of my will and purpose with no end in sight.

Funnily enough, it was the moment I realized Zhao Rui had left me for good. I stared at the card for a long moment before I picked it up.

I rarely ever thought back to that moment at all. I thought I had found a home in Zhao Rui. After he left, I was a complete mess for weeks. There wasn't a single moment I wasn't sobbing, with some stranger pitying me being the only way for me to put food in my mouth.

It was even more miserable than when I ran from home. Because when I had run away, I never had a taste of the life I could have lived if things had been different for me. But, when I met Zhao Rui, it was the first time I realized that I could be something sensational.

When Rui said goodbye and never came home, that all shattered. I was reminded that I was to be damned for the rest of my life.

There would never be a time in my life that I would meet Zhao Rui again. I came to accept that the moment Ruoming rejected me. I looked down at the card with a solemn smile on my face. In that case, I would rather live believing that Zhao Rui left, but forget that I was burdened by his absence for months on end.

> **How would you like to alter this card?**

> **Give the card to another entity.**

> **Who would you like to give this card to?**

I turned away from the blue screen momentarily, keeping it in my field of vision.

The balls of dark energy were just behind me now. I had seconds before I'd be blown to smithereens, and all I had was a theory of a plan.

"Hey, Zhige. You need to do something . . . very important for me," I said desperately, fearful that the blade might turn down my request.

"I need you to leave me behind. Okay? Don't come back for me. Go as far away as you can as fast as you can, and find my party once the damage subsides."

Zhige's red eye trembled back and forth in a firm rejection, but I quickly shushed it, continuing.

"You have to do this, or nobody is going to make it out of this arc." I took off my Boundless Bag and sifted through it, pulling out my dao. I then sealed the bag and tied the long straps around Zhige's hilt, ensuring it was secure and nothing would be lost.

"I'm going to sit on the throne, and I'm going to let Hundun kill me. You're going to let it happen."

I took in a steady breath, looking down at my tattoo.

"Zhige, if I die, it's all your fault. I'm really counting on you and this damn tattoo you gave me."

First, spiritual energy was innate to every single entity, whether they were a ghost, divinity, demon or even a disciple. And gods could create a "core" of spiritual energy, which would be their most vulnerable point.

Since the Tower tattoo served as a reserve of my spiritual energy, it was an optimal choice for me to place my core, especially since the tattoo seemed indestructible and could offer additional defense to my core.

Second, the Minor Arcana cards were correlated to living entities. Thus, it must be tied to their spiritual energy. A being with absolutely zero spiritual energy would not have any Minor Arcana cards, since they would not be alive.

I placed the dao in my non-dominant hand and drew in a deep breath, biting down on the fabric of my hoodie. I brought the blade to my elbow and, with a sharp inhale, sliced through my arm.

I let out a brutal but muffled scream, blood pouring from the wound. The cut had stopped at the bone, which would take much more effort to saw through. I was about to vomit from the pain.

> **Divinity Great Sage Equaling Heaven watches in shock.**

> **Abyssal Kraken of Black Seas is pleading with you.**

> [Observers Chat]
> **Socrates:** Jia Li?? What are you doing???
> **Socrates:** Jia Li, I know things seem impossible right now, but please don't do this again!

I moved my screen back in front of me, finishing the Card Dealer skill.

> **Give card to Liu Peijin alternate.**

With these two things in mind, I could move my spiritual core into my arm, and my Minor Arcana cards would follow. All except for the Ten of Wands, which I would transfer into the rest of my body using Card Dealer.

Effectively, I would be a god split in two. My true body, with all my spiritual energy and core memories, would be in my arm. However, in my main body would be the Ten of Wands card and some remaining spiritual energy, which would let me mislead Hundun and complete the arc.

Since both my arm and my main body were intact, I would have access to all my spiritual energy and memories until my main body was destroyed, in which I would lose the Ten of Wands.

With all my willpower, I cut off the rest of my arm. I let out a loud scream, the fabric of my hoodie falling from my mouth. I grabbed my amputated forearm, staring at the tattoo, before I shakily moved it forward.

> **Ten of Wands has successfully been given to Liu Peijin alternate.**

Blood poured from my arm, splattering all over Zhige. I was grateful Zhige didn't have a mouth. Given how frantically its eye was spinning, I was certain it would be screaming louder than I was.

Holding onto my forearm, I carefully pierced it on the tip of Zhige's blade, like it was meat on an oversized skewer.

I must have looked mad.

"Whatever you do, don't lose my arm. Is it secure enough?"

Zhige's eye spun wildly with no direction, and I instantly scolded it.

"Answer the question. Is it secure enough?"

Zhige's eye gave a reluctant nod. I didn't bother to use my spiritual energy to slow the bleeding of my arm, knowing I was about to die anyway. I threw the dao away, unable to untie the strings of the Boundless Bag to store it.

"Good. Ah! My hoodie!"

I moved to tug it off with one arm, but the hoodie instantly revolted, seeming disgusted to get more of my blood on it. It easily removed itself from my body and tied itself around Zhige's hilt.

I didn't have time to be offended by the hoodie's reaction. Now, I just had to pray this would work like I planned. I looked down and saw the throne just beneath me. I turned to Zhige.

"Goodbye. I'll see you again."

I leapt off the blade, looking like a maniac. I looked up, staring at my arm hanging from the tip of Zhige as I fell backward toward the ground. The balls of dark energy followed suit without missing a single beat.

Ding!

Ding!

Ding! Ding! Ding! Ding! Dingdingding!

More and more appeared, Hundun growing frustrated by its pursuit of me. I looked down, and just before I could crash into the ground before me, Artemis sent up massive hawks to slowly break my fall.

They slowed my descent enough for me to land with only a few seconds to spare and with no further injuries. Blood was still pouring from my amputated arm, and I was only wearing my original button-up shirt from when the apocalypse began.

"I suggest you return home now," I said simply, meeting the eyes of Athena and Artemis. They looked like a complete mess themselves, and I could tell they wanted to inquire about my now missing arm, but they heard my warning at the sight of the rapidly descending attacks and vanished instantly.

I placed a hand on the throne. The poor thing had no clue what was happening, only that it had been subject to a horrific amount of torment.

"I'm going to sit on you and end this, so don't move."

I turned around, facing the dozens of dark energy balls spiraling toward me, and I shut my eyes, leaning back into the chair when all the energy crashed into my body.

I felt no pain before everything went dark.

CHAPTER THIRTY-FIVE

When I regained sensation, the first thing I felt was excruciating pain. I wanted to writhe and kick or scream, but I could do none of those things. It felt like I was in a straitjacket, blinded, deafened, and also gagged. I tried to move, but I couldn't tell which direction I was facing or where my limbs were moving. In fact, I couldn't tell if I had limbs at all.

I gave up, ceasing my struggle. There was no point in it, not when the only thing I could detect was my own suffering. I wondered if maybe I really had died. Perhaps this was the afterlife of the apocalypse.

I waited and waited, but still, nothing improved.

Was this how Wei felt in his dungeon room?

I began struggling again, straining to pick up anything else outside of my own body but failed.

Finally, I could hear the faintest noise.

It wasn't dialogue or anything close to it. It was a faint buzzing like the sound of an insufferable fly that just wouldn't go away.

But, I centered all my focus on that one sound, trying to latch onto it in the dark abyss that I was trapped in. I was grateful to have any kind of relief from my current agony.

The buzzing turned into faint mumbling. Sometimes it was louder, and other times it went away, causing me to panic. Finally, I began to make out individual words.

"... back ..."

"... ghost ..."

"... train ..."

If I had a head to bang, I would be doing just that. It was infuriating not being able to understand more of the conversation.

"Peijin ... Chang'e ..."

"... no ..."

"Never ... listen ..."

I gulped at the last phrase. I couldn't quite make out whose voice I was hearing, but they definitely were not happy with me.

"Are we sure ... Is everything?"

"... have to go ... now!"

"The ... torn apart!"

Finally, I could twitch parts of my body. I could now sense where my arm was, and most importantly, I saw light bleed in through the thin skin of my eyelid.

I peeled my eye open, and I couldn't make out a thing happening around me. My vision was far too blurry.

"S-She just opened her first eye!"

"Huh?!"

I saw a number of figures pop up above me. I blinked rapidly, trying to make out who they were. I wanted to speak to them, but I had yet to regenerate my mouth.

"Quickly, we don't have any more time left!"

I could recognize Feiyu's grating voice anywhere. What did he mean there was no more time?

I tried to roll my head over to make out where I was. I finally blinked away most of the blurriness, and what I saw made me want to return to that state of nothingness I had just escaped.

It was complete and utter chaos.

We were on the back of Amelia's serpent, though it had shrunk significantly. Where the throne and heart had originally been was a massive crater. It must have been at least fifty feet wide, and the entire edge was black, like it had been burnt to a crisp.

"Jiejie," Feiyu said, looking down at me. "Do you have everything? Can we leave?"

I blinked in confusion and remained trained on my surroundings. The entire ground beneath us was covered in a deep layer of black goop, and thunderous booms continuously rang out. The sound was so powerful I could feel the deep rumble in my chest.

"Hun ... dun ..." I finally said. I sounded like a forty-year-old chain-smoker.

"The arc is over. The gods are gone, and Karma sucked Hundun away."

"Then, what's that sound . . ." I began before I finally realized what it was. The outer god was swinging its massive tentacles frantically, smashing them into the ground and throwing rubble all over the arc in hunt of its beloved pet.

With each failed search, lightning erupted from the outer god's entire body, and it smashed into the ground, destroying anything that dared cross its path.

For a moment, I almost felt bad for what I had done. The poor outer god was more preoccupied by the idea that its pet had died, and it was a terribly human and rational thought process.

Some of its tentacles moved to attack the serpent, but Wei, Ruoming, and Feiyu would drive it back while Amelia would guide the serpent to evade its attacks. We were playing an entirely defensive game now.

But, it wouldn't be long before the outer god's sorrow, grief, and confusion turned into a rage we would be victims of.

"Then . . . what are we waiting for?" I croaked.

"You won't survive the journey back to the station."

I groaned in annoyance.

"Well, since my Jiejie looks like she'll live, it's a wrap for us," Feiyu said, standing up and smacking his palms together like he was dusting them off. Ruoming was standing behind him, and I realized that Cheng was the one trying to patch me up.

But, at the sight of his party leaders leaving, Cheng quickly abandoned me, and I let out a frustrated groan. Qijing and Yuan were also overlooking me, but they turned to Feiyu.

Feiyu stretched languidly. "Don't take too long. You wouldn't want that outer god coming after you."

Ruoming gave a curt nod before turning his back. From far away, a cloud of blue sparks was rapidly approaching them.

The sparks wrapped around their bodies, lifting them into the air. It dissipated bottom up, and it was unsettling to see their legs vanish with the sparks, while their upper bodies still remained.

I caught Ruoming's eyes. He stared at me before lowering his gaze and turning away. The sparks reached his head, and he vanished only seconds later.

I stared at where he was standing only moments before, bringing my hand up to rub my new eye.

"Ah-ah!" Yang instantly panicked, forcing my arm down. "Heal first."

"I'll be fine," I murmured.

"You're going to be the death of me. I mean it."

"Don't worry," Yue interjected. "She'll get us all killed anyway, so we don't have to worry about that."

I kept my eyes trained to the place Ruoming had been. For some reason, my brain felt horribly foggy when I looked at him.

Why did I dislike him so heavily again? I combed through my memories, remembering that I was highly critical of him after he'd mentioned that he wasn't related to Zhao Rui in any form. But even so, I didn't know why I passed that judgment onto him.

I let out a heavy sigh, squeezing my eyes shut. Even trying to think about it was more than exhausting. I just wanted to go to sleep.

Yue slapped my cheek. "Hey, hey. Don't go back to sleep. Come on, we have to go home. Like, right now. Do you see the state of this place?"

Yue was absolutely right. Not only was the outer god still wreaking havoc all around us, but it was clear Hundun had as well. Aside from the crater, part of the the ground beneath us was partially cleared of debris. A large radius in the center was absolutely spotless.

That must have been from Hundun's storm. Another part was completely charred, likely from whatever fire Hundun released. Another part was completely flooded with muddied waters.

Not even the sky was spared. With the presence of the outer god only increasing each second, then sky was crumbling like a delicate sheet of ceramic.

Return Peijin's World Dominion to the station?

Yes/No

I tried to sit up, but I was still missing my other arm and an entire leg. I grunted in pain. I wasn't actively bleeding, but it was still a completely open wound. My tattoo was glowing vibrantly as well, doing its best to distribute my spiritual energy through the rest of my body.

Furthermore, an oversized black button-up shirt had been wrapped around me to cover me up as I regenerated. I carefully slid it on, as well as the shorts on the ground.

Zhige nuzzled up against me. At the base of the weapon was my hoodie and my Boundless Bag. I held onto both for now, but once I regenerated more of my body, I would throw on the bag and tie the hoodie around my waist.

I lifted my hand gingerly and patted the sword lightly. I undoubtedly expended much of my spiritual energy reserve to pull off this move. And with all my observers turning their backs on me, it would be much harder to recover than earlier.

Thankfully, I could still try and sell myself to lowly ghosts or demons. Any divinities who didn't already like me were unlikely to start.

"Just hold onto me as we travel back. I'll be able to survive the journey. We'll die if we're here or any longer," I said.

As if to emphasize my words, a giant bolt of lightning shot down from the sky, signifying the outer god's increasing rage as it began to realize that its cherished throne was truly gone for good.

"Peijin . . ." Yang muttered.

"I'm serious." I turned to Wei. "How much longer until you can't hold off the outer god, especially without Ruoming and Feiyu?"

Wei pursed his lips.

"Hold onto me," I ordered. "All of you just need to prop me up until we return."

Return Peijin's World Dominion to the station?

Yes

The flurry of blue sparks returned. I wrapped my arm around the back of Yang's neck, and I hobbled on my one leg. Amelia moved beneath me, holding me up beneath my back. Yue lifted my leg, and Wei guarded the side with all my injuries.

The sparks appeared, and although it was easy to get separated in their whirlwind, my party's grip on me remained steadfast. Still, I couldn't hide how painful the experience of being transported was, wincing at each jerky movement.

Furthermore, I could tell that my party was doing their best not to say more to me. If I wasn't still in such a horrific state, then I was sure they would have already berated me for throwing away my life so carelessly.

But, for now, they bit their tongues and did their best to steady me.

A feeling of weightlessness took over, and I accepted it, finding temporary relief in the sensation. I let out a heavy sigh, looking down at my wrecked body.

In all honesty, I was entirely surprised to be alive.

I had taken my biggest gambles so far in this arc. And although I was still a winner, I knew there would come a day when I would lose, and that was what my party members were already dreading.

But, for now, I survived.

As we were transported, the world around us melted away into nothing but fast-moving drops of light and darkness. I didn't say a word, just staring at everything going by in silence. An overwhelmingly solemn feeling had settled over me after my brush with death.

Divinity Ears That Hear What Comes on the Wind is lending Disciple Peijin spiritual energy.

> **Divinity Great Sage Equaling Heaven is lending
> Disciple Peijin spiritual energy.**

> **Demon Abyssal Kraken of Black Seas is lending
> Disciple Peijin spiritual energy.**

> **Divinity Spirit of the Jade Moon is giving
> her best wishes to Disciple Peijin.**

> **Demon Great Sage Who Pacifies Heaven is
> lending Disciple Peijin spiritual energy.**

Despite the massive influx of spiritual energy, I could hardly say that it had much of an effect on my rate of healing. Perhaps it subdued the pain, but the only thing that could heal me in my current state was time.

Finally, the world around us began to materialize once more. I could make out the doors of the trains and the colorful signs denoting the platforms. My party braced around me, ensuring that the landing wouldn't be too difficult on my body.

I was hit by a wave of exhaustion, and I could feel thick beads of sweat trailing down my forehead. I let out a shaky breath, shutting my eyes as my head lolled to the side.

> **Divinity Blessed Martial Guard of Salvation is lending
> Divinity God of Fate and Fortune spiritual energy.**

"Is she falling asleep?" Yue asked, her grip on me tightening.

"Hey, Peijin," Yang said, gently shaking my arm. "Peijin."

Their voices were fading and growing more distant.

"Hey!" Yang exclaimed, slapping my healed cheek. "Peijin, come on."

CHAPTER THIRTY-SIX

With the spiritual energy from Wei, I forced my eyes to open, but a terrible bout of fatigue hit me. I'd have done anything to go to sleep right then.

"I'm fine," I said softly, more sweat breaking out all over my body. "We're almost there, right?"

"Just a few seconds," Yang reassured me.

"Okay," I replied meekly.

My breathing became more and more ragged. I forced my eyes open and found that we were fully in the station now.

"Why isn't she better?" Amelia whined, kneeling down next to me and gripping my shirt tightly.

I forced myself to look at Amelia and smile at her, entirely relieved. Our relationship had been so damaged this past arc that I was truly concerned she no longer cared about my presence in her life. At her concerned words, I gently grabbed her hand and ran my finger over her knuckles.

"I'll be fine. I'm just tired," I croaked.

Most of my body had healed by now, but the pain was still unbearable. I could hardly breathe.

Yang signaled something to Wei, which I couldn't hear. But Wei stayed by my side, continuously lending me more spiritual energy as Yang left.

"Where did Yang go?"

"Sh. Don't speak."

"Answer."

"He's grabbing Cheng."

"I'm fine."

"Sh. I don't want to have to tape your mouth shut."

I didn't say another word.

When Cheng returned, he looked down at me, worry etched on his face. He then pricked me with a needle to get a reading on my current condition.

I jerked away from him, knowing nothing good ever came from Cheng poking someone with a mysterious needle.

"Don't worry. This one isn't poisoned."

He took my blood and activated one of his skills, quickly assessing it before the Azure Dragon Store opened up before him.

"When moving locations, time doesn't work in a linear or consistent fashion," Cheng explained. "Sometimes time can pass by faster when teleporting. Because of that, the bodily processes also move faster. So, Peijin has a very advanced infection."

"Oh, really? Well I feel great, actually," I wheezed out.

I groaned in pain, writhing on the ground while trying to catch my breath. I wanted to collect my award from the arc, but it looked like it would take a moment before I could check the screen.

For the first time in a long time, Chang popped into existence just beside me. He was sniffling dramatically, and he hobbled over toward me to grab one of my fingers in the palm of his clawed hand.

"Peijin."

"You're the absolute last person I want to see right now, Chang."

"I would have come during the arc, but there wasn't a single safe moment for me to descend. I would have been blown to smithereens for being in your line of sight."

"True—" I pulled back slightly as another wave of pain moved through me.

I could see Cheng purchase an entire arsenal of elixirs and terrifying looking instruments right beside me. Running out of space, he held onto a small glass vial holding a lime green elixir, looking awfully studious.

Scathing Reviewer activated!

I frowned slightly as I looked at Cheng. "You should be in school."

He turned to face me, eyes wide, and started laughing. Then he turned to Yang and said, "It seems like she's suffering from hallucinations, too."

Yang's expression fell. "Isn't that a terrible sign?"

Cheng pondered for a moment, looking up and bringing a hand pensively to his chin. "It does improve her attitude."

Cheng was incredibly lucky I was dying of some horrible infection.

The little dragon at my side shuffled closer to my face, peering at me. "You lost a lot of observers."

"I know."

"And your rating went down. A lot."

"I know that, too. It's fine."

"A lot of the gods like you."

"Well, considering I almost killed half of them, they better like me, unless they want to die next."

"I'm trying to say that things are still looking up for you, Peijin."

"My luck is still bad."

Chang's tail waved back and forth like he was in a pleasant mood. He looked up at Cheng. "She's already feeling better. She's much more talkative."

Cheng puffed out his chest with pride. "I'm a very good healer. Especially after this last arc. Peijin put me through such agony and stress that I've never learned faster. If I hadn't, I definitely would have died an absolutely brutal death at both of your hands," he said, smiling brightly at Yue and Wei.

Wei gave the young kid a pat on the back, clearly holding no hard feelings. Yue, however, shifted in discomfort, casting Cheng a more than judgmental side-eye.

"I think you almost killed me. Multiple times, actually," Yue grumbled in annoyance.

Yang playfully bumped her shoulder. "But I'm a pretty good healer, too, aren't I?"

"No. Chang'e is a good healer. I could have executed her instructions myself if I wasn't the one dying."

Yang deflated instantly, and Cheng had a cheeky grin on his face as his eyes darted back and forth between the duo.

Despite the playful scene before me, I was still feeling rather abysmal. I looked at Chang, shifting slightly to meet his gaze.

"I can't promise you that I'll bring in more money next arc," I said simply.

The entire basis of my relationship with Chang was that I would put on a good show, and in return, Chang would reap millions and millions of stars from my viewers.

However, now that the observers had discovered my identity, it was only a matter of time before everyone else did as well. One word from Ruoming . . . one observer message bypassing Karma . . . and it would all be over.

There would be no way of talking myself back from that one.

I struggled to sit up, and I instantly had a dozen hands on me trying to push me back down, but my gaze remained locked on Chang's. I couldn't read his expression at all. Maybe it was because he was a dragon.

"Peijin," he began, "I was only a bottom-tier streamer. I didn't have anything to lose in the first place. But now"—Chang held up a finger—"I'm first."

"Congratulations. You're first out of all the ones that existed in China before they were brutally wiped out."

"Bigger."

"First in Asia?"

"This is the number one broadcast on the planet. It might even become number one in the entire broadcasting system."

". . . Well I guess I should pat myself on the back for all the hard work I put in."

Chang flashed me a toothy smile. "Recover quickly. The next arc will always be worse than the previous one."

"Thanks for the reminder."

I could hear Chang laughing to himself, thinking he was the most entertaining and witty broadcaster to ever exist, before he vanished in a cloud of sparks.

"Well," I began, "I'm certainly feeling better now. I didn't think I'd have to worry about something as silly as an infection."

Cheng shook his head, helping me slowly sit up. "It's only when you're going between locations. You don't know what you might get exposed to, and with such severe wounds as yours, it's always a dangerous move."

"Thanks, doc," I said, smiling and patting the boy on the shoulder. He was really cute and sincere when he wasn't trying to kill everyone I knew.

Cheng nodded and stood up, brushing himself off before he turned back to speak with Yuan. Yuan had been standing far off to the side, eyeing us during our entire interaction.

I could practically feel his eyes boring into my skin the entire time, but I didn't want to make Cheng uncomfortable by calling it out.

Although Yuan was one of my original characters, I'd hardly had the opportunity to interact with him. Because of that, it felt unusually cold between us. Given that one of his only impressions of me was using Archangel Michael to try and kill his sponsor, he probably didn't like me very much.

However, when I faced my own party, it didn't feel much warmer now that Cheng had left.

Yang began the inevitable conversation. "I think, at this rate, we should tie Peijin down for the next arc and handle it ourselves, since Peijin has a very large desire to die at every possible moment."

"That's not true," I retorted. "It was the only thing that could work in that situation. That poll and the heart's defense significantly altered my original thinking."

"Enough that you had to die?"

"It was a sacrifice. That's how these things work, Yang. You know that.

Nobody can truly win an arc. It's always a give or take, and that's what it took this time to win it."

"It's not a victory if you're not there to celebrate it."

"Well, I am here, Yang. I don't see why you're so caught up on what *didn't* happen."

"Because it *will* happen, Peijin, if you continue acting like this."

Yue didn't berate me nearly as much as Yang or Wei did when we had these arguments, but this time, she refused to even meet my pleading gaze.

"You scared Amelia," Yue said, and my heart clenched in my chest.

I looked down at Amelia, who was still glued to my side, trembling slightly. "I'm sorry, did I scare you?"

Amelia shook her head.

"I'm sorry," I said, bringing up my weak arm to wrap around her body and pull her close, rubbing her back gently. "Don't worry. If I promise you I'll be back, then I'll be back."

Wei's eyes never left mine. "It is a bit morbid when your blade is all alone, and it comes flying back to us with only your amputated and tattooed arm attached to the end. You might as well have stuck your head on a stick."

"Well, I had to make sure it was safe and secure," I said sarcastically. "Besides, I might as well use all of my abilities if it means we can survive another day. If I'm a god, I should use that. And if I have this godforsaken tattoo, I should also use it. It's the same thing as using a skill."

Wei sighed loudly, bringing his hand up to rub his temple. "You're too stubborn for your own good. There's no point in arguing with you. Peijin, I trust you, and I know you'll always fight your way back to us. But, I also wish you would take better care of yourself, for our sake."

I bit my lower lip before turning away, shakily getting to my feet. Yue immediately jumped to my aid.

"I'm just getting the housekeeping done. Don't worry."

I opened my system, and I was at once bombarded with what looked like a million different notifications. It was like I was a corporate worker returning from the weekend and answering emails on a Monday morning.

> **Congratulations! You have completed the arc.**

> **Arc #3 - Battle of the Ascension Citadel has concluded!**

> **Due to an error with the proper ending of the arc, winners have been decided based on party involvement. Party Peijin's World Dominion had the greatest influence over the outcome of the arc. Thus, they are the decided winners and leading party of China.**

> **Stars Received: 100,000 to each party member.**

At once, Yue lit up just beside me.

"O-one hundred thousand stars?!" Yue exclaimed, giant dollar signs practically popping out of her eyes. "This is what it's all for!"

Yang looked at the same notification that appeared for him. "This might just cover your medical expenses."

Next came all of the messages from the gods . . . and there were a lot of them. I skimmed through most, only looking at the most important ones.

CHAPTER THIRTY-SEVEN

> Divinity Ears That Hear What Comes on the Wind is incredibly relieved to see Disciple Peijin alive.

> Divinity Ears That Hear What Comes on the Wind apologizes for not doing more to help Disciple Peijin.

> Divinity Ears That Hear What Comes on the Wind promises to work harder to support Disciple Peijin.

> Divinity Ears That Hear What Comes on the Wind apologizes for not giving a proper goodbye to Disciple Peijin.

> Divinity Supreme Commander of the Heavenly Hosts says there is no need since they will meet again.

> Divinity Supreme Commander of the Heavenly Hosts apologizes for getting injured.

> Divinity The One Who Fights in Front is still enraged by the actions of Disciple Peijin.

> Divinity Far Shooting Queen of Beasts says it's not Disciple Peijin's fault they all got injured.

> Divinity Great Sage Equaling Heaven nods in agreement.

> Divinity Great Sage Equaling Heaven states it shows weak devotion from the supporters of all Greek gods instead.

> Divinity Far Shooting Queen of Beasts reminds Divinity Great Sage Equaling Heaven he couldn't even descend.

> Divinity Great Sage Equaling Heaven says it's because he's far too strong to bypass karmic restraints.

> Divinity The One Who Fights in Front says it's due to his lack of spiritual energy.

> Disciple Spirit of the Jade Moon is taken aback by how much the gods argue.

> Demon Abyssal Kraken of Black Seas casts Disciple Spirit of the Jade Moon a sheepish look.

> Divinity Spirit of the Jade Moon is still crying.

> Demon King of the Nine Hells is still cursing Disciple Peijin.

> Divinity God of Thunder is prideful that he won Poll #3 despite being outnumbered by the other gods.

> The World is surprised by the degree of infighting within this timeline.

It seemed as though the gods hated each other more than they hated me for almost getting them all killed, and that was a very good thing. Archangel Michael and Shunfeng'er, however, were far quieter than I would have expected, given how much they sacrificed to help my party.

Perhaps they were madder at me than I expected, and they were just trying to mask their disappointment.

The observers, however, were not nearly as understanding.

> [Observers Chat]
> **Socrates:** Jia Li??
> **Socrates:** Jia Li, you didn't really die, did you?

> **Socrates:** Jia Li, please answer me.

I felt guilt growing in me with each passing second. These must have been the messages that Socrates tried to send me right after watching me blow apart from Hundun's attack.

I quickly scrolled past the rest of them—there were far too many for me to read through, and by now, Socrates knew that I was still kicking.

> **[Observers Chat]**
> **Aslan:** If none of you decided to mass-vote against Peijin JUST because you suspected she was Jia Li then absolutely none of this would have happened. Literally insane thing to do
> **Routined:** It's not a suspicion. She is.
> **APCase29:** Since when were we supposed to play the role of bringing justice? This is literally an apocalypse, and she's meant to entertain us
> **Peenut:** She's been taking us for granted this entire time. Did you see her worried at all when poll 3 came out? Nooope. Only after all her naive gods got a hole blown through their chest did you see her react properly
> **SonYon:** Because she thought we'd rescue her again lol
> **Aslan:** Or it's because she had multiple gods and all their followers on her side.
> **LostintheSky:** And she still lost! Now imagine what that says about her actual character. Not her facade
> **TarteJuice:** Didn't she manipulate all of us the entire time? I don't see a problem reclaiming it
> **MoldyBlanket:** ^^
> **Aslan:** You guys are no better. This is insane.

The chat kept going for what had been dozens upon thousands of more messages, but I didn't want to read the conversation further. It was clear how I stood among them, and there was no point in torturing myself by reading through the rest.

> **[Observers Chat]**
> **Socrates:** You're alive.

The newest message appeared with that familiar name. I stared at the message before murmuring inaudibly under my breath.

"Yeah. I guess so. Thanks for worrying about me."

I clicked the X on the screen and officially slid it out of my vision, catching up on enough to properly assess where I now stood.

Unable to catch a break, I heard the familiar footsteps of Feiyu approaching. I turned around expectantly.

"Jiejie looks much better now. I told you Cheng was the greatest," Feiyu said with a large grin.

I turned around to face my party, bowing my head slightly to indicate that I was going to speak to Feiyu. I took my first step forward shakily, having to relearn how to move my limbs again.

Feiyu had changed into much nicer clothing. My eyes moved up and down his figure. He bought himself new black dress pants, a black button-up shirt, and a black coat. He made absolutely zero aesthetic changes, but at least the clothing wasn't ripped up anymore.

I suspiciously looked down slowly at the oversize black button-up I was wearing, not saying a word.

I pointed at the collar of his button-up shirt. "Do you leave the top three unbuttoned for extra stars?"

Feiyu looked embarrassed and quickly buttoned up only one more. I snorted before I began walking beside him.

"Where's Ruoming?" I asked.

"You're already asking about him?"

"He seemed pretty mad at me. And you for letting me go through with my plan."

Feiyu shrugged. "At least we got out of that crisis. Not that I ever doubted Jiejie."

"Of course not," I said facetiously, going along with the stupid nickname.

At this point, I knew Feiyu was never going to call me by my name again unless he was forced to. And I hated to admit it, but he practically conditioned me. Now, whenever I heard "Jiejie" ring out, I instinctively looked for Feiyu like a dog being called.

I scrunched my nose. The more I thought about it, actually, the more I disliked it. Scratch that, I was not going to accept the title yet.

"Don't call me that. What happened to Bohemian Grove?"

"All the disciples have already returned. There's no leader anymore, but they're reassimilated into the station hierarchy. Nothing is special about them without Owl's guidance."

"Thank god I killed that man."

Feiyu chuckled slightly. "What are you going to spend your glorious one hundred thousand on?" Feiyu asked, a slight competitive tone in his voice.

"It's just a drop in the bucket. I have too much money anyway."

Feiyu pouted slightly, turning away. "Well, since Jiejie is so rich, you should buy all of us a celebratory dinner."

"What?"

"You were basically reborn earlier. And since none of us died, doesn't that mean we should celebrate?"

I argued, feeling very cheap all of a sudden. "Isn't the junior supposed to pay for their senior's meal? If I'm your Jiejie, you should be spending every dime spoiling me."

Feiyu frowned, digging his hand into his pockets to flip them inside out. "I have no money compared to Jiejie. I'm just a poor, incompetent disciple. Jiejie is so wealthy."

"Why should I pay for *my* rebirth dinner?"

"Fine. No celebration then."

I went silent for a couple strides, staring down at my feet.

"What type of cuisine do the people in your party like?"

Feiyu flashed me his brightest smile yet, nearly blinding me. I instantly flinched and turned the opposite direction.

"You're too easy, Peijin."

"Excuse me?!" I instantly shouted, smacking him firmly on the back of his head. "That's no way to talk to your senior! Besides, I'm only doing this for the benefit of my party. Being on the good side, especially of Cheng and Yuan, will save my party members in the future. It's just a strategic move." I babbled on and on, sending Feiyu into a fit of laughter.

"Yeah, yeah, of course. Just professional networking. Should I have all of them bring their business cards?"

Feiyu opened the Azure Dragon Store, swiping all the way to the back, where there were a plethora of food options. It was in the very back of the store because no idiot was stupid enough to cook a feast in the middle of a fantasy apocalypse.

He brought his index to the top right of the blue screen, clicking the "filter" button. Then, he sorted by price from high to low.

I was going to kill this man.

He smiled and pointed at the most expensive option. It was five hundred thousand stars for a single serving.

"Oh, Jiejie, doesn't this look incredible? Sea serpent caviar from the Caspian Sea, aged Kobe beef seared in spices from a dragon's blood . . ."

"I am not buying that for you, Feiyu."

"It's not for me. It's for all of us."

"No. Now you're not getting anything."

Feiyu deflated on the spot. "No sense of humor. Fine." He removed the filter and scrolled through until he found a quick and easy barbecue meat set.

"We can do Korean barbecue," Feiyu declared, bringing up a thumb to point at himself. "And, I'm not sure if you know this, but I'm a really fantastic chef."

I could hardly stop myself from rolling my eyes.

I wonder who made you such a great chef . . .

"Fine. We can do it. How many stars is it?"

"Fifteen thousand should be enough for all of us."

"Isn't this supposed to be a celebration?" I peeked over his shoulder, looking for more food options before I pointed at a cake. "Let's do this one. I think the kids will like it because it has ice cream in it, too."

"Whatever you say, Jiejie. After all, you're the one paying for everything," Feiyu said with a massive grin.

"We might not have time for dinner. The next arc might start."

"We will. I already checked with Chang. There's sponsor selection, and the next arc will be tomorrow evening. We have an entire twenty-four hours."

"Of rest and solitude," I clarified. "Not partying and socializing."

"Seniors need their rest."

"Whatever."

I had been walking in tandem with Feiyu the entire time without a destination in mind, so I hadn't even processed where he was leading me. I now saw Ruoming leaning casually against a railing before a staircase and met his eyes.

"I'll see Jiejie at dinner," Feiyu said, grinning ear to ear. Then, he turned around and left me alone with Ruoming.

I swallowed audibly. So Feiyu had picked me up only to bring me to Ruoming, and on the way, he decided to force my hand into paying for his meal. What a cheeky bastard.

"Why did you drag me here?" I asked Ruoming, keeping my distance from him. A part of the reason was my feeling of existential dread seeing him, which I couldn't quite place.

Although I always found Ruoming terrifying, I now also felt foggy when I looked at him. I couldn't pinpoint why, though.

"I wanted to see if you actually survived."

"Well, obviously I did, considering that you approved of Cheng healing me."

"I don't tell any of my party members to do anything."

"What a benevolent ruler."

I expected Ruoming to bristle at my snarky comment, but instead, his wide and light-colored eyes stared at me blankly. It unsettled me even more.

Ruoming fiddled with the fabric of his sleeve. "You agreed to my dinner plans."

"It was your idea?"

"I sent Feiyu because if I asked, you would've thought I poisoned all the food."

I hid my surprise. "Ha-ha. Very funny."

"Liu Peijin," he said, now gripping his sword and tapping it against the hard ground. "Do you realize you could have killed every single one of us with your stunt last arc?"

"I get this lecture from my party members every time. Don't worry."

"Peijin. If you die, you will never come back. You aren't immortal."

I sighed heavily. Now Ruoming was scolding me, too. "Aren't you more interested in how I pulled it off? In all your past runs, have you ever done what I just did?"

"You could have killed *my* party." Ruoming's voice was deep and low, almost a threat.

"*Your* party stood on the sidelines trying to slaughter mine. Last time I checked, the only one who actually died was me."

"You gambled, and you got lucky. That's all you did."

"Me? Lucky?" I said, pointing at myself. "No one has ever used that word to describe me."

"You were lucky because your idea of a hypothesis of a plan worked. But, if you were wrong anywhere along that chain, you would have died."

"It's a good thing I'm the god of fate and fortune," I said with a cocky expression. "That's what you're really curious about, right? You called me here because you wanted to pick my brain for any information you can get about *that*. Whether or not the observers were lying earlier."

"Tch. So cocky."

I laughed, walking up to stand next to Ruoming. I grabbed the railing he was sitting on with both hands and swung myself so that I was seated right beside him.

"There. Now I'm close enough that you can kill me easily if you want to," I half-joked.

Ruoming ignored me, preoccupied by Owl's claim of my true identity. "I don't want an answer. I can only hope that it's not true."

"What will you do if it is?" I asked, turning to him. "I'm the reason you've been tortured to death for millennia, aren't I?"

My tone was obviously bitter. At the start of the apocalypse, especially in my dungeon room, I felt as though it was a great injustice that Karma blamed me for every negative thing in the world. I had no control that my novel would become everybody's reality.

However, now, after witnessing the way I caused the people around me to suffer, I was beginning to think that I did deserve my karma.

If I was in Ruoming's place, I would have killed me the moment we met. There was no reason to keep me alive. I was cocky, self-centered, dangerous to myself and others, and most importantly, I was the worst thing to ever happen to Ruoming.

"*Even if you lived a billion years and only committed good deeds, you'd never be able to pay off your bad karma.*"

In that sense, Karma was entirely right. I'd have to begin by paying off my

Karma to Ruoming. That alone would take me an eternity, and I'd never be able to atone.

Ruoming finally spoke up. "No. You couldn't have known better."

I froze at his words, slowly turning to face him. I didn't even know what kind of expression I was making.

"This is my first time seeing you, so it must be your first time going through this. It couldn't have been your fault," Ruoming said softly, like he was trying just as hard to convince himself.

"Maybe I just stayed hidden the whole time and decided to appear now."

"Then keep it a secret, or else I'll kill you the moment you reveal it."

I laughed solemnly, running my hand through my hair. Ruoming cut me off before I could say anything back.

"Have you figured out what the tattoo does?"

"Nope. It gave me some spiritual energy, though."

"It allows you to tap into the reserve of other Major Arcana members if they're active near you."

I perked up, cocking my head. "It gave me more during my fight with Hundun."

"Right."

"You have that much energy?"

"Not right now, I don't. That's the problem."

"Do you think another member of the Major Arcana was there? The World was spectating, so it could have been her."

Ruoming shook his head back and forth. "No. She's still recovering from her fight with Karma."

"Then who?"

Ruoming shook his head. "I didn't recognize any of the other members there."

"You mentioned that they could come from past runs, too, right? Maybe it's someone from the previous runs that you didn't know about."

"It has to be someone from the arc."

"Are you suggesting . . ." I said trailing off, my eyes darting up.

"Yes."

"Who?"

"Thanks to you, there was too much interference to tell."

"Archangel Michael, Shunfeng'er, and Chang'e were all heavily involved."

"I've never seen Shunfeng'er in a previous run, but his power was immense. It is nearly impossible to become a member this early on and amass such power. But I feel as though Archangel Michael or Chang'e would have told one of us."

"The angel? I can ask, but he would have told me."

"I'll figure it out," Ruoming said, tapping his foot restlessly. His mind was still working at a thousand miles per hour, even though this was supposed to be a brief period of rest.

"I don't get you at all," I sighed heavily. "And I don't have the hardest time deciphering the essentials of people."

"I haven't lived like a human in a very long time."

I smiled at Ruoming, playfully nudging his shoulder. "Oh, come on. I'm sure that Feiyu kept you company."

"Feiyu saves everybody."

I snorted at the implication of his words. It was true—I had written Qiu Feiyu to be the most perfect protagonist, and there wasn't a single person he couldn't understand.

"I understand. That bastard can be insufferable sometimes. Especially in the shoes of someone like you or me. Hasn't he been hovering around us for most of our lives? And he doesn't even know it."

> **Many gods are confused by your conversation with Disciple Ruoming.**

"I'd rather have him in it than not," Ruoming confessed.

I turned to him, my head cocked. "Is that related to one of your big regrets?"

"Yes. It is."

"Well, then, I won't ask you more about it. Tonight, let's just celebrate new beginnings for everyone here. Congratulations on becoming a human again, you heathen."

The tension had dissipated. I slapped his shoulder repeatedly while laughing softly, surprised by the sudden humanity that Ruoming was displaying with me.

He had seemed so walled off that I would never be able to understand him, but it seemed like we were far more similar to one another than we'd initially thought.

I jumped off the railing and walked just ahead of him, extending my hand.

"Song Ruoming, I want you to be my partner."

CHAPTER THIRTY-EIGHT

"Your mind hasn't recovered from your injuries yet." Ruoming walked around me, fully ignoring my extended hand.

"Huh?"

[Observers Chat]
Spearmint12: LMAOO
MGirl193: What did you think he was going to say . . .
Ahoy987: Omg i have to look away

I stood there frozen like an idiot, my hand still extended. I initially thought I was about to look very cool and suave, but of course, Ruoming had to ruin my incredible theatrics.

"I said your mind hasn't recovered from your injuries yet."

"No, I know. I heard you."

"Then retract your hand."

"I'm a little embarrassed, though. Can you shake it out of courtesy?"

"No."

Divinity Great Sage Equaling Heaven bursts out in laughter.

Divinity Supreme Commander of the Heavenly Hosts turns away in complete embarrassment.

> **Divinity Supreme Commander of the Heavenly Hosts reminds you that Disciple Feiyu would hear you out.**

> **Divinity Ears That Hear What Comes on the Wind agrees with Divinity Supreme Commander of the Heavenly Hosts.**

> **The World cringes at the rejection.**

> **Divinity The One Who Fights in Front criticizes such nonsense.**

I coughed into the hand I outstretched, pretending that I suddenly had something stuck in my throat to try and save some face, but there was no use. I looked like a total loser.

"I'm leaving," I declared, heading back to the kiosks without waiting for any response from Ruoming. And, he didn't give me one. The moment I was certain he couldn't see my facial expression, I brought my hands in front of my face and groaned into them, bright red.

I thought we were on friendly enough terms to declare a partnership between our parties. Clearly, I was incredibly mistaken.

> **The final round of sponsor selections will begin shortly!**

I hurried back to my party but was stopped by Feiyu, who was waiting for me at the mid-point.

"Good chat?" he asked.

"Ruoming is a cruel, brutal, and wicked man. He has no empathy in his cold, desolate heart. None for the damned or for the righteous."

"Oookay. I take it that it went very well."

"Obviously. Why are you following me?"

"The rest of my party is right next to yours . . ."

"Sorry. I'm a little flustered. I think my worst social interaction to date just occurred."

"That's saying a lot for Jiejie."

"I know. That's why I'm distressed, Feiyu."

"Ruoming isn't a social butterfly, either," Feiyu shrugged. "Don't let it bother you."

"Are any of you planning on picking up a sponsor?"

I figured most of Feiyu's party would be without sponsors, given that Feiyu and Ruoming were disinclined from being influenced by any bodies of power. Yuan and Cheng had ones, and I doubted that Qijing did, given that her skill was in firearms.

"Nope."

"Figured. Then I'll see you afterward. You're cooking. I'm not going to stink of barbecue."

Feiyu smiled softly, turning toward his party. "You won't have to lift a finger."

I returned to my party, letting out a deep sigh as I slumped on the ground, resting my head in Yue's lap.

I flipped over so I was lying on my back, looking up at Yue. The rest of my party was circled up together.

"You look bad from this angle," I commented.

"You look bad from all angles."

I huffed and rolled to my side, my eyes landing on Amelia.

"Feiyu-shushu is going to cook you a big dinner tonight," I whispered to her before grinning.

Instantly, Amelia's face lit up. "Really?"

"That's what a little birdie told me."

"Huuuh?" Yue interjected. "Is he going to make me a serving, too?"

"Yes," I answered. "He's cooking for everyone to get on our good side."

"Well, he's already on my good side," Yue said, practically drooling already.

Wei, knowing why I was really here, turned his head toward me. "What were you thinking about for the sponsors?"

I lazily pointed a finger at Amelia. "This girl here is very popular. She's going to get a lot from the Greeks."

Amelia corrected me. "Only two."

"That's more than most of us ever had," I said proudly. "Artemis and Athena both really want you."

"Which one should I pick?"

Divinity The One Who Fights in Front looks at Amelia expectantly.

Divinity Far Shooting Queen of Beasts looks at Amelia expectantly.

Demon Abyssal Kraken of Black Seas nervously looks at Amelia.

Well, that was a new option.

"You . . . might have even more options than that," I confessed. "Pick whoever you think you have the most synergy with."

"Synergy?"

"Who you like the most and are most compatible with. This is the god that will be at your side for the rest of your life. Not only should you like their character, but they should possess skills that align with where you want yours to be. You can also stay sponsor free."

"I want a sponsor."

"You'll only have good picks. Don't let somebody sway your opinion."

I yawned, for once feeling incredibly lazy.

That wasn't right. For once, I *could* feel incredibly lazy. What a relief.

Wei turned to me, waving his finger back between him and me. "What about us?"

This was the part I was a bit more nervous about.

Now that both Wei and I had enough spiritual energy to be considered gods, we could also sponsor disciples this time around. I cleared my throat, trying to make my suggestion sound as neutral as possible.

"I'm going to sponsor Qijing."

Amelia frowned slightly.

I continued with my explanation, hoping to alleviate any tensions. "It's a purely strategic move. It'll ensure that someone in Ruoming's party is under our party, and it also means that they don't get another god on their side. Even though they're avoiding sponsors as much as possible, it's always better for us to try and snag a share."

Yue let out a frustrated groan, flopping backward onto the ground. "Do we have to keep fighting?"

I instantly jerked my head up to look her in the eyes. "Did I hear that right?"

"I just want to laze around for a while."

"Maybe you're not cut out to be a demon . . ."

"Huh?! W-Wait, no, we absolutely should. We should kill them all if we have the chance to again. Yang, don't they get on your nerves?"

"Not really."

"Well, they get on mine."

I gestured to Yang. "What do you think?"

"Qijing likes you, although kidnapping her in the last arc may have been a bit damaging to your relationship."

Amelia crossed her arms, interjecting. "I don't like it."

"Amelia," I began, "it's not a personality thing. It's just about making the best moves in the long-run."

"You said personality matches and synergies were important."

"They are for you. But, since I'm the sponsor, I don't care as much about who my disciple is. I'm not truly invested in Qijing's cultivation. I just would rather her be in our hands than in Ruoming's."

"You pinky promised me that you wouldn't choose her first."

My brow furrowed slightly.

When did I do that?

I remember pinky promising Qijing that I would reunite her with Feiyu by the end of the arc, which I did. I also remember forcing Zhige to promise he wouldn't snap and get me killed.

Nowhere did I recall ever making a promise with Amelia.

"Oh . . . yes. That's right, I did. And I meant it."

"You said if you lied to me," Amelia said slowly, "you would cut your pinky off."

"Ha-ha . . . really?"

What kind of morbid lie was that?! I would never say such a thing.

I sat up now, not wanting to make it seem like I didn't care about Amelia's input. "Amelia, do you remember how you rode on my back at the end of the third arc?"

"Yes."

"If you're worried about being replaced with Qijing in all those important moments, don't be. You're irreplaceable. There's a reason you were there with me the entire time, not her." I reached across our little circle and ruffled her hair. "Besides, Qijing might not even pick me if Ruoming or Feiyu can help it."

I turned to Wei. "What about you?"

Wei shook his head back and forth. "I need to master the Thirty Aethyrs. If I had a disciple, I wouldn't want to neglect them if I were too busy to care for them."

"How responsible. How old are you again? I want to see how long it takes before I become this wise."

Wei rolled his eyes playfully at me, and I chuckled.

SECONDARY SPONSOR SELECTION
Difficulty: F
Task: Select a sponsorship from any of the gods that have made offers. Once you have picked a sponsorship, declined gods may offer to other members in your party.
Time: 15 minutes
Reward: Sponsor

Unsurprisingly, it was the exact same set of instructions as the first time around.

However, this time I got to be on the other side of the process.

As the God of Fate and Fortune, you may take on a disciple.

Would you like to send an offer to a disciple?

Yes/No

> Yes.

> Which disciple would you like to sponsor? Please select their name from the dropdown window below.

> Disciple Zhang Qijing.

> You have selected Disciple Zhang Qijing!

> You may only sponsor one disciple. Confirm Disciple Zhang Qijing?

> Confirmed.

> Thank you for submitting! Your offer has been sent to Disciple Zhang Qijing of the Major Arcana party.

I slid over to Amelia on my knees, peeking obnoxiously at her screen. "Toggle your screen settings so the whole party can see your list," I said eagerly.

Amelia followed my instructions and flipped the screen around. I grinned at the extensive list she boasted. That was my girl.

> **POTENTIAL SPONSORS LIST**
> The One Who Fights in Front
> Far Shooting Queen of Beasts
> Spirit of the Jade Moon
> Abyssal Kraken of Black Seas
> The Horned One

"Who's the last one?"

"I think that's Cerununnos. He's also a god of nature and animals. Out of this list, he's the most similar to Artemis, if that gives you a good gauge," I answered.

Amelia hummed softly, looking at her list intently.

"Geez," Yue grumbled. "It's way longer than mine was."

"Amelia is the only available candidate in the best party. Of course she'd be highly desired among the gods who are still looking to pick up a disciple to call their own."

> Divinity The One Who Fights in Front is regrets trusting you.

> Divinity Far Shooting Queen of Beasts is watching with bated breath.

> **Demon Abyssal Kraken of Black Seas says he hopes his offer doesn't add stress to Disciple Amelia's decision making.**

Finally, Amelia made her decision.

> **Congratulations! Disciple Amelia has selected 'Far Shooting Queen of Beasts' as her sponsor!**

CHAPTER THIRTY-NINE

I cheered loudly, quickly embracing Amelia in a tight hug, practically suffocating her in my arms. The rest of my party quickly joined me, celebrating Amelia's new sponsor.

She looked terribly embarrassed, her cheeks turning their signature rosy color at all the praise she was suddenly receiving.

"Don't worry about any potential backlash. You made the choice you thought was best for you," I reassured her.

Divinity The One Who Fights in Front is watching in silence.

Divinity Far Shooting Queen of Beasts feels rewarded for her previous sacrifices.

Divinity Far Shooting Queen of Beasts promises to be an involved sponsor.

Divinity The One Who Fights in Front asks where Divinity Far Shooting Queen of Beasts was prior to sponsorship selection.

I turned away from the screens, not bothered by their bickering. Athena was still tied to me by virtue of our contract. And Artemis was a logical choice—not only did she mesh well with Amelia's beast skills, but Artemis was also associated with bodies of water, like rivers. Thus, she'd be of help in the next arc as well.

"Then it looks like we're done here," I said, standing up and stretching. I walked over to Zhige, picking up the blade and untying my hoodie and Boundless Bag.

Yang turned to me. "What about Qijing?"

"I didn't get any notifications. It's fine. If I was in Ruoming or Feiyu's shoes, I would've freaked out seeing my name pop up in Qijing's potential sponsors' list."

"It hasn't been fifteen minutes yet."

"They're decisive. They might not even be taking any sponsors."

I sifted through the Azure Dragon Store, looking for any other clothes instead of my current black button-up and shorts. Since I had the hoodie, I bought a simple tank top, and as for pants, I bought a nice pair of jeans that would further boost my physique stats.

> **16,999 stars used!**

The plain white tank top and jeans plopped straight into my hands. I walked into one of the bathrooms and took off my current clothes. I stared down at the black button-up, rubbing the fabric in between my index and thumb.

I instantly threw it away. I quickly changed before returning.

> **Physique level 33 → 38**

"Does it look good?" I asked Yue as I stepped out of the bathroom.

She glanced up briefly, gave me a thumbs up, and then returned to whatever speck on the ground had her preoccupied.

I cleaned my hoodie and threw it on, feeling the familiar, soft fabric hug me. Although this break was only for a day, it was truly the most peace we'd all felt since the apocalypse began.

> **Congratulations! Disciple Qijing has selected you as her sponsor!**

I froze at the message, blinking at it absentmindedly a few times before my eyes drifted to where Ruoming's party was huddled together. Feiyu and Ruoming were off to the side, whispering to one another, but Qijing instantly met my stare.

She gave me a small, shy nod of her head. I smiled and gave her one back.

Yang appeared behind me, peeking his head over my shoulder. "She picked you?"

"Surprisingly."

"I told you." Yang said with a smile, sharing the news with the rest of the party.

They all reacted in a variety of ways, but I couldn't hear any of the words they were saying.

Finally—finally, after all of these years resenting my mother for abandoning me, I could at least say that one good thing came from it.

I looked down at the ground, still feeling completely serene. There was a genuine, soft smile spread across my face.

"Let's get that dinner now," I said happily.

My party made its way over to Ruoming's, all of us chatting pleasantly now. We moved past the massive crowds of people in the station, many from Bohemian Grove. Some of them were cheering, finally getting a sponsor after gruesome days without any.

Others seemed exhausted, failing to get a sponsor for their second and final time. But, regardless, the system that Feiyu had established in the station was still running effectively, even if we no longer had the time to supervise it constantly. Everybody would have access to the necessities.

From now on, the arcs were going to be far more exclusive. Thus, not everyone had to participate and put their lives on the line. Only the top disciples did. Some previous Bohemian Grove members sulked throughout the station, but the moment they caught a glimpse of me, they just as quickly scurried away.

Some of them may have heard Owl's words over the sound of their party members being slashed apart by Feiyu. If they did, then they also heard the sound of his skull crunching and his organs oozing out of his body when I trampled him.

We found a large, empty hallway. Ruoming didn't mind buying the table and seats, and Yang, feeling bad about not contributing anything, bought all of the proper decorations. Yue sat back lazily. Wei worked with Cheng to establish the proper atmosphere by changing out the sickly white lightbulbs for more relaxing yellow ones.

It almost felt like we were creating our own little underground restaurant with how cozy it was. I was sorting through the Azure Dragon Store, buying all of the necessary ingredients that Feiyu had demanded from me. Once they appeared, I laid them out on a cheap countertop nicely.

Yuan approached with Qijing in tow. I looked back at the two of them. "Are you here to alleviate my financial burden for all this food?"

Yuan let out a low chuckle. "You haven't greeted your disciple yet."

"Well," I said, turning back to face my little sister, "I know she's very shy. I figured she should approach me first."

Yuan grabbed a chair and sat down next to me. He watched me work meticulously, intrigued by the way I could create such elaborate setups with my dexterous hands in comparison to his, which were calloused and broken beyond repair.

"Do you have siblings?" Yuan asked. He was trying to meet my gaze, but I stared intently at the assortment of ingredients before me.

"Nope. I grew up alone, and I didn't have the best parental figures."

Yuan let out a gruff hum. "It's tough on you kids now."

I wouldn't really call myself a kid at the grand age of twenty-four, but I went along with it anyway.

"Sure is. I think my life would look a lot different if my parents had taken good care of me."

Yuan watched as Qijing did her best to peek over the counter and look at what I was working on. I stepped to the side so she could get a perfect view. Although Cheng was by far Yuan's favorite, he evidently had a soft spot for the little girl as well.

"The only thing you or I can do is take care of those younger than us," Yuan declared simply. "Every child should know that they are a miracle. Since the beginning of the world and until the end, there will never be another child like them."

"When I get all old and gray, will I be able to whip up such moving quotes like that at some random dinner party? Or is it a skill only you have?"

"By the time you're my age, you'll spend years thinking about what you regret. I'm just saying what I wish I'd said back then."

"Geez," I groaned, "I already have years of regrets. Don't get me too excited for my future."

"When you don't have to deal with the past, memory is the most wonderful thing."

I pursed my lips. For Yuan, that must have been the philosophy he lived with. The memories of his daughter continued to live on in his mind. But with each recall, he was reminded of the fate she met at her own hands.

"I don't think about my past much," I said simply. "I have nothing positive there. The only thing I can say with confidence is that we're meant to take care of those younger than us."

"Is that why you sponsored the girl?" Yuan said, jerking his chin toward Qijing, who was listening intently to our conversation.

"Yes. It is. I'm older than her, after all. And you're older than Cheng. It's how things should go. One day, all I can hope is that Qijing will also take care of those younger than her."

I stepped back, sighing heavily. "Finished!"

I pointed at the massive array of meat. "Yuan, do you know what you're looking at? Fifteen thousand stars of every beef cut they had. Feiyu's greed is insatiable."

I reached down and placed my hand on top of Qijing's head. "Do you like Korean barbecue?"

"I've never had it."

I gasped audibly—partially for drama, partially genuine. "Really? Well, Feiyu is about to cook you the most delicious meal of your life."

I walked over to Yuan. "Be honest. Why did you come over? Qijing could have come to me herself just fine."

"Not everyone has ulterior motives."

"Yeah? Well, you sure do. So, spit it out."

Yuan's eyes followed me as I began cleaning up and popping open the grill I'd purchased, preparing it. I had never set this up on my own, so I was frantically flipping through the instructional manual to make sure I wouldn't accidentally blow up the entire train station.

"I wanted to remind you to take care of your disciple. And I wanted you to know that I'll take care of you, too."

I faced him, wagging the instruction manual at him. "You know, both you and Feiyu do this one thing that I don't understand one bit. You say you'll look out for me. But I can think of multiple times where you both definitely tried to kill me and my party members."

Yuan looked a bit uncomfortable, shifting in his seat. "That was during the arc before we were familiar with one another."

"Yeah, but I'm starting to think I'm the most honest person here, and that's a dangerous thought to have because I'm a massive liar. At least I tell you guys when I want you dead."

"I'm sorry."

"I'm not being serious. We all do what we need to do. I also saw how well you looked after Cheng. I'm jealous."

"You said your childhood was tough?"

"I ran away from home at fourteen, and my mom left my family even earlier. I stayed with a stranger a while after, but then . . ." I trailed off, my mind going blank. And then what? At some point, I moved out of Zhao Rui's apartment, but I had no recollection of why or when. "Sorry. I'm blanking."

"It's all right. It's the opposite for me. My daughter took her life, and I got divorced after. Crazy how all those bad things happen all at once, huh?"

"I'm sorry for your loss," I responded, filled with guilt.

It grew quiet between us for a second. Sensing the awkward atmosphere, I gave Qijing the instruction manual and set her on a bench in the corner, asking her how to operate the grill, which I was miserably failing at using.

I turned back to Yuan, a comforting smile on my face. "Don't worry. I'll spoil Qijing rotten. She'll be drowning in so many riches that she'll forget she's even in an apocalypse."

"That's how it should be," Yuan said, laughing. "I'm sorry for dragging down the mood. This was supposed to be a celebration, but it became so solemn."

"It's okay."

Yuan stood up and walked over to me, patting me on the shoulder. He gave a friendly smile, and my heart twisted in my chest.

He reminded me so much of Dad.

"It's good for us to talk about it openly," Yuan remarked. "Better for us to do a good job now than lament over the past."

"Yes. You're right. Thank you."

"Qijing really does like you, even if she doesn't show it. Ruoming was mortified to see your name pop up on the sponsor list. I think we all were."

I laughed. "Really? Did I have a lot of competition?"

"On paper you did, but not in Qijing's mind."

"You don't need to flatter me."

"I mean it. I was sworn to secrecy about this but . . . after that stunt you pulled in the last arc, you should have seen how everyone reacted. Ruoming practically begged me to protect all your party members, and when I saw them, all that was left of you was your skewered forearm. They were all sobbing, pleading with Cheng to do something."

I flinched at his words, and he instantly picked up on it.

"What I'm trying to say is, don't be careless with yourself. You talked about ending the cycle, right? Well, it begins with you and your party. You've saved their lives over and over, but whenever they take your hand, they watch you sink down into the same trap that almost killed them. It's miserable."

"I'll be so careful from now on that you won't even see a bruise on my skin," I grabbed his shoulder reassuringly. "Thank you."

Yuan gave a curt nod and hobbled off as if the entire conversation didn't leave my mind reeling.

CHAPTER FORTY

My social battery was entirely drained by this point. I had no clue how I was going to sit through an entire dinner. I yawned, rubbing my eyes. I waved Qijing back over, who was already watching me intently, despite hardly speaking a word.

"I'm done setting up here. Do you wanna see the decorations everyone else is working on?"

Qijing nodded, walking beside me as I headed over to the table and waved at everyone setting things up. Yang and Yue were working together on decorating the massive table. Yang struggled with where to place the artificial berries or what glasses to pick, leading Yue to sigh loudly and correct him.

"I didn't know you were such an artist, Yue," I teased.

Which was true. I never wrote that Yue was an artist or anything of the sort.

"I'm not. Yang is just exceptionally bad."

But, Yue's set up and design looked incredible, and I found it hard to believe her words despite being her creator. I pointed at the one seat where the decorations seemed entirely complete. "Do I just need to replicate that?"

"Don't fuck anything up."

"I'll replicate it. Qijing, do you want to help me?"

Qijing nodded, and I bought all of the necessary items. I placed them all on the table right before her. "Set up the napkins and utensils last. Do the table decorations first."

Qijing followed my instructions perfectly, diligently working to replicate Yue's complicated set up.

"Have you ever done this before?" I asked Qijing.

"No . . . my family never celebrated holidays."

"Mine didn't either," I said, smiling at her softly. "Why did you pick me as your sponsor?"

Qijing refused to meet my gaze, embarrassed by my question. "Because Gege likes you."

". . . That is absolutely not your reason."

"Why? It is."

If this was Yue, I would have already whipped out the Lie Detector. But given that this was my dear disciple, I decided just to dismiss the validity of her words.

"Feiyu bullies me. He might be your Gege, but most of what he says is nonsense. It's probably better to never listen to a word he says, to be honest," I shrugged.

"Jiejie!"

I practically jumped out of my skin, slowly turning around to see Feiyu standing behind me with a menacing smile. "Jiejie, did you buy the ingredients yet?"

"Yes . . ."

"Then, I'll get started. I can't wait."

I gave him a tight smile and nodded my head painfully, cursing myself. Feiyu knew very well I had been organizing this entire time. He was just eavesdropping on my conversation and wanted to remind me of my place.

Qijing smiled while watching Feiyu turn around. "Gege never says nonsense."

"No, he says a lot of nonsense."

"He doesn't."

"Do I say nonsense?"

She remained silent, and I gasped dramatically. She really did like Feiyu more than me. Had she had the option to pick between Feiyu and me as her sponsor, I knew with complete certainty she would have chosen Feiyu.

But it was hard to stay angry when the incredible smell of meat cooking was wafting through the air.

Yue looked up, sniffing like Amelia's dire wolf. "That smells so good!" she exclaimed brightly.

She shoved everything that she was holding into Yang's hands, running over to the grill that Feiyu was operating. Feiyu had removed his coat and unbuttoned the third button of his collared shirt again, although this time he had a reason to do so.

Smoke blew up from the grill, carrying the delicious aroma all throughout the room. Everybody paused to let out murmurs of excitement.

Yang walked up behind me, still holding all of Yue's newly ordered decorations. "I can't believe we get to eat like this."

"It'll be a good way to recharge our energy before we begin the next arc."

"You're already thinking about the next arc?"

"Always."

"Enjoy your day off. At least you're here to celebrate it."

"You're right, you're right," I said, laughing.

Qijing and I quickly finished the rest of the setup as Yue shoved her face with the freshly cooked slices of meat that Feiyu had made.

"I-It's so good!"

"Wait until we're seated at the table!" I exclaimed, mostly out of jealousy. In *Surviving My First Run*, I had spent pages upon pages just describing how good Feiyu's cooking was.

It was simply another one of the protagonist's strengths. Of course, I had to make him perfect at everything.

"Peijin, you don't even understand how good it is," Yue said, practically in tears. "It's so good. I haven't had a meal like this in forever."

Feiyu put his hand up against her head, pushing her away from the grill. "Jiejie is right. Wait."

Yang practically dragged Yue away from the grill. Amelia approached next, cautiously, and Feiyu instantly gave her a piece. Amelia took a bite, and her face lit up instantly.

"It applies to you, too!" I shouted toward Amelia. She giggled, putting her hand in front of her mouth as she walked back to the table. "It really is so good. Feiyu-shushu, can you make some extra for the wolf?"

"As long as Jiejie buys more ingredients."

Amelia slowly turned to face me, and I let out a loud sigh, walking over to Feiyu and buying whatever ingredients he started rambling off.

The table was fully set now, and we all took our seats, leaving one empty for Feiyu as he completed platters of food with incredible efficiency.

It was odd to be seated across from people who just hours before were trying their best to take your lives. But still, the clinking of plates and forks as everyone got settled made it feel like we were celebrating a grand holiday.

I was a bit giddy at the feeling of sitting at a long table like this. I had never had any large family get-togethers, and I never celebrated a single holiday—not even Chinese New Year.

So now, being seated across from the only people I could ever consider family, I found a small smile creeping onto my face.

"Do we want drinks, too?" I asked, looking up at everyone and trying to hide my expression to avoid being teased to death.

"Oh, hell yeah!" Yue exclaimed, slamming her fist on the table with excitement.

I immediately regretted my question, knowing that Yue was going to drink until she dropped, and probably bleed me of all my stars doing so.

I opened the Azure Dragon Store and bought Maotai, the most well-known Chinese liquor. I poured myself a shot and then passed the bottle around the table.

Amelia, who was seated beside me, stared at the bottle as it went by. "Can I try some?"

I handed her my shot glass. "Sure. Just take a tiny little sip first. It tastes just like water."

Amelia brought her lips to the glass and stuck just the tip of her tongue into the drink, but she instantly retracted, spitting it out with a disgusted expression. She put down the glass and picked up her water, chugging it down.

I burst out laughing, pulling her into a tight hug. "Don't drink. It's bad for you."

I turned to Qijing, waving the shot glass in the air. "Do you want to try some?"

Qijing, looking utterly mortified, quickly shook her head back and forth.

I snickered, putting down the glass while I waited for everybody else except for Cheng and the kids to pour themselves one.

"Wait for me," Feiyu called out, quickly rushing over with plates upon plates of deliciously cooked food.

He put the first plate down, and I looked at it in complete and utter shock. You couldn't even consider this Korean barbecue anymore. It looked like something that would be served in a world-renowned restaurant.

There were plates of thinly sliced and marinated meats. Others were entire filets, cooked to a perfect medium rare. There was a wide assortment of vegetables, soups, and rice, all plated to perfection.

I began drooling on the spot.

Yuan laughed, calling out my expression to the rest of the table. "Peijin looks like she's about to eat the whole table."

"I've never had a meal like this," I muttered, truly in awe of the sight.

Before the apocalypse, I went hungry more times than I could count. Even the night I interacted with MolaMola, I was still eating just steamed rice and pre-packaged pork.

Wasn't there formal etiquette for these kinds of things? I looked around the table, waiting for someone to make the first move before I messed it up.

Yue, however, was worried about no such things. She instantly grabbed her chopsticks and loaded up her plate as high as she could.

"Y-Yue!" Yang exclaimed.

"Don't care," Yue said casually, grabbing more food. "I'm fucking starving. Hey, thank you, Feiyu! You're the best!"

Feiyu slumped down in the seat across from me and beside Ruoming.

"Don't thank me," Feiyu said. "This was all Peijin's idea. I just threw food on the grill."

He lifted his chopsticks, perfectly forming little wraps with the lettuce and meat. I copied his movements exactly, though it was embarrassing to be learning formal conventions from my creation.

I brought the wrap to my mouth and took a bite. At once, my eyes widened, and I savored each bite. The meat was so tender it practically melted in my mouth, and the seasoning was incredible.

I never even knew food could taste this good. I quickly shoved the rest of it down before I started assembling my second, third, and fourth. The table became completely silent as everyone was too preoccupied enjoying their meal.

After I finished my third wrap, I poured Feiyu a drink and slid it over to him, not saying a word. A little smile appeared on his face, but he stayed silent.

Yue was practically crying between each bite. "Peijin, you should keep doing stupid things so we have a reason to celebrate."

"No, no, no," Yang quickly interjected. "I cannot keep playing doctor."

Suddenly, Yang sat up straight and slowly turned to face Cheng, the implication clear.

"M-Me?" Cheng said, pointing a finger at his own chest. "I'm already busy all the time with healing my party. And you guys seem to be much more injury prone."

"It's good to learn time management from a young age," Wei said with a teasing smile.

Cheng turned to Yuan for support, but Yuan was looking down too intently at his food. Cheng slumped in his chair, and we all laughed.

Feiyu was resting his chin casually on his hand, a lazy smile on his face. "Let's just enjoy tonight. I'm sure things will only get worse from here, so we can party harder with each one."

I snorted.

"I mean it. How many timelines have there been before us? We're not the first or the last, and we're certainly not the most important." Feiyu stretched out before he leaned back in his chair and kicked his foot to rest on the opposite knee. "We appear, we disappear, and we're important to each other. But really, we're just passing through."

The table quieted at his words. Feiyu usually didn't say profound things.

I grabbed my shot glass, lifting it up into the air. "Cheers. To just passing through."

Everyone lifted their glasses, reaching over the table to cling them with one another.

"To passing through."

"To passing through."

I leaned my head back and took the shot, sticking my tongue out after. "Oh god. It's still awful."

> **[Observers Chat]**
> **Nipon23:** this is the last time you'll ever be able to sit with them like this

Yuan chuckled, and then the dinner truly began.

CHAPTER FORTY-ONE

Even after all the food had gone cold and we had gone through bottle after bottle of liquor, we were still at the table, laughing and telling jokes.

Cheng purchased a pack of cards and showed Qijing and Amelia a magic trick, completely blowing them away. They gathered at the corner of the table, playing various games as Amelia and Qijing fought over who guessed the card first.

I had pulled out the cake, and before I could even slice it up for everyone, Amelia, Cheng, and Qijing finished the entire thing with their bare hands like barbarians.

Somehow, a drunk Yue had successfully challenged Yang to a drinking game, which he lost terribly. He was completely asleep at the dinner table, prompting Yue to buy a pen and draw on half of his face.

Yuan was leaning back, telling Ruoming, Feiyu, and me about the most memorable moments of his life. Ruoming and I knew this speech by heart. Ruoming because he had read and lived it; me because I wrote it.

Feiyu, however, was utterly enthralled, practically jumping out of his seat every time Yuan would tell a thrilling story. It sent me reeling back with laughter to see his childish excitement, and Ruoming watched quietly with half-lidded eyes.

My head was spinning by this point, and I knew I wouldn't remember a thing in the morning. By this point, my cheeks were aching with how much I was smiling.

Still grinning, I turned to Ruoming, my voice soft. "How does this compare to all your previous dinner parties?"

"I don't know."

"What do you mean?"

"I never went to one. There was always work to do."

I instantly sat up before I let out a bright laugh. "So I should feel very honored that you came to mine, right?"

Ruoming didn't say a word, just downed another shot while watching Feiyu.

"Ha! You're not as wicked as I thought."

"It's my first time losing this arc."

"Huh? Really?"

Ruoming nodded. "Maybe I lost it when I first started, but it's been a long time since then. I can't even recall it."

"So, not only have I successfully dragged you to sit at this table, but I'm also better than you at surviving the apocalypse?"

Ruoming didn't answer me, and I snickered.

Not long after, our celebration came to an end. The kids had fallen asleep in their chairs, every single piece of food was gone, and Yue and Yang were also completely knocked out on the table. Even Ruoming had shut his eyes.

I stood up shakily from the table, still swaying slightly. I began cleaning up all of the plates and drinks.

"Why did Yue and Yang buy all these decorations . . ." I grumbled, not knowing what to do with them.

I opened the Azure Dragon Store and purchased another Boundless Bag, this time in light pink. This would be my junk bag. I placed it on the ground, opening it as large as it could go. I began to throw all the decorations and furniture in.

"Let me help you," Feiyu said, stumbling over.

"You are going to fall over," I warned him.

"Then we both will. Look at the state you're in, Jiejie."

I normally never laughed at anything Feiyu said, but in my haziness, I chuckled at his words. Feiyu took all the dishes and quickly washed them before tossing them into my bag. It only took a few minutes to clean up the entire thing.

The bigger concern, however, was what to do with all the party members.

Feiyu snapped his fingers. "Futon!"

"You're buying it."

An enormous futon appeared in his hands, and with one whip of his arms, it was perfectly laid out in the empty room. I lifted Amelia and Qijing into one arm each, placing them down on the futon beside each other. Feiyu handled Cheng.

When I got to Yue, her eyes blinked open.

"Peijin?"

"Good. You're up. Move to the futon on your own. This floor is disgusting."

Yue hummed mindlessly, repeating my name over and over again under her breath.

"What? Are you stupid—"

Yue then vomited all over me.

I remained frozen, staring down at the complete mess she'd made of my brand new clothes. Even my poor hoodie was squirming like it wanted to get off of me.

Yue fell asleep right after.

"You're already a demon," I said, aghast.

I waved Feiyu over, sniffing dramatically. He panicked at the sight and moved Yue out of the way, cleaning her up. I moved to the corner of the room, quickly cleaning up my clothes with various skills.

I pulled off the hoodie and apologized, setting it on a chair until I was sure it wouldn't fall victim to such a heinous thing again.

I moved Yang next, and of course, there were no issues. Feiyu moved Yuan and Wei at the same time, throwing one of them over each shoulder.

However, when we got to Ruoming, we both stared at one another.

"You should do it," I said. "You're in his party."

"I'm more drunk than you. I might drop him."

"What? Are you serious? Just do it."

"I'm not doing it."

I gawked at Feiyu. "Then let's just leave him in the chair."

"He'll kill me if he wakes up with back pain."

"So? That doesn't have to do with me."

Feiyu clasped his hands together. "Please, Peijin."

"No. If his back hurts, he can wake up in the middle of the night and move by himself."

"Ruoming has very bad insomnia. He hardly ever falls asleep for more than a few minutes. This is the best I've ever seen him."

"Then leave him on the chair!" I exclaimed.

"Let's settle this with rock, paper, scissors."

I stared at him, thinking he was joking. When I realized he was serious, I sighed and went with it.

I threw scissors, and he threw rock.

I let out a loud groan, sulking over to Ruoming. I gently grabbed his shoulders, trying to move him without stirring him.

At once, Ruoming jolted awake. He punched me across the face, knocking me out.

After a few moments of darkness, I woke up in a dream, where I was standing on a beach. I looked down and saw myself wearing a light blue dress that was flowing with each gust of wind.

There was nothing and nobody on the beach except for me. I walked along the sand barefoot, the water occasionally lapping at my feet and sending a shiver up my spine.

Behind me, the sand faded into snow. The sky above me was a pale gray. It was the dead of winter, but I didn't feel cold at all. If anything, I was more taken aback to see sparkling snow on a beach.

I continued walking, having no clue where I was supposed to be headed until I saw a figure ahead of me. I ran up to it, stopping as I got closer.

I could recognize that red dress anywhere.

Although Karma stood with her back to me, when I finally got close enough to recognize her, she slowly turned around, swinging her leg as she did so.

"Hello, again."

I instinctively reached for Zhige before remembering this was all a dream. "You're not real."

Karma giggled, skipping over until she was nose to nose with me. At once, her expression fell. For the first time, there wasn't an unsettling smile spread across her face.

"A corpse is talking."

Her cold, monotone voice sent chills throughout my body. I instantly tensed and brought my hands up before me, ready to defend myself, even if it was just with my fists.

Karma smiled again like nothing had happened. She grabbed onto my wrists, pushing them down. "No need for all that. I'm only here for a moment to tell you something."

"Get out of my head."

"My, my! Look who's saying that now!" Karma laughed, twisting my wrist up above my head and forcing me to twirl.

"Liu Peijin," Karma said with a grin. "You best say your goodbyes."

"What?"

Karma smiled sweetly. "The situation is far worse than you can imagine. You've bitten off more than you can chew."

I stared at Karma blankly before she suddenly thrust her arm forward. It pierced straight through me, and when she pulled out her arm, she dangled my heart in front of me.

I gasped, collapsing to the ground and bringing my hand up to touch my chest in complete shock. Blood immediately poured out of my mouth, and I kicked the sand and snow, trying as hard as I could to scramble backward.

Karma smiled and slowly stepped closer before leaning down just before me. I shook in fear, my hand clenching my chest. Karma leaned in and grabbed my neck.

At the sound of my spine crunching, I jolted awake with a scream. I brought my hand to touch my chest and neck frantically, looking around completely confused.

I looked down, finding myself on the futon. My hoodie was back on, and both of my Boundless Bags were placed beneath my head nicely like a pillow. Feiyu's large arm was draped over my torso, and Ruoming's head was resting on my lap, his drool on my jeans.

My breathing was rapid, my gaze locked straight ahead. I could see the vague figure of Karma smiling, leaning down to stare straight in my eyes. She brought two fingers up to her lips and blew me a kiss.

"See you soon, Liu Peijin."

ABOUT THE AUTHOR

BananaDragon is the author of the Scathing Reviewer series, originally released on Royal Road. Adventurous at heart, she loves taking pictures of the vast outdoors with shaky hands and painting portraits with mere, scattered brushstrokes. She also enjoys sitting under her backyard's vast oak trees on a soft pink blanket with a pen and notebook in her hands, sipping a sweet iced coffee. BananaDragon lives in Chicago.

RESPAWN YOUR CURIOSITY
follow us on our socials

 podiumentertainment.com

 @podiumentertainment

 /podiumentertainment

 @podium_ent

 @podiumentertainment

www.ingramcontent.com/pod-product-compliance
Lightning Source LLC
LaVergne TN
LVHW041622060526
838200LV00040B/1392